BIOGRAPHY
ALI CARTER

Ali lives in Sutton, a small village up on the Norfolk Broads, with her husband, who as a retired Met. Police Officer was a great help in assuring legalities in *The Delegate* are as accurate as possible.

Her debut thriller – *Blood List*, and its sequel *Dead Girls Don't Cry*, are her first two crime thrillers in the DCI Harry Longbridge series. *The Delegate* is the third and a fourth is currently underway.

Ali loves to hear from her readers and can be contacted below:-

Website:– alicarterauthor.com
Facebook:– @alicarterauthor
Twitter:– @alicrimewriter
Instagram:– alicarter.author

'She had the pâté, he had a broccoli and stilton soup. This would have been a convenient vehicle to receive the syringed hemlock, but only being the first course he had no need of the men's washroom to give her time to administer it. Annie ate her food, tasting nothing. The blurring hum of the restaurant's diners floated around her as she nodded, smiled, drank her wine and generally tried to engage with her dining companion. A man she had no real grudges against, who had no idea why he was really there, but who she was required to kill that evening…'

To Sue,

THE
DELEGATE

Welcome to the web...

Enjoy?

[signature]

ALI CARTER

4·2·2023

Matador
Unit E2 Airfield Business Park,
Harrison Road, Market Harborough,
Leicestershire. LE16 7UL
Tel: 0116 2792299
Email: books@troubador.co.uk
Web: www.troubador.co.uk/matador
Twitter: @matadorbooks

ISBN 978 1803135 687

British Library Cataloguing in Publication Data.
A catalogue record for this book is available from the British Library.

Printed and bound by CPI Group (UK) Ltd, Croydon, CR0 4YY
Typeset in 12pt Adobe Garamond Pro by Troubador Publishing Ltd, Leicester, UK

Matador is an imprint of Troubador Publishing Ltd

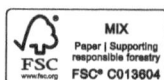

To my dearest friend Sue – besties always x

MESSAGE FOR
MY READERS . . .

Although *The Delegate* takes place between June 2020 and May 2021, I have deliberately chosen not to mention the pandemic other than to vaguely refer to a local 'sickness bug'. References to various organisations being short-staffed due to related employee absence is as far as I've gone. I hope you feel as I do that we read fiction for pleasure, to get away from our daily lives, and would prefer not to be reminded of what was, for many, an exceptionally difficult and upsetting period.

PROLOGUE

RAMPTON HIGH SECURITY HOSPITAL

JUNE 2020

Charlotte was a little perplexed she had a visitor at all. She never had visitors. Not surprising really, it's something she'd come to get used to . . . *again*. But not today. Today the request sent out many times before had finally been accepted, and she'd agreed to see her. *Two months of secret correspondence had paid off.* Well, secret as far as one person was concerned, anyway.

When the door to the lounge area opened and the woman walked into the room, for the first time in a good number of years, it was Charlotte Peterson who looked surprised – *or maybe not....* They weren't so different, she and her.

The orderly indicated a chair for the woman to sit down, there were other people in the lounge and she acknowledged a thank you with a slight nervous snatch of her head. She looked about her and took a seat opposite the patient she'd come to see. The two women initially observed each other silently, an oblong table set between them. For a few moments the orderly stood to one side, and then left them to observe from a desk further away.

"H – Hello, Charlotte," said the visitor, picking at her nails, eyes now darting between their misshapen edges and Charlotte's waiting stare. "I've been. . . I've. . . it's. . ."

The former doctor eased forward slowly, leant elbows on knees and made a bridge with her hands against her mouth. She then looked closely into the very soul of her; closely enough to see it was severely emotionally scarred, *and thus vulnerable. Vulnerable, ripe and ready.* The corner of her lips tugged into that famous half smile – her eyes remained cold. Charlotte breathed a whispered, slow reply into her hands so as not to alert anyone nearby.

"Hello, Annie. . . what took you so long?" And as Annie Longbridge smiled nervously, biting her lip, beginning to wish she'd never come, never written that letter, never got involved in *any* way whatsoever.... Charlotte Peterson knew she'd found her. She had found *'the one'*. Exactly the *right* one for her very, very important work – she had found **The Delegate....**

ONE

KIRKDALE, CUMBRIA UK

JULY 1ST - ONE MONTH LATER

It was July again. The weather was still mixed and the scenery still glorious. Two full years since that summer when the murders had begun; well, the ones on home turf anyway. Retired DCI Harry Longbridge was still mooching about the house wanting back '*in*' at Kirkdale nick, and spending more time than ever with his black Labrador, Baxter. At least *he* appreciated his old police buddy, his wife, Annie, *not so much*.

He waited whilst Baxter did the necessary. This was basically digging another 'Baxtery' type hole to Australia from somewhere within the local woods by the River Kirk, which was where they were at that moment. He wasn't in view but Harry could hear him snuffling and scraping not far away. *Not reached Australia yet then, Baxy boy*, he thought, smiling as he swung the leather lead and turned left on the footpath towards the digging sounds. When he'd decided the Lab had had enough excavation time, he called him using his new 'Acme' whistle an expert at training club had recommended. When that didn't work he used the foolproof way of getting him to heel. Biscuits....

"Baaaax!! Bis bis!! Bis.....cuits!! Baxter!! Come *on* boy, *BIS BIS!!"* This always got him back in half a second flat. To be fair to the lad, so did a couple of blasts on the '*Acme'. . . usually.* Not today though. *"BAX-TERRR!!!* Where the hell *is* that dog?" Harry followed the now unmistakably over-excitable whining noises and quickened his step. When extreme agitated barking filled the air he began to run. Through a mixture of treelined paths, heavy undergrowth and damn near breaking his neck on several concealed stumps, the closer he got, the louder the barking became – until – until it just stopped. The scene that met his arrival would haunt him forever. Wagging his tail proudly, Baxter stood regally foursquare. . . *an arm dangling from his mouth.*

* * *

Since their return from New York after the tracking and re-capture of ex GP and serial killer Charlotte Peterson, Harry and reunited ex '*Canon Row'* partner DI Fran Taylor had only met up a few times. Most contact had occurred through text and phone calls the last three and a half months, and of course he'd felt guilty about what had happened out there. *The whole damn thing was a mess.* His leaving London seven years previously was entirely down to their getting too close, and his wife's suspicions and pressurising had led them to move to the Lake District in the first place. He'd honestly never expected to see Fran again.

When Charlotte Peterson had escaped on a day release from Rampton, and Fran having 'coincidentally' relocated to Kirkdale, they both knew what might happen, *especially Fran*. No longer a DS, DI Taylor had specifically requested Harry be called back in to shed light on the newly re-opened Peterson case. *Officially*, because he'd acted as senior investigating officer in 2018, *unofficially*....

Given their depleted numbers, similar to most of the country, Chief Super Chris Hitchings had grudgingly acquiesced against his better judgement. At the end of the day he knew Harry would get the job done even if he did 'go a bit rogue' on occasion. Several occasions had actually come to mind, mostly involving a lot of shouting, throwing insults about and ignoring protocol. However, Harry and Fran *had* got the job done, *together*, and Charlotte Peterson was safely ensconced back inside Rampton Psychiatric Hospital.

Fran had made it quite clear she was keeping the baby. Conceived stateside during a weak moment both had wanted to happen, no blame could be laid at her door. Or for wanting to keep the baby come to that. *The truth of it?* He was over the moon she was going to have his child. *The reality....?* Whatever his feelings towards her, he knew damn well despite being inevitable, their one-off liaison in New York had been wrong. And yet he didn't regret it. Not one bit.

It appeared her ex-husband had never wanted kids. To be fair to computer analyst Josh Taylor, neither had she in their early years of marriage, but at nearly forty-three, Fran felt it was likely to be her only chance of motherhood and she was taking it. She also intended on having her police career. Despite her, at times, flippant granite-style attitude (Harry had always assumed it a Scottish trait), it seemed she no longer wished to go through life childless. And neither did he. But there of course was the crux of the problem. *Annie....*

* * *

Understandably Harry didn't recognise the desk sergeant's voice when he put the call in directly to Kirkdale Station rather than dialling 999, so was pleased when Joe Walker arrived on scene. He was even more pleased to see Fran following, picking her way carefully across the tree roots and uneven stony ground. They'd had to leave the car up on the road in a lay-by at the wood's edge. There was no way it could have been driven down to where Harry was walking his overly enthusiastic, and apparently '*newly promoted*', seek-and-search dog.

Despite seniority, at nearly four months pregnant he could see Fran wasn't going to risk a fall by striding in ahead as per, and they were not far from the slippery water's edge either. He also knew there was no way she'd accept any help.

"Joe, it's good to see you again, lad." Harry's arm was outstretched to receive Joe's already extended hand,

and he clasped his forearm as the two greeted each other warmly. They had met up briefly in January before the New York trip, but even so, the younger man seemed to have grown in maturity again and was certainly a good deal more confident than a couple of summers ago.

Sergeant Joe Walker had been a raw PC in 2018 with Harry as his detective chief inspector. He remembered many occasions where he felt his boss had been a little unfair in the summing up of his abilities and the way he'd dispatched his duties. Despite that, it was some of Joe's ideas and discoveries that had led to solving the Peterson murders whilst in Harry's team, earning the surprised if grudging respect of his senior officer. At the end of the day Joe had still held his past DCI in high regard, and it was no secret amongst his colleagues he wished Harry was still in the job.

"Sir, you too, sir!" replied a smiling Joe, addressing his old boss in exactly the way he always had.

"No need for the sir stuff anymore, son, I'm just one of the rabble now."

"And a right shame it is, sir, I was only say—"

"Okay boys you've had a nice cosy reunion," interrupted Fran. "Harry..." She nodded towards him in acknowledgement. "Where is it then?"

Forthright as ever he thought. Harry had managed to get Baxter to drop the severed arm (having silently thanked his obedience trainer for persuading him to persist with the 'drop' command). Obviously with no evidence gloves on him as a member of the public, thankfully there'd been no need to handle it himself. He never *had* enjoyed the mucky end of policing.

"I got the Lab to leave it over there." He pointed to a large old yew on the upside of the path away from the water. "That's not where he found it, though. It was further into the woods off the track because he'd disappeared on me. I was having a devil of a job getting him to come to heel and that rarely happens these days. Well, as long as I've got biscuits on me." At the sound of the 'word', Baxter had his head in his master's pocket, whimpering and pawing at his hand. Harry delivered a couple of gravy bones onto a happy wet tongue.... "You're going to have to get a search team up here, Fran; Baxter's forelegs are covered in soft mud. That means he's been digging – and in freshly dug earth. The rest of the body could be anywhere in here. It's definitely a 'him' by the way."

"Yes – *thank* you, Harry. I *do* remember how to set up a crime scene and make initial observations. Pregnancy hormones haven't entirely robbed me of my faculties." Harry flushed and glanced briefly at Joe. *Did the lad know anything? Had Fran told anyone who the father was? No. Not in a million years. He was just being neurotic.*

"Yes, of course, I didn't mean—" He stopped as Fran walked over to the yew tree to take a look at the severed arm. Joe followed after throwing Harry a 'you know how she gets' look.

"I agree, definitely a man's arm by the look of it, the hand's still intact and animals haven't had a go at any of it yet. It couldn't have been there long with the earth being freshly dug, unless it's been moved. There's even a signet ring still in place." She bent down to pick up a thin piece of fallen branch and used it to turn the hand slightly. Joe paled – *he wasn't so great with hacked-off body parts either*. "Leaving that sort of evidence behind is pretty unusual," she said leaning in closer. Fran could now see what she was looking for, possible initials on the signet ring. There were two – J.J. in a scripted style. She threw the branch down and straightened up. "Whoever did this was either in a hurry or just plain sloppy, not in need of spare cash either. Joe, call the station and get Sergeant Moorcroft to organise a SOC team and then cordon this area off."

"Yes boss." As he started to walk back to the car for crime tape, he put in the call to Suzanne Moorcroft's direct line. She answered immediately....

"Suze? It's me, Joe. It's definitely the real thing, male by the looks of it, complete with gold signet ring. The DI wants SOC down here ASAP." He paused.... "Yep. . . and plenty of shovels." Then he turned back towards Harry and Fran, who by their body language were now clearly discussing something other than a severed arm and the whereabouts of the rest of the body. "And Suze. . . reckon you're right. You're going to be winning that bet on who the father is."

* * *

Annie Longbridge sat in the lounge of what had become, *much like her mind*, a confused, untidy and very disorderly place. She did, however, have her spare laptop in front of her, clean, shiny and in perfect working order. *More importantly her husband had no knowledge of it.* It had become a lifeline, an extended family. Lately she'd discovered her particular online world a much friendlier place compared with her real one, and it was where she'd been spending an awful lot of time whilst Harry walked the dog and did other 'Harry-type things'. What those things *were* exactly she wasn't entirely sure anymore. What she *was* sure of, however, absolutely *certain* of, was he was hoping to be recalled yet again, back into the job. . . in order to work alongside that woman.

She'd tried so hard not to think about it. Harry and Fran together. But it had been front and centre the entire time they were in New York as they'd tracked down and apprehended the *third* woman in Harry's life, escaped killer Charlotte Peterson, and it had continued since their return.

Of course her recent covert visits to the woman in Rampton, the psychiatric hospital home of that serial killer, hadn't helped. In fact, it had had an effect. *And not in a good way.* Annie hadn't even wanted to go there, not at all, but there'd been a distinct psychological pull, some kind of unspoken connection between her and the deadly doctor. When the original visiting request arrived soon after Harry had got back, she'd simply binned it. And the second. . . and the *third*. When they didn't stop coming she'd eventually caved. Harry had no idea of course, he was always out first thing with Baxter so never saw the post. It was the last one a month ago, the most recent, that Annie had finally accepted.

That woman seemed to understand how she was feeling. . . and thinking. She listened carefully and thoughtfully to Annie, validated and gave consideration to her worries and insecurities. She empathised. Charlotte was, after all, a trained medic. It had been her job to do *exactly* that, and despite obviously now being struck off the register, was still very good at it. Charlotte Peterson was also good at obtaining anything she wanted through the people she was living with – instigating special favours, like acquiring the home address of the retired police officer who'd put her away – *twice.*

Annie deftly worked the keys and mouse pad. Her hand hovered above the keyboard for a few seconds, then her fingers began to drum gently, randomly, not pressing hard enough to actually type anything, as if she was not quite able to make the decision to proceed. When red splashed down onto her laptop Annie realised she was biting hard into her lip. Despite the hesitation, she had felt nothing and merely wiped the blood away with the back of her hand before eventually typing the link. The site opened up, bright, blue, and orange. She stared at it for a few moments. . . then logged in to her account. The first picture came up. Not bad, she thought, and carried on slowly, pausing occasionally to begin with. *Two?. . . Three?. . . Four?. . . Five?* No, definitely not five – too old. Her head began to throb impatiently, in anticipation. And then she saw him. Well, well, well, who'd have thought it? Number six – *what* a surprise, and so soon.... Yes, number six. He would do. . . *he would do nicely.*

TWO

KIRKDALE, CUMBRIA, UK

Whilst he'd been grateful for the extended leave for New York in the early part of the year, Andrew Gale had not really been satisfied at work for the last eighteen months or so. In truth, ever since his involvement with the first Charlotte Peterson case, and becoming, if not exactly close friends with now *finally* retired DCI Longbridge, certainly a very close acquaintance. The combination of the two had noticeably increased his interest in the police service month on month.

Despite the fact (and maybe because of it) that Gina's *second* near-death experience, and Charlotte's second batch of murders and attempted murders in Manhattan had obviously been horrendous experiences, he felt journalism could no longer hold his interest enough to pursue it. Harry had let slip a couple of times he believed Andrew had what it took to be a good detective; maybe he should just bite the bullet and do something about it?

He was only thirty, still young enough to apply, surely? His keyboard remained silent as he tapped his fingers on the desk.

"Daydreaming, Gale? Not like you." Peter Gray was walking up the *Courier*'s office from the little kitchen, two full mugs chinking in his left hand. He'd operated this local newspaper, his and wife Stella's, from the converted double cottage for the last thirty years. He placed one mug down for Andrew, and facing him, leant against the empty desk in front.

Andrew smiled briefly and picked up the coffee. "Thanks, boss."

"So. . . what's ailing my ace crime reporter this morning? Burglaries and car thefts not happening often enough to keep you busy?" Peter took a sip of his three-sugared black and waited. Andrew gave a half laugh as he stroked the handle of his '*Crime Journalists Hit Better Deadlines!*' mug. He'd been with the paper pretty much since leaving university. There was a reason why there'd been no attempt to try and progress to a national as his experience had grown. Peter and Stella had become very good friends, almost like family. When the crime of the decade hit in the summer of 2018, and the paper's 'senior PA' Rachel Dern had become Charlotte Peterson's first victim, Stella had relied heavily on Andrew to sift and sort any and all information that had come up. He was the sports columnist back then – she the crime reporter at home with a broken ankle. Andrew got his first bite at Stella's job by attending all the murder scenes in her place, literally learning on the job. It soon became apparent he was a natural. Rachel was the daughter of Stella's dearest school friend who'd passed away when the girl was in her teens. Stella had promised Rachel's mother she'd keep an eye on her, which is why Rachel had been given a job at the *Courier* despite not owning great IT skills. . . or frankly any relevant skills or experience pertaining to the running of a newspaper at all.... Rachel hadn't been strong emotionally and it was her murder that had got Andrew involved with the Peterson case in the first place, and the police – *specifically Harry Longbridge.*

"I've been having some thoughts, Peter, about the police. The government's opened up recruiting again as you know, increasing by twenty thousand they say. I'm. . . well, I'm thinking of applying."

Peter Gray choked on a mouthful of coffee as half went down the wrong way and the other got royally spat down his shirt. He certainly wasn't expecting *that!* Gale's young fiancée, Gina, was expecting their first child and he obviously knew all about their horrific experiences in the States. If anything, he'd expected him to ask for some more time off because Gina was still suffering stress. This was something else entirely. He mopped the front of his shirt with a hanky.

"Are you sure about this, Andrew? I mean. . . it's a big step, a completely different direction altogether."

"Well, as sure as I can be. Don't get me wrong, Peter, I've loved working here, it's just that—"

"Just that you want to be chasing the criminals rather than writing up reports about them," his boss finished for him.

"Yeah. . . basically, yes. After being on the inner rim of two big cases, I think I want to be fully involved investigatively, although I know in all reality I'll probably end up writing up burglaries and traffic reports! At least the writing side won't come as a shock." Andrew took a sip of his coffee, not his favourite Italian from Café Calisé, but still hot and sweet. One of many images mopping up Rachel's tears and sharing a kitchen coffee break, floated briefly....

"Well, you've got plenty of experience in that regard, son, and from what I hear there's an awful lot of paperwork." Andrew smiled and was just about to take another mouthful when his mobile rang. He picked it up from the desk and swiped the screen.

"Andrew? It's Harry. I've got something for you."

* * *

Annie Longbridge checked the kitchen clock as she dried her glass. He'd be home with Baxter soon. She'd need to return the spare laptop to its hiding place – and quickly. At the end of that thought a ping echoed from the lounge. *A new email.* Annie slipped off the high kitchen stool and winced as she put the bottle back in the cupboard. Drinking alone at home in the middle of the afternoon had become more than a regular habit. It was only one or two, and of course she could stop any time she liked. . . she definitely *could*, it was just....

Her inbox showed a reply to her request from the site. *Already? Jesus. I must look better than I thought.* Annie checked her watch. *Three forty-five, only about fifteen minutes or so....* She turned back to the screen and clicked on the message. The email opened up with a link to check her account. She'd have to switch to a second phone if they were going to come through this quickly. Annie clicked through and logged in again. She opened the photo attachment and swept his facial features. *Not bad. Not as nice as the one I chose but. . . well, maybe that's a good thing.* Her eyes quickly swept the brief description and then checked her watch again. Three fifty. She flipped the lid down and made her way out to the hall, heart thumping. She expected Harry back any minute and it was imperative to get the laptop securely hidden.

At the top of the stairs she stopped. The window wall that overlooked the front garden held a large photo of their wedding. She hesitated briefly, feeling the weight of the laptop under her arm and a muddled sensation in her head, before turning to continue down the landing where she stopped at the spare room. It was a bit of a junk room in all honesty. If anyone stayed over (rare), they would use the middle bedroom next to theirs. It was just what she needed, though.

She pushed the door open and inched past the numerous bags of old clothes and shoes she'd kept meaning to take to the charity shop, the exercise bike and cross trainer she'd never used, and the aeroplane paintings Harry had inherited from his Uncle Bill and still not found anywhere to hang. There was no bed in this room which is why she ironed in it.... *sort of.* The board was always up and in situ, and she had to squeeze past that as well. It may have been a messy room, but it had its uses. . . like *still* not being decorated yet so no fitted carpet, and loose floorboards under the bike.

Annie put the laptop on the ironing board so she could pull the redundant *'Slim Cycle'* away from the wall. Crouching down she felt along the end edge of one of the floorboards where her fingers found the narrow gap. She lifted the wood panel out then removed four more. The space below was just big enough to hold the spare device. As she stood up to take it off the ironing board, Annie thought she heard Harry open the front door and Baxter's panty 'post-walk breathing' in the hall. She quickly replaced the loose floorboards and repositioned the bike on top before leaving the room and shutting the door behind her. Running quickly along the landing to the banister at the top of the stairs, she leant over to look down into the hall. No Harry, no Baxter. Annie strained to hear any sounds from below but heard absolutely nothing. *Must've imagined it* she thought, puzzled. *Guess I really should try and cut down. Well, maybe. . . but maybe it's time for those other changes too.* With that, she backtracked up the landing and turned into the bathroom.

* * *

RAMPTON HIGH SECURITY HOSPITAL
NOTTINGHAMSHIRE

Charlotte sat in the leisure room eyeing the activities of the other women. Some were reading, some were talking to each other and some were just sitting staring out of the window with a glazed expression on their faces. She was particularly taking note of Zoe Zandini bobbing here and there between them, a member of staff watching her as she went. Charlotte was also monitoring her every move in between dropping her eyes to the magazine in her lap, to keep her observation discreet. She knew it wouldn't be long before the younger woman approached her. . . again. *That* Charlotte was sure of.

Thirty-year-old Zoe (nickname *Stabby)*, had been her link to the outside, a link to what she *now* knew was the Zandini organisation. The mafia-like group who'd sprung her en route to her mother's funeral at the end of the previous year, and enabled her escape to the US – the considerably *dangerous* group to whom she now owed a king's ransom with not the slightest idea of how she was going to settle that debt. Her mother's inheritance (Charlotte believed) had initially been frozen, but as it turned out, Cynthia Krane had changed her will following her daughter's murderous rampage, leaving Charlotte penniless. This little nugget of destitution had been revealed by her mother's solicitor, Christopher Mogg, on the top floor of the Bellevue Hospital in New York. It was here Charlotte had finally been cornered and taken into custody – *for the second time.* The additional surprise sprung on her that day was truly a masterpiece on Mogg's part. . . and frankly if it wasn't for the fact it had majorly affected her, Charlotte could have hugely respected his entire plan. It had transpired Christopher Mogg was also the brother of the overly excitable would-be actress, her now ex-husband, Miles, had gotten a little too close to. Charlotte had 'dispatched' Mogg's sister because of it whilst posing as a mobile luxury makeover consultant. It was her belief that Susie Sarrandaire's *(real name Danielle Mogg)* solicitor brother, must have persuaded devastated widow Cynthia Krane to change her Last Will & Testament, thus leaving Charlotte with no future income. She'd long ago conceded the incredulous fact he'd managed to infiltrate the Zandinis' plans by getting his hairdresser/beautician partner to swap with their own makeover artist, and followed Charlotte to New York with the intention of tracking her down to kill her, was sheer genius. But diverting her *inheritance?* To some third-rate second *cousin?* That was something she could *not* concede to. . . *or forget.*

Charlotte's eye twitched. It was only the tiniest movement. Unusual for her, as she'd been trying hard to control her tick and the meds they had her on helped. Most people wouldn't have noticed, but Zoe Zandini was *not* most people – and was now looking straight at her. She suddenly smiled broadly, hurrying towards her idol, the wonderful Dr Charlotte, the woman she admired more than any other – the woman she followed around at every opportunity and modelled herself on. The woman she'd helped to escape and longed to be....

Zoe was in Rampton for similar reasons to Charlotte Peterson, albeit not quite as elaborate in their execution. It appeared she'd stabbed her social worker (hence the nickname), and three neighbours, all in one busy afternoon for absolutely no reason other than she was having a bad day. All survived. Three years previously Zoe had set up home with someone outside the family, which hadn't gone down well at all, meaning 'finances' had been withdrawn. Her partner (Jimmy 'the Lash' Johnson), had gambled and lost the best part of a week's wages on an online seven-horse accumulator, and the neighbouring kids had been playing their drums in the garden – *for two solid hours.* By the time the social worker had staggered outside and called the police, Zoe was back in the house from next door making them both a cup of tea, half-heartedly apologising and lighting up a cigarette. No, she was not *quite* in Charlotte's league. . . but somewhere in the back of her warped mind she'd like to be.

Zoe also knew she had to press her dear one for information about money again, for the New York debt. Her Uncle Raiffe had already been to see her on a visit and was getting seriously impatient for news. Being heavily pressed from 'above' was making him exceedingly uncomfortable.... He'd understood there would be delay, but the papers had got wind of Charlotte's lost inheritance, and delay had led to doubt, and doubt to disbelief. In the Zandini family, disbelief *always* led to despatch. The twin brother of Jimmy 'The Lash' had been despatched..... Zoe was worried.

"Charrrrlotte!!! There you are!! I've been looking for you *everywhere!!"* The younger woman beamed as her head jiggled agitatedly from side to side, long ginger spirals springing up and down from each temple, eyes scanning Charlotte's own noticeably uncomfortable features. Zoe's sickeningly cloying manner made even Charlotte squirm. Now with one arm extended as she approached, it was all Zoe could do to stop herself from stroking her idol. She snatched back the extended hand to let it fall by her side as Charlotte lowered her copy of *Psychology Now* and visibly flinched, her fingers scrunching the page in slow motion…

"Zoe…" The magazine was brought back up following the brief acknowledgement as Charlotte tried to imply she wasn't in a chatty mood. She fixed her attention on a picture in the article she was 'reading' as Zoe immediately pulled up a chair and sat down in front of her.

"Uncle Raiffe's been in again." The older woman's eyes didn't engage. Zoe looked down at her hands and began to pick round her bitten nails. "He was really upset, Charlotte, kept telling me to let you know things are getting serious now…" She lowered her voice and glanced furtively around as she spoke. "… with regards to…" Zoe leant in and pulled Charlotte's magazine down slowly with her forefinger… *"the money,"* she whispered. Charlotte let the magazine rest on her lap and smoothed out the crumpled page with a sigh. This conversation was just one of many they'd had about her uncle and his. . . *organisation,* since her re-admission.

"I don't know what to tell you, Zoe. You know the score, nothing's changed. My mother's will was altered without my knowledge. I haven't a penny – not a groat, not *anywhere.*"

Zoe initially looked puzzled at the old-fashioned word for coinage, decided against asking its meaning and began to roll her bottom lip in addition to the nail picking. Her fingers began interlocking back and forth, hands moving continuously over and under each other Uriah Heep-style. She'd already been anxious about bringing the subject up, but she also knew what Uncle Raiffe would expect her to do, and *that* was what was bothering her. Dr Charlotte was her hero. She was clever. She was beautiful, she was bold and exciting. She was a walking friggin' *legend* to Zoe Zandini. *Zoe really didn't want to have to mutilate her....*

THREE

Before he'd set off for home, Harry had waited for Andrew
to join him at the crime scene in Kirkdale Woods. Much
of the SOCOs' work had been completed just as St
Peter's struck five in the distance. They started to clear up
beneath a sky now broadly stained with blue-grey hues,
and Andrew glanced up at the threatened shower as a
breeze cut across the river. He carefully picked his way
along the uneven terrain towards the group, staying clear
of the sloping river's edge.

"Harry – hi – how's things?" he called out. Three white-
coated crime scene investigators looked up at the sound of a
new voice as they collected the last of their equipment, and
Joe Walker waved whilst dismantling the cordoned area.

"Andrew, hi, good to see you. Yes, fine thanks. How's
Gina? Everything okay with the baby?"

"Yes, all good, baby's on course for a September
birthday!" Fran glanced over at Harry who flushed

awkwardly. In that moment he'd forgotten there were three babies conceived during their combined US excursion. Andrew's fiancée, Gina, their friend Molly Fields who'd apparently had a fling with a keep-fit guru – Tai something or other (Harry hadn't kept up with naming formalities of the oriental arts) – and of course he and Fran had got closer than they should have....

"That's good, son – glad all's well," he replied, snatching a sidelong glance at Fran as Andrew bent down to an excited Baxter who'd come to greet him. He sat at his feet where a confused whine escaped having checked Andrew's pockets and discovered Dad's friend had arrived without treats.

"Sorry, Bax, I'm all out!" He held his hands palms upwards to the disappointed Lab and Harry called him back to put him on his lead.

"Andy, I have to get back – I've been out twice as long as usual and Annie will wonder where I am but. . ."

"*Won't* she just..." murmured Fran under her breath as she passed them to speak to a member of the team. Andrew threw a raised eyebrow at Harry to be met with a tight smile, and Joe flashed a supportive glance. Male sympathy bonding was certainly alive and well on the riverbank that afternoon.

"Baxter here's dug up an arm," continued Harry quickly, unable to stop a second glance at Fran as she continued her conversation with one of the forensics. He put an arm across his shoulders and walked Andrew over to where the limb had been packed into a cool bag. "Gave me a right start, I can tell you. Never did like finding the fresh stuff – and this one's pretty new." Andrew took out a notebook and began scribbling as they walked. "Strange thing though," Harry went on. "Had a signet ring on one of the fingers, it was engraved too, but we don't want that going in the papers. Okay, son?"

"Sure – you know I'd never write anything that could interfere with an investigation." Longbridge smiled and patted Andrew's shoulder. If he'd had a son, he'd want him to be just like him. He was a good man – one he could trust.

"You want to take a look then? Sure you're ready for that?" Andrew nodded and Harry pointed to a white cool box. The arm now lay inside it in a clear, sealed, marked and numbered evidence bag. For a moment Andrew hesitated, then remembered he'd just had a conversation with his boss about wanting a career change. He took a deep breath as Harry opened the lid. The two men looked at each other for a moment over the top of the container – then looked down. Andrew leaned in closer, stared in amazement at the arm inside the transparent forensic bag and thought how incredibly realistic it looked. Then he felt a bit of a dick and glanced around awkwardly as though his thoughts had been overheard. *This isn't a film set for God's sake....*

"Nasty," was all he could manage as he straightened up and jotted a couple of lines in his notebook. Then. . . "Obviously a man's. Was there anything else? Any other body parts? Clothing, personal effects, more jewellery and so on?"

"Not that they've found so far," Harry answered as he pointed in the direction of the trees Baxter had emerged from earlier. "Dog found it in the woods away from the riverbank here – stood there proud as you like with it hanging from his mouth. Pleased as punch, he was. Well. . . that's a Labrador for you!" The two men smiled as Andrew pocketed his notebook. Joe Walker passed them on his way back up to the car.

"The dogs will be out to cover that area tomorrow, Harry. Reckon young Bax here would like another go at that!" He crouched down to tousle the Lab's ears and immediately got a face wash. Laughing, he stood back up. "Love this boy of yours, sir, want to get a dog just like him one day."

"Can't do better than a Lab, son. They need training, mind, but they're a fine fit for a copper!" Joe smiled and continued to walk slowly in the direction of the car with the crime tape and poles under his arm.

"Don't forget you're my driver today Walker!" called out Fran from behind them. *"I don't want you disappearing and leaving me on a bloody riverbank, thank you!"*

"Yes, of course, ma'am – sorry, ma'am."

Harry winked at him as he saw the old 'Joe blush' spreading across the sergeant's face. "No 'arm done, Joe lad, no 'arm done...."

Fran groaned loudly, shot a look at her old partner that clearly stated, *'Really* Harry – *really?'* Then turned back to the forensics, dropped her head low and wrapped her arms tightly across her chest to hide the laugh that threatened to escape.

* * *

Harry shut the front door and took Baxter's collar and lead off. The Lab ran through to the kitchen and immediately began slurping noisily from his water bowl. Harry then pegged his jacket in the cloakroom having first fished out his mobile and switched it back on. After his walk had become somewhat extended, the battery had run low so he'd turned it off, and now wanted to check if Annie had rung him before he got accused of not answering her. As the music and lock screen sprang into life, it echoed around the large, airy hall.

He couldn't hear any noises from the kitchen other than Baxter digging around in his bed, so assumed there was no dinner on the way. . . *again.* A quick check revealed no calls were received from Annie whilst he was out, and he breathed a sigh of relief. Life had become an eggshell walk lately; another showdown over being late home he could do without, though late for what exactly was anyone's guess.

It was then he realised he could hear soft movements and TV noises coming from the bedroom. He was just about to climb the stairs when his wife came padding down in her dressing gown, a black towel on her head. A glance at his watch showed 6.10 p.m.

"Early night, love?" he asked, smiling, hoping that was an okay thing to come out with on a not so late Sunday evening.

"I'm not going to *bed,* Harry, I just wanted a nice relaxing bath. And now I want a nice relaxing glass of *wine.*" She flashed an expectant smile. *His* smile slowly faded as he just stood there. "What? *What?! I haven't had a drop all day! I'm entitled to an evening glass or two!*" Annie Longbridge returned her husband's concerned and somewhat doubting gaze with her usual fiery one. They both knew she hadn't got through the day this far without a drink. She swept haughtily past him into the kitchen, the black towel on her head a stark contrast to the escaped ash blonde tendril that, as of half an hour ago, had replaced her natural, much darker shade. As she rounded the door into the kitchen and disappeared, he caught sight of the blonde wisp. She'd changed so much in her behaviour and personality over the last six months he barely recognised her, but despite being a stylist, in all those years since they'd met, his wife had never changed the colour of her hair so dramatically.

His back stiffened. Suddenly the tick of the lounge clock tolled like Big Ben as Harry slowly followed. From the doorway he watched her reach up to the cupboard for a bottle of red and a bucket-sized glass that was soon filled, emptied and refilled. Harry put an arm out at the second filling then let it fall hopelessly to his side. She put the glass on the counter, turned round slowly and holding his eye line ripped the towel from her head. Even though mostly wet he could still see the excessive lightness of the blonde waves that tumbled past her shoulders. She reached behind her, picked up the glass and held it high towards him.

"*Cheers Harry – meet your new wife!*"

Dinner was a quiet affair. Well, if you could call beans on toast dinner. Harry chased the last few around his plate like his life depended on it. Annie just picked at a small cheese salad and then pushed it away. The clock on the wall crawled slowly round to 7.30 p.m. and Baxter sat expectantly by the sliding door to the garden. Harry got up to take his plate to the sink and let the Lab out on the way. He leant heavily on the counter top watching him from the window as he trotted round the garden looking for a favourite pee spot – which was basically everywhere. Harry just prayed he didn't start digging again, another row over bomb-site lawns he could do without right now. The tension was palpable.

"Coffee?" he asked optimistically to the back of Annie's bright blonde head. He reached for two mugs, hesitating...

"Yes. . . thanks..." she replied tightly, not turning round. Both felt drained, unhappy, disappointed with the other, but only one had the beginnings of unhealthy fleeting images ricocheting around their mind. Only one was stumbling, falling, victim to their recent experiences.

Harry let Baxter back in and picked up the two coffees from the work surface. He put one in front of his wife and hesitated before sitting back down. There was so much he needed to discuss with her; not just needed to, *wanted* to, but didn't know where to start. Or even *how* to start. He knew he couldn't tell Annie about Fran and the baby. Realistically he'd *never* be able to do that, although he knew it was always possible she'd hear through the grapevine. But he *did* want her to see someone about the post-traumatic stress she was quite evidently still experiencing.

Since the kidnap by recently released Kenny Drew, a vengeful ex-con he'd put away years before, his wife hadn't been the same person at all. Occurring whilst he'd been in New York tracking down the escaped Peterson woman, it had been a double nightmare for her. This was completely understandable, but trying to get her to see anyone about it, anyone at all, had been met vehemently with a brick wall. Harry knew the official route would be a complete no go, she'd always avoided anyone in a white coat, but even to try and get her to talk with friends had resulted in a flat refusal. Now she was drinking more heavily than ever, and appeared to be radically changing her outward self as well as her mental and emotional one.

Unbeknown to Harry, for Annie the kidnap had gone much deeper than Drew's connection with the bank heist her husband had sent him down for. Kenny had also known Annie during their teens. He'd raped her after a school dance which had resulted in a child, Michael, who her parents had insisted she have adopted. Michael Morton had initially been involved with the kidnap after tracking down his birth father. Kenny had spun him a story of Annie and himself being engaged, but that she'd deliberately chosen to abandon him as a baby whilst Kenny had wanted them to be a family. Michael was basically a good, if gullible, young man. He hadn't enjoyed the best childhood with his adoptive parents, and he'd also needed money. Kenny had promised him a good deal of it from the proceeds of the kidnap, but after seeing how Kenny had treated Annie during her captivity, and on learning the truth of his birth, Michael had got her away from the abandoned lock-up where she'd been held. During a dramatic escape Michael had shot and killed Kenny, and mother and son had escaped to her family home in London. *Harry Longbridge still had no knowledge of Michael Morton being Annie's son, only that he'd rescued her on that snowy March night....*

"Annie . . . can we talk – *please?"* He was standing at her shoulder holding his coffee, she was still at the table looking down into hers watching it go cold. Her thoughts lay firmly with her plans for the morning, one of the arrangements she'd made online a few days before.

"We *could*, Harry," she said drily, turning around to look up at him, "but that of course would involve you listening – and that's not something you really excel at, *is it?"* Annie pushed her chair back sharply, and leaving the kitchen went straight upstairs to her bedroom.

FOUR

Gina had just got in from work and having made a cup of tea, placed it on the side table and eased herself gently onto the sofa. The baby was due in a couple of months and had been lying awkwardly most of the day, now she just wanted to relax, if she could *just* avoid going to the loo for half an hour. Maternity leave was starting to look really attractive although she knew she'd miss some aspects of working at The Carpenters Arms – seeing more of her closest friend, Molly, for a start.

The other doctors at the Peterson's surgery had completely understood when she hadn't wanted to return following a break in the autumn of 2018. Everyone had been knocked sideways after the truth had come out, but for Gina, even though Miles had left and moved away and Charlotte was in Rampton, it was still a place that carried too many painful memories. She'd worked a few temporary positions throughout 2019, but since returning from

New York and recovering from all that had entailed, she'd accepted the offer from Molly's parents to work at the pub.

When her grandmother had gone into a home, she'd been fostered by the Fields' from age fourteen until meeting and ultimately moving in with Andrew. It had therefore felt right. She felt very comfortable, and more importantly, *safe*, plus the two friends were both expecting their first babies together, although in all likelihood Molly would be going it alone.

Gina *was* occasionally in touch with Miles, but it hadn't been easy and she still wasn't entirely comfortable with the relationship. It had been enough of a shock to discover why her mother, Emily Stone, had abandoned her and run off to America when Gina was only two, leaving her with her grandmother, then finally meeting and spending time getting to know her over the last couple of years. When she'd been told the husband of her murdering boss (who'd nearly killed her twice) was also her *father*. . . well, that had been a whole other mountain to climb. Miles Peterson hadn't exactly taken late parenthood in his stride either, but after the shock of learning the results of his university fling, he'd actually been quite pleased to discover he'd got a daughter. Charlotte had never been able to have children. It was the less than fatherly thoughts he'd harboured about Gina every morning as he'd passed her at the reception desk for nearly a year that had taken a lot longer to forgive himself for – that and the fact her mother had been his wife's closest friend, from primary school all the way through to their university days....

As she lay on the sofa stroking her baby bump and pondering the past, Missy cat came softly padding down the stairs from the bedroom (she always slept there when they were out), and jumped up beside her to snuggle down for post-work Missy 'cattention'. Initially Andrew's, the white Persian was now also very much Gina's, even before they'd bought the small townhouse and moved in together.

And so it was, when Andrew put the key in the door and let himself in, he was met with the sight of the two most important people in his world, cuddled up beneath a throw on the sofa. . . both snoring like warthogs.

"You comfortable there, Missy?" he whispered. "Keeping Gina company? Good girl." Andrew ruffled the top of the cat's head and walked past them into the kitchen to make a coffee as he churned over the day's events. Another murder in Kirkdale was unsettling to say the least. Charlotte Peterson aside, it wasn't a usual occurrence. Kirkdale was a smallish town with no history of any really serious crime, well not 2018 BC anyway *(Before Charlotte),* as the locals had started referring to it. Who the hell could it be? And just an arm! It was bizarre to say the least – and had Andrew completely hooked.

He walked back into the lounge having put the kettle on, and plonked down on one of the armchairs sighing impatiently. His brain was racing as it always did when a puzzle presented itself. Glancing at the clock, he noticed the time and picked up the control to turn on the local news. As the noise of the TV broke into the room, Gina stirred and he quickly lowered the volume. The report was top of the programme...

"Police were called to the lower part of Kirkdale Woods late this afternoon, after a local walker reported their dog had dug up a limb which is believed to be human. No details have been released as to whether it is male or female, and no other body parts have as yet been found. The entrance to the area has been cordoned off from the road and is now out of bounds to the general public until further notice. A full search using police cadaver dogs will commence first thing tomorrow morning...."

"Andy...? What was that about a limb being found?" Gina half sat up and threw an anxious look at her fiancé as she reached for her tea and wrinkled her nose on discovering it was now cold. Missy hastily jumped to one side as Gina's feet disturbed her snooze.

"That's where I was just before I came home," Andy replied getting up and walking over to the sofa. "Harry called me – Baxter dug it up. It was an arm." Gina's eyes widened followed by her mouth.... "I'll get you a fresh cup," he said as he picked up her cold tea and walked through to the kitchen.

"Thanks, I can't seem to stop dropping off as soon as I sit down these days, God knows how many cups of tea I've made and not drunk!" She looked for Missy to pick her up for a comfort snuggle after the 'arm news', but having seen her favourite person in the whole world enter the kitchen, Missy had immediately followed in the expectation of dinner. Andrew made Gina's tea and his coffee, and nearly tripped over the white cat who was now doing her twirly in and out leg thing as he walked round the kitchen reaching into cupboards.

"Yes, *okay*, Missy, I haven't forgotten *you – look!*" He held up a tuna sachet, waved it at the impatient feline, and grabbing a matching handful of biscuits from their box, proceeded to place each in separate silver dishes, mashing the fish with a fork. Only the best for the pickiest Persian in Kirkdale, and only when they were both placed on the floor did she leave his legs.

"They've not said on the news," he called out, "but it was definitely a man's arm and there was a signet ring on one of the fingers."

Gina grimaced. "Sounds utterly disgusting. You didn't actually *look* at it did you?"

"Well. . . yeah, I did actually. Thinking about this police recruitment lately, thought I wouldn't be much use if I couldn't face the awkward stuff."

"True," Gina agreed with an acknowledged nod. Andrew came through from the kitchen, passed the fresh tea over the back of the sofa, and sat down next to her. He wrapped his mug with both hands and blew across the top. Gina stared at what she could see of the bright red letters that hid between his fingers. Placing her tea on the table, she unpeeled Andrew's left hand from his mug...

"What?" he asked looking puzzled as Gina smiled knowingly.

"You've bought *another* one, haven't you?" she teased as she read slowly out loud – "*I – could – MURDER – a – coffee!*" He laughed and tweaked her nose gently.

"Oh, you *know* I can't resist a new caption mug!"

* * *

THE CARPENTERS ARMS PUB

Molly was on an evening break following a bite to eat. Sprawled on the couch in the private quarters of the pub, idly scrolling through her Facebook newsfeed, she began to feel ever so slightly guilty about the large portion of treacle pudding and custard that no longer sat in her bowl. However, she was also pregnant. Only four months but had recently started to feel a lot better after almost eight weeks of constant nausea – *hence the treacle pudding*.

"Make the most of it, my little Brooklyn baby," she said looking down and stroking her belly, "that was a one-off treat – don't go expecting *that* every day!"

As she lazily continued scrolling, a friend request suddenly appeared in her notifications. Molly clicked on it half-heartedly, expecting another foreign brain surgeon, admiral in the navy or other equally fake scammer. There had been a lot of those lately. Suddenly her heart stopped.

She swung her legs off the couch and sat up. Now well alert she switched to the person's timeline to make sure . . . and there it was in plain evidence....

* * *

Molly couldn't sleep. It was now 3.00 a.m. and she'd seen every ten minutes since getting into bed at midnight. The friend request had been on her mind all evening, so much so she'd poured two incorrect pints and double changed at least three customers. Luckily they were all regulars and very understanding – and *honest!* What should she do? It had just been a holiday fling. Not even a fling really, more of a. . . she hated to say it, and in fact had pushed it to the back of her mind, but at the end of the day it was what it was – a one-night stand. *Or two or three...* He *was* a lovely guy and had she been living out there would definitely have wanted to see where the relationship went but....

She turned over impatiently for the umpteenth time, picked her phone off the side cabinet and looked at the friend request again. There had been no expectation on her part to ever hear from him after she'd left New York, but there it was, clear as day. *Danny 'Kwondo' Kellerman.* There had been no mistaking it; even had his Taekwondo nickname. Molly lay on her back holding the phone in the air staring at his lovely smiling face, remembering their first meeting on the mat at the Brooklyn Dojang class. Then with a tense sigh she dropped her hand and held the mobile to her chest, biting her bottom lip as she drummed her fingers over the back of it. Her brain was hotwired now. *On a scale of one to ten. . . just how crazy would it be to accept his request? What might it lead to? And where...?*

This was exactly the sort of thing she would have shared with Gina had she still been living at the pub. Having her working alongside the last couple of months had been wonderful, but it had seemed an age since they'd lived together during their teen years, and Molly hadn't seen as much of Gina after she'd moved in with Andy. She'd missed her friend's company – Gina was closer than a sister, now it was almost like old times again – although at first she'd had to keep an eye on her attempts at serving draught! It had taken a good few shifts for Gina to pull a pint of beer for the punters as opposed to a pint of froth! She'd never actually worked in the bar before. But it was the hard decisions, the out of the blue surprises they'd always shared with each other she missed, often at the end of the day or in the middle of the night. Boy, did she wish she could pad down the landing and share this one with her right now.

Molly refreshed the screen. She was just about to press 'confirm' in a final act of rash decision making, when something bigger got her attention. Something much, much bigger.... She lowered the phone very slowly, and swallowing hard stared straight ahead. The air in the room had suddenly turned ice cold. She could feel a light breeze against her skin, moisture on her forehead – taste the iron. It hadn't happened for a *very* long time but it was happening again now. Not as dramatic a wound, but the blood was still running, still the same rich colour. . . and it meant the same thing. Only this time the vision wasn't a woman...

And she knew him.

FIVE

JULY 2ND

Annie Longbridge drove the ten-year-old Range Rover Sport slowly past Kirkdale Woods, and casually glanced at the scene that had sprung up overnight. The news report she'd watched in the bedroom the previous evening came to mind.

Billowing tape cut the public off from the gravelled parking area at the top of the slope leading down to the river – it was clearly making a statement. It catapulted her thoughts back to breakfast that morning, and the statement *she'd* made very clearly to Harry....

Annie had sat Monroesque at one end of the table, bed-head blonde waves and a glass of something clear, effervescent and distinctly less alcoholic in front of her. Harry, as usual, had been at the other end nursing a strong black coffee in his Arsenal mug. The air in the kitchen had been heavy with questions, the pain in Annie's head piercingly real, and the Alka-Seltzer in her tumbler several fizz decibels too loud. Baxter, bless him, had watched suspiciously from his bed between both front paws.

"*Why*, Annie?" he'd asked. The question had floated somewhere between the smell of burning toast and the Alka-Seltzer playing a drum solo. She knew he knew the answers, he just needed to hear her say them out loud – accept them, deal with them. . . get help.

"Why what?" she'd asked, lifting her head disinterestedly from staring inside the glass to meet his confusion. There'd appeared to be genuine concern in his eyes. She hadn't been sure, so had gazed at them for a little while, at the worry that seemed to hover there and above, buried in deep frown lines. Annie remembered Harry's head tilted on one side, his concentrated 'trying to understand' expression looking back at her, just before the explosion....

"You know damn well what! The hard, brittle attitude, the drinking. . . the, the. . . " (She remembered he'd palmed a hand upwards at this point, gesticulating sharply towards her) ". . . the bloody *hair!!*"

She'd taken a deep breath then and let it out slowly, still looking at him. The table wasn't that big, the one they'd sat at together and eaten breakfast most mornings for years. *That* morning it had felt at least a mile long. She'd picked up the tumbler, drunk it dry and stood up arrow straight and with cool detachment....

"Identity, Harry. . . identity – I no longer had one. *Now* I do...."

Oh yes, she thought crisply, looking hard at the road ahead – *that I definitely do.*

The cordon was left rattling in the wind behind her as the Range Rover wound its way down the hill towards the bridge and out of town.

* * *

She was sitting at the back facing the door. Annie knew it was him from his online profile. Naturally he wouldn't be able to share similar knowledge of her – not now she'd changed her appearance so dramatically.

Annie smiled calculatingly behind a large mug of tea, wishing it was anything but. She watched him closely as he entered. Medium height and build, around forty with a shock of auburn hair skimming the collar of his tan leather jacket. He hesitated and scanned the cafe from the doorway. Looking a little confused, possibly even a little agitated at not being able to see her, he checked his watch. Enjoying his confusion, she didn't move as a flop of hair shaded his eyes when he looked down at his wrist. Not being familiar with the area he hadn't exactly arrived early. Maybe she'd given up and gone? The hair was pushed back impatiently with a large hand as he bent to look through the brown painted *Cally's Café* signage splurged across the huge window. His eyes squinted up and down the pavement and over to the village green, but neither brought any information. He was beginning to feel awkward, standing as he was in the walkway of the cafe. Waitresses squeezed either side of him as he dithered between two rows of imitation light-oak table and chair sets.

Annie continued her summing up from the back of the room. She was already learning to think differently – *to wait.* To collect more detail. To be thorough, sharp, like a sniper – like a predator. That much she'd absorbed from her Rampton meetings. Finally, when it looked as if he was about to leave, she stood up. Revelling in the control but smiling now, she waved him over. His expression was unsure and he paused as a waitress behind him sighed impatiently, holding a tray of used cups. He turned round, apologised and breathed in to let her through, then looked back at the platinum blonde waving at him; this unfamiliar woman who clearly knew *him*, but was certain he didn't recognise. Seeing his hesitation she grabbed a handful of hair, shook it wildly and grinned, rolling her eyes in laughter by way of an explanation. Realisation slowly dawned. He smiled back, and edged his way slowly between the tables, *walking happily but naively towards her. . .*

* * *

Darcy and Deefa sniffed and scurried, nose down exploring the earth, tree roots, bushes, mossy mounds, criss-crossed pathways and tracks, leaving no area unchecked for human traces. . . *human remains.* They had been working hard for the last couple of hours, and as cadaver dogs the two yellow Labs knew they had a job to do. They were specifically trained to find as many stages of decomposition as possible – and all that went with it.

Bones, flesh, blood, tissue, semen, clothing and other materials stained with human bodily fluids, or maybe chemicals. These and much more could be found by an experienced forensic-evidence search dog. They were the first such dogs in the area, and their handler was very proud of them.

"Good lad, Deefa, good lad, Darcy, track him – track Ted!" DS Suzanne Moorcroft encouraged the two Labs she'd bonded closely with after specialising in the dog unit the last two years. She was a good handler.

"Anything?" called out Fran from a camping chair she'd brought in case it was going to be a long job. "And who's Ted? We don't have any info on the arm yet."

"I've trained them to 'track Ted' rather than 'find the body', just in case anyone's around," she replied. "It's a bit more sensit—" Suddenly her hand went up as Deefa began to whimper and whine, getting very agitated. Having nosed a huge sweep of the area, he was about a hundred feet from where the arm had been unearthed by Harry's dog the previous day. At Deefa's raised alarm, Darcy had run over to where his team mate was frantically digging. Suzanne gave a *'Stand by!'* command to both dogs and they immediately stood back – alert and ready to receive a small liver treat for their efforts.

Fran waved a couple of PCs with shovels in the general direction of the activity. With anticipation of further remains being discovered, she hoped there'd be something, *anything* belonging to the same as yet undiscovered male body. If not, it would mean a second murder for Kirkdale.

When the PCs reached her, Suzanne pointed to the specific area the dogs had scented, and the two officers began to take it in turns to make use of their shovels. Luckily the earth was quite soft in the spot the two Labs had sniffed out. It was easy to dig.

Now late morning, the sun had come out and was shining directly onto their backs, having found a gap in the branches. There was only a sparse covering of trees in that area. This now got Fran thinking. Surely anyone burying a body, or parts of a body, would have chosen a much deeper and denser part of the woods, nearer where the arm had been found? *Strange....*

Twenty minutes later and with a fairly large hole and two piles of earth either side, there was still no 'Ted'.

"Could they have made a mistake, Suze?" called Fran, feeling the heat and wiping a hand across her forehead, although as DI not actually involved with any shovelling activity....

"No – definitely not, there'll always be something, not necessarily what we'd be looking for though. It could be a—"

"Dog bone!" finished Rob McPhail, the shorter and stouter of the two, grinning above his ginger beard and moustache as he held up the very old, very dirty marrow bone – "Clearly more sheep than Ted, ma'am!"

"See – told you, there's always *something!*" called back Suzanne crouching down ruffling the two Labs' heads as both dogs looked up at her very pleased with themselves.

"Well, that was a waste of two hours," declared Fran to herself checking her watch. "Now I need coffee and a plate of pas—" She fished a ringing mobile out of her pocket and hit the answer button. "DI Taylor. . ." She looked over at Suzanne and the two PCs who'd begun walking towards her with the dogs, and beckoned them urgently. "Yes, yes, I've got that. When exactly? Okay. . . yeah, right, do you have any idea of time? *Really?* Interesting – thanks. I'll be in touch."

"Ma'am?" Suzanne now stood in front of her DI, with Darcy and Deefa sitting calmly at heel waiting to get back in the van. Having just seen her governor's face though, she wasn't feeling quite so calm.

"That was Penrith," replied Fran. "Seems they have a man's leg in the local morgue..."

* * *

Molly had not been at all happy that morning. With no visions experienced for a good two years, it was not something she wanted recurring. Whilst having a natural sense of 'knowing' about certain things was kind of nice, and frankly quite useful sometimes – dead bodies floating in her bedroom at night again was a definite no-no. Of course she hadn't enlightened her parents of the latest news, but she *had* rung Gina – as soon as she'd got up.

"... yes I know. I *know*, Gee, you don't have to tell *me* that, I've only just got past the vomiting stage!" Gina being Gina, was worrying about Molly's early pregnancy and the stress she could now be under if it all started up again.

"*Why* though, Molls – why *now?* Unless. . . unless it's to do with—"

"You saw the news last night too, then?" replied Molly, shoving four slices of white in the toaster, pushing the lever down and flicking the kettle on. She was regularly famished now she could eat properly again. "Thing is, Gee. . ." She hesitated, not entirely sure she was right because there'd only been the one meeting but . . . "The thing *is* – I think I know *who.*"

"Oh my God, you *are* kidding me!?" Gina rushed down the phone. "You never actually *knew* any of the others two years ago. So come on – *who the hell is it?!!*"

Molly swivelled the kettle round and picking it off the base poured the boiling water on a teabag and spooned in three sugars. Despite getting her appetite back and no longer throwing up every morning, she still couldn't face any coffee, but her sweet tooth was well out of hand – particularly with her tea.... "No, no, I didn't – this one is a complete surprise to me I can assure you."

"*And. . .?*" Gina prompted impatiently. "*Who* then – *who did you see?!!*"

"You remember when we were at the top of the hospital when – when. . ."

"Of course, I could hardly forget I nearly *died – again!*"

"Well, the guy that ran in at the end, the one who was really hysterical because Charlotte had murdered his sister that summer – *remember?*"

"Yes – yes, get to the point!"

"It was him. Susie Sarrandaire's brother, the solicitor that did for Charlotte Peterson with her mother's will. Got her mum's money diverted to a distant cousin or something. *It was him – Christopher Mogg.*"

SIX

RAMPTON HIGH SECURITY HOSPITAL

RETFORD, NOTTINGHAMSHIRE, UK

Charlotte was in the flower garden with a few other residents, under a watchful eye of course but it *was* summer and at least it was outside. Gardening was hardly a passion, but a change of scenery did help a little, and today's scenery was very interesting indeed.

She watched the man carefully as she dug little holes for the Busy Lizzies with a plastic trowel. No metal or sharp implements were allowed. This was a shame given the number of irritating people she found herself living with again....

Kneeling on the grass holding a small pink plant above the earth, plastic trowel poised, her eyes narrowed in tense thought at the man walking slowly towards her on the path from the south wing. Charlotte held her breath. She didn't recognise him but could guess by his stature, his walk, his Mediterranean complexion – *this was Raiffe Zandini.*

As the steps got closer Charlotte dropped her head and concentrated hard on the job in hand. She placed the flower into the hole, held it carefully and scooped the soft earth around its base, patting the soil down purposefully with her fingers. The gravel scrunched louder, until it sounded like a whole army of boots fell on it, until her ears rang with it. . . *until it stopped.* She froze.

Hearing several voices, Charlotte looked up and now saw Zoe Zandini holding a tea tray and talking with the man and one of the warders by the wooden picnic tables. These were set on a flag-stoned area about twenty feet from where Charlotte was working. Her closet admirer glanced over very briefly. Charlotte thought she looked anxious, worried even. The warder stepped back to settle on a wall bench to read, whilst the man and Zoe sat down with their drinks at a table. Zoe had made sure she was facing her idol and the man had his back to her. She didn't want Uncle Raiffe to spot Charlotte, unless she was pressed to tell him the woman was just a few yards away. He already knew what she looked like – that was dangerous enough....

"Soooo.... tell me, Zozo, vhat is zhe current seetuation viz her?" Raiffe Zandini spoke in a heavy, low and thickly accented voice as he looked stonily at his niece. Zoe noticed there did not appear to be much in the way of caring in his eyes, but that he still used his childhood nickname name for her. She squirmed awkwardly on both counts. The wooden seat suddenly appeared harder and distinctly more uncomfortable, and her eyes glanced everywhere in an effort not to look directly at Charlotte, who was a damn sight closer than she would have liked. This was an unusual thought for Zoe, but considering her visitor the situation merited it.

"It's just the same, Uncle Raiffe. I told you, she *has* no money. It's been diverted to some distant cousin somewhere she's not seen in *years*."

"You assured me zhis voman vas reech, Zozo, *ve-ry*, *ve-ry* reech, zhat zhere vould be no reesk in investing in her. . . and her. . . *beesiness*."

Zoe leant forward pretending to blow the heat off her tea and spoke low and fast.... "She *was!* Or at least was about to be. Her parents were *millionaires!* How was I supposed to know a pissed-off brother of one of her victims would turn out to be her mother's solicitor?" It all came out in an exasperated rush. Zoe's cheeks flamed. She'd begun to feel pressured in the last few months since Charlotte's recapture and re-appearance at Rampton, but had no desire to anger her uncle. Raiffe Zandini said nothing. He did not have a very understanding expression on his face, and after taking a large gulp of tea, Zoe resorted to her anxiety crutch as she began to pick her fingers.

Raiffe slapped her hands. "You *know* vhat zhis means if she does not find a vay of paying her debt to us. You know how it vorks in zhis fam-eely, Zo. You vere zhe introduction agent. Eet is *your* reesponsi*beel-ity* to make sure zhere are consequences – repercussions, understandings. Zhey must not be fatal. . . at first. Ve still need to try and recoup zhe debt after all. Zhis voman, zhis . . . *Charlotte Peterson.* . . she vill know vhot it means to cross a Zandini. To take vhat is not hers, to have no honour in beesiness, to laugh at and have no fear of zhe largest, most powerful family in Eet-aly!" As he finished with a flourish snapping his fingers in the air, his voice, now raised, attracted the attention of the concerned warder. Her expression gave a warning. Raiffe smiled broadly at both her and his niece, and dipping his head to the woman in acknowledgement, now cradled and patted Zoe's reluctant hands instead. The Zandinis were indeed the most powerful family in Italy. Raiffe though had been born to a Ukranian mother and spent much of his early life in Russia. His Italian father had taken him back to his home country when she died, and try as he might, Raiffe could never shake that Slavic accent....

Zoe pulled her hands slowly away from beneath her uncle's and started to shake. Her mouth felt dry despite the tea. Since the newspaper reports of her lost inheritance, she'd always known this would be the result of Charlotte's dilemma. It would be bad enough whoever it was, but her dear one – her special, wonderful friend? *How could she bear it?*

"Please, Raiffe, *please* don't make me do this," she begged. "It would be near impossible to find a way in here anyway, and if I were to be—"

Raiffe slid his large, strong hands back slowly over both of hers and squeezed hard. "You vill find a vay, Zozo. . . *a Zandini alvays finds a vay...*"

Zoe winced in pain. A little more than was necessary in order to steal a glance at Charlotte, hoping Raiffe wouldn't notice. But a member of the Mob, from wherever in the world, has heightened reactions, almost vampiral senses. He swivelled quickly in his seat. It was a fast, snatched motion – and then he saw her. The woman in the flower garden. The woman looking in their direction. *The woman who owed him a very great deal of money.*

* * *

Harry had not been happy about the situation at breakfast. *Or the night before come to that,* and he hadn't heard from Annie all day either. It was now five o'clock and he was sitting in the Carpenters Arms with a pint – phone in front of him. His finger hovered over the call button and the number displayed was Fran's. He took another swig of his beer and attempted to press the connection again but didn't quite make it. He'd already had three stabs at it and now it was getting silly, but since seeing her in the woods the previous day, it had stirred things up again. Not that his feelings had waned any, just that being in her company. . . it had brought it all back; their work partnership, their closeness in New York. His thumb stroked the screen and he gave a deep sigh....

Kirkdale Woods had been the first time they'd seen each other since their return, and although he'd rung in the arm discovery *(courtesy of Baxter)* directly to her without any problem at all, this was entirely different. He wasn't in the job anymore. Phoning Fran to find out what was happening with the case now would look lame, like he was trying to get back in, get back on the team, to work with her again – *which of course he was.*

One finger traced the line of the pint mug handle from top to bottom then began to tap the phone screen incessantly, but not quite hard enough to make the call.

"Hey Harry – why so glum?" Molly had swung round the corner of the bar into his favourite 'cubby hole' where he was sitting. "Not found a retirement hobby yet then?"

"Ah. . . Miss. . . Fields, how are you doing? And er. . . no, no I've not found a hobby as yet."

"It's *Molly!* God, you don't need to call me Miss *anything* now, not after all *we've* been through." Harry acquiesced, smiling softly over his glass. "You know what I think, don't you?" she continued quickly wiping down the table in front of him. *He didn't but sensed he was about to.* "*I* think you should get in touch with Fran, see if you can come out of retirement permanently. You're *way* too young to be put out to grass anyway!"

"Thank you. . . *Molly.* I happen to agree with you on that as it goes." He smiled again, and taking another sip of his pint actually felt a little more decisive about the conversation he knew he had to have.

"Reckon that call will come before you know it – decision made for you, as it were," Molly replied, clearing the table beside him now and smiling to herself. "Let me know if you'd like anything to ea—" And there it was. Harry's *Law & Order* ringtone filling the air as

Fran's number illuminated the screen. He turned to look incredulously at Molly and mimed a pointy hat and mouthed 'witch', as the phone vibrated on the table. She grinned knowingly, tapping her nose....

"Fran. . . it's Harry!" he said excitedly.

"Yes, I know, Harry – I just rang *you*. . ."

"Oh yes. . . *Sorry* – yes, of course. How are you?" he replied as Molly laughed and then mouthed *'cheese ploughman's?'*. He nodded and gave a thumbs up.

"Fine, thank you. I just thought you'd like to know what happened this morning with the cadaver dogs, given it was Baxter who'd dug up the arm." Not a sentence that would get many people worked up, but Harry's heart skipped a beat....

"Yes, definitely, did they find anything else connectable? Well, not exac— "

"It's all right, I know what you mean." Fran couldn't help a small smile escape as she turned her back on her blind-free office window. "Unfortunately, or fortunately depending on how you look at it, they didn't find anything else *connectable,* just an old lamb bone. A local dog had probably buried it to return for it later. Not Bax I take it?"

"*Nooo*. . . *God* no, Annie would never let—" He stopped short.

"*Anyway*. . ." continued Fran pointedly, "after that I had a call from Penrith. As luck would have it they've had a leg turn up. It's now in the hospital morgue. I'm waiting on blood tests on both to see if there's a match."

"And if there isn't we have—" interjected Harry.

"*We* have two bodies – so far, yes." She accented the '*We*'. Harry was always right back in there, and as much as she knew that's where he wanted to be, where he belonged really, he wasn't. *Well. . . not yet anyway.* She was working on that one but couldn't say anything officially yet.

"Fran. . . do—" She knew what was coming and didn't want to go down that particular road till she'd worked her little bit of magic.

"Look, Harry, I really have to go. I've a meeting in ten minutes before I head off home and I need to grab a coffee first. It's going to be a tough one."

"Oh right, okay," he said resignedly. "Well, good luck with that then." He paused... "Just keep me in the loop if you can, you know I like to hear how. . . well, you know. . . how things are going for you."

She smiled, dropped her head and stroked her belly. She was beginning to show now and with Harry on the other end of the phone it was like a little captured family moment. "Sure, of course I will. *And Harry. . . ?*"

"Yes?" he replied hopefully...

"Don't go joining any golf clubs just yet." She hung up, and pocketing her mobile, walked out of the office to go upstairs to Chief Superintendent Chris Hitchings' rather more impressive suite. *It was time to bring Harry in from the cold.*

SEVEN

Andrew was not long back at the *Courier* having interviewed a restaurateur who'd been vandalised at the weekend. He was just about to pull up his report on the arm found at Kirkdale Woods when Gina came bursting through the office door. She was panting as though she'd been running for at least fifteen minutes although at seven months pregnant could achieve the same state in only five....

"An – Andy, yo – you're not going to—" She aimed for the nearest desk, supporting herself with her left hand, and rubbing a painful side stitch with her right.

"Hey – *heyyy* – what the hell?! Gee? Are you okay?" Andrew jumped up from his chair to reach her, quickly checking her over for any injuries whilst one of his colleagues went to get Gina a glass of water. "Why on earth have you been running? You're in no fit state to go marathon training, you know!" Still panting she glanced up at him sarcastically with a *'yeah, very funny'* look on her face – *he* genuinely concerned and confused, helped his fiancée into a chair, then picked up her hands after bobbing down to kneel in front of her. Sally Coombs returned from the kitchen with the water, and smiling a thank you, Gina drank deeply before continuing. Grabbing Andrew's forearms, she got her breathing under control and when she could speak coherently enough to tell him, Andrew knew he'd never forget her news....

"Molly rang me earlier. I tried to get you but your mobile went to Ansaphone."

"Sorry, Gee, I must've left it in the car, I was out on an interview. What on earth did she *say?*"

"*Visions*, Andy, she's got them back again. She had one last night." Andrew paled visibly as his brows lifted in conjunction with widening eyes....

"Go on. . ." he said quietly, glancing up as Peter Gray hurried down the office to join them, equally concerned having seen Gina's flurried entrance.

"Gina – Andrew. . . are you okay?. . . *Is* she okay?" he asked, babbling and turning from one to the other. "Do you need a glass of – oh, you've got one. Good."

"No, no, I'm fine – Sally got me one, thank you Peter," replied Gina smiling appreciatively.

"You were saying, sweetheart? About Molly...?" Andrew encouraged.

"Yes. . . she had one of her visions late last night when she was in bed. She couldn't sleep. It was a massive shock because she'd not had any for *two years*, not since. . . since—"

"*Since Charlotte. . .*" said Andrew and Peter in unison.

It was 8.00 p.m. Molly had the night off and was now sitting on Gina and Andrew's sofa with Missy cat in her third favourite place, on *her* lap. In fact where fish and chips were concerned, Molly's lap was her *first* favourite place because Molly usually had rock salmon as it was her favourite. This was just as well because it was also Missy's favourite.

"So. . . Christopher Mogg," said Andrew from an opposite chair, dipping a large chip in tomato sauce.

"Does it really matter *who* it was, Andy?" questioned Gina. "I mean obviously it's a bit *extra* creepy that we sort of. . . *know* him but...."

"It's the fact they've come back at *all*," finished Molly as another piece of rock salmon disappeared down Missy's throat.

"*Exactly*" continued Gina stroking her bump protectively. "It means things are starting up again. But it can't be *her*, can it? I mean. . . she's still inside. She *is* still inside, *isn't* she, Andy?"

"I think Harry would've rung me if there'd been any change to that, and I'd be bloody surprised if Rampton managed to lose her a *second time!*"

"I saw Harry this afternoon actually," said Molly passing Missy cat to Gina so she could eat some supper. "He came into the pub for a pint and a bite to eat. Looked a bit on the agitated side actually, think he was trying to decide whether to ring DI Taylor. He was staring at his phone with a finger hovering over it then *she* rang *him!* Although I *did* sort of tell him she would."

"How'd you mean? Or given your resumed talents is that maybe a stupid question?" asked Andrew.

Molly pulled a face. "We had a chat about how he hadn't found a hobby yet and I told him I thought he should give her a call – see if he could sort of come out of retirement as it were. Dunno if that's even possible, especially a second time, but you know what he's like when he's not working, he gets bored stiff."

"You know it was Baxter who found the arm in the woods, don't you, Molls?" called Gina from the kitchen, having placed a disgruntled Missy on the floor and now getting them all drinks. "Andy was there with Harry yesterday collecting information for the *Courier*. Actually, Harry called him to the scene."

Molly shook her head then swallowed quickly saying, "Wow!! Go Baxter!!" before shovelling in another piece of fish much to Missy's disgust, and eating like she'd not been fed in weeks.

"Yeah, he did, and I was," said Andrew. "Seemed absolutely fine then. . . although—"

"He was back in his environment though, wasn't he – *see?*" said Molly, hands palms upward. "*That's* why he was looking so agitated in the pub today. He needs back in or he'll go nuts."

Since their reunion in New York under even worse circumstances than Charlotte's rampage of 2018, the three had formed an unusual friendship with Harry whilst he was in the service. One which may not necessarily last an entire *lifetime*, but they'd probably all share for a good few years yet.

There was general agreement at Molly's assessment of Harry's current demeanor as Gina awkwardly passed her their teas with one hand, held out a bottle of lager to Andrew with the other, and then eased herself down onto the sofa again next to Molly. Missy immediately jumped back on her lap, and discovering it was getting smaller and smaller these days, finally settled between them, nose back in Molly's fish bag.

"*Such* a traitor, Missy cat, soon as the girls are here!" said Andrew winking as he picked up his beer.

"Andy's been thinking of joining the police, haven't you?" said Gina looking at Molly, more as a statement than a question.

"Really?" her friend replied looking at Andrew. "Are we seeing a bit of 'Harry encouragement' at work here?"

"Well. . . initially I guess. He did mention something about it in the middle of events two years ago, and it's been niggling me ever since. After our experiences in New York I must admit it's been on my mind quite a bit."

"You should," said Molly firmly, picking up her tea. "You *absolutely* should. He'd be great, wouldn't he, Gee? When are you going to apply?"

"I'm still thinking about it. I'd like to but with the baby due in September and the wedding planned for Christmas. . . well, I think I need to put it off for a while to be honest."

"Takes a long time, though," said Molly, "from start to finish I mean. A friend of mine down south got accepted last year and it took about six months from applying to actually starting at Hendon. I imagine it'll be the same or at least similar at Penrith." Andrew and Gina exchanged glances. Gina looked at her bump and back up at him.

"If you're sure it's what you want, Andy, then go for it. If Molly's right then it'd be January before you even got into training, and by then Molly's baby will be here too."

"*Exactly!* We'll both be supporting each other, the kids will be like *siblings!*" added Molly excitedly.

"Actually. . ." Andrew ran his tongue nervously over his bottom lip, "I did have another look at the Constabulary website the other day. Several times last week in fact...."

Molly and Gina looked at each other and rolled their eyes....

"*Just do it!*" they both chimed out loud as they shook chips at him. Missy took this lax moment as a final opportunity. A white fleshy chunk protruding from Molly's bag proved far too tempting, and grabbing it neatly, she jumped off the sofa and disappeared into the kitchen.

* * *

Fran Taylor knew she'd have a damned hard job convincing Chief Superintendent Hitchings to consider asking Harry to come out of retirement again, and because of it had prepared her case with great care. She'd pointed out he'd only really been away for four months anyway since the New York job, so would it really be that difficult to arrange, especially with what appeared to be a big case brewing and several officers off with a serious sick bug, a couple of which were senior in rank and that would mean bringing help in from Penrith anyway?

She'd already got some inside knowledge on who was likely to get transferred down to Kirkdale, and from past conversations knew that for all his misgivings, Chris Hitchings would rather have Harry Longbridge back in (better the devil he knew), than either George Jenkins or Douglas Judd. Worse than that (she'd pointed out in glorious Technicolor), if things *really* took off they could end up with *both* of them. Douggie had been giving her boss an insufferable caning on the golf course the last ten years and enjoying it exceedingly, and George. . . well, George Jenkins was twice as bad as Harry for not working to the book, plus he liked his whisky far too much.

Now with the sight of Hitchings' jaw almost hitting his clasped hands in dread, Fran was already planning where Harry's desk would sit....

"DI Taylor, I'm not quite sure *how* or even *why* come to that, but it seems you've managed to persuade me to consider reinstating DCI Longbridge *again. . .*"

"Well, sir, I was beginning to get concerned, what with the size of the team shrinking due to this bug that's hit us, my maternity leave will start in three months, and with the early stages of 'Operation Bonaparte' – the body parts case – I thought it best to get some real experience back in the squad. . . *sir.*" She'd made her case perfectly. It was absolutely watertight and they both knew it.

"*Hmmm...* well, I won't be putting up with Harry doing *anything* outside the box, *do you hear me, Taylor?* He *will* toe the line and he *will* do everything by the book. *Do you understand?* I don't want a repeat of the escalation in New York, *or* the lack of reporting that followed his poor wife's abduction and incarceration in South London."

"Yes, sir – I mean – no, sir, of course not, sir. . . I'll make sure of it."

"Well, you'd better had, Taylor, because I'm making you *personally responsible!*"

"I understand, sir, so. . . I can, make arrangements then?"

Hitchings tapped a pen several times on the pad in front of him staring long and hard at both before looking back up at her. He had a strong feeling he was going to regret this....

"Tell Longbridge to come and see me first thing tomorrow – I want him in this office at 8.00 a.m. – and without an attitude!"

Fran could barely hide the upturn of her mouth. She was desperately trying to stay serious and professional. "Eight o'clock it is, sir – I'll make sure he's informed."

Hitchings harrumphed, quite convinced he'd been set up once again by his relatively new DI, and absolutely no real clue as to how she'd managed it either time. He *had* noticed however, Fran had already backed out of his office as quickly as was decently possible before he could change his mind.

With a huge grin now and a spring in her step, she was soon back in her own office collecting her things, then down to reception and out into the station car park. Sitting in her car she punched the air and pulled out her mobile to make the call. Harry was back on board. . . *and so was their partnership.*

EIGHT

Annie Longbridge hadn't exactly enjoyed the meeting with her first online date. Admittedly it was only coffee and cake in a small cafe (*out of town of course*), but electrifying it definitely wasn't. None the less it had served its purpose. He wanted to see her again. They'd made arrangements to meet up for a meal a couple of nights later at a little Italian in Penrith, although at the end of the day the type and setting of the restaurant was completely irrelevant. She just needed to make her own special arrangements for the end of the evening. . . *and not make a mess of them.*

Now back in Kirkdale and walking the supermarket aisles, Annie had been reflecting on that liaison. Hesitation set in at the wine section. Her breathing quickened and lips rolled tensely before she pushed the trolley straight past, walked round the end to frozen foods and irritably slung in a bag of chips and a pizza.

It was the fact he'd spent the majority of the time waxing lyrical about his *poor* dead sister, clearly demanding empathy across his latte and custard slice instead of showing interest in getting to know *her*, that she felt it was going to make her job a damn sight easier. At first, when he'd introduced himself and sat down he'd appeared to be quite pleasant. . . for all of ten minutes. Then the conversation had quickly descended into *Danielle this and Danielle that....* Of course Annie had known the subject may come up – it *was* after all why she'd chosen him, or rather why Charlotte had instructed she hunt him down through any means necessary and set up a meeting. A colossal amount of googling, and frankly sheer luck, had turned him up on a dating site soon after first locating him through his Facebook and LinkedIn profiles. Social media – always the first port of call when stalking someone.... She'd cross-referenced his details after seeing his photo during a flick through of '*Switched On,*' just to make sure it was definitely the same person. Luckily it was – *not for him though, obviously.*

Annie continued on through the freezer section and turned at the end back to where she'd come from, pulling three bottles of red down after absentmindedly scanning the shelves. She added them to the items in her trolley. Annie hadn't a clue what they were, but the familiar and comforting 'chink' sounded as she cruised on autopilot to the checkout.

* * *

When Harry received the second call from Fran in a little under two hours, he had just been about to leave the pub and go home. He'd left it as late as he'd dared, although with dinner having less than a remote chance of making an appearance when he got there, he hadn't a clue why he should be worrying about time.

"*Fran?* Do you have news about the blood tests on those body parts already?"

"*Nope!* I have news you need to be in Hitchings office at 8.00 a.m. sharp tomorrow morning." She was smiling so widely, heart thumping so hard as she awaited his reply, she had to stuff a fist in her mouth to stop her gabbling in excitement. Not that she'd really let him *hear* that, of course.

Initially there was silence from the other end – first time in a long time Harry Longbridge was finding it hard to speak.

Fran removed her fist.... "Harry? Are you – can you hear me? Did you hear what I just said?"

He finally found his voice (somewhere below the lump in his throat....) "I heard you. Just can't believe you pulled it off a second time – and I'll be there. *Of course I'll be there!*"

She smiled, head leaning against the window of her car. It had started to rain again, the screen definitely looked blurry. Or maybe it was just her....

* * *

TWENTY MINUTES OUTSIDE PENRITH

The little sixteenth-century church stood in the valley behind the dry stone wall that ran alongside the road's verge. To the left flowed the river, behind and to the right the huge hills climbed almost endlessly, a vast vampire cloak beneath the night sky.

Built by ancient hands from slate and stone, St Martin's had three small lead glass windows evenly spaced down each side, one at each end and a heavy wooden door beneath a peaked roof that faced the road. With a little modern help over the years in one place or another, it had stood the test of time. But behind the rear wall of the building and a bit further beyond, aged and mossy headstones of those long gone slouched at sunken, awkward angles.

It was here that two tiny red lights glowed in the dark, up in the air then down. Up, down, repeatedly like little fireflies. There was no traffic moving along the road, but an owl hooted loudly in the trees overlooking the graveyard making one of the red dots leap suddenly.

The men had been digging quite hard for a while now, maybe an hour, and were having a rest. The ground wasn't hard but the hole needed to be deep and it had been raining. Sometimes too soft was as bad as too hard. Flooding had also occurred earlier in the year with the ground totally under water for days. It had remained spongy ever since. The resident owl had spooked the wiry shorter man who'd dropped his cigarette and jumped up from the wall he'd been resting on....

"Je–*sus*, that bloody well got me good 'n' proper!"

The larger, taller man laughed, flicked his dying Marlboro in the air, grinding it into the grass with his heel when it landed. "Daft bugger, it's only an *owl*. They're beautiful birds – *the best!*"

"That's as maybe, still shook me up," his mate replied grudgingly, looking for his lost smoke in the grass embarrassed by his nervy reaction.

"Here – your shovel," the big man answered throwing it in his direction. "We gotta get this done before sun up. Start digging."

The wiry man gave up on his search, and grumbling, picked up the shovel before walking back to the hole. It wasn't a usual size for the area. It wasn't that long and it wasn't that wide, certainly not the length and width of any coffin – even a small one. After about a further half an hour's digging they both stopped and leant on their shovels.

"That should do it. Where's the package?" asked the larger man.

"Here," replied his mate reaching behind him. "What exac—"

"*Shut it!*. . . We've been paid to do two things, dig – and bury. That's it. We don't question *anything*. The less we know the better."

"Aren't you even a *tiny bit* curious? Just a *little* bit?" his partner asked, one hand fingering the tape that secured the weighty parcel.

"Of course I'm bloody curious, you cretin!" he spat in a low hurried rush, "I just don't want to get my fucking head blown off – or worse!" He snatched his shoulders forward and back in an agitated move and blew an angry sigh, the irony of his words lost on them both.

"But how will they even *know?*" his mate wheedled....
"Look around you, there's nobody here but us." His fingers
were now eagerly and quickly picking at the heavy-duty
gaffer tape.

"Just chuck it in the sodding hole! I want to go home
to my bed – *and ALL IN ONE PIECE!*"

The thin man had begun to wrinkle his nose and sniff
the package. Feeling something sticky now, he turned his
left hand away palm upward. It definitely didn't feel like
tape adhesive. . . or smell like it.

"What's the matter, *for Christ's sake?*" asked the other
getting angry now as he moved towards the outstretched
arms of his accomplice who was now awkwardly holding
the seeping package. The big man couldn't see the problem
clearly, but his mate could feel it, and was now beginning
to stammer....

"Thi-this. . . it. . . it isn't money or. . . or drugs or any
kind. . . it's—"

"Oh for God's sake – just *give* it to me!" The larger
man snatched the package out of his friend's hands
causing the bottom seam to split where the tape had
been loosened. The smell and tackiness that exuded
resulted in him heaving violently, flinging the package
into the hole and, hands on thighs, letting his dinner
follow it. Staggering away from the edge he fell on his
backside cursing loudly. His colleague stared at him for a
moment, and with both thumbs in his mouth began to
chew at his nails nervously before quickly walking over
to where the other man was sitting, and offering him a

hand up. It got smacked away angrily as he scrambled to his feet.

"We've been paid. Once we've refilled that hole I don't want to hear anything about tonight again – ever. *Got it?*" His friend's head nodded, fast and furious....

They started shovelling.

* * *

Annie couldn't sleep. It was now 3.00 a.m. and even an entire bottle of red that evening hadn't done its job. She was seeing Charlotte the following day, and always got nervous before a visit. *That* and keeping everything secret from an ex-police officer husband.

Obviously Rampton had the strictest procedures in house, although the fact Charlotte had been sprung en route to her mother's funeral the previous year *had* obviously caused them huge embarrassment. Annie hated the whole procedure. The prior bookings and timings of everything, the pat-down routines when passing through the various walkways and rooms, providing proof of ID and address, (*particularly her address with Harry having been directly involved with Charlotte's case*), just being in that environment. It was all hugely stressful. But it was necessary, *it was worth it.* She practically inhaled Charlotte's shrewdness, her mental abilities, her steel resolve and control, every time she saw her. She was getting stronger. At least the visiting form had to be returned immediately once completed and signed so she had no need to hide it in the house. And as yet, remarkably, nobody had made the connection to her husband.

Annie turned over for the umpteenth time trying to get comfortable. She flung the duvet off and then pulled it back on again, lashing out frustratingly with her foot in the process. Harry's snoring from the bedroom along the landing was just an added problem. She winced. A fleeting moment of warmth took her by surprise before she scrubbed it clean from her heart.

Well, if sleep was going to elude her she should use the time to plan. There was the need to research for a start. Annie was no gardener. Certainly not where the plants she would need were concerned. The word 'hemlock' danced around her mind connected to a vague memory of a school history lesson or an old film, she couldn't remember which. She liked the sound of it though. . . *hem-lock*. It would be a good place to start. The following half hour or so was spent googling exactly how powerful it was, how it could be used and where it could be found. *It seemed gardening was quite interesting after all.*

Eventually her eyes began to wince against the light on her phone, her lids felt heavy and breathing got lighter as finally elusive sleep stole the night. Her head dropped back on the pillow and the mobile slipped from her hand....

She awoke to her phone buzzing. It was a text from Michael, her estranged son. Sleepily Annie screwed her eyes at the screen until she could make out the words. Then she just kept staring at them till they became a jumble. A messed-up Scrabble-bench of letters, each fighting for a place in the dying remnants of rationale in her mind.

> Hi Annie, hope you're well, it seems ages since we last met. I'm not working at the moment so thought I'd take the opportunity to come up to Cumbria! I take it Harry still doesn't know about me so will find a B&B. Arriving next weekend, love Michael x

She read it three times. It didn't alter. At least she thought it was three, it could easily have been thirty-three her heart was thumping that wildly. What should she do? What *could* she do? A cold sweat broke out on her forehead. This was not good. *This was not good at all....*

NINE

JULY 3RD

Harry waited for the second time in six months to be called up to Hitchings' office. He wasn't exactly looking forward to the ritual fifteen minutes of sadistic sarcasm, something he'd been used to experiencing quite often in the past. Hopefully though, there would only be this one tiny torture to suffer and then he could get back to work. His usual *'thank the Lord for criminals'* mantra flashed through his mind.

"Chief Superintendent Hitchings will see you now, sir," said Joe Walker beaming his head off, "and it's so great to see you back!"

"Thanks, Joe – might be a bit presumptive though, keep your fingers crossed eh?" winked Harry, as they both walked towards the lift that would take him to one of several conclusions. Either it was going to lead to a good few months of being back in the job, a complete long-term reinstatement, or far more likely.... *'You've got a fortnight to prove I'm not making a horrible mistake, Longbridge!'*

After Joe had returned to his own floor, Harry continued on to the top. The lift juddered to a halt and the doors slid open with a grating squeal. *No change there then.* He took a deep breath, ridiculously excited yet nervous nonetheless, and walked briskly along the whole length of the cream and grey corridor, turning left at the end to Hitchings' familiar office. A little further down he saw Fran who was pacing hard and checking her watch. She looked up when she heard his approach, flashed a smile and gave him double thumbs up. He returned the gesture before she disappeared into another room, his heart leaping for just a second....

Harry turned back to the job in hand, and as he knocked on Chris's door began to wish he hadn't pushed his luck so regularly and flippantly in the past.

"Come in, Longbridge...."

He sounds almost resigned thought Harry as he grasped the handle. *Was that good or bad?* He was about to find out. He walked in with a confident air and smile, shut the door behind him and held his hand out in greeting. "Good morning, sir, good to see you again after such a long—"

"Sit down, Harry," Hitchings interrupted whilst remaining seated. He waved him towards the chair in front of his desk. Harry sat in it as his former boss clasped his hands together, then repeatedly clenched and unclenched his hands before speaking. Harry swallowed hard....

"I don't know how you've managed to persuade DI Tayl—"

"Oh I can assure you I've not—"

"Be *quiet, Harry!*" Hitchings just about managed to refrain from palm-slamming his desk and re-clasped his hands. "As I was saying. . . you and DI Taylor have clearly. . . hit it off, if rumour has it right and in more ways than one whi—"

"Sir, that's—"

"*Longbridge, for God's sake, shut up and let me finish!*" He glared across the desk and Harry decided for the first time in years it might be better to keep his mouth zipped for a bit. Hitchings sighed, steepling and unsteepling his hands. "Look. . . you and I both know you're a *damn* good copper… (Harry nearly fell off his chair at this seismic admission) … and you went too soon, *far* too soon. Your old team won't have a *bloody word* said against you, even young Joe Walker. . . who by all accounts had his first months on the job made pretty *grim* by you. And you always get the job done, even if it's not strictly by the book. But there's the *rub*, Harry – *right there, the book.* This time there *must* – **must**, Harry, be a distinct and permanent change." He stopped, surprised more than anything that his soon to be reinstated DCI had not continued to interrupt his flow.

Harry remained quiet. He was still gobsmacked over the compliment. *Chris Hitchings said he was a damn good copper?!* In all the years he'd been up from London with him as his boss, there'd been nothing but friction and ball busting from that direction.

"Harry? Did you hear what I said? You *must* play it by the book, especially this big case Fran's working on. You'll be partnering her and back with your team."

"Thank you, Chri. . . *sir* – I really *do* appreciate this. It's what I want more than anything." He lifted his chin and threw out his most responsible expression. "The book will be played, sir – *to the page, to the letter.*" He meant it as far as he felt he reasonably could, but knew there'd be occasions where things might not pan out quite as 'book-like' as they ought to. This was why the forefingers of both hands were tightly crossed on his side of the desk.

* * *

Annie had pretended to be asleep until she'd heard Harry's car pull out of their drive that morning. Before leaving he'd popped his head round the bedroom door to say he was going into town. She'd barely grunted a response in order to convey something quite different from her actual status. He'd quietly shut the door and walked downstairs, but she'd waited until the BMW's engine had fired before leaping out of bed and dragging underwear and clothes out of drawers and wardrobes. Then she headed for the shower. She couldn't be late.

It was the day of her journey to Rampton. A long six-hour round trip on a good run. She was now on the A1 and the run was indeed so far very good. The booked visit was for the 2.00 p.m. to 4.00 p.m. slot; she would have had to stay overnight for the morning one and that could prove awkward. As it was she would be inventing a day trip to a friend's that would correspond with her mileage and fuel consumption, but it would be rare for her to stay over. It occurred to her in that moment she may well have to start doing that though, *despite the creepy attentions of her friend's husband.*

Annie glanced at the satnav; one hour down, two to go. She turned on the radio and pushed the volume up a notch. . . *which was precisely why she never heard her phone ringing....*

RAMPTON PSYCHIATRIC HOSPITAL RETFORD, NOTTINGHAMSHIRE

Charlotte had just finished lunch. Well. . . if you could apply the phrase 'cheese sandwich' to an item that was more than a little sparse on cheese and made from thinly sliced white bread, to the word '*lunch*'. The tomato soup hadn't been too bad, but she longed for the delicious beef and lamb roasts, garlic salmon pastas and pulled pork and smoky barbeque sauce she and Miles used to enjoy at their local. No chance of *that* anytime soon, *and certainly not with Miles.*

A quick glance up at the clock in her room revealed Annie would be arriving shortly. She hoped she would have good news as there was a lot to get through and Charlotte was impatient. Not being able to finish the '*List*' herself was irritating. In fact it was more than irritating; *it had become a permanent mental scar*, one she picked at daily.

They kept her on meds of course, to keep her calm and as rational as possible, but then she didn't always take them. She'd managed to get more than a little shrewd on that score lately. It wasn't hugely difficult to outsmart the average security warden or nurse, they were currently low on numbers and that had helped considerably. That, and the fact they were quite simply not that committed to the job.

Half past one.... She should be arriving about now and going through the security procedures – *soon then.* Charlotte got up from her table and walked over to the chest of drawers. Bending down to the bottom one she pulled it open slowly and felt around beneath the jumpers at the back. Nothing. Then she began scrabbling anxiously, sweeping her hand left and right across the base of the drawer. *They weren't there! Where were they?! No! No! No!* She glanced up at the clock again, ten minutes till another pre-visit warder check. The first jumper to fly out and across the room was a cherry-red rollneck, followed by three black, two grey 'v' necks and another two black ones, before the little sachets revealed themselves. She sat back on her heels and with hands on thighs heaved a sigh of relief. The three slim brown paper tubes that had once held instant coffee and now held her unused medication, sat snugly inside a rolled-back sleeve of a chunky autumn knit. She picked them out of the jumper cuff and slipped them into her pocket. It had taken weeks to save the right amount of meds by only taking a third for herself. *She would need these.*

After being searched and signed in, Annie had been through at least five different doors. Each was locked behind her as she walked accompanied by a warden, CCTV following her every move through a long line of corridors. Of course the cameras weren't so much for *her* benefit, but knowing why she was there and the plans involved, it felt like they were.

All the patients she saw along the way were escorted by two or three officials, either wardens or medical staff. Several inmates were obese, some vacant, others fairly calm, some looked directly at her. She suddenly felt quite cold, pulled her jacket closer and gripped the strap of her shoulder bag tightly.

At first, Annie wasn't sure of the *exact* reason she felt so uncomfortable; whether it was the environment, the cameras, the people, or simply just who she was coming to see. But as one foot followed the other along that last corridor, she knew. In the pit of her stomach and as her palms began to soak, she knew. It was all of it. . . *all of it.* Plus the knowledge that if she wasn't careful, it could one day become her new residence.

Soon the last door was unlocked ahead and relocked behind her. The warden directed her to a sofa in the corner of a lounge area and told her to wait. She sat down holding her bag on her lap, then lay it beside her, then back on her lap again. She was just about to move it to the arm side of the sofa when Charlotte appeared with another warden at the entrance of the lounge. The two women's eyes locked fast as if they were transferring data telepathically. Charlotte almost glided to the chair opposite and sat down. There was a table between them and the new warden took a seat by the door. The first one left and returned to the reception station to help receive and check in other visitors.

There were other people in the lounge area, family visiting family, friends visiting friends. *Probably no other amateur assassins visiting their mentors though*, Annie thought glibly.

"So. . . how has it gone thus far?" asked Charlotte, her back against the chair, arms and legs crossed, eyes steady.

Annie let her gaze loose around the lounge before answering. She took in the warden glued to a phone, tapping away and clearly not interested in overseeing her obligations and duties. Then there was the mother earnestly questioning her disengaged son as to how his treatment and IT coursework were going, and on the opposite side of the room, the strange ginger-haired woman with a round face and ruddy complexion, sporting oddly long, springy curls either side of her head. The one who was sitting on her own. The one who was staring straight at *her*....

"*Well?*" pushed Charlotte intently. "What sort of progress are you making?!" She hissed the question under her breath, low and urgently as she leaned in towards her across the table.

Annie dragged her eyes away from Zoe Zandini, not an easy task, and answered. "We met – at a café" she glanced briefly back at Zoe who was still eyeballing her.... "and arranged to meet again for a meal in a couple of days."

Charlotte looked to the left and over her shoulder following Annie's line of vision. "That's Zoe. Nickname's Stabby on account of the number of people she despatched by knife in a single afternoon." She turned back round. "Craziest bitch in this wing but she's got her uses, or at least she *did* have."

"Oh? Why?" replied Annie forcing herself to look back at Charlotte with interest. . . *hoping it was also without irony.*

"Zoe's a Zandini. She's the niece of *Raiffe* Zandini." Annie's questioning expression led Charlotte to roll her eyes in irritation before speaking through gritted teeth. "The Zandini's are the biggest mafia-style family in Italy. Raiffe organised the finances and paperwork for my little American trip." Suddenly things slotted into place. Annie had heard all about Charlotte's escape from Harry, just didn't know who'd arranged it. She was pretty sure *he* didn't either.

"She looks a little. . . *odd*," said Annie, unable to stop herself from stealing several more glances at Zoe *'Stabby'* Zandini.

Charlotte raised a tired eyebrow. It spoke volumes given the establishment they were both sitting in. "She's more than a little *odd*, Andrea, Stabby is a pain in the fucking arse. Yes, she helped me get the money I needed because she has the connections, but the bloody woman's *obsessed* with me! And worse, keeps nagging me about my debt to the Zandini family – which I can't actually pay. And *you* know *why* I can't pay it...."

Annie did know. It was partly why she was there. "Well, that *why* will soon be removed," she replied quietly, "although it won't help your situation with . . ." Annie flicked her eyes over at Zoe, who was now stretching and pinging a long, springy screw curl whilst chewing gum with impressive panoramic dedication.

"Clearly not – but it will make me *feel* a whole lot better," said Charlotte reaching into her pocket. "What's the warden doing now?" Annie lifted her eyeline to that of the bored woman, still head down tapping away.

"Probably scrolling Facebook – she's not looked up from her phone since you sat down. *Why?*"

"When I indicate, drop a tissue on the floor on top of the three brown sachets I'm about to throw under the table near your left foot." She spoke very quietly and with a completely normal expression on her face. Annie smiled and nodded as if listening to an interesting conversation. (From across the room Zoe Zandini certainly thought it looked *very* interesting.) Charlotte's fingers closed around the pill sachets and she casually drew her hand from her pocket. A moment's rest on her leg, then she leant forward and dropped them under the low coffee table. Annie simultaneously took a tissue from her handbag, dropped it over all three, scrunched the tissue up and pretended to dab her nose before placing the tissue and sachets into her bag. All of this happened just as another visitor passed in front of Zoe, who saw nothing....

"I'll visit the ladies before I leave," she said. "An undercover transfer is probably a good idea – *yes?*"

"Very," replied Charlotte leaning back and crossing her legs. "*Deep* undercover – if you get my drift.... "

TEN

Tucked inside the top of her pants, the drug-containing sachets scratched uncomfortably against her skin. Annie drove slowly down the drive and out of the entrance, turned left and pulled up as soon as she could to rectify the matter. After quickly glancing up and down the street, she undid the zip of her trousers and transferred the three offending 'tubes' to her handbag. Sitting quietly for a moment, she pondered on the last two hours inside Rampton Hospital. It was not somewhere she wanted to be on a permanent basis that was for sure. The inmates alone were enough to keep a person on the straight and narrow. *Not that straight and narrow was exactly where she was heading, she knew that. However, stealth and shadows would have to help her out, be her only friends in this. Annie had no intention of ending up in a high-security hospital – that one or any other....*

It was a long drive home. By the time she arrived Harry was already out with Baxter for his evening walk.

She knew this because when she let herself in, their Lab hadn't come hurtling through the hall to greet her, or whoever else he thought might be at the door. It felt oddly quiet. As she hung up her coat, a distinct aroma of bacon and egg floated through from the kitchen. Annie followed it and stuck her head round the doorway to see a variety of used frying pans chucked haphazardly in the sink, and a dropped egg shell adorning the beige tiled floor. With pursed lips she exited hotly and marched straight up to the junk room where she kept the spare laptop under the floorboards. Moving the slim cycle aside and taking the three drug-filled sachets from her bag, she knelt down to remove the loose wooden slats, and placed them on top of the laptop hidden beneath. There they lay, three little brown sachets full of pills. Annie sat back on her legs and stared at them for a moment. It was only then she realised she had absolutely no idea what the drugs were, their strength or how many Charlotte intended her to use on each recipient. *Oh well, I still rather like the idea of hemlock,* she thought as she replaced each board one by one, and dragged the barely used exercise bike back over to cover them. *Maybe I won't even use them.* Just then she felt her mobile vibrate in her pocket and pulled it out. A swipe across the screen revealed a text message had been left. Annie felt the hairs on her neck flick up as she read. Her estranged son, Michael, would be arriving earlier than planned – in fact he would be there in only three days....

* * *

JULY 4TH, PENRITH

The following morning, Fran Taylor and Harry Longbridge met in the car park of Penrith Hospital. With Harry now officially reinstated, although in all honesty more in an experienced consultancy role, he still managed to retain his old DCI status. Fran was in theory below him as a DI, but as a serving officer, still running the body parts case.

"This is a bit like when Lewis was brought back out of retirement to assist Hathaway, isn't it?" grinned Fran as she leant against the bonnet of her shiny red Polo, holding out a bag containing breakfast. Harry locked his rather tired but classic silver BMW, and pocketing the key as he walked over, looked quizzically at her whilst pulling a custard doughnut from the bag.

"Come again?" he said before guiltily taking a bite.

"Lewis! Hathaway! *You knowww. . .* Inspector Morse and co., set in Oxford. You must've wat.... oh *never mind.*" She gave up (as she often did), and shook her head smiling. Harry was so. . . well, *Harry!* But Fran was just glad he was back, back on the inside and more importantly back working alongside *her*, and hopefully this time for considerably longer than a couple of months. Their partnership, being together again, was what she'd planned from the beginning. When she'd first wangled a transfer up from Canon Row after her marriage break up, Fran hadn't been entirely sure *what* would happen. When the opportunity had presented itself to work with Harry again following the Peterson woman's escape, she'd decided then, nothing was going to prevent her getting things back to 'normal'. The baby, though, that *hadn't* been part of the plan....

"Mmmm.... good doughnuts," said Harry appreciatively. "You'll get me *shot!*"

"Come on, they're waiting for us," she said licking her fingers one by one before reaching through the window of the car for her stash of hand wipes. She pulled one out and offered the pack to Harry who did the necessary before handing them back.

"They still just got the leg then?" he asked as they began to walk towards the entrance of the hospital. "I take it nothing else has turned up?"

"Well, I've not been notified so assuming not. How was Hitchings by the way? I take it he didn't make things easy for you?"

Harry harrumphed. *"Does he ever?!* No is the answer to that one. To be honest, Fran, I just gave him what he wanted to hear and crossed my fingers under the desk. Didn't want a repetition of his beetroot face on my mobile in that New York B&B – *remember?"*

"I remember. . ." she replied softly. Another memory from that time together flashed briefly through her mind where Hitchings' face definitely *wasn't* present.... "Not promising to always play it by the book then?" she asked, a smile breaking across her lips.

"Something like that. Well. . . *for God's sake*. . . the man knows damn well what *real* policing's like, and it's not pulling page forty-seven, subsection '4a' of PACE into your brain when you're in a tight spot, especially with no back-up or firearms available. Or anything else come to that."

"That *is* actually what it's all about though, *isn't* it, Harry?" Fran pointed out pushing the door open into the reception area as they both walked into the hospital.

"I'll remind you of that next time we're in the area car and you turn into your racing-driver brother!" whispered Harry close to her ear.

"Can I help?" asked the woman behind the desk.

It was a long walk to the mortuary. Fran had met sixty-year-old Marcus Ventnor on a few occasions, and in truth wasn't looking forward to another visit. His trademark quip when meeting someone for the first time was always the same: '*Marcus Ventnor – Ventnor as in the Isle of Wight!*' Only he often forgot when he'd already met you so it got repeated – *a lot.* He was thrice divorced (currently single as far as she knew), largely due to his drinking and gambling habits which had ended all three marriages, was endlessly sarcastic, had gained 40lbs since his last divorce, was rude, crude and totally sexist. None of this however seemed to affect his excellent work as Penrith's senior forensic pathologist. His two grown-up sons from his first marriage that he rarely saw, lived in Aberdeen, and rumour had it he wept for every child that found their way to his table. In summary, Marcus Ventnor was a seemingly forgetful, crass, loud and short-tempered yet emotional man, who longed to be reunited with his boys, and whose greatest fear was of growing old alone. He reminded her of a cross between Robbie Coltrane's classic *Cracker* character Fritz, and larger than life actor and singer Brian Blessed. However *sometimes. . .* sometimes he could surprise. *How did Fran know all of this....?*

"Fran!! Good to see you, it's been *ages!!* We should grab a coffee sometime – actually, scrap that, make it a drink, we need a thorough catch-up so you can fill me in on your wild trip to the States – *in detail!!"* The blue eyes of coroner Holly Cairns widened collaboratively as she flashed a sidelong grin at Harry. He took a deep breath as his cheeks flushed....

"I'll go find some coffees whilst you two—"

"No, it's okay, Harry," interjected Fran. "Holly, this is DCI Harry Longbridge, we're—"

"You're here for the leg that came in?" guessed Holly correctly, interrupting her friend as she ran an eye down the list on her clipboard.

"Yes," chorused her audience in unison.

"Look, Holly, it's great to see you but we'd better go. You know what Ventnor's like," added Fran.

"Indeed. Have you met him yet, DCI Longbridge?"

"No, I don't believe so. Sounds like a bundle of fun." He checked his watch and then raised an eyebrow at Fran. She took the hint.

"We *must* go. We're actually due *now.* I can just imagine the reception we'll get if we're late." She rolled her eyes as the two women said their goodbyes and the tall willowy figure of Holly Cairns carried on up the corridor, her shaggy Halle Berry pixie cut gleaming in the bright overhead lights. Fran gazed after her for a moment, sensing every ounce of her growing waistline, and as she saw it, boringly straight mid-length bob.

"Sooo. . . this Marcus Ventnor...." said Harry breaking the moment as the two of them continued at a smarter pace towards the pathology block, Fran doing her best to shake off the negativity.

"You'll see, Harry, you'll see," she replied knowingly as they rounded the corner to the mortuary, and found its senior pathologist waiting at the open door.

"*Franeee!!* Good to see you, although you *are* five minutes late!" scolded Marcus tapping his wrist. There was no watch there but he still knew – mainly because of the large clock they discovered behind him after entering the room. "*And* I notice expecting something of a *surprise?* You kept *that* quiet!" His facial expression feigned hurt as Fran internally winced. She chose to ignore the pointed hint at her pregnancy.

Harry raised a more than surprised eyebrow. In fact, both shot up, first at the elongated and intimate name given to Fran, and then elevated further as Ventnor leant in for a hug and kiss on her cheek after his personal comment. To a very relieved Harry, Fran skilfully dodged both. Having recovered himself, Marcus turned to him as she introduced her long-time colleague.

"Marcus – this is DCI Harry Longbridge."

"Ahhh – *Longbridge!!* Ventnor, Marcus Ventnor – *as in the Isle of Wight!*" He held out a hand as Fran pursed her lips in suppression of a grin. Harry shook it firmly – but *briefly*.

"I'd heard you were back on the scene; thought they'd finally put you out to grass after that US business."

"How the he—" began Harry, dumbfounded he knew anything about him at *all*, because he certainly had no information on *him!* If there was one thing Harry hated more than anything else, it was someone having the upper hand.

"We have a mutual friend, Harry," said Ventnor tapping his nose now. "Kay Winford and I go back a long way; met on a river cruise up the Rhine in 2001. Jolly good holiday as I recall. I caught up with her on a pathology Zoom meeting a month or so back, said you'd not be satisfied with retirement, especially after the Manhattan business. Well done by the way – *both* of you. Nasty case, well, times two rea—"

"Marcus, can we cut to the—" interrupted Fran. (At this point Harry was still struggling with the phrase 'Zoom meeting'.)

"Yes, yes, of course, the *leg!* I understand you have an arm over at Kirkdale General? Suppose you'll be hoping there'll be a match, otherwise...."

"*Exactly* that," said Fran. "Another serial killer is definitely *not* what we need."

"Quite. Well, I've got it on the bench so to speak, so come on through and you can have a look. It got washed up at Pooley Bridge about five miles away. I take it the arm you've got at your morgue was black too, as in from a person of an ethnic minority?"

Fran and Harry exchanged frozen looks. Nobody had

mentioned anything about the leg not being white when the report had come in.

"No, it bloody well *isn't!*" exclaimed Harry. "Why the hell didn't that get relayed to us at Kirkdale? It would have saved us a trip — this is a Penrith case! They won't thank us for stomping all over it, you can be sure of *that!*" Harry now looked slightly sheepish at the irony of his last sentence. "Pun not intended..." he mumbled awkwardly.

Fran now glared at Harry as Marcus hunched his shoulders, hands palmed upwards in a gesture of ignorance before removing the sheet from the limb lying on his table. It was a right leg, had been hacked just above the knee and clearly from a very dark-skinned person, almost certainly male given the hair, muscle and size of the foot.

"Reckon this poor chap was butchered with a heavy cleaver," Ventnor said leaning over the table pointing out the fairly clean cut edges to bone and muscle tissue. "No sawing here, do you see? It's also not newly removed. This happened at least six months ago."

Harry and Fran *could* see. They could also see that having learned it was not from a white Caucasian, it appeared they did indeed have a serial killer on their hands. . . *unless. . .*

"Can you tell the age or height of the person from just a – a single *leg?*" asked Fran. "And we're all assuming here that both the original owners of the arm and leg are dead."

"Good point," said Harry. "It's likely, of course, but not inevitable. Have there been any reports of missing black men in the area?"

"Not that we've been told, but it could be someone killed in another part of the county. If more parts turn up elsewhere, they could be spread throughout Cumbria or even further. We can analyse the leg to try and develop a biological profile of the victim," replied Marcus. "The profile will include approximate age, height, weight and possibly other evidence of trauma, plus of course the blood group. I'll have a report sent over to you – *save you a journey.*" Ventnor looked directly at Harry as he delivered *that* little nugget.

"Okay, well, I think we're done here," interjected Fran quickly. Things had been decidedly tense as they often were with a visit to Ventnor. "Thanks, Marcus, we'll wait for your report." She and Harry headed for the exit.

"You're welcome, should be about a week – two tops. Hope it's the last part that turns up. Any more and you could have another long and unpleasant case on your hands."

Marcus Ventnor saw them out, and Harry noticed the man at least had the decency to pull back from actually placing his hand on the small of Fran's back as she approached the door. Longbridge balled his fists as they walked through to the corridor. He needed to get out of there. How Kay Winford could have spent any amount of time with this man on a river boat, or anywhere else for that matter, was beyond him.

Alone again Marcus placed the severed leg back into the correct fridge drawer and turned to the one next to it. He stopped for a moment and ran a finger over the label.

It was quite difficult to read on account of the blurring in his eyes. He took a handkerchief from the large square pocket of his lab coat and dabbed several times before returning it. The label was clearer now, although he knew he'd need the service of that hanky again in the next hour. He pulled the drawer open slowly – and rolled out five-year-old Dylan James MacAfee . . .

ELEVEN

That lunchtime Andrew had completed his application to join the Cumbrian Constabulary. His finger now hesitated over the 'Enter' key as he thought of the changes he would be making to his life, to Gina's life and the life of their unborn child. He'd been a journalist, albeit on a small town paper, for nine years since leaving university, and had thought nothing would change that. If the last two years had never happened he felt sure he wouldn't be staring at the Constabulary website now. He withdrew his finger, making a fist for a moment, but then vivid pictures of New York's Bellevue Hospital with Charlotte Peterson holding a knife to Gina's throat, eyes cold and cruel, flashed sharply in his mind. *He pressed the key.*

* * *

Andrew wasn't the only one staring at screens. Annie Longbridge was digesting a text whilst having a quick cut and blow-dry in what used to be a competitor's salon. This was an irony in itself considering hers had gone down the toilet after twenty odd years of planning and sheer hard slog. The training of a dozen or so young people over that time, most of which had upped and left the moment they'd qualified, had just been another kick in the guts. She could dye her hair blonde, red, black, blue or whatever the hell she felt like, but taking a pair of scissors to it was another matter entirely, particularly the back – she wasn't risking that.

Suddenly Ace of Base's 'Beautiful Life' was bouncing off the walls as she quickly hit the green phone icon. Smiling awkwardly she mouthed sorry to the other customers.... she also made a mental note that despite being an old favourite, it was altogether too. . . happy.

"Annie? It's Michael. As in your Mi – your. . ."

She recognised the number. "Yeah – hi, Michael, I know, I know it's you, I umm... I'm at the hairdresser's. Can I call you back?"

"Sure, I just wanted to let you know I've booked myself in to a B&B near to that pub we had a drink in once, *The Carpenters Arms?* It's a little way up the road from there. I'm arriving about 2.00 p.m. tomorrow."

Annie tensed. *"Tomorrow?!"*

"Um – well yeah . . . is that a problem? I know it's sooner than I said. I mean if you're busy I can always lose mys—"

Annie began chewing the inside of her mouth. She needed to think quickly. When was she seeing her first...

despatch again? Despatch? *Despatch? Where the bloody hell did that come from?* She shifted uneasily in the chair before answering… "Let me ring you later, Michael." She spoke quickly and softly into the phone. "My stylist's waiting – we'll speak then, must go – bye." She snapped the cover shut and slipped the phone into her floored bag. Things were starting to get complicated, as if they weren't bad enough already.

Thirty minutes later Annie was leaning back thoughtfully against the headrest in her black Range Rover Sport. At least she felt human again now her hair was trimmed up and looking sharp. She flipped the mirror down and turned her head from side to side as she always did post cut. Carly was a bloody marvel in all honesty. At more than ten years Annie's junior, 'Beaut' was already more successful than most salons in the area including her own – and it was still going. Carly was the best in the business. Annie should know – she'd taught her all she knew. Sighing resignedly, she started the car. Bleating on about the failure of 'Chic', was pointless; the past was the past, done and dusted. Now it was time to prepare for the present. There was work to be done – *and it began with hemlock.*

* * *

The cordon tape around the parking area had gone. As soon as Annie neared the mid-section of Kirk Hill, she'd noticed its absence. On reaching the top, she swung the Range Rover left onto the gravel and aimed it at the furthest point away from the road. The tyres barely scrunched across the worn stones as Annie brought the car to rest alongside the path leading down to the river. She killed the engine and sat quietly for a moment. After a quick glance around the perimeter of the car, she pulled a plastic bag containing thick rubber gloves and a knife from under her seat, and stuffed it into her jacket pocket.

The afternoon sun cast long, sparkling shadows on the water as she picked her way carefully along its edge. This was all knew to her. The researching of plants that most people would call gardening (which she hated), was for her, a little different. Annie recalled the detailed information she'd gleaned from the Internet... She was looking for *a specific type of long bright-green stem, hollow, grooved and hairless, with a collection of tiny white flowers. It was known to grow up to seven or eight feet tall, and when cut, exuded a yellow staining liquid. The triangular leaves, also bright green and a bit fern-like were shiny with two to four pinnate divisions. It also had a scent resembling sweet parsley....* Yes. . . she'd learnt a very great deal about 'dead man's fingers' or 'water dropwort', or '*oenanthe crocata*' as it was scientifically known. However, it didn't really matter to Annie *what* it was called as long as it did the job. It was hemlock – *the most poisonous plant in the UK.*

Once well away from the car, Annie removed the bag from her pocket as she walked, took out the specially purchased heavy-duty gloves and held them in her left hand ready to use. It was imperative she didn't touch any part of the plants she was about to cut and collect – the species was *that* deadly. The knife in her right hand was an old one she'd found in the garden shed. She twirled it over and over in a now sweaty palm as the late afternoon sun shone down on her. But Annie knew it wasn't the sun that made an old shed knife slip and slide between her fingers....

She'd been walking for about ten minutes and surprisingly still hadn't seen anyone else. *Maybe the news of the buried arm had scared people off walking there,* she thought. *They had a point.*

Her phone sat in the back pocket of her jeans, a picture of the plant downloaded and displayed in her photo gallery. It would ensure no mistakes were made with anything similar, flat-leaved parsley or water celery for example. There was, however, absolutely no guarantee hemlock would even be growing on the banks of the Kirk. Annie just hoped she'd get lucky.

It had only been a few short months ago she'd been abducted from the same woodland area to the left of the riverbank she was walking along now. The very path where Kenny Drew had stepped out from behind a tree and pulled a gun on her was not far away. She stopped for a moment as the memory hit. Annie's breathing became erratic as she let the emotions wash over her from that snowy February afternoon. Looking up and away from the riverbank, she saw the track where she and Baxter had walked that fateful day and first realised her estranged son, Michael, had been deceived by his biological father, the man who Michael had traced to HM Prison Belmarsh, the man who'd convinced him Annie was the one who'd abandoned Michael as a baby. The painful memory of what had happened all those years ago seared down her back. The way it always did when she remembered the jutting stones of that flint wall pressing mercilessly through her thin dress, sharp and cruel whilst Kenny Drew had raped her....

Her mind whiplashed into the present. Michael. She hadn't rung him back since he'd called during her hair appointment. She put the knife into her other hand, pulled out her phone and thumbed up the call log. As the line connected she carried on walking along the riverbank continuing her search for hemlock; the plant she would use to destroy, in order to heal *herself*....

* * *

Back at the station, having stopped off at Bella's Buffet on the way, Harry and Fran had bacon baps and Styrofoam coffees spread across their desks, just as Hitchings walked into their office.

"Things never change, do they, Harry?" observed the senior officer, raising an eyebrow. Looking at Fran he said, "Don't let him get you into bad habits, Taylor, he's very good at that although I'm sure you're aware...."

Fran immediately tidied up, removing her lunch to a drawer. She would normally go for a healthier option (apart from their shared love of custard doughnuts), but since becoming pregnant had weirdly adopted Harry's love of every fattening carb, sugar and fat product Bella Bray could provide. This was exactly why a giant chocolate muffin was sitting in her bag for later, mocking her for not using a gym properly in weeks.

Harry took a big bite out of his bacon bap, ketchup dripping from his chin, before deciding it might be prudent to follow Fran's lead. Swallowing quickly on engaging her warning stare, he whipped out a hanky to remove the sauce and re– wrapped the offending bap, before also shoving it in a drawer.

"Hello, sir," he said, smiling enthusiastically, "just grabbing a quick spot of lunch bef—"

"I can *see* that, Longbridge, I'm not *blind*. Scattering it across one of our constabulary desks like a children's picnic however, is, *as you know,* neither professional *nor* necessary. Not in my book." Hitchings turned to Fran who was playing it cool. Harry pulled an irritated expression behind his back.... "DI Taylor, what was the outcome of your trip to Penrith this morning? I hope it was fruitful."

"Well, sir, turned out the leg they have in their morgue is from a black male, not white, so obviously not related to the arm found on our patch. Marcus Ventnor's running tests. It's also at least six months old, not recently found and washed up under Pooley Bridge. Technically it's Penrith's, so unless we get asked to help them out . . ."

Hitchings sniffed. The day he helped out George Jenkins and Douggie Judd would be a day too soon. He'd rather have ten Harrys on his team than either of those two, which was exactly why he was sitting opposite his DI right now due to low manpower, instead of either of *them*. "Right, well, keep me informed of anything that comes up with either of the. . . er. . . limbs. What's happening re the arm your dog sniffed out, Longbridge?"

"Nothing else came from the cadaver search DI Taylor set up in the woods, sir. The morgue at Kirkdale General has it and we're waiting on tests there too."

"Nothing from missing persons?"

"I've got Joe and Suzanne on that, sir," said Fran. "Nothing as yet."

"Right, right. . . well, keep me in the loop – and Longbridge. . .?"

"Sir?"

"At least *think* about eating something healthy from time to time. Consider your condition. I don't want you collapsing on the team at an ultimate moment. *And try to do it more tidily.*" With that he swept from the room and out into the corridor, to return to that lofty floor where those with multiple pips ruled in their altogether smarter, more affluent and distinctly *tidier* offices.

* * *

Annie Longbridge stopped dead in her tracks. Ahead of her was an array of white flowering water dropwort – *hemlock.* She shivered a little despite the warmth of a summer's day. Swallowing hard and moistening her lips, Annie pulled the phone out of her pocket and checked the picture against the plant. It was identical. She replaced her phone, put on the gloves and readied the bag. Above her a pair of buzzards hovered silently on the wind, their eyes on a proposed kill far below. As she neared the tall plants and leant forward to cut the first of the bright green stems, the birds dropped in tandem, stone-like and utterly focused on the unfortunates beneath.

TWELVE

JULY 5TH

Michael Morton dumped his bags beside the chintzy double bed, and bent down to look out of the low-set window next to it. The B&B cottage he'd booked into was old, quaint and genuinely rustic. It also enjoyed the most fabulous views he'd seen for a very long time. Wide blue skies soared above the majesty of the mountains that tumbled down to the grassy valleys, long, low cobbled walls as far as the eye could see, and the River Kirk snaking its way in the distance. There hadn't exactly been much time to do any sightseeing the last time he'd been in Kirkdale. *That* memory brought him up short, immediately making him redden in shameful remorse.

He sat on the bed, kicked off his shoes and swung his legs up on to the duvet. It had been a long journey and it was good to stretch out and relax. Lying back against the pillows, he focused on the intricately patterned ceiling rose surrounding the lampshade. Michael knew he'd never forgive himself for his part in his mother's, Annie's, abduction just a few short months ago. The fact the story they'd both concocted and delivered to the police had actually been believed, was in itself a miracle, and for him hugely fortunate. He knew very well he could have, and *should* have done time for what he'd done.

It had all started when he'd traced his birth father, Kenny Drew. Drew had just been released from prison having served fifteen years for his part in a city bank heist. Believing the lies he was told surrounding his birth, and Kenny's hatred of Annie's police officer husband for sending him down for that bank heist, it had all seemed so believable he and his father should be vindicated. Had Annie stayed with Drew like he'd told Michael he'd wanted to happen, and kept him instead of giving him up for adoption, Kenny would have stayed on the straight and narrow. Of course none of that was actually *real*. The fact he'd forced himself on Annie all those years ago had been conveniently omitted, they'd never been in a relationship at all because she'd barely known Kenny. It had led Michael to aid and abet Annie's kidnap, helping Drew take her to a lock-up in London, demanding a ransom and in the midst of it all discovering the truth. A risky and dangerous escape for them both had followed, and very nearly failed. With himself wounded, finally shooting his father dead, and his mother having suffered terror and humiliation at his hands, it was a time he would never get over and never forget. However. . . if none of it had happened, if he hadn't been sucked into the lies and the hatred because of his unhappy childhood, if he hadn't gone along with Kenny's vengeful plan, he may never have found his mother. The fact she'd forgiven him, patched up his shoulder and driven them *both* to her parents where a great deal of explaining and omittance had occurred (particularly his part in their daughter's kidnap), was the *second* complete and utter miracle. He had initially orchestrated their escape, which with her dog in tow hadn't been easy, but she could still have told them *and* the police the part he'd originally played.

It was the snoring that woke him. On realising it was his own, Michael checked his watch. He'd dropped off, sleeping soundly for the best part of two hours and it was now after five in the afternoon. The six-hour drive from Beckenham in London to Kirkdale had obviously left him more tired than he'd realised. Now he felt refreshed, *and hungry*. Much as he would have liked to meet Annie for a meal, he knew she'd still not told her husband about her estranged son. Despite the ordeal they'd shared in February, Harry Longbridge had only been told of Annie's abduction by Drew with Michael only being referred to as her rescuer.

Still lying on the bed, he thought of the two short conversations he'd had with his mother the previous day. One where she'd said she was at the hairdressers and couldn't talk, and the other where she was apparently walking the dog. At least he'd assumed Baxter had been with her. He *thought* she'd mentioned that, but hadn't actually heard him barking, panting or running, nor her calling and generally playing with him. In fact she'd seemed very edgy, distant even. Not herself at all. This had puzzled him. They'd been getting on really well since Annie had returned from staying with her parents in London following the abduction. Her forgiveness of his actions, *her* insistence that she wanted to keep in touch and meet up whenever possible, had both pleased and surprised him. They had emailed and phoned each other several times, and she'd repeatedly said she wanted him in her life for good now they'd been reunited. So why did he sense her reticence when he'd contacted her to say he was coming to Cumbria for a holiday? The only thing he could come up with was she had yet to tell Harry about him. At the end of the day though, she'd been through a terrible experience in her youth resulting in the birth and loss through adoption of him as a child, and again at the hands of the same man more than thirty years later. *Surely* her husband would be sympathetic and understanding?

His stomach began to rumble. Michael made the decision to go out for a meal alone and contact Annie in the morning. Hopefully she'd seem more welcoming by then.

* * *

At the far end of Millbeck's popular Italian bistro, Annie had deliberately chosen a table as far from its high street window as possible. Conveniently she was also in the darkest corner shielded by an enormous cheese plant.

The decor was rustic with rich russet and amber colours and lights set low. Music played softly in the background so as not to disturb diners' conversations – all in all, the ambience was just right. A successful family-run business, it had grown over the years from one small unit to three, and it was here that Annie had agreed to meet the first of her 'dates' for the second time.

She had deliberately arrived early in order to calm herself and feel in complete control. Running a finger around the top of her wine glass she reflected upon the only bit of 'cooking' she'd done in months. The chopping, boiling and liquidising of her special bright green herb had proved a bit of a nightmare if she was honest: Making sure Baxter was in the utility room so nowhere near the hemlock in the sink, wearing rubber gloves (which she hated because they made her hands sweat), and chopping the leaves and roots as miniscule as possible before tipping them into an old saucepan she'd earmarked for the job. Its sweet parsley smell was quite surprising given its deadly toxicity, but she'd still given the kitchen a liberal spraying of neutralising air freshener. She thought it prudent to remove any remaining aroma before Harry had returned home – *just in case.* Now several little bottles nestled snugly beneath the loose floorboards in the spare bedroom, along with her laptop and the coffee sachets containing Charlotte's unused medication.

She took a large mouthful of red wine and swallowed. The syringe containing the bright green liquid sat patiently at the bottom of her bag inside a plastic box. Knowing it was there and what it could do – what it *would* be doing. . . both fascinated and horrified her, and yet. . . there was a strange tingling excitement beginning to grow deep down. It made her shiver a little. It was like a seed trying to push its way up to the light, but not just any seed, this was destructive. Demonic. It had been planted by another when Annie had been at her weakest, her most vulnerable. She was now Charlotte's marionette – *and she knew it.*

Suddenly Annie was no longer alone. Her 'date' for the evening had arrived in a rush and after initially looking around the restaurant wondering if this would be a repeat of last time, was finally standing in front of her in a fluster, apologising for being late.

"Noooo... you're *fine!* I was early. Drink?" Annie flicked a slightly longer blonde strand over her shoulder, and smiling widely, gestured her arm towards the chair opposite. Christopher Mogg had replaced the casual tan leather bomber and jeans from their previous meeting at Cally's Café, with a smart black fitted jacket and grey trousers.

"Er... yeah, that would be lovely – a lager would be great, thanks."

Annie turned round, got the waiter's attention and ordered his drink as he pulled out the ebony hooped-back chair to sit down.

"Nice restaurant," he said, taking in the general decor and atmosphere. "Have you been here before?"

"No, thought I'd try something new. Italian's my favourite, though."

"I'll have to remember that," he replied. "My sister, Danni, the one who..." Annie's expression tightened as her eyes flicked sideways and she shifted uneasily on her chair. The thought of spending the entire evening hearing about Charlotte's murder of Susie Sarrandaire (birth name Danielle Mogg), yet *again*, would be just *too* much. Although on the other hand, she thought, psychologically it might help, given the reason she was there. *If he bored her brainless with the repeat story first....*

"Sorry... *sorry,* I know I go on a bit about her. I still find it. . . difficult. I was just going to say Italian food was my sister's favourite too. She used to *love* pasta, always smothered it in just about any flavour sauce, and plenty of the strongest parmesan available!"

Annie bit on the inside of her cheek and inhaled deeply as she looked at her wine, twisting the stem of the glass backwards and forwards. Slowly she released the captured breath and said, "That's okay, it must have been. . . *awful.*" Christopher half smiled, half winced, before downing a mouthful of the lager a waiter had just placed in front of him. There was a distinct air of tension. On the one hand Annie didn't want to hear him chatting on endlessly about Danielle, on the other, all the time he *was*, she didn't have to think up topics to talk about. At the end of the day she wasn't there for idle chit chat, and it wasn't easy sitting opposite someone you're planning to kill whilst swapping pasta sauce preferences of your siblings. Not that she had any now either since losing her brother in Iraq. A brief image of Mikey in his soldier's uniform swam inside her head. *Mikey, whose name lived on in her son...*

At that point the waiter thankfully appeared from nowhere, hovering a little uncertainly at the silence and holding two menus aloft. Annie snapped out of her trance, as thanks were offered and both taken. She swiftly scanned the choices wondering which would conceal the taste of hemlock most effectively, and hoped *he* liked his pasta smothered in plenty of the strongest parmesan too...

She had the pâté, he had a broccoli and stilton soup. This would have been a convenient vehicle to receive the syringed hemlock, but only being the first course he had no need of the men's washroom to give her time to administer it. Annie ate her food, tasting nothing. The blurring hum of the restaurant's diners floated around her as she nodded, smiled, drank her wine and generally tried to engage with her dining companion. A man she had no real grudges against, who had no idea why he was really there, but who she was required to kill that evening.

"... and so that's how I ended up moving to Cumbria," Christopher Mogg finished. He had just given a fairly detailed explanation of the last two years of his life as he chased the remainder of his *'safe'* soup around his bowl. *"Annie?"* He blotted his mouth with a napkin as she stared blankly somewhere past his right shoulder.

"S. . . sorry – *what?"*

"I said that's how I ended up moving to Cumbria – because of dealing with my sister's house clearance and sale, and then falling in love with the scenery of the area.

You really can't beat....." He followed her eyeline then, looking over his shoulder. "Is something—"

"Yes – I mean *no!* No – nothing's wrong. I was blindsided for a moment – thought I saw someone I knew walk past the window outside," she lied. It was becoming easier and easier lately. Finishing her starter, Annie placed the knife back on the plate and leant back for the waiter to remove it along with Christopher's soup bowl. She smiled nervously. This wasn't going quite as smoothly as she'd hoped. Her heart was thumping wildly despite the wine which normally completely relaxed her, but she didn't dare drink to her normal excess given the sleight of hand that would become necessary at some point during the evening. Quite when, she wasn't sure yet, but it was definitely going to have to occur during this tedious meal. A third run was quite out of the question.

"So you've settled here, have you?" she asked, with an overly bright smile hopefully disguising her bored face behind her huge wine glass.

"Yes, very much so, I can certainly see what Danni saw in the place. I couldn't live in her house though, not after. . . well...."

"No, no, of course not, quite understandable," Annie empathised quickly as she drank deeply, forgetting the need for a clear head for a moment. "So where did you decide to live then?" she asked trying to show an interest, one she didn't have given the true purpose of his company.

"I found a little croft cottage in Martindale. It's up on the hillside, overlooking the church. Needs work but I figured it'd give me something to focus on."

"You were very close to your sister, weren't you, Christopher?" It was a statement more than a question.

"Yes. Yes, I was. She was my *little* sister – twelve years younger than me, a late second child for my parents. I always looked out for her as she was growing up. Twenty-three is far too young to die." He paused for a moment before shaking his head clear and forcing a smile. "Anyway, this is getting too morbid. I promised myself I really *would* try harder at our second meeting – sorry for ruining the atmosphere by talking about her death again."

"No problem," replied Annie, lifting her wine once more. "No problem at all."

THIRTEEN

JULY 6TH

It had been five days since Molly's vision and nothing had happened. She was pondering this behind the bar in the Carpenters Arms as she dried a pint glass and put it back on the shelf. Either it was obviously good news nobody was about to die, *(or more specifically, someone she slightly knew),* and she'd imagined it all, or for some obscure reason *(as if having visions wasn't obscure enough...),* they were arriving much earlier than the event itself. She was sure she hadn't imagined it given her many previous experiences, but if that was the case and it was the *second* reason . . . why would....

"Two white wines and a pint of bitter... *please!*"

Molly jumped at the rather sharp drinks order and then pulled a sarcastic expression seeing her dad standing customer-side of the bar, giving her that '*look*'.

"Daydreaming again, Molly Moo?" Since she'd announced her pregnancy, Ron Fields had rekindled his daughter's toddler name, and even more embarrassingly started to use it... "Come on, snap out of it, love, we have customers. It *is* lunch time you know." Her mother frowned from the other end of the bar, wagging a cross finger at him as he rolled his eyes and turned back to his daughter to whisper... *"Please, sweetheart?* Just for an hour and then go rest that precious little baby bump."

"Sure, Dad." Molly smiled at her portly father as he limped back round to the dining area, his leg certainly starting to give him some gip, she thought. "You rest that dodgy knee of yours this afternoon as well!" she called out after him. He lifted an arm in acknowledgement as he disappeared around a pillar towards the kitchen.

* * *

It was later that afternoon Molly met up with Gina for coffee and cakes at Café Calisé, following Gina's antenatal class at the local clinic. Andy had taken an hour off for it too and was about to return to work, but Molly persuaded him to stay for a cup of his favourite *Calino.* As it was sunny they decided to sit outside at one of the wooden bench tables with a view over the River Kirk. Gina made a (slow) beeline for the one with the biggest umbrella....

"It's so hot I need as much shade as I can get these days!" she exclaimed, dumping her bag on the bench and waving an ineffective hand in front of her face as Andrew placed the tray of drinks on the table. "Oh thank heavens, I'm *gasping* for an iced coffee!"

"Just as you like it, sweetheart," he said grinning. "A large scoop of vanilla ice cream on top with plenty of chocolate sprinkles and a long straw." Gina scrunched her face into a happy smile and blew him a kiss as she took the iced drink and one of the jam doughnuts beside it.

"Andy. . ." said Molly thoughtfully as she reached for her drink, "I take it you've heard nothing untoward re Christopher Mogg? Not that I *want* there to be of course, it's just tha—"

"Oh yes, of *course!*" Andrew jumped in. "Your *vision!* That must be. . . what? Four days ago now?"

"Five," replied Molly, biting her lip as several nearby heads swivelled her way at the word 'vision'. "Beginning to wonder if I've lost the knack," she said dipping her head a little and lowering her voice. "Not that I'd begrudge *that* at all!"

"Nothing's come up so far, not that I've heard. I think Harry would've given me a tip-off if there was."

"There's been enough gruesome blood and stuff lately, what with that arm Baxter dug up," said Gina grimacing right before licking the bright red strawberry jam dripping from her doughnut, and sighing ecstatically. Molly and Andy both glanced at her in unison trying not to laugh. "*What!?* Can't a girl feed her baby bump a decent squidgy cake?"

At that moment someone sitting nearby got up to go and threw a national newspaper down on the table they were leaving, only for it to miss and land close to where Molly was sitting. She picked it up, read the words splashed across the front page and lowered her cup slowly onto its saucer.

"Molls. . .? What's up?" asked Andrew, reaching for the paper and sliding it round to face him. He dropped his gaze to read the headline.

Former doctor and convicted murderer Charlotte Peterson, isolated for her safety after Rampton inmate attack.

Gina leant over her to see what was so interesting.

"Well, I for one won't be crying over *that* witch's problems, she deserves all the trouble she can get – *and then some!*" Given she spoke quite loudly, this earned Gina a few swivelled heads in her direction as well.

"Agreed," replied her fiancé, sliding a supportive arm around her shoulders, "but it's interesting none the less. She lost access to her inheritance following her arrest, and then it came out about Christopher Mogg persuading her mother to leave it to some distant cousin… She must owe someone an *awful* lot of money to have been sprung on the way to her mother's funeral, *and* fund her US trip to find your mum and Jenny Flood. I reckon that *'someone'*, is none too happy about their lack of reimbursement."

* * *

KIRKDALE STATION

Sergeants Suzanne Moorcroft and Joe Walker had spent the last couple of days going through the MISPER (missing persons) files for the county. There were several thousand, many who'd been reported missing for decades but were always considered an open case until found, whether that was safe and well, or sadly not. However, they'd come up against a complete blank with regard to matching a male with the arm their newly reinstated DCI's dog had just dug up. This was mainly because the limb was not very old and there'd been no recent reports of anyone of either sex missing. Both of them were now standing in DCI Harry Longbridge and DI Fran Taylor's shared office delivering their findings, Suzanne also with a report from Penrith hospital...

"So basically nobody from the locality or even the county then," said Fran sighing impatiently.

"Sorry, ma'am, no," replied Suzanne. "There's nobody within the last few weeks, which of course it would have to be given the... er... freshness of the arm."

"Quite," replied her boss. "It could of course have been frozen somewhere first before burying it; unlikely I suppose but we shouldn't rule it out." Joe and Suzanne glanced at each other.

"We hadn't thought of that," he added, "but did feel we should go further out, contact the MISPER database for Northumberland, North Yorkshire, County Durham, Lancashire, etc. It would make sense for the perpetrator, or *perpetrators*, not to dump on their own doorstep anyway."

"Exactly so, son," answered Harry firmly, eyeing Fran who nodded in agreement. "Don't forget the leg up at Penrith that belonged to an IC3 (black male) either. You're looking for two missing men in recent weeks, assuming of course a freezer wasn't used with one or both of them."

"Yes, sir," acknowledged Joe and Suzanne.

"Has a call come in from Marcus Ventnor at Penrith Hospital yet? We're expecting a report from pathology on blood type, and projected height and weight for the black guy." This from Fran....

"Ma'am," said Suzanne, holding out the report she'd received earlier that morning. "It came in about half an hour ago. I was going to bring it straight down but we were nearly at the end of the MISPER list, so—"

"That's fine, thank you, Sergeant," said Fran smiling and holding her hand out whilst rolling her eyes. "I really wish Marcus would use email like everyone else, he's *such* a dinosaur."

"Bit more than that, ma'am, *if* you know what I mean...?" replied Suzanne, now rolling *her* eyes.

"Hmm... yes, well, I'm sure he's harmless. However, anytime you have to attend pathology at Penrith and feel uncomfortable, for *any* reason at all, you come and tell me – you hear?"

"Yes, ma'am – thank you."

"Okay, that's all then, unless you have anything you want to add, Harry?"

"Only that we need to keep an open mind about these two limbs. Neither of them is old and that worries me. Also there was a signet ring on the hand of the arm my dog found. Initials were J.J. if I remember right?"

"Yes, sir, I believe so," said Joe.

"Run a check on anyone known to us with those initials – it's just an outside hunch. If anything else turns up, and I think there's every possibility it might, we may just have some kind of gangster war on our hands."

"Yes, sir – will do."

"Also, chase up the pathology report from Kirkdale Hospital on the arm re blood type, etc. We've not heard anything about that yet either."

"I did chivvy them up yesterday," said Suzanne, "but I think they're a bit short-staffed at the moment."

"Okay, well thanks both of you. Off you go, and keep us up to speed with what you find out," Fran concluded.

After the two young officers had left the room, Harry was thinking about taking the opportunity to ask Fran about something he had on his mind since first seeing her after she'd told him about the baby. She was four months pregnant and although he knew she'd want to do everything *her* way, as indeed she should, he still cared, and was interested in the health of both her and the baby. Just as he summoned up the courage to do so, she suddenly clutched at her stomach and began wincing in pain....

"Fran? Are you okay?!" He was up out of his seat and in front of her in a second, pulse racing and heart thumping.

"Yes. . . I. . . er. . ." She held both hands over her bump and pressing her lips together in concentration, head down, began breathing in and out slowly and rhythmically. Gradually the pain eased off until it was mildly uncomfortable. "*Ohhh*. . . well, *that* wasn't exactly the greatest," she said quietly.

Harry by this time was crouching on the floor and looking up into her face. He moved a strand of hair out of her eyes and stroked her cheek softly. They stayed like that for a moment, faces close, eyes holding each other, his hands now both cradling hers as they covered their hidden, unborn child.

"Are you sure you're okay? I've actually been meaning to ask if you've had a scan or anything yet."

"Yes, I'm fine, honestly, it's gone now, and no, I've not had a scan. No time for bloody scans with bits of bodies turning up everywhere and a major case, *or cases* to run."

"Why don't you go home, grab an afternoon off at least? I can take over here, that's if you're happy for me to do that?" Fran thought about it for a moment. She *was* still feeling a bit odd, but didn't want to admit it. As soon as she did that, she knew she'd be taken off the job. Maybe a quiet afternoon with her feet up wouldn't be such a bad idea though.

"I might just do that," she said smiling and squeezing his hands. "Thanks, Harry. Don't go telling everyone the reason though. I don't want to be put on desk duties." Harry grinned and stood up just as there was a knock at the door and Joe Walker stuck his head in.

"Sir – ma'am? We've just had an email in from Kirkdale Hospital. The blood group from that arm is AB negative and very rare apparently with only 0.6 per cent of the population having it. When we ran a CRO check for a male with that blood type and the initials J.J., it came up with a James Johnson."

"Not Jimmy *'the Lash'* Johnson by any chance?" asked Harry.

"Well, I've not heard of him but. . . yes actually, that was the acronym beside his name."

"No, you'd be too young. I remember a colleague mentioning him when I was at Canon Row. Nasty little shit, bad gambling habit from what I recall. Not big time, well he wasn't back then, I suppose he could've progressed – probably *did*. Mainly aggravated burglary, car theft and ran a small-time drug racket twenty years ago. Maybe he short-changed the wrong person their stash once too often."

"Harry, I'm going to make a move," said Fran. "I'll leave you the info from Marcus re the leg at Penrith, and see you in the morning." She picked up her bag and turned to Joe. "Good work, PC Walker, hold the door and I'll follow you out."

"Ma'am," replied Joe smiling, opening the door wider and stepping back for her to pass.

"Walker. . ." called out Harry as Joe started to close the door, "I'm putting you as team lead below me for the Jimmy Johnson case. I want to know who his family is, how many, where they are, what they do, how they like their eggs for breakfast and anything else you can find out. That goes for his friends too."

"Yes, sir – I'm on it!" replied Joe smiling. At last he was going to be leading something and he was going to be doing it with the officer he respected the most, DCI Longbridge – *the Magpie!*

FOURTEEN

Annie Longbridge lay uncannily still. Along with Harry's snoring from his room along the landing, she could also hear the ticking of the hall clock from her bedroom. It would soon strike midnight. She waited knowingly. It always *had* been irritatingly loud and rather ugly too if she was honest, *but it had belonged to Harry's mother so....* She held her breath slightly. Just to add insult to injury, each tick now appeared to punctuate every tiny detail of the previous evening, and the chimes would soon do the same. Injury. . . *hmm....* not quite strong enough a description given the events that had occurred in that restaurant, events initially planned by Charlotte, but detailed by – *Dong!!. . . Dong!!. . . Dong!!. . . Dong!!....*

CROFT COTTAGE, MARTINDALE - TWENTY-FOUR HOURS EARLIER

Christopher Mogg wasn't entirely sure he'd be seeing that particular lady again. He hadn't rated the evening very highly, certainly not the food, although the soup was quite good, but the second course. . . not great. He wasn't really a parsnip fan anyway, yet there it was. Such a heavy flavour too, and in a peppered steak sauce – quite wrong. It had kept repeating on him as well, but hey, you live and learn. He made a mental note not to re-visit the restaurant either, no hardship there.

There was something about his date, though, Annie…. He couldn't quite put a finger on it but it was like she wasn't 'all there' during the meal. In fact, the whole evening when he thought about it. She'd changed from that first meeting in the café. Vacant? Yes, that was it, she seemed vacant. As if she was waiting for something, or someone. . . very strange. Maybe he'd just bored the pants off her constantly talking about Danni. He'd tried not to talk about his sister so much to people over the previous couple of years, he really had, but it was just so hard. He found it too difficult not to. It was as if. . . if he stopped talking about her, everyone would forget her. She'd be forgotten altogether – truly gone forever.

After he'd returned from the restaurant washroom he felt he'd definitely made an effort to ask Annie about herself, what she liked to do, where she liked to holiday, favourite bands, work, etc., but it was still a bit stilted. No, he wouldn't be seeing her again. He could always check out the dating site later, see if anyone else looked like a possible.

Christopher hung his jacket up, fished out his phone, made a coffee and took both through to the lounge. Placing the mug on a side table, he dropped down on to the squashy burgundy sofa he'd saved from Danni's house after selling everything else. She used to love that leather couch so much, it just felt right to keep it. With Facebook open on his phone he began flicking through it, his various groups and other social media. Reaching for his coffee and then sinking comfortably into the large velvet cushions, for the first time that evening Christopher finally started to relax.

It had started to rain. It was quiet at first, spitting lightly against the windows as he drank and casually played with his phone barely noticing the weather. But it was then he sensed the numbness in his toes. Absentmindedly, he wriggled them a bit to stave it off as he continued to scroll through his newsfeed, occasionally flipping over to a friend's timeline. The strange feeling was irritatingly persistent though. He began to shake then stamp first his left foot on the floor, then his right, trying to bring the circulation back. It was puzzling. He'd never suffered from severe tingling, numbing or cramps before. He laid his phone on the sofa, now also wiggling his fizzing fingers and shaking fully affected hands, took his shoes off and began massaging each foot in turn as best he could. . . but the numbness quickly increased in his hands and began creeping up his legs, wrapping his muscles in an increasingly tight pain that was now beginning to concern him. His mouth dried. He reached for his coffee only to find his arms were now copying his legs. . . and his chest. Now he wasn't concerned, he was seriously scared. *The mug bounced off his useless hand and hit the stone floor smashing against the tiles, sharp, jagged little pieces skittering and bouncing until his numb body slumped forwards to join them – blood now running from a gash in his temple.*

Lying there, he was now aware of the rain. It was becoming louder. The wind had whipped up, sending an eerie tune down the chimney as his eyes blurred in terror on a lakeside pattern of broken shard. Mobile well out of reach, Christopher made a last desperate attempt at inhaling, drew in a final constricted breath until it squeezed and wheezed inside his asphyxiated lungs, until it stopped halfway. . . until it fell silent.

The rain lashed against the glass and the clock ticked one excruciating minute after another as a terrified rictus grin stole his mouth, stole lips that would never speak again, never whistle or kiss again. And with one final thought of Danni. . . it froze his face completely.

* * *

JULY 7TH

Annie had fallen into a fitful sleep. By morning there was only one thing on her mind, to report to Charlotte and give her the news she knew she'd be so eager to hear. The man who'd persuaded her mother to divert her substantial inheritance to a distant cousin, was now almost certainly dead. However, she knew one thing would have to happen first for Charlotte to be satisfied; Christopher Mogg's body would need to be found – and in the news. It was then Annie realised she didn't actually know much about him, mainly because she hadn't bothered to find out. *Big mistake.* Who would miss him if he didn't turn up in the morning? Did she need to know? Would there be anyone she should avoid? Annie began wracking her brains to try and remember if he'd mentioned work or friends or any hobbies or groups he belonged to. Would anyone know he was going to be at the bistro, had he told anyone about her? She vaguely remembered him saying something about an enforced break from work, but that was from two years back after Charlotte had murdered his sister, Danielle – *aka model and actress Susie Sarrandaire.*

The buzzing of her mobile shook Annie from her thoughts. Reaching over to the bedside cabinet, she pulled out the charger and swiped the screen. . . then hesitated. It was Michael. This time she would *have* to make an arrangement to see him. It wasn't that she didn't *want* to; she did, very much. He was her son after all and they had a lot of time to make up for. It was just that she was scared. Scared he'd be able to see straight through her, see what she'd become. Annie didn't want him to hate what he saw. *Or see what she was planning.* A swipe right on the screen brought them together again. She took a deep breath....

"*Michael! I'm sooo sorry!* I've been ridiculously busy since you've arrived – how *are* you? Did you find a nice bed and breakfast?" She winced at her overly bright voice, realising it was also too shrill, too loud. *(Luckily Harry had already left for work.)*

"Hi Annie, yes, I, er. . . I did actually, not too far from the pub." Michael was more than a little surprised at the sudden change in her reception. Obviously whatever had been bothering her was now no longer a problem. He also thought he'd told her where he'd be staying several calls back.

"That's good. . . *great!* We must meet up then." She swung her legs out of bed and ran a hand through her still unfamiliar hair, catching its new shade in the mirror as she grabbed her watch off the dressing table. Ten to nine – *late again.* "I'll meet you in Gino's the other side of town – say about noon? Do you know where it is?" She moved quickly round the end of the bed, side-stepping several hangers as she launched herself towards the en-suite.

"I'll find it. Annie. . . are y—?"

"*Great!!* See you at twelve then. Must go. Baxter needs his walk." At the other end Michael could now hear the sound of water.... She snapped the phone shut killing the call and slung it backwards through the doorway onto the bed behind her. As Annie stepped into the shower to let the warm spray run comfortingly over her body, she leant against the tiled wall and sighed heavily. *She was about to channel her inner actress like never before.*

* * *

Charlotte's head hurt. Her head hurt, her arms hurt, her legs hurt; *everything bloody hurt.* As she lay in the hospital's medical wing she was also still trying to get over the shock if she was perfectly honest.

When Stabby (Zoe Zandini), had come towards her with that weird droopy look on her face, bottom lip quivering, head hung a bit low, she thought she was in for a long, miserable chat from her stalking idoliser. True it would have made a change from the sycophantic 'love-in' she usually had on offer, but Charlotte really *had* had enough. It would have been preferable however not to have had to put up with either.

Her eye twitched. It hadn't done that for quite some while, certainly not since she'd been sent to Rampton for the second time and on top dose calming meds anyway. However, since she'd been reducing those meds herself and hiding the surplus, to a) give to the Longbridge woman, her *delegate,* to continue her crucially important work, and b) because she didn't *want* to feel fucking *calm* every *fucking* day of the week *thank* you very much, Charlotte's eye tic had returned – and with it a very noticeable part of her identity.

She lifted a bandaged arm to reach her water and winced, not only with the pain, but also the memory of what had occurred in the main dining room two days before. Zoe had been walking down the hall towards her, and although Charlotte had clocked her sullen expression, she hadn't noticed the two kettles of boiling water held low as she walked between two rows of fully occupied tables. How the hell Stabby had even managed to get her hands on them was surprising enough. When she'd reached where Charlotte was sitting (trying her utmost to enjoy a lifeless pineapple pizza), and began sloshing scalding water over her arms and legs, all hell broke loose. The scorching of Charlotte's skin as the water hit and soaked through her clothes had engulfed her in pain like nothing else on earth – surely a flamed match to petrol on her couldn't have hurt any less? The screaming from deep inside had seemed to go on forever as women had started scattering, warders had started running, yelling for jugs of cold water, wet tea towels and medical staff, the alarm system shrilling and mad Zoe Zandini dragged off crying her eyes out declaring (loudly), she hadn't *wanted* to do it, she'd been *made* to do it. But later, when Zoe had been asked by whom, she wouldn't say. She'd just sat on her hands, shaking her head from side to side, those long corkscrew curls bouncing wildly around her tearstained mascara-ridden face. Zoe's terrified glassy eyes had related quite a lot though... That afternoon she got sedated.

Charlotte had been told that in time she shouldn't have any scarring. Luckily she'd been wearing jeans, and most of her legs had been tucked under the table. It was her arms that had suffered the worst. *At least Stabby hadn't slung the contents of either kettle over her face – thank God.* Her headache now was purely stress, both at the situation and the fact all visiting would now be cancelled and she couldn't see Annie for an update, or even make a phone call. Mobiles were not allowed and landlines were in a main public area, not wards.

She sipped her water thoughtfully. There could only be one reason why Zoe had done what she'd done. Knowing the woman adored her, Charlotte knew she wouldn't have chosen to damage and hurt her like that, deliberately have caused her so much agony. No. Either Zoe was jealous because of Annie's visit the other day, or. . . Raiffe Zandini was giving her a warning. The trouble was – Charlotte had no use for warnings. It wouldn't matter how many times Raiffe ordered his niece to hurt her, Charlotte had no money. She had no money, no assets, no way of paying her debt to the Zandini family. And that was the most frightening thing – because for the first time in her life, *Charlotte Peterson had zero control over her enemies.*

FIFTEEN

After the painful stomach spasms she'd suffered the day before, DI Fran Taylor had decided maybe an afternoon off work wasn't long enough. She'd been resting up at her flat as best she could, which wasn't easy for a woman who, although four months pregnant, normally led a busy CID team and was happier in the field than at home on a computer or reading a book. She'd still been going to the on-site police gym a couple of times a week but only to gently use the treadmill; she'd decided against anything more physical than that. Swimming wasn't really her thing, and unlike Harry, although she could turn her hand to most ball sports, since coming up from London had yet to find someone to team up with on a regular basis. So it was with a great deal of self-control that Fran was lying on her couch, arm outstretched with a remote at the end of it pointed in the vague direction of the TV. The other was stroking her bump as she flicked through a dull Sky planner when thankfully her mobile buzzed to save the day....

"Fran, it's me, just checking you're okay."

"Hi Harry, not too bad, bored to death of course but otherwise. . . bit achy but nothing untoward has happened since yesterday. Baby *Taybridge* remains safely on board...." Holding her breath for a minute, a smile darting across her lips, Fran surprised herself with the conjoined nickname she'd apparently just given their unborn child. At the other end Harry felt a warm, fuzzy glow he thought he should probably try and shake off, but found he didn't want to.

"We've had an interesting development," he said, still glowing.... "The arm as you know definitely belongs to Jimmy 'the Lash', defined by the rare blood test. Whether or not the rest of him is in a pub somewhere or scattered halfway across Cumbria we've yet to discover."

Fran raised her eyebrows at the dry quip.... "*Harry....*"

"*Welllll.* . . he's a. . . was, is, *whatever*, a seriously unpleasant piece of sh... Anyway, that's not the most interesting bit. His partner is someone called Zoe Zandini. Now it's been a long time, but I vaguely remember he had a girlfriend, equally unpleasant, with an. . . *interesting* name."

"Yeah so, what's the problem with a foreign-sounding name? Please don't go all anti on me, Harry!"

"Nothing wrong with the name, not at all, it's a *nice* name as it goes..."

Fran sucked in a large breath and let it out slowly.... "So. . . what's the score then?"

"Ms Zandini is a long-term guest at Rampton – same wing as Charlotte Peterson...." There wasn't a response from the other end.

"Fran...? Did you hear me? I sai–"

"Arrrr..... owww!!"

"Fran? Fran, are you all right?!"

Fran looked down at the red stain that was slowly seeping through her pale grey tracksuit bottoms. Mesmerised for a minute with both the pain and the blood, she suddenly 'came to' as the vice-like grip shot around her abdomen and cramped down again.

"I-I've got to-I'm. . . I'm...." She dropped her mobile and clutching at her stomach staggered through the lounge to the bathroom, whilst Harry, who suddenly realised he didn't actually know where she lived, zigzagged and circled their office, in total panic!

Fran sat on the floor, legs now naked, wet and apart, her back propped up against the bath. Tears streaked down her cheeks as the blood streaked down her thighs. She stared downwards in shock and despair, feeling utterly helpless at the tiny foetus that lay on the white tiles between them. In fact, on only *one* smallish white tile....

She wasn't sure how long she'd been there, but when a banging from somewhere filtered through to her brain she looked up, then back at the blood on her hands, her legs, the floor.... The banging was soon joined by repetitive urgent ringing and Fran suddenly tuned in. She began to ease herself up to a standing position, then realised she'd need to get to the front door before Harry had the neighbours complaining. She knew it would be Harry. Of course it would, although she hadn't remembered ever mentioning her address. It had never come up considering they weren't officially seeing each other.

She rinsed the blood off, then dried her hands and legs, grabbed fresh underwear and sanitary protection, and once sorted, pulled yesterday's joggers from the linen basket. The frenzied banging and ringing increased as she gingerly put them on and then made for the door. When she finally opened it, an exasperated Harry fell through to the hall in a lock-busting shoulder barge, just managing to prevent a collision by immediately enveloping her in a bear hug.

"What the hell *happened?*" He briefly moved her away from him to look at her face. "Oh my God, you look as white as a sheet!" He pulled her back into his arms and stroked her hair, rocking her gently as Fran began to sob into his shirt, holding on to him as if she'd never let go again. Finally, looking up into his distraught face she managed to say it....

"Taybridge – *I've lost Taybridge....*"

* * *

Michael Morton found he was actually quite nervous of seeing Annie again – seeing his estranged *mother* again. He'd initially been looking forward to this trip to Cumbria to spend time with her, but although their last conversation had been a little more positive and upbeat, therein lay the confusion – she was way over the top in the '*bright and breezy*' bracket. Something was up. He didn't know what it was yet, but something was definitely not right.

He was sitting at one of 'Gino's' white filigree pavement tables, hands wrapped round a cold lager. The weather had cleared up over the last couple of days since the heavy rains earlier in the week and it was now warm and sunny. He thought the wine bar Annie had chosen was pleasant enough, but it was over the other side of town well away from where she lived with her husband. She still hadn't told Harry about him, and whilst Michael had initially understood why *(his being involved in her kidnap wouldn't exactly endear him to anyone),* he was beginning to feel a little hurt at being hidden away from her family. Although he'd spent a couple of days at Annie's parents following their escape from Kenny Drew, they had also only been told Michael was Annie's rescuer, not her son. At the time this was completely understandable and necessary given the situation, considering he'd have been arrested had the truth come out. Now though, he wanted to feel part of her family. . . the good part of his *real* family.

A glance at his watch showed she was ten minutes late. He was just going to ring her when he saw a woman crossing the road headed straight for him. Dressed in a crisp white shirt and tight black jeans, she walked confidently in red patent heels matched with a glossy red smile. He looked to his left and right before realising the woman was smiling directly at *him*. There was something familiar about her, but the pillar-box red lipstick, spike heels and frankly almost bleached white hair, was throwing him right off. She now stood right in front of him expectantly, and Michael had to do *something*. So he stood up.

"*Annie?*"

"*Michael! It's so wonderful to see you again!*" She pulled him to her in a surprising embrace, then drew out the spare chair from under the table and sat down.

"You look so. . . *different*," he said, his stunned gaze trying to absorb the complete transformation from when they last met. Now he understood why she sounded so unlike her normal self on the calls, she *wasn't* her normal self. It wasn't just the hair and clothes, it was like her whole *identity* had done a runner.

"I just needed a change," Annie replied brightly, "a new *me!*"

It was certainly that, he thought. "I'll get you a drink. What would y—?"

"Anything red – *thank* you, I'm *parched!*"

Michael disappeared inside the bar and soon reappeared with a large glass of Merlot. On the way out he'd noticed Annie was looking up and down the street, eyes darting around the other tables, lips rolling anxiously.

"Everything okay?" he asked putting the wine down cautiously in front of her, glancing around questioningly.

"Thanks. Yes, yes – all good," she replied after taking a large mouthful. "So Michael, how've you been keeping? How's the shoulder now? Has it healed up well?"

"Not bad, still a bit stiff on occasion but I can live with it. Don't fancy having to take another bullet though," he said with a wry smile picking up his own drink and noticing her Merlot wasn't going to last long. They sat in awkward silence for a moment remembering the chaotic and horrific scene outside the Stratford warehouse, where Kenny Drew had caught them trying to escape and had shot Michael. Luckily the bullet had only winged him. At one point Annie'd thought Baxter had taken a hit too, but thankfully he'd been allotted a guardian angel that night.

"I don't think either of us could ever forget what happened," said Annie searching his eyes closely. "At the end of the day the whole event brought you back to me for which I'll always be grateful – however ghastly the experience." Michael sat quietly looking at his lager for a moment. *Would now be a good time to mention it, the fact his mother still hadn't told her husband about him?* He twisted his glass around in circles pondering the idea, before bottling it.

"Fancy some lunch? I took a look at the menu when I was getting your wine. They do some nice looking pasta dishes."

"That would be lovely, the food here is great. I'll have the ravioli and green salad with parmesan on both. Actually, let me get this, my treat. What would you like? I can definitely recommend the ravioli, it's Gino's special recipe. Well, it was his mother's actually but we don't remind him of it – *not that often, anyway!*"

She was smiling more naturally now thought Michael. Maybe it was just nerves on her part too. Maybe.... "Sounds delicious. Could I get some crusty garlic bread with that?"

"Sure – the bread's homemade too, you're going to love it," called Annie over her shoulder as she disappeared through the door. Once inside she took a deep breath in and let it out slowly. Things were going okay. They were going more than okay. She could do this.

Over their meal Annie began to relax and Michael noticed. They chatted easily, swapped more usual topics like hobbies, holiday plans and work, something that had not been appropriate during their first encounter. His initial thought of her radically different appearance was beginning to seem like nothing more than her wanting a change, just as she'd said. But why a change in such complete opposition to the type of woman he thought she was. . . *that* was what still bugged him. It was only when a news media video began playing on a mobile at the next table it became more than something just bugging him. Michael jumped up at the sudden sound of glass smashing and the neighbouring customer shot round in her seat to join him in his surprise. *Only Annie, who was no longer holding her wine, sat transfixed – unable to drag her eyes away from the woman's phone.*

SIXTEEN

Harry sat by Fran's bedside at Kirkdale Hospital, heart heavy for them both and the child they'd lost that afternoon. However, they were also stunned at the revelation of the ultrasound Fran had just undergone, and what it would mean for the immediate future.

"Who'd have thought?" whispered Harry as he held her hand, stroking it gently. "At lea—"

"Don't say it, Harry – just *don't!*" Her eyes flashed wildly through a film of tears. They both fell silent for a moment. Harry dropped his head. Just as she was about to speak again, a nurse entered the room tapping her watch and raising her eyebrows...

"Ahem. . . time for your partner to leave now, Fran. You need your rest and it's my job to make sure you get it. There's going to be a lot of that in the next few weeks, especially with your being considered an elderly primigravida." Fran barely managed an acknowledgement.

Flushing at the nurse's assumption of their relationship however, and confusion over the perplexing *'primi'* thing, Harry stood up and bent over Fran to kiss her forehead, all fire gone to be replaced with an expression of what he could only describe as struggling hopelessness.

"I'll see you tomorrow. It'll work itself out, it will – *I promise.*" He let his fingers brush her hair as she slid further down beneath the covers where confusing, swirling emotions enveloped her.

* * *

Annie Longbridge was now back behind the wheel of her Range Rover in the parking bay across from Gino's. Given the shock at what had just happened at her favourite wine bar, she'd amazed herself how coolly she'd switched to apologising for having a 'blonde' moment in forgetting a prior arrangement. A swiftly invented dental appointment had created an excuse to beat a retreat as naturally as possible. She'd left Michael more than a little perplexed at the pavement café, even with a sweet smile, a wave goodbye and a promise to call him later.

She sat tensely, recalling the moment the woman's phone had suddenly played the news bulletin uncannily loud. When the report had come on about a body being found at Martindale, Annie's guts had felt they'd quite literally plunged to the pavement, quickly followed by her very large, fairly empty wine glass. The smash of it had cut through the shock and wrenched her eyes from the mobile.

Amidst the following confusion, where Michael and the woman had instinctively jumped up, cleaning tools requested and apologies given from Annie for startling everyone, no one had actually heard the details of the news report *accurately.* Including Annie.

Now, despite almost two large glasses of wine inside her, she put the key in the ignition and started the car. All she wanted was to get home as quickly as possible and have an uneventful evening, although the news of the body would no doubt be on TV. Harry may even be aware of it. *How would she react if he was?* A tide of adrenalin washed through her as she pulled out from the kerb and tried to concentrate on the road.

The rush hour traffic had started to build up a bit on the outskirts of Kirkdale, and in the stop-start queue she found herself in, Annie began to drum her fingers increasingly fast on the wheel at the thought of Harry returning home. She desperately hoped he'd be in a reasonable mood and there'd be no arguments. Tired and going to bed early would be even better. The last thing she needed was her DCI *Magpie* husband eyeing her quizzically – or worse.

She had yet to come to terms with what she'd actually done three nights earlier; the fact she had, as Charlotte would say. . . *despatched* someone, and would have to do so again. Annie felt confused and agitated. She had done for quite some time now. Her right thumb found its way to her mouth and she repeatedly ground her teeth down the side of the nail. On the one hand there was a certain thrill and control to the whole thing; certainly in the choosing and planning of the dates, the anticipation of the suffering, the need to lash out against something or someone – *anyone* to numb the pain she'd been feeling the last few months. *Years* if she was honest. On the other. . . somewhere in the back of her frenzied mind, Annie just wanted her old life back.

So much had happened since those days in March. To her, with the abduction and meeting of her estranged son *(and those two being intertwined),* and to Harry out in the States hunting Charlotte with. . . *that woman!* Now he was back in the job, and *again* working with *that woman!* Much had happened to both of them, but it wasn't Harry who'd been drastically let down at the most vulnerable time of his life, and Annie would never forgive him for not coming home to her after the sheer hell she'd suffered in that deserted lock-up – courtesy of Kenny Drew. She shivered. At that moment she just wanted to forget about them – *all* of them – Kenny, Harry, Michael. . . *no, not Michael,* not him. Christopher Mogg though.... He was haunting her now and she needed to delete that night from her conscious thought, to feel refreshed, find a blank page. A clear head had to be resumed, because despite her confusion, her agitated state, Annie sensed she must be calm and ready for when Charlotte contacted her again. . . *as she knew she would.*

The traffic had started to ease up away from the town. Aware she'd taken a couple of corners a bit wide as well as running a red light, she was lucky to get most of the way home before hearing a siren. At first it was way behind her, but it soon increased and the flashing lights indicating her to stop were suddenly shooting through her rear window, then the marked car was alongside with an officer gesticulating to pull over. *Damn!!* She slammed her hands on the wheel in temper and yanked the car left at the first opportunity in order to comply. *Damn!! Damn!! Damn!! Harry wouldn't be happy about this at all. In fact, he was going to be absolutely livid – and he was bound to find out.* The officer was out of his vehicle and now approaching her car.

She rolled down the window. Thankfully it was nobody she recognised.

"Afternoon, madam, you seem to be a little. . . *uptight*. Are you aware you just ran a red light and took that last corner overly wide. . . and in completely the *wrong* gear?"

"Sorry, Officer – brain somewhere else for a moment, plus a hideous migraine. It won't happen again." Annie flashed her most appealing smile whilst holding a hand against her temple. The appeal went straight over his head....

"Could you step out of the car for a minute, please, madam?"

Annie knew where this was going and prayed she'd eaten enough to absorb almost two large glasses of Merlot she'd sunk back at the bar. At least she wasn't only a spit over five feet like a couple of her friends. Once outside, trying not to lean against the car, she was subjected to a breath test, her first ever surprisingly, *given her love of alcohol.* Even more surprisingly she blew under. . . *just.* After a short lecture on choosing designated drivers or public transport for the future, and a fine for the red light, she was on her way.

When she put the key in the door at six o'clock, Annie hesitated for a moment before opening it. She fully expected Harry to be home already, and with no food sorted (as usual), and having had no job to go to, would have to figure out which of her friends she'd be using as cover for her lunch date. Especially as it was obvious she'd been drinking. However, his car wasn't in the drive, and the house was empty apart from Baxter who raced out of the kitchen and leapt all over her to deliver his special Baxter-style welcome. These days she didn't mind the hair and slobbery kisses, not after his loyalty and protection against that spawn of the Devil, Drew.

It was another half hour before Harry turned up. Sitting at the kitchen table, the black coffee she'd made after feeding Baxter and loading the dishwasher got clasped a little tighter. When Harry's key turned in the lock, the Lab's ears shot forward and the rest of him responded by jumping out of his bed and dashing into the hall to greet the most important person in his small world.

"Hello, boy, you missed your old dad then, eh? Have you? Yesss.... '*course* you have. We'll go for a run later – okay?" A gravy bone fished out of his pocket was swiftly delivered and quickly devoured. It was then a case of a deep breath, keeping calm and preparing for whatever lay ahead in the kitchen, both psychologically as well as gastronomically.

He found her in her usual teatime spot – at the table nursing a mug of coffee. Although there was no aroma of dinner (not even a burnt one), he was at least grateful it was a mug and not a wine glass in her hand. Just to be sure there *wasn't* wine in it, he surreptitiously eyed the contents over her shoulder on his way round to the kettle.

"Hello, love, how was your day?" he asked brightly, although not *too* brightly. Judging how to converse in a vaguely happy manner without *actually* implying he'd been having too much of a good day *himself*, was now becoming a real art. Particularly given he was back at work, and until today, assisting his wife's perceived nemesis on a major case, or indeed possibly *cases*, plural. As he waited for the kettle to boil, he realised he'd have to accept the word 'perceived' was probably no longer valid. . . or even vaguely correct. As it was, that day had been the shittiest he'd had in a very long time, but clearly he couldn't tell her that.

He soaked the teabag in his Arsenal mug for a good three minutes, and was just going to pour in the milk when he noticed there was a chip on the rim. His day was getting shittier by the minute. He also noticed Annie hadn't answered him.

She hadn't replied because of frantically trying to think of someone she could tell him she'd been with for the afternoon. Someone he didn't really know and wouldn't create a long, detailed 'interview' about. Finally it snapped into place....

"It was Carly's day off – we had some lunch and mooched around town for a bit of window shopping. Sorry, I just realised I've not—"

Harry vaguely remembered the name of her old trainee hairdresser, and had already dismissed it as well as guessed at the absence of dinner. "No worries, love, I picked up a pie at Bella's on the way home," he said smiling. "Just fancied a bit of steak and kidney." It was a lie, but it was easier that way despite his diabetes.

Grabbing the biscuit barrel he took it to the table with his tea and sat down. He'd not done a glucose check since that morning, only had a sandwich at lunch and was now feeling tired and heady. Picking up the TV remote he dipped into the digestives with one hand whilst flipping through the channels to find the news with the other. With the channel found, Annie immediately got up and began busying herself wiping down the work surfaces. Harry glanced at her briefly, surprised at the sudden cleaning burst, and then went back to the TV as the newsreader began....

"Human remains have been discovered below a croft cottage at the back of St Martin's Church in Martindale, Penrith. Police were called to the area this afternoon where it is thought that due to heavy rain three days ago, and the now exceptionally soft ground, the land has become waterlogged enabling the remains to come to the surface. It has not been confirmed, but the remains are not thought to be connected to any of the graves. The area has been cordoned off and is now...."

At that point (having updated his ringtone), Harry's pocket began playing the theme music to *Line of Duty*.... He pulled out his mobile and on first checking it wasn't Fran, answered on loudspeaker...

"Longbridge..."

"Sir, it's Joe. We've just had another one called in – by a *vicar*, would you believe? This time it's not an arm or a leg though." Annie stopped cleaning.

"Just watching the news now, son," interrupted Harry. "St Martin's, up at Martindale, the church in the valley below the old croft cottage. That makes it Penrith, not far from where the leg turned up."

"That's the one," replied Joe. "They've been instructed not to say anything in the media yet but. . . well, it's definitely murder, sir. It had been buried and emerged from the ground due to the heavy rains we've had."

"*And . . .?* So what've we got, lad? Another arm, another leg, foot, *what?*"

"*Sir*... it's a man's. . . *head.*"

A tight squeal of hysteria sounded. Annie didn't know whether to laugh or faint.

"I said it's a . . ."

"I heard what you said," replied a disturbed Harry – now staring at his wife.

SEVENTEEN

JULY 9TH

9.00 A.M. CHIEF SUPERINTENDENT HITCHINGS' OFFICE

He'd received the call at 7.00 a.m. telling him to be in Chris Hitchings' office first thing. It had temporarily shelved concerns over Annie's frankly bizarre reaction to the news report the night before, although he was obviously going to have to bring the subject up. In fact, he was beginning to wonder if he should suggest some kind of therapy for her again considering she'd refused all help since the abduction.

The wait outside Hitchings' office had been a long one. Harry had arrived early wanting to be punctual as he knew his boss had a big 'thing' about timekeeping; amongst a whole host of other specific things it had to be said, but time was right up there, and this meeting was going to be completely different from the previous one only five days ago. *This one* resulted from Fran's unexpected sick leave. With her out of action, Harry knew Hitchings would need to let him run 'Operation Bonaparte' – the body parts case. *And so did Hitchings.*

At *exactly* nine o'clock, Harry walked into the office when his boss called through to his PA, and waited for the chief super to look up from his computer. As usual he made him wait....

"Ah. . . Longbridge. . . yes, well, I'm sure you know why you're here."

"Sir?" answered Harry questioningly, standing up very straight, very properly and very respectfully. This threw Hastings for a second. He simply wasn't used to it.

"Sit down, Harry, no point in changing the habit of a lifetime, and it feels too weird having you standing there like a real policeman."

Harry let the sarcasm slide. It *was* quite funny and he even thought he saw a smidgeon of a smile at the corner of Chris's mouth. "Thank you, sir, don't mind if I do." He sat.

"Right. . . Now – with DI Taylor unfortunately indisposed for the next few weeks, I'm going to have to ask you to head up the 'Bonaparte' case."

"Oh, *really*, sir?" replied Harry feigning surprise.

Hitchings gave him *'the look'*. "I think you know full well there's no one else who could take on such a huge operation, Harry. Despite shall we say. . . an occasional *Gene Hunt* approach to the service, I'm well aware when it comes to serious crime you're probably the best DCI I have." He began to shuffle a few bits of paper before finally stacking and shoving them into his drawer, a fumbled attempt to cover his embarrassment at this admission.

Harry nearly forgot to speak and was doing a good impression of a goldfish – such praise was completely unheard of; *well, for him anyway.* He was also suitably impressed his boss even knew who Gene Hunt *was.* He was under the impression Hitchings spent most of his TV time watching André Rieu, Brian Cox and *Country File.* Finally he found his voice...."Thank you very much, sir! I really appreciate that, sir, giv—"

"Yes, okay, Longbridge, no need to *revel* in it. Just don't let me down. *You won't let me down, will you, Harry?*"

"Absolutely *not*, sir."

"I mean it, Harry. I've gone out on a limb here, had to give you my full backing and approval to the chief constable."

"Yes, sir, than—"

"You are *clear* on what that means, aren't you, Harry? You remember who the new chief constable actually *is?* She'll have my balls dangling from the rear mirror of her recently acquired turquoise Bentley if you even *think* like *Gene bloody Hunt!*"

"Don't worry, sir, I've got the message, loud and clear, super clear – *as crystal.*" Harry smiled reassuringly across the table at a *not* so reassured Hitchings.

* * *

The emergence of the head in the grounds of St Martin's churchyard had not been 'seen' in any dream or vision by Molly Fields. Like the rest of the country she'd watched the news the night before stating the find as 'human remains'. Unlike the rest of the country, she'd been thanking her lucky stars she'd not experienced any kind of premonition with regard to how they got there.

In fact, her visions were pretty random these days and she could only put it down to pregnancy hormones. There had been several grisly news reports lately all in and around the Kirkdale or Penrith area, none of which she'd sensed or predicted. It was all very confusing. Whilst she didn't *want* any creepy experiences, it meant she couldn't relax one way or the other, either to get used to them as a full-on psychic, or not at all. The only death vision she'd had recently was about that solicitor who'd persuaded Charlotte Peterson's mother to change her will, and nothing had been reported about *him*. Well. . . not so far.

The strange thing about that news item though, just as she'd watched the police being interviewed in the church grounds, the camera had panned the hills above the valley. It had been then that she'd seen it. It was small but it had definitely been there, and now she couldn't stop thinking about it. Her eyes had kept homing in on a cottage way above the church. Molly had been drawn like a magnet, because on screen it looked like it was literally glowing in the hills, which of course was ridiculous. She had even changed channels and gone back again, turned the TV off and on again, checked there were no lights in the lounge shining on the screen, but that cottage had kept right on glowing with an intense, pulsating light . . . *and she hadn't been able to tear her eyes away.*

Now in the bar of the Carpenters Arms the following lunchtime, her thoughts were firmly on that glowing cottage, even more than the gory news report itself. In fact it had been on her mind constantly. She was very glad when she saw Andrew in the bar on her return from the till to get a customer their change.

"Hi, Andy – are you in for lunch? Is Gee on her way or is this a solo visit?"

"No, just a fly-through, Molls, only time for a quick cheese and pickle sadly. I've got an appointment in half an hour. I could have really downed one of your mum's pies too." He scrunched a sad face.

"I could always box you up a slice of steak and mushroom to take away. Think the spicy shepherd's pie might prove a bit messy to take out!" They laughed at the possibilities of that as Molly pulled him a pint of his favourite lager, wrote up the sandwich order for the kitchen and gave it to one of the girls to take through. She put the pint on the bar waving his money away smiling. "That's okay, my treat, you got the coffees the other day. Actually, Andy. . . I'm glad you've come in. Did you see the news last night, about the human remains found in Martindale?"

"Thanks – yes, we both saw it," he replied after taking a long drink. "Gina went quite green, nearly threw up on the cat – Missy was most upset being thrust off her lap!"

"Did you notice the cottage up in the hills above the church?" continued Molly leaning on the bar towards him.

"No. . . don't think so. Why? I was just looking at the crime scene and listening to the police interview. They weren't giving much away though, didn't say it was a body, or parts, just kept repeating the phrase *human remains.*"

"Yes, I noticed that too. It's just that. . . something was pulling me towards that cottage. Mainly because it was. . . *glowing....*"

"Glowing? How'd you mean. . . *glowing?!"* replied Andrew genuinely confused.

"Exactly that – it was *glowing!* Really bright. . . the whole *thing* was pulsating with a golden hue. I just felt. . ." She leaned in closer and lowered her voice, "It felt like it was trying to *tell* me something."

Now a few years ago Andrew would've thought his friend was losing it big time, but since the Peterson murders in 2018 when Molly's visions had first started, he knew this might actually mean something. He thought for a moment.... "Like what? Have you had any more visions sin—"

"No – no, nothing. . . *Oh my God!!"* Molly's hand flew to her mouth. She began to whisper fast, eyes in wide realisation, flying left and right to check customers in earshot. *"The solicitor! The solicitor Christopher Mogg, the one that—"*

"What about him, *and why are you whispering?"* asked Andrew now also whispering....

She pointedly raised her eyebrows, tipping her head sharply at the full bar then waited until a few people moved away to their tables. "That's *it.* There's not been a single thing out there about his. . . *death.*" (This last word she mouthed silently.) "*Nothing since I had the vision of it a week ago,*" she quickly whispered again as two more customers approached, catching her eye. "What if that cottage is where he lives. . . *or lived?*" Molly left Andrew mulling over that possibility whilst she served the couple who'd just walked in.

Later on she took a break in the pub's private lounge quarters, and putting her feet up for a bit, took out her phone and skimmed through her contacts. Since seeing Andy earlier she'd been turning it over and over in her mind. Should she or shouldn't she? It was only the once this time, and several days ago now. Had she imagined it? She was starting to wonder. She tapped the phone on her chin and sighing, chewed her lip in thought. The thing was, Molly had been here before, *exactly* here, and not knowing whether to report a psychic incident during a murder investigation or not. This time however it was different; there was an understanding between them and he'd learnt a thing or two about not rubbishing clairvoyant events. Molly looked back at the screen, pulled up his number and hit connect.

* * *

7.00 A.M. - BEFORE HARRY
HAD LEFT FOR WORK

Annie showered, dressed, stuck her hair up in a towel and made her way downstairs for a much needed coffee. Standing on the small halfway landing before the second flight, she was immediately alerted to the snap of the letter box. A familiar brown envelope met her gaze over the banister. It lay at an awkward angle on the black paw-print mat, looking up almost accusingly. She stared at it for a few moments, more shocked at the postman having arrived two hours early than knowing precisely where it was from. Guessing its contents and realising exactly what she was going to do with it, on hearing Harry moving around in the bathroom she ran down the rest of the flight to the door, swept it up and stuffed it inside her jeans pocket. Her heart was thumping wildly as it always did when they arrived, partly with excitement, partly with terror – *always with anticipation....*

Two weeks later she was back inside Rampton.

EIGHTEEN

TWO WEEKS LATER

THE FLOWER GARDEN - RAMPTON HIGH SECURITY HOSPITAL

There was a light breeze and the sun was shining brightly. It was pleasant to be able to sit outside for a change instead of always meeting in the visitors' lounge. Charlotte winced as she leant forward to pick up her coffee from the table, take an awkward sip and replace it. The effort was still immense and the pain evident. Annie was visibly horrified when she saw the swathes of bandages on her arms and heard what had happened; no amount of pleasant sunny afternoons could make up for that. It also occurred to her that despite Charlotte's controlling and coercive personality, it hadn't stopped the Zandini woman attacking her.

"It must hurt *terribly*," said Annie sympathetically, turning in her chair and looking around awkwardly as if Zoe might suddenly rush up to them and repeat the assault, but this time on *her*.

"*It's fucking agony*," spat Charlotte through gritted teeth and holding herself awkwardly. "That bitch won't make old bones. One way or another I'll make sure of that." It wasn't only the eye tic that had reappeared on occasion recently, her renowned shark stare had returned since reducing her meds, all so she could hide and then pass the drugs to Annie for their 'work'. Her face was home to it now. The lead eyes stared cold, somewhere way beyond rational as she mentally sealed Zoe's fate with her promise.

Annie sucked in a deep breath then let it out slowly. Lifting her tea to her mouth she took a sip and laid the plain white cup back in its chipped saucer. The beverage wasn't exactly enjoyable. She was just wondering if she should mention the Christopher Mogg despatch as it would surely please her, when Charlotte spoke first, quietly and with a tinge of warning. Judging by her mood, Annie could tell it wasn't going to be pleasant....

"Well? What have you got for me? Anything? *Anything at all?* I'm very much hoping the recent news on those body parts is something to do with you? *Is* it? *Is* it, Andrea?"

"Er. . . no, not exactly, that's to say I—"

"*No?! What do you mean NO?!*" Charlotte hissed before clocking the narrowing eyes and one step forward of the nearest orderly. She threw her a quick 'everything's fine' smile and twisted her chair slightly, scraping it on the flagstones.

For the first time Annie felt threatened. Suddenly the reality of her association with this woman was pricking at what was left of her own sanity. She gave a small gasp at the verbal attack, and resorted to nervously picking at her nails. This had become a regular habit.

Charlotte had noticed Annie's anxiety resulted in agitated nail picking, at their very first meeting. She wasn't stupid. She didn't want to lose her delegate – not so soon anyway. Although it wasn't in her nature, she decided to drop the accusatory tone....

"Look, I didn't mean to get snarky. I'm—" The word stuck in her throat . . . "Well, I'm. . . I'm *sorry*, if I sounded, you know. . . a bit *irritable*." She managed a small, thin smile which of course did not reach her eyes, then paused for a moment. "Andrea, you do *know* how much this is going to help you, don't you? Give you back your *confidence*, put you back in *control*. . . make you feel *strong* again." A repeat of the linear smile... It wasn't a question, and the constant use of her full name reminded Annie of her mother.

She thought back to how she'd prepared the hemlock: Chopping it finely, simmering it in the old saucepan, allowing it to cool, straining the liquid into little glass bottles and hiding them under the loose floorboards in the spare room. It was true, there *was* a kind of power to that. The planning of it, the measuring, the art, the control, the completeness.... even if she *did* have to wear those horrible sweat-inducing rubber gloves. Annie's mindset shifted. Charlotte was right. It *had* made her feel stronger to know she was in the driving seat for once, and not the one being moved around like a chess piece on its board. *Not that Annie had told her about the hemlock of course....* She smiled slowly then, head on one side, a smile that reached both of *her* eyes as realisation sunk in.

"How did it go then?" asked Charlotte more gently. "Has your first been accomplished?"

"Yes, yes it has," replied Annie, now staring at her tea, running a finger up and down the handle of the white cup, studying its shape and strangely no longer afraid. She looked back up at Charlotte. "Do you want to know the funniest thing?" Her eyes widened then, and a tiny hysterical laugh escaped the same way it had that night the remains had been reported behind St Martin's Church; the night Harry had been watching the news in the kitchen.

"Go on. . ." said Charlotte, intrigued now by the sudden change in her demeanour....

"My husband still hasn't found him, that solicitor, that *boring* Christopher Mogg who never stopped going on about his *bloody* sister. Harry simply hasn't a *clue!*" Annie blew a satisfied sigh, exuded a malevolent grin and lifted her cup. The two women's eyes locked. Charlotte wasn't quite sure what had just happened. The idea a power swap had hovered in the air for even a moment was of course quite out of the question, but she wasn't going to examine it too closely either. The man, who'd diverted her inheritance by persuading her mother to leave it to a distant cousin, was apparently now dead. It was good enough. She would of course need to see proof of it in the media before celebrating the fact, but for now it was positive news.

Breaking eye contact, Charlotte reached gingerly forward for her own cup. *It was only at this point she realised she'd been holding her breath.*

* * *

ST MARTIN'S, MARTINDALE

Despite his previous experience of Molly Fields' mediumistic talents, Harry's phone conversation with her two weeks earlier regarding the glowing cottage above St Martin's Church had been firmly shelved. With Hitchings' warning still ringing in his ears about doing everything by the book, he simply couldn't justify sending a forensic unit out to investigate, or even a couple of officers. Not solely on the basis of a psychic's TV observations, even if she *did* have form. *Especially one that lived in a pub.* However.... there had now been a MISPER reported by one partner of a local solicitors, and it turned out the other lived in a croft cottage. . . out at Martindale. When he was told the missing person was Christopher Mogg, Harry had actually put in a call to Rampton to make sure Charlotte was still there.

Strictly speaking, it was Penrith's patch, but the law firm and partner who'd rung it in were both nearer Kirkdale, so it had fallen in Harry's lap. With no answer from Mogg's mobile and bad rains from two weeks before causing difficulty in the property's approach road, nobody had been to check on him.

The drive over had been quite memorable. With Fran still convalescing after losing the baby, Harry had taken Joe Walker with him. It had been a long time since they'd officially been out on a case together, with the last time having been when they'd raided the Petersons' farmhouse to arrest Charlotte. She hadn't been there of course, and Harry had arrived to discover Joe's stupid mistake of leaving her husband, Miles, alone in the bathroom, without taking his mobile first. This had led Longbridge to apoplectically explode at the rookie officer's actions, especially as it was later proved Miles had messaged Charlotte to let her know the police were after her.

"It's been a while," said Joe looking sideways at Harry as they drove to Martindale. He had huge respect for his boss and was also thinking of that time at the Petersons' farmhouse where he'd messed up. Luckily his saving grace that day had been spotting a major clue that had led to Charlotte Peterson's conviction.

"Indeed," replied Harry, "and unfortunately I've a horrible feeling *this* search *is* going to prove fruitful."

"What do you think we'll find, sir? I mean realistically he could've just decided to take a holiday and not even *be* there. He *is* an adult after all."

"Maybe. . ." replied Harry thinking about Molly's phone call. "His business partner appears to think otherwise though. Apparently our Mr Mogg is extremely reliable and dedicated to his work, even given his past difficult history."

Joe snorted in surprise. "Not sure I'd want to be working with a guy who spent months plotting to kill someone and fly three thousand miles across the pond to do it. Even if he didn't get actually get convicted of attempted murder – even if it *was* Charlotte Peterson he was after."

"Rumour has it his best mate put a word in with this current firm after he left a Northampton practice, and moved up here to settle his sister's estate," replied Harry, indicating left and taking the road for St Martin's. "It was after 'doctor death' got sent to Rampton and *before* the US stuff this year."

Joe suppressed a laugh at the *doctor death* reference, not that he probably needed to; there'd be no chastisement from Harry given his dry sense of humour.

"His partner told me he'd decided to keep him on after what had happened out there because he'd accepted therapy – *and he's a damned good solicitor*," continued Harry. "Christopher's a wills and probate man, not a criminal lawyer, so doesn't have the stress of court. There's plenty of work in that sector and he's apparently still seeing a therapist once a month."

Harry had turned off the A66 and was now in the tiny village of St Martin's looking for the slip road up to the croft cottage. They'd just passed the old church with its five hundred year-old yew tree in the grounds, and he'd taken his foot off the gas a bit so they could both search for Croft House Lane...

"*There!*" Joe pointed to the road sign having dropped his head slightly to read the partially covered name.

Tree branches hung low over it and it was worn by the elements. In all likelihood it hadn't been replaced because only one house sat at the end of the lane, and the fifty or so locals knew exactly where it went. Harry turned the car into the stone-walled road and changed down a gear ready for the muddy climb.

"Try his phone," said Harry digging out a piece of paper from his pocket with one hand and expertly steering through the road's muddy surface with the other. Like everything from his pockets the note was covered in sugar from barley sweets. Joe shook it off, took out his mobile and punched in the numbers. The car's wheels occasionally spun in the wet mud from the recent storm, lurching along the winding unmade road through overhanging trees and sheep grazing either side of the flat stone walls. The sun had disappeared behind a cloud and it looked like the rain might return. Joe put the mobile on speaker as the line connected and then eventually rang out. Harry dipped back into his pocket and popped one of the sweets in his mouth. Lunch missed again, he was starting to feel the effects. "We'll need to grab some food after this, lad, I'm not feeling so sharp."

"I can drive, sir, not to worry," said Joe, beaming a hopeful smile at his boss.

Harry looked at him like he was mad. Nobody ever drove his beloved old BMW – it would be utter sacrilege.... He turned back to the road automatically wiping his eyes as if it would ward off the weariness creeping up on him, then threw another barley sugar in his mouth. If Fran was with them there'd be a big bag of custard doughnuts on the back seat; always thinking ahead that woman. *He missed her*. The thought of Fran reminded him he must call as soon as he'd dealt with Croft Cottage, where he sincerely hoped he would not find its owner in an unfortunate predicament. . . *or worse.*

As soon as it came into view Harry felt his guts clench, and it wasn't from hunger. Mogg's car was out front. A fairly respectable-looking blue Volvo saloon, one that looked like it hadn't been moved in days, maybe a week. There were no tracks down to the hill road, and there would have been given the mud. The car had a pearl finish and it was pretty spotless. The two men looked at each other.

"Doesn't look great, sir, not if Mr Mogg's as reliable as we've been told – car's clean too."

"No, no, it doesn't," agreed Harry, scanning the cottage and front of the property through his windscreen. He emitted a deep sigh. This reminded him of the Peckham high-rise in '89. A seventy-five-year-old woman had passed away in her flat and wasn't found till two weeks later when a social worker had phoned her in as a sudden death. Harry had been barely twenty years old, a rookie – it was his first corpse. He'd never forgotten it, found it difficult then and every time since. Removing the keys from the ignition and gripping the handle, he fixed Joe with a meaningful look. "Okay – let's get this done."

As they walked up the gravel path a light breeze passed across the back of Harry's neck and Joe looked up to have a few wet splashes land on his face. The heavens were about to open. All they could hear were the leaves rustling on a single Rowan tree and the scrunch beneath their shoes as they continued towards the front door. Harry pointed at the windows. The curtains appeared to be closed. There was an eerie feel about the place even though it was mid-afternoon, and despite all the windows *also* being shut, on reaching the door the curtains seemed to be moving slightly. A flashback made Harry pause for a moment and he drew his hand back from lifting the black metal knocker. Indicating to Joe to stay quiet and standing very still, he realised he was right. He could hear a very faint, very steady hum.

His heart sank.

NINETEEN

Joe stared after his boss as he marched back down the path to the BMW, watched him open the boot, take out a large jemmy, then march right back up again.

"Sir, are you going to—"

"Yes, Walker, I am. I don't know about you, but I've a feeling he's not going to be answering that door anytime soon."

"But how d—"

"Listen. Do you hear that noise?" asked Harry.

Joe looked puzzled, and when Harry inclined his head towards the house, put his own head closer to the door. His eyes widened then dipped. He sighed heavily before looking up.

"Exactly," said Harry as he hooked the claw end between the door lock and frame and yanked. It was old wood which needed replacing so gave way pretty much immediately. A vision of Chief Superintendent Hitchings flashed out of his head the moment it flashed in. He hesitated for a moment. "Will this be your first, son?"

Joe nodded, looking a bit anxious. Harry knew exactly how he felt; he'd never got used to it even after all these years. A reassuring pat on the back would have to do.

"Ready?" asked Harry looking at his rather green-looking sergeant. Joe nodded and Harry pushed at the door slightly. The vile stench that greeted them made both men heave and face outwards to the fresh air, and the faint hum that could be heard on the outside was now much louder with the door open. Harry took a deep breath and turning back round stepped into the small hall, followed by Joe.

Covering their mouths and noses as best they could by lifting the front of their jackets, they took a few steps towards the nearest room with the closed door. The noisy vibration from inside left Harry unsure whether or not to enter, despite knowing he needed to officially confirm the obvious. The flat in Peckham began to swim in and out of his head, and his hand hovered over the handle before he stopped to take a packet of latex gloves from his back pocket.

"Don't touch *anything*," he instructed as he removed two pairs from the packet, shoved it back, and handed a pair to Joe. Both men eased the disposables on. "Ready?"

Joe nodded, heart beating fast as Harry depressed the handle and slowly eased the door open, left arm holding his jacket front across his face. Apart from the lung-invading stench, despite the daytime hour it was also immediately noticeable the room was strangely dim. They both moved carefully inwards, looking about them as they went, conscious not to touch anything in case it turned out to be a crime scene. So far there was nothing to suggest it was. There was no sign of a break in (apart from Harry's contribution), nothing was disturbed and everything appeared to be upright and in its place. Everything was normal apart from the flies and the god-awful smell. Neither man spoke for good reason — it was not advisable to open one's mouth.

The sofa was set away to the left of the lounge door with its back to them, as they entered shielding their faces as best they could. A square oak table with four chairs around it stood immediately in front, an older-looking bookcase was against the wall ahead of them with a blacked out window to the right. The stone walls were painted a light cream and a black log burner sat inside a brick fireplace in front of the seating area.

The flies were everywhere. They not only fed on the body of the man they now found prostrate on the floor in front of that sofa, but they learnt the reason for the curtains being both closed. . . and '*moving*'. They weren't drawn across the windows at all, the glass was swamped with bluebottles blocking out the light and creating their own furnishings. Plenty more filled the room as both men swiped at the air around them with windmill arms.

Harry indicated to Joe that he recognised Christopher Mogg despite the rotting flesh, an unearthly amount of maggots present that were still to evolve, and the blow flies that flew in and out of his mouth and what was left of his nose. He stabbed his finger at the door they'd entered through and beckoned Joe to come away from the scene out into the fresh air.

"That's definitely Mogg," said Harry. "I recognise the 90s' Patrick Swayze hair, except Mogg's is auburn."

"Patrick who?" replied Joe brushing a fly off his jacket.

"Never mind – *it's him.*" Harry pulled the door to as best he could, given he'd busted the frame, fished his mobile out and tapped in the station number as they walked back to the car. He waited a minute or two for the call to pick up.... "It's Longbridge. I'm out at the croft cottage, top of St Martin's checking a MISPER." *A pause....* "Yeah, the one phoned in earlier by the lawyer. Well, I found him. It's definitely Christopher Mogg and he's definitely dead. My guess is a week or so but forensics will give us the detail." He unlocked the car and they both got in just as the heavens opened. "I can't see any disturbance, no false entry, nothing to suggest foul play but. . . well, we'll find out more with an autopsy." *Another pause....* "Right, yeah, we're coming back now, just get a team out here, will you? Okay, yep, thanks. . . bye then – bye – bye." He flipped the case closed and returned it to his pocket.

"You think there's foul play, don't you, sir?" It was a statement rather than a question.

Harry turned to his sergeant and popped another barley sugar. "I almost always suspect foul play, Walker – almost always, until I'm proved wrong. *Now. . . I need feeding.*"

* * *

RAMPTON HIGH SECURITY HOSPITAL
NOTTINGHAMSHIRE

Zoe Zandini had been in solitary since the boiling water incident. It had hurt her deeply to injure her special friend, her idol, the wonderful Dr Charlotte. . . but Uncle Raiffe had insisted, he'd *made* her do it. She'd begged him not to but he'd reminded her Charlotte owed the Zandini's a great deal of money and nobody made a fool of their family. Now Charlotte was understandably very angry with her and Zoe had no special friend, no dear one. She was banged up most of the day in punishment and on top of that hadn't heard from her partner Jimmy in weeks. *That* was worrying her a great deal. The Zandinis had already 'disappeared' his twin brother the previous year for messing up on a job, and Zoe had lived in fear for Jimmy ever since. He was not from within the mob, *the family*, so would not enjoy any special forgiveness for a job poorly done. He was a loud-mouthed, gambling drunkard and not the sharpest tool in the box, but he was *her* blunt-tooled loud-mouthed gambling drunkard. They had an accepted understanding between them. It wasn't all moonlight and roses, *hell it was never moonlight and roses*, but people like Zoe and Jimmy never expected that kind of life.

She lay on her bed quietly morose repeatedly pulling on the long ginger 'spirals' that fell either side of her face, and chewing on a very old piece of now tasteless gum. Outside her room in the corridors, the echoing sounds of various bells for meals and buzzers for locking and unlocking doors compounded her loneliness and loss. *She was about to discover just how much loss from the knock that now fell on her door.*

A key turned and an orderly walked in. It was Rita Lemon, the one she cared for least, although in truth she didn't really like any of them. Sour as her name suggested with skin pallor to match, the woman stood beside the entrance with her back to the wall, a bunch of keys in hand. The key to Zoe's room was fixed firmly between thumb and forefinger, her expression difficult to read, but it certainly wasn't full of the joys of spring. Zoe pushed herself up slowly to a sitting position.

"Zoe. . ." began Rita hesitantly, "I'm afraid I have some. . . *difficult* news for you." A male orderly slipped in behind her but remained quiet. Rita continued having acknowledged him. "It's about your part—"

"*Jimmy?*" said Zoe, alarmed now, having swung her legs off the bed, eyes wide. "What's happened to him? Where *is* he? Jimmy's not visited in *ages* and he's not rung either." Her anxious expression flashed between the two tense orderlies.

Rita took a deep breath, stepping to one side so her colleague would have a clear path if Zoe kicked off. "I'm *really* sorry, Zoe, but we've had information from the police today that a Mr James Johnson, your partner, has been confirmed as. . . as having passed away." She waited as the woman on the bed initially looked puzzled before appearing to try to assimilate the information.

"*What?. . . No!* But. . . but *how? Why?* No, no... *NO!* It can't be – not *Jimmy?! He's the strongest bloke I've ever met!*" Behind her, Rita's colleague Cal slipped a hand into his pocket. It was then that Zoe jumped up, and on finding her legs gave way, fell back on to the bed and started breathing erratically, rocking backwards and forwards, moaning and shaking her head in denial.... "Who's *done* this – *who's killed my Jimmy?!*"

"We don't know yet I'm afraid. . . nobody knows," answered Rita calmly and slowly, trying to keep things from escalating to God knows where. *She just prayed Zoe hadn't managed to get hold of and hidden any blades given her media nickname – 'Stabby'....*

"Where . . . *where* did it happen? *How* did it happen?" She looked through a veil of tears that now coursed down her cheeks soaking the ginger spirals as she swiftly wiped her eyes in order not to appear vulnerable in front of them.

"Well. . ." Rita hesitated not wanting to reveal too much. "All we know is that Mr Johnson had a very rare blood type and that has helped in identi—"

Zoe knew exactly what that was likely to mean. She knew the Zandinis, she knew her family – Jimmy had never been accepted. Hands over her ears the rocking became stronger as she began to emit a low guttural noise that gradually climbed to a crescendo.... "No, no, no, no. . . *Nooooo!!*" Cal Davis moved forward swiftly with a preloaded syringe as Zoe reached for a lamp and with Rita on one side of her and him on the other, delivered a sedative that would give this particular Zandini a very long, very heavy sleep.

"Good job you didn't tell her the complete story," said Cal as they lay her in the middle of the bed and pulled a light cover over her before walking out.

Rita blew a sigh of relief as she locked the door behind them. "Christ, if I'd mentioned the *head*, one of *us* could've ended up jabbed with that Lorazepam."

* * *

The weather had taken a turn for the worse, but the forensic team had just about managed to negotiate the mud slide that was Croft House Lane. The end result of several hours' specimen collection had on the face of it, not found anything unusually suspicious, but still necessary given it was a sudden death and the county was in the midst of the *body parts* case. It looked like Harry Longbridge had been right though – *an autopsy was going to be necessary to determine how solicitor Christopher Mogg had died.*

TWENTY

On the way back to the station, Harry and Joe stopped off at Bella's Buffet for bacon rolls and coffees, the consumption of which quickly cleared Harry's head and sharpened his thoughts. Now pulling into the station car park and seeing the empty space, Harry couldn't help but think of her. On top of dealing with Annie's recent escalating and frankly disturbing behaviour, plus now leading the Bonaparte case, he knew somehow he had to make time for Fran too. Not that this was unwanted in any way, not at all, just that it involved a lot of juggling. And he wasn't very good with anything to do with balls. . . not even metaphorical ones.

"She'll be fine, sir," said Joe quietly, followed swiftly by a distinct feeling he shouldn't have said anything. It *was* after all the elephant in the room, or in this case – car. Everyone knew Harry and Fran were some kind of unofficial item, and that Harry was the father of her baby (or *had* been, the rumour mill had most people guessing why Fran was off work), but it was not generally acknowledged and never mentioned directly to either of them, or even in their hearing. He could feel his throat constricting for a moment as Harry parked the car in silence. Joe was used to dry humour, sarcasm, lots of shouting, but not this. Harry pulled on the handbrake, turned to him and was just about to speak when Jacey Pearle, a first-year trainee DC, came running down the station steps swiftly followed by the dinosaur of the nick, DC Terry Hackett. Jacey slowed to a normal pace when she noticed Harry's car, and emitting a nervous smile approached it as he rolled down the window....

"Everything okay, Jacey?" he asked whilst purposefully giving Hackett his look reserved for the low-life plankton that harassed female officers, particularly the rookies. Although ten years younger than himself, like Harry, Terry still harboured some old-school tendencies. However, unlike him, the man was without any basic good manners, especially when engaging with female officers. He certainly possessed zero empathy or respect with regard to anybody's emotions or sexual orientation. Hackett, who had now decided he wasn't going in the same direction as Jacey after all, averted his eyes and switched his route to the other side of the car park. Jacey briefly looked after him before answering Harry. Joe leant forward and offered her a sympathetic smile. He'd suffered a bit from the snide comments of Terry Hackett himself, despite Joe being a sergeant and Terry never getting off the bottom rung. In fact it was probably a mix of this and the fact the older man was a full-blown homophobe.

"Hi Joe." Jacey had leant down to the window. "Yes. . . thank you, sir, it's just that he's. . . Terry, he's just a bit full-on. I keep trying to ignore him, but the more I do the more he makes me look an utter *plank* in front of the department."

"Does he now...? I take it you won't make an official complaint about his behaviour though, or—"

"No, *no, sir,* it's not worth going there. I'm sure it'll all blow over in time, he'll soon move on to someone else. . . hopefully." Jacey broke another nervous smile in response to Harry's understanding nod. After a couple of minutes' support chat, she said her goodbyes and made her way to the car park entrance. She didn't look too hopeful thought Harry dryly as he watched her go, but knew she was right. If an official complaint went in, whilst it would be dealt with, the end result might not go favourably for her amongst colleagues, and *that* could affect her even more. However, she was a determined young woman, and even if slightly less confident than some, certainly one with ambition – and *definitely* one that did everything by the book. Probably why Hackett was trying to squash her confidence, especially as he'd noticed Hitchings beamed approval on the few occasions he'd seen him talking to her in Hackett's presence. Hitchings liked Hackett even less than he approved of Harry – but at least he respected Harry for his clear-up rate, even if it wasn't as squeaky clean as Jacey's approach to the job.

"Can't stand that bastard," said Joe tersely, narrowing his eyes. "*Waste of bloody skin!*"

Harry turned to look at the young DS, his own eyes wide in surprise now. He couldn't remember ever hearing him swear before, and with such *venom* too. This he'd always put down to his devoutly religious father dishing out an intensely strict upbringing. Joe rolled his eyes, looked out of his side window and snorted in disgust.

"Sometimes even *I* can't hold it back. Hackett's a nasty piece of work, sir, came over from Penrith whilst you were in New York. I wish to God he'd go *back*."

"Indeed, son, beginning to realise we'll have to keep an eye, especially where Jacey's concerned. Now you need to get inside, there's work to be done. Someone's got to track down Christopher Mogg's family and contact his business partner which will have to be your call. I need to be elsewhere..."

* * *

Whilst he'd been on the phone to Fran as often as possible since her miscarriage and following scan at the hospital, Harry had only popped in to see her a couple of times since. Given the unspoken 'upgrade' in their relationship, he knew this was very remiss of him. Now back in Keswick standing on the doorstep of her new-build off Stanger Street, Harry hesitated, thinking sadly of the mayhem and heartbreak that had brought him to her door two weeks ago. Finally he rang the bell and waited. Despite it only being about thirty seconds it felt too long and he rang it again – twice. The second of those pushes he kept his finger on the button until he heard her footsteps running down the stairs.

"What the *fu-? Harry?!* It's a doorbell, not bloody blues and twos!"

"Sorry, I, well. . . jumped the gun a bit, I guess," Harry replied sheepishly. They looked at each other for a moment, Fran holding onto the door and he holding on to her gaze, remembering how it felt to stroke her hair....

"Come in – I'll make some coffee." She opened the door wide and Harry followed her upstairs in silence to the first-floor open-plan lounge/kitchen/diner, and stood awkwardly in the middle of the mainly grey and silver-toned room.

"How are you feeling?" he asked. "Physically I mean, I know that. . . well..." his voice faded. "Look, do you fancy a late lunch?" He checked his watch, it was almost 4.00 p.m. "I've had a snack from Bella's but Annie's on an away day, gone to see an old friend. We could go over to the Carpenters for a bit, I could do with thanking Molly for—" He stopped, realising Fran hadn't been around for Molly Fields' visions, either in 2018, or recently.

"Thank Molly for what?" she asked with the kettle in her hand.

"Grab your coat, the weather's turning again by the looks of it. You're okay to go out now, aren't you? I mean I haven't a cl—"

"I'm fine, Harry." She spoke quietly, placing the kettle back on its stand and disappearing into the cloakroom off the lounge and re-appearing with a black leather jacket. "Let's go – you can tell me in the car."

* * *

Sitting in the snug area of the Carpenters Arms, Harry and Fran looked up as Molly appeared with some drinks, followed by Gina with a couple of plates of chilli. Gina was technically on maternity leave, but had popped in to see her friend and was briefly helping out because one of the staff had rung in sick.

"Thanks Molly," smiled Harry, "and, er. . . also for the tip-off. You were right about your latest. . ." He shifted uncomfortably even though he was now used to her. . . "You know, that *thing* you do..."

Fran picked up her Coke and winked at the girls who smiled knowingly back. Harry had always felt awkward about having to accept Molly's random psychic abilities, and had explained about her visions (none of which had happened in New York), to Fran on the way over. Molly had put it down to the fact Manhattan was extensively hurried, loud and noisy, whereas at home her life was much slower and she was surrounded by trees, lakes and hills. The setting simply hadn't been right in the US, and truth be told, she'd been relieved not to see any floating dead people out there.

"You're welcome. Was it him? The solicitor?" asked Molly.

"Yes, but you keep that to yourselves, I've got officers contacting family and friends as we speak."

"Yes, of course," replied Molly. "Well, enjoy your meals, and if you can fit it in, the Spotted Dick is unbelievably good. Mum's used chocolate pieces today instead of fruit!"

Gina playfully punched her arm. "*What?* You never *said!*"

"You've got a wedding dress to fit into at Christmas – I'm doing my best to help you achieve that even if you haven't had the baby yet." Gina pulled a face but followed it with one that said, 'okay I *knowww*'.

Harry discreetly glanced at Fran given her current situation, and was relieved to see she appeared unaffected by it. The two girls then left them to eat, both wondering as they walked back to the bar just exactly how that bolognaise of a relationship was going to pan out.

Half an hour later Molly was pulling a pint for a customer when something bright caught the corner of her eye. Glancing up to look, her mouth fell open and she became locked into the glow as a steady stream of Loweswater Gold rose up and poured over the rim of the glass, her hands and was soon decorating the floor. Her father, Ron, yelled from the other end of the bar to no avail, and with Gina having a break in the Fields' private lounge, it was left to him to limp painfully across the pub to get her to release the pump. Molly couldn't hear him though; in that moment she wasn't really aware of anything except the glowing aura that hovered clearly around Fran Taylor's head....

Later that evening, Gina was still technically working the bar with Molly, although Molly was a tad jittery after her latest 'experience', and Gina had promised Maisie Fields she'd start taking things a lot slower given she'd only got six weeks to go before the birth. She'd already been there since lunchtime, and because of this was now doing a lot more chatting at tables and just taking a few meal orders, rather than actively serving drinks and carrying plates of food. It took her longer to get about than the other waitresses too, so in all probability it would be her last shift and Molly was a great deal quieter than usual. There hadn't been much time to discuss Fran Taylor's 'attachment' so the atmosphere in the bar was a little tense.

It was whilst Gina was chatting to a couple who were sitting on her favourite couch in one of the bays, she noticed a middle-aged fair-haired man at a wall table next to the chalkboard menu. He was drinking alone. The long floppy fringe now replaced by a neater, altogether more classic style from a couple of years previously, framed his naturally tanned face. Still present though, the familiar crisp-cut blue shirt, expensive blazer and tailored trousers, and an equally tanned Rolex-adorned wrist. The fact he looked up from his red wine to smile at her *(albeit in a completely different way from back then)*, and that she knew exactly who this man was, made her reach for the top of the nearest chair. She gripped it firmly, practising newly learnt breathing techniques as uncomfortable memories of him mixed with '*her*', the darkness beneath the lake, and New York's Bellevue Hospital echo swirled inside her head. Even though there had been contact since that bombshell two years ago, some stilted phone calls, texts, the odd Facetime. . . she still found it difficult. And now he was in the pub. Right there in front of her. Smiling...

Dr Miles Peterson was back.

TWENTY-ONE

Miles was a changed man. Not that he'd had any kind of epiphany, just that he was no longer hitting on every attractive female that appeared in his eyeline, certainly nobody under the age of twenty-five anyway. Discovering two years previously that his former employee *(the young woman he'd been leering and winking at in his surgery reception every day)*, was in fact his own daughter, had definitely had an effect. Even on him. It was undeniably enough to tailor his past vacuous behaviour, because in all honesty he couldn't rule out a second, or even possibly a third similar car crash event. Several teenage affairs at university had tripped through his mind since the revelation he was not only a father, but a father who'd been lusting after his own flesh and blood....

After Charlotte's court case and inevitable sentencing in 2018, Miles had moved away from Kirkdale. Despite discovering Gina was his daughter, *although eventually pleased given Charlotte had been unable to have children,* the initial shock and disgust he'd felt about his conduct towards her albeit unknowingly, had fuelled a need to get away and find some space. He also thought she would understandably not want him around with the case hitting the national as well as local press. This was of course on top of the fact he'd learnt he'd been married to an insane serial killer, and had absolutely no clue prior to Charlotte's arrest. That fact alone had sent him reeling and in need of psychiatric help, help that had quite literally put Miles back on his feet because for a time he hadn't even wanted to get out of bed. So much so, he'd decided he might look at diversifying, or even leaving the NHS altogether and privately study for and set up his own exclusive counselling and natural nutrition service. To achieve this through the official route would obviously have taken him years, certainly the counselling side, *which of course is why he didn't....*

Following the divorce, which in itself was initially at least a double-edged sword given Charlotte's vast (if theoretic) inheritance, he'd set about getting himself well again and training (online) for his future business. To be fair, Miles genuinely believed that after his experiences, he could provide substantial and beneficial help by offering counselling, either in person or online, to those who had gone through, or were living with, difficult situations. Quite frankly though, in addition to that, he'd been looking for a way out of the NHS for a variety of reasons for quite some time, not least the burgeoning daily

pressure of a growing patient list. Being expected to give correct prescriptive help and advice in a ten-minute time slot had become increasingly frustrating, not to mention extremely unsatisfying. Latterly he'd begun to see people as individuals. Each having varying requirements that may not respond to being told they all had to *'wear a size five shoe . . .'*, basically the broad umbrella of the prescription pad that treated everybody as a 'body' and not as a person. It was not how he wanted to treat his patients. The conveyor belt approach had begun to bother him....
The way he was planning on running his new business meant he could allow an hour or more for each client, and truly feel he was helping with their issues. The money side wasn't to be sniffed at either, and since Charlotte was no longer the beneficiary of her parent's financial assets (and he'd divorced her anyway...), well. . . 'needs must' as his ex-psycho wife used to say. He was entitled to make a living and felt this was as good a way as any. It kept him connected to health which he wanted (on his terms), and made him feel he was doing something positive to relieve his guilt. It also put him firmly back in the driving seat of his sorry life.

Now it was time to build a relationship with his estranged daughter – *properly*. Not just the odd phone call, even if some had been on screen. Thanks to Emily telling Charlotte about his affair with her at uni all those years ago, and who Gina was, she'd been through hell. That was bang out of order and should never have happened, not when it could have, and *had* put their daughter in danger. Em hadn't even told *him* for God's sake!! However, it appeared she'd suffered enough for that landmark confession, so he'd no intentions of jumping on a plane to New York to confront her. What was done was done. Now there was a baby on the way for Gina and Andrew, and unbelievably he was going to be a grandfather in a few weeks. That much he *did* know. Now was the time for new starts – for all of them.

And so he now found himself sitting in the Carpenters Arms pub with a glass of red, and his daughter across the room looking anxiously at him. He would have to tread very carefully.

Gina had calmed herself sufficiently to allow her to let go of the chair she'd been clutching so tightly. She knew she had to get a grip on her nerves once and for all. She was going to be a mother in a few months and these nervous episodes could not continue. Taking a deep breath and standing tall, she walked over to her father with a smile as confident as his and sat down. It was time to talk as family....

JULY 25TH, KIRKDALE GENERAL HOSPITAL - TWO DAYS LATER MORTUARY AUTOPSY ROOM

The late afternoon sun filtered through the window bouncing off the three vacant steel tables like a camera flash. The fourth was occupied. With staff laid off because of the local sickness bug, pathologist Marcus Ventnor had been seconded from Penrith to help out, and was preparing for his last autopsy of the day. Once scrubbed and gloved, fully gowned and paperwork checked, he walked over to the occupied table. Christopher Mogg's body lay partly covered with a mortuary sheet. His face, like all his muscles, now relaxed, flaccid and pliable, its grotesque rictus grin that had frozen his final expression, now long gone.

Marcus pulled down the sheet to the top of Mogg's thighs and picking up his chosen scalpel, began cutting the typical 'Y' insertion from just below his right shoulder. He worked confidently, methodically and alone, a seventies' classic rock CD playing 'California Dreamin'' on a 'Bose' quietly in the background. He liked music. It helped him concentrate, just like it had when he was twelve doing his homework, and later as a med student writing endless theses and dissertations. It was a lucky break that Kirkdale's absent inhouse pathologist clearly mirrored him – hence the Bose and stack of CDs, although he'd had to dig for a decent album what with Kelly Novak being almost half his age, and sadly, a Coldplay fanatic....

Forty-five minutes later he was snapping his gloves off and leaning against the wall units, mobile in hand waiting for a connection to Fran Taylor's office landline. It was picked up by Harry who'd insisted Fran took a few more days off before returning to work after the miscarriage.

"Longbridge – how can I help?"

"DCI Longbridge, it's Marcus Ventnor, Ventnor as in the Isle—"

"Yes, yes, I remember – do you have some results for me?"

"I do as it happens. Is Frannie okay, by the way? I was expecting to spea—"

"She's fine, got a few days off. Now what do you have for me?" Harry's clipped yet slightly dismissive tone had not gone unnoticed by the man on the other end, but he chose to ignore it....

"Your solicitor fellow found in the croft cottage – Mogg, Christopher Mogg...."

Harry leant forward on the desk, now gripping the phone. *This* he was interested in. It was the most incongruous looking body he'd found so far in his career, certainly with regards to his face. Nothing Ventnor was about to say would surprise him, however wacky. "Go on," he said tensely.

"Hemlock," stated Marcus simply. "That's what killed him, also called dead man's fingers, official scientific name, *oenanthe crocata*. Nasty stuff, took me by surprise, to be honest. Don't think I've ever had any—"

"*Hemlock?*" repeated Harry, now up and walking around to the front of the desk to open the door. "What the fu. . . *hell is hemlock*? Some sort of weed, isn't it? How on earth…?"

"Very effective poison if prepared carefully," interrupted Ventnor, seemingly almost impressed with the cause of Mogg's death, if not actually with the poisoner themselves. "I would be very surprised if he took it deliberately, as in a suicide attempt – no, I believe he ingested it unknowingly. If it was hidden in very rich-flavoured or spicy food, well. . . although the smell and taste would be pungent, very like parsnips, it's quite possible he may not even have noticed it. *Not at the time anyway....*"

Ventnor was, if exceedingly irritating especially where Fran was concerned, obviously very knowledgeable, thought Harry. He consoled himself with the fact he'd probably done a whole lot of online research to sound extra impressive, making doubly sure before ringing him. Harry quickly conveyed his thanks, *whilst deflecting more questions about Fran*, and said goodbye.

After he'd caught up with Joe Walker and Suzanne Moorcroft to make certain Mogg's relatives and colleagues had been notified, despite his hesitancy, Harry knew there was a need to have a serious sit-down discussion with Annie – whether she wanted it or not. He'd not forgotten about his wife's erratic and frankly at times bizarre behaviour of the last few weeks. The drinking, the god-awful practically bleached white *hair*, the downright eerie squeal of hysteria in response to the news report about the washed-up head at Martindale.... It all made the general bad mood, continual disappearance and lack of anything resembling even remotely like 'dinner', look positively normal by comparison. As he left the station and jogged down the steps to the car park, he pressed her mobile number and waited for her to pick up.

* * *

Annie sat, *unusually for her,* with a coffee in the lounge. She was at least *trying* to cut down on wine during the day although not necessarily for health purposes. It was more for keeping herself mentally sharp and aware. Juggling the craziness of what was going on in her life, Charlotte's demands, avoidance of Harry's questions, seeing Michael when she could (and trying to appear normal), and fighting the nagging guilt in her head over that boring but innocent solicitor Christopher Mogg, was all taking its toll. She'd decided a need to be 'clean', at least during the day, was important. She would try anyway. At the same time though, she felt invigorated. The thrill of knowing what Harry did not, the challenging way she'd responded to Charlotte on her last visit to Rampton, *and Charlotte's badly hidden surprise,* the insane power she'd felt as she'd watched Mogg literally dig his grave with his teeth. . . it was all, undeniably, giving her a kick.

Her phone rang just as an interesting advert in the rapidly shrinking classified section of the magazine *Psychology Today* caught her attention. Her stomach tightened on realising it was Harry, who rarely rang her during the day anymore....

"Helloooo...." she answered with a distinctly bored tone of someone being interrupted from not doing anything particularly important.

"Annie? It's me," replied Harry.

"I guessed."

"Right. . . yes, well, I'm just ringing to suggest we go out to eat tonight. It's been ages since we've had a nice dinner somewhere. What do you say?"

"Well, I wish you'd mentioned it earlier, Harry," said Annie with mock annoyance, "I've cooked a full roast beef dinner with all the trimmings!"

There was silence from the other end. Harry wasn't quite sure how to respond to this without sounding either a) ungrateful or b) condescending. He opted for somewhere between confused and grateful.... "Oh. . . right. That sounds. . . lovely."

"Don't be stupid, Harry, of course I haven't," Annie sighed, rolling her eyes skyward.

"Right. . . well. . . let's get a roast and a nice bottle of—" he stopped before the word 'red' realising her increasing wine habit would be forming part of his conversation. "Well, a nice slap-up meal at the Carpenters anyway, yes?" he continued awkwardly, hoping she'd not noticed. "I'll meet you in there about six, okay?"

Annie fiddled with the corner of the magazine, folding it backwards and forwards thoughtfully, wondering what was bringing this on, this 'slap-up' meal out of the blue. Before answering him she picked up a pen and circled the advert. "Yes. . . go on then. Your shout though, I'm flat out." She cut the call and checked her watch then switched her attention back to the classifieds....

– 'NATURALLY YOU' –
Feeling Depressed? Anxious?
Increasing Anger issues? Stressed?
eating disorders?
RELATIONSHIP PROBLEMS?

Not in control of your life?
Borderline personality disorder?

Let us help you become – *Naturally You*
Affordable, Drug Free, Positive & Private Therapy
Dr Miles Peterson:– naturallyou.com
Email:-mp@naturallyyou.com

Opening the web browser on her phone, Annie swiped some pages on the site until she found what she wanted, the site owner's profile picture. Annie smiled. She found the contact list on her phone and added the contact details of *Naturally You.*

Charlotte was going to be very – *very* happy....

TWENTY-TWO

Annie walked into the Carpenters Arms and immediately had flashbacks. It was where she'd met Michael in March after he'd turned up out of the blue at the house, and she'd only been in the pub a couple of times since. The memory always triggered. In turn of course, it inevitably led to all the other disturbing and devastating memories of what had followed, before arriving at where they all found themselves now. Unfortunately her husband hadn't exactly shined during that period, and the resentment still burned long and slow. . . *like a crematorium furnace....*

As she rounded the arch to the snug, Harry was sitting at exactly the same corner table she and Michael had shared that first time. Was her husband still unaware his wife had a son? More specifically, if not, did he know who the father had been? Or, *God forbid*, had he discovered what she'd done more recently? That was far worse than having a secret child. Annie's heart began to thump wildly as a heavy congested eel-like sensation slid through her gut.

Harry sat with his back to the wall and on seeing her, jumped up smiling to pull out a chair for her to sit down. At this point Annie decided maybe he wasn't going to grill her about Michael (or Christopher Mogg) after all – he was actually trying very hard to be nice. She noticed there were a couple of slim glasses already on the table containing something brown. They looked suspiciously non-alcoholic. The word *Coke* splashed in red across them was a bit of a give-away too.... *Harry had thought he should play fair and not have a beer so had ordered them both a soft drink*. She sat, dropping her bag off her shoulder, stared at the two glasses and shot him a *'what the hell?'* look – palms upwards. Harry opened his mouth in order to explain when at that exact moment her bag began to play muffled thunder and lightning sounds from the floor, sounds that crashed louder and clearer as she pulled out her phone. She checked, then immediately killed the call, returning the mobile to her bag.

Harry looked at her expectantly.

Quick as a flash she said, "It's nobody. Just a friend. The one from school I stayed with the other week in Nottinghamshire. I'll call her tomorrow."

"Thunder and *lightning*? Bit *dark*. What happened to your favourite Ace of Base ring tone?" Harry replied, half-teasingly, half-surprised, *and just a touch uneasy*.

"Oh. . . just got *bored* with it – needed a change," Annie quipped, taking a long drink of her Coke.

"Anyway. . ." continued Harry, "I thought we could cut down on the booze for a bit," he said gently. "Actually, love, I wanted to have a chat with you about. . . about the whole *wine* thing, and one or two other concerns I have, about, well, about you. . . about *us.*..." He waited for the fallout....

Annie winced, and not only at the word love. He hadn't called her *love* in a very long time. No wine was also a significantly justified reason to wince. However, she quickly reminded herself of her recent decision to cut down on that particular weakness in order to remain clear-headed, razor-sharp and supremely efficient. Considering the plans she was juggling, even plain water might have proved safest. Only during the day, though. It was now the evening and there was only so much 'sharpness' her brain could juggle.

Annie raised her drink. "*Cheers for that!*" She rolled her eyes sarcastically as she swiftly searched the room above the rim of her glass. Nobody here she knew, thank *God*. The last thing she needed was to have to be jolly and amusing with friends and acquaintances, not that there were many of those these days.

"I thought I'd order the roast beef for both of us as well," said Harry nervously, thankful for the relative ease with which his idea of their alcohol reduction had been received. "I know it's your favourite and it's not like we have a roast that often."

"We don't have one at *all*, Harry, not unless we go to my mother's, and we've been up in the Lakes for seven years, plus you're always working, so...." She lifted her glass and drank again. . . wincing.

Harry's mother had Alzheimer's and lived in a home in London. His father was dead. Although he did occasionally visit his mother he never talked about either of them.... "No, quite, well, we'll enjoy it all the more then, won't we?" he said smiling broadly.

It was very clear to Annie he was trying exceedingly hard, *too* hard. *Where exactly was he going with this?* She was about to find out.

"Annie. . ." Harry began tentatively, "I know things have been really hard the last few months, for both of u—"

"*Excuse me!?*" she threw at him, aghast after nearly choking on her wine-free Coke... "Did you just say *both?*"

"Well, no. . . perhaps not so much *me* in actual fact," Harry replied, sensing this wasn't exactly how he intended this to play out. "I just meant we've not been, well, as close as we might have, and with everything that happened to you, your terrible, *awful* experience with that leech Kenny Drew...."

At least he was acknowledging it she thought, stroking the side of her glass....

"I do understand how. . ." Harry took a deep breath, swallowing awkwardly, "... how let *down* you must have felt when I couldn't get out of New York, with the snow stopping the flights an—"

She looked at him like she was going to explode. "Harry, you *stayed* there even after the planes were *flying again!* You could've come home, joined me at my parents to give me support at the very *least*, you know, like any other *normal husband would have done!*"

Harry shifted uncomfortably. There weren't many tables in the snug, which is why he chose to sit there, but there *were* other diners and they'd started to flick them the odd glance. He used his eyes to nudge her awareness of the situation, adding softly, "Annie, could you take it down a couple of notches? I *am* trying here, you know."

She sighed and reluctantly drank a little more of her brown fizz wishing it could do something. Harry took a deep breath and started again....

"Annie. . . I know I've mentioned it before but...."

She tensed.

"Have you given any more thought to seeing someone? Get things off your chest so to speak instead of bottling things up so much. PTSD can be really hard to deal with, I'm sure it would help." He let the sentence tumble out all in one go instead of delivering it with the usual nervous hesitation he'd come to use with her lately. The hard, glassy stare that looked back at him was impossible to interpret. "It's worth a try, don't you think?" he continued, looking around anxiously in preparation of an outburst. "Just maybe give it a short trial – see how you feel?"

Her response surprised him, in as much as she didn't flip out completely. He always knew it was a possibility, but hoped even Annie wouldn't lose it in the middle of their local. Eventually she visibly relaxed and looked almost calm when she replied.

"It's in hand, Harry. I'm just as tired of dealing with the memories as you appear to be."

He breathed out slowly in grateful relief, and thankfully their meals arrived soon afterwards.

* * *

The other occupants of the snug weren't the only ones who'd noticed the tension at the corner table. The bar was directly in front, and Molly had been serving someone else when she'd first seen Harry come in alone. She was quite surprised to see his wife had joined him shortly afterwards, where things had started looking heated almost immediately and were still iffy when the waitress arrived with their food. Although she'd seen her before and knew who she was, Molly hadn't actually *met* Annie Longbridge, and to be honest couldn't imagine Harry with anyone other than Fran. She prayed the atmosphere would calm down a bit though and decided to do a smiley walk past to ask how their meals were....

"Is everything okay? Can I get you anything else at all?" she asked brightly.

Harry looked at Annie who actually gave a genuine smile back before answering.

"It's really very good. We should come in more often."

Molly thanked her and resisted looking at Harry who she obviously knew was in there quite regularly.

Holding up her now half-filled glass of Coke and smiling even wider, Annie added, "Put a double Bells in that for me, would you?"

Harry immediately began coughing, having apparently swallowed something the wrong way. He had *never* known

Annie to drink anything but wine, usually red, but never spirits. She smiled at *him* too – in triumph. Molly left her glass with her saying she'd bring a fresh one with the whisky in, and raising her eyebrows on turning round, approached the bar for the order. *It was clearly going to be a tense evening – in the snug at least.*

Whilst she waited for her dad to change the bottle on the optic, her mobile sounded a notification. She pulled it from her pocket and tapped the WhatsApp icon. Her heart started thumping – *it was Danny.* Since she'd returned from the States he'd surprised her with an initial contact through Facebook and they'd then messaged occasionally, even Zoomed a couple of times, but she still hadn't told him about the baby. Now he was talking about coming over for a visit....

"Molly. . . ? Molly. . . *Molly – whisky?!*"

"Sorry, Dad." She hastily pocketed her phone and took the glass. "Thanks – table 121's a tab." With the whisky delivered to Annie, Molly told Ron Fields she was taking her break and disappeared into their private family lounge. She had some serious thinking to do.

* * *

ONE HOUR LATER . . .

It was fair to say Michael Morton was confused. Very confused and very disappointed. Since his arrival in Kirkdale two weeks ago, he'd only seen Annie once, and even then she'd made a sudden excuse and run off halfway through their lunch at the wine bar. Although he genuinely understood how difficult it must be to tell her husband about him, he felt sad and disappointed that not only had she still not done so, but that she'd also been avoiding his phone calls. It hadn't been easy, but in light of everything, he'd made the decision to go home in the morning and had been packing before going out for his final evening meal. *Probably his last in the Lake District for the foreseeable future....*

By the time he reached the car park it was about seven fifteen. He'd already rung her an hour earlier from the B&B. He killed the engine and thought he'd try her just once more. If she didn't answer him or call back later, Michael promised himself he'd forget it for good. He should have got a taxi, he thought, sensing a depressive drinking session coming on as he punched in her number. Listening to the call connect he held his breath, until it was cruelly cut short. Pocketing his phone, Michael got out of the car and slamming the door, walked swiftly towards the opened entrance, through into the pub and headed directly for the bar. As he leant against it waiting for his drink, he turned round and pulled out his phone staring at it thoughtfully. *Just once more.* Biting his lip, he rang Annie once again, promising himself it really *would* be the last time....

A realistic sound of crashing thunder and lightning filled the air exactly as her number connected. It was an unusual ring tone and it was moving closer – then it died. His arm fell, his head was pulsating, people were chattering, stretching over the bar to pay for drinks, walking past him in both directions. . . *then he saw her.*

Their eyes locked.

TWENTY-THREE

INCIDENT ROOM - KIRKDALE
POLICE STATION
8.00 A.M., JULY 26TH

The room was packed. True it was partly due to the fact it wasn't a huge space, but nevertheless there was a full complement of Kirkdale's finest in attendance – it was rumoured even Hackett had *some* skills.

Now bored stiff following two weeks off after losing the baby, Fran had insisted on returning to work with strict instructions she wasn't to be asked about her loss – not by *anyone*. She was joined by Harry, who'd kept her up to speed, Sergeants Joe Walker and Suzanne Moorcroft, gentle giant PC '*Big Mac*' Rob McPhail, who though not strictly crime squad, at forty-five was no rank climber but had stellar experience, particularly of the area. An excellent team player with zero angles to him he'd gained Harry's respect, and in his DCI's book was good enough to be there. Longbridge wanted him briefed – *end of.* The nauseating Hackett ('*Tacky Terry*'), sat at the back, and young TDC (trainee detective constable) Jacey Pearl was also in attendance. Jacey ensured she was as far away from TT as reasonably possible, which placed her at the front of the room to the left of Harry and Fran who were standing together. There was a general mumbling, a scraping of chairs to get comfortable, and the familiar scent of someone's night-shift Chinese still lingering in the air.

The whiteboard facing them was central to the room. It was plastered with enlarged pictures, above which the sentence – OPERATION BONAPARTE – THE BODY PARTS CASE was penned in large black capitals. The photo of the head recovered from behind St Martin's Church, sat next to the one of the white left arm dug up by Harry's dog. The retained hand clearly showed a gold signet ring on the central finger, where on closer inspection the initials 'JJ' could clearly be seen. The arm had already been corroborated as belonging to known criminal, 'Jimmy the Lash Johnson', through Joe checking the CRO (Criminal Records Office) numbers after cross-referencing with the rare blood group forensics had come up with. All necessary investigations. . . *until the head had turned up.* This had eradicated any doubt of a remote chance Jimmy the Lash could still be alive, and his torso had yet to be found. The picture of the black right leg had a red question mark on it and was a lone find that clearly had nothing to do with Johnson. Penrith were technically dealing with it as it had been found on their patch. However, Kirkdale were still liaising with Penrith, and it was still attached to the body parts case so had to be included.

Then there was the Christopher Mogg photo....

"Okay. . . can we have a bit of *hush*, please...?" Fran walked towards the board and turned to face her team as the room began to quieten down. "Right. . . from a combination of DS Walker's investigations and the forensic blood reports, we already know both the arm and head are a match for a James Johnson, aka Jimmy the Lash Johnson. He was a small-time gangster originally from London, but with known links to Retford in Nottinghamshire, and also our own county town of Carlisle. What we still *don't* know obviously is who killed him or why."

"Did I hear right, ma'am, his partner's in Rampton?" This from Jacey Pearl....

"Yes, she's been notified by Retford, I believe," replied Fran. "Why do you ask?"

"I'm sure I read somewhere that her surname's Zandi—"

"*Zandini!!*" interrupted Harry, shooting an arm out to point at her whilst holding his chin in thought. "Excellent, Pearl, well done – *well remembered!*" He and Fran already knew this information a fortnight ago, but given Hackett's recent tacky behaviour towards her, Harry was determined to bolster the young officer where he could. Jacey smiled feeling a little more confident. She regularly spent a lot of time, sometimes even outside of work, scanning the Internet and researching big stories of the past as well as the present. Sometimes, like then, it paid off. The exuberant praise however had not gone unnoticed. She heard a loud harrumph from the back of the room and saw Terry Hackett, arms crossed, smirking....

"More *pearls* of wisdom, eh Jacey?" he scoffed, laughing at his own poor joke as a few moans and raised eyes rippled around the room.

The pathetic jibe didn't get past Harry who flashed him a distinct warning with the Longbridge glare, whilst most of the team just looked puzzled at the Zandini connection. Fran, who also disliked Hackett intensely, narrowed her eyes and played along with Harry and the name Jacey had come up with. Turning to him she said, "That's not the same Zandini family who were running a drugs racket across the South East about twenty years ago, is it?"

"The very same, DI Taylor, the very same," he answered, smiling. "Maybe Mr Johnson did something to *hack* them off." Then turning to Terry continued with, "Eh, *Hackett?*" He called out, "What do *you* think?" More groans echoed around the room, together with a few loud and exaggerated hacking coughs that hit the air until Fran called for quiet again. Hackett just hunched his shoulders, looked away and sniffed in irritated annoyance.

"Jacey, call Retford CID after the briefing, will you? Confirm the name of Johnson's partner and get back to me."

"Yes, ma'am, will do."

Fran turned to Harry...."Harry, do you want to add anything, or request any further information from Retford regarding a possible Rampton connection – given your 2018 Peterson case?"

Harry was about to answer when DC Hackett stood up and crossing his arms, made it clear he wanted to ask a question. At that moment this was more interesting to Longbridge. He could always ask Jacey to run a couple of extra things by Retford CID later on if needs be. He lifted his chin up and stared straight at him... "Go on, Hackett. . ." (*He couldn't stop the words 'make my day' popping into his head...*)

"Why is Mogg's face on the board?" Terry replied in a challenging tone. "He's surely not part of this case; his body was found entire, no parts were removed and we've not even had a pathology report yet stating unlawful death."

From the centre of the room Rob McPhail raised his hand slowly into the air. Harry gestured with a wave of an open palm for him to add his contribution to the meeting....

"In all likelihood, he's up there because he was called in as a MISPER around the same time the body parts started turning up. Nobody yet knows whether or not he would have been sliced up had he not been found, because nobody yet *knows* how or why the murderer or murderers are operating. Until the Peterson case two years ago, nothing major like this had ever happened here in the last two decades I've policed Kirkdale and the surrounding area. Not even in Penrith, which you should be well aware of, Terry, having worked most of your service over there until February this year. It could *well* be the same person or persons responsible for all these crimes – but as yet we don't *know*."

For the second time in half an hour Terry Hackett had been made to look a fool, but Harry hadn't finished with him....

"And that's *exactly* why I wanted you in this briefing, Mac. I know you do a great job out there on the beat, but please give thought to applying for CID – it's never too late."

Rob McPhail looked thoughtful, acknowledging the request. Maybe he should, *maybe he would when things were more settled at home.*

Then looking to the back of the room again, Harry added... "And the reason you think the pathology report isn't in yet, DC Hackett, is because you were off duty yesterday and haven't bothered to *catch up!*"

This now left the riled officer flushed with anger. It was an 8.00 a.m. briefing, how the *hell* was he supposed to have caught up?!! He bit the inside of his mouth, a newly developed stress habit he'd acquired. Jacey Pearl had made him look stupid and now Longbridge had played bang out of order – *or that was how he saw it.* If it wouldn't have made him look worse he would've stormed out of the briefing. As it was he remained seated and cheated. . . and seethed. His time would come.

Like the rest of the room, Fran had remained quiet during the stand-off, quite surprised at Harry's aggression towards Hackett despite the officer's unpopularity. She also realised Terry couldn't possibly have known of the pathologist's report on Mogg from the day before, and would point this out to Harry in private afterwards. Hitchings had given Harry temporary lead whilst she was off, but she was back now and in charge of her team. She mustn't let Harry slip back into their old Canon Row DCI-DS roles. He'd been her boss back then; seven years wasn't really that long ago and he found it all too easy to revert to their original partnership. Fran reminded herself Harry had only been brought back in as a specialist consultant because of the sickness bug laying people off, and Hitchings' outright anathema of the only available senior officers likely to be loaned from Penrith. It had been her wangling that had got Harry back in, and she *did* want to be working with him again, but she knew she mustn't let him take over. Easier said than done though when she was a DI and he'd technically retained his old DCI status. It didn't help them being in a complicated personal relationship either. All of this swam around her head leading her to release a heavy sigh before speaking to the now very quiet room.

"Okay, everyone, so let's now concentrate on Christopher Mogg." Turning back to the board to tap Mogg's picture with her hand, she continued. "It's been concluded through the autopsy that solicitor Christopher Mogg was poisoned. There were no big surface wounds or bruising to his body, other than a small cut to his head presumed to be from a shard from a broken mug on the floor where he was found. However, hemlock was discovered in his stomach. We've been advised that consuming hemlock is a particularly nasty way to die, one that nobody would likely choose as a way of committing suicide. *Hence we are treating this as murder.*" She now also served Hackett with a glare before turning back to the board.... "As Mac has so eloquently pointed out, we can't be sure our culprit, or culprits are different from whoever's responsible for the body parts with regard to James Johnson's murder, and the unknown owner of the black leg. In light of this I want you to keep an open mind when talking to people and sifting through any and all information that comes our way. The other point of interest here is that Mr Mogg was the solicitor employed by Charlotte Peterson's mother, and intelligence suggests he convinced her to leave her entire estate to a distant niece. Given she was nigh on a millionaire, this would clearly have caused Peterson considerable resentment."

Another hand went up and Fran invited them to speak. This time it was Joe. "Thank you, ma'am. Is the implication here that Charlotte Peterson has a reach extending beyond Rampton? People prepared to do her dirty work for her?"

"I wouldn't rule anything out where that woman's concerned," cut in Harry. "She managed to pull off her escape and get to New York. Controlling someone to do her bidding from within Rampton's walls wouldn't surprise me in the slightest."

Fran caught Harry's eye and gave him a hard stare for jumping in, before turning to Walker. "That's a good question, Joe, and an avenue I'm examining. Charlotte Peterson certainly has a very controlling personality, and as such I don't think we can rule her out, particularly with the other connection of James Johnson's partner Zoe Zandini being an inmate."

"There was also the boiling water incident, ma'am," added Suzanne Moorcroft, hand half raised, who up until then hadn't contributed. She was sitting next to Rob McPhail – they often worked together and got on well.

"Excuse me? What boiling water?" replied Fran.

"Zoe Zandini slung a kettle of freshly boiled water over Charlotte Peterson about three weeks ago. It hit the papers."

Fran and Harry looked at each other. "*Okayyy.* . . I didn't actually know that – good call, Moorcroft."

"Ma'am...."

Fran took a marker pen and added Zoe Zandini and Charlotte Peterson to the bottom of the whiteboard with two arrows pointing upwards. She wasn't sure how this was going to tie in yet, but something told her it would. *And she damn well needed to start reading a newspaper.*

* * *

12.30 P.M., STORM CAR SALVAGE - CARLISLE

"Okay, Jez, swing it this way, big lad. . . no. . . left, left a bit more. . . I said *LEFT!! For fuck's sake, Jerry, you're wide off the mark!*" The man on the ground had been using his arms to direct the new operator in the air, but now held his head with both hands. "Fuck's sake, man, you'll have that Jag on me office roof if you're not careful!! *Friggin' 'ell....*"

"Okay, okay, don't sweat it, Stormy, me ol' mucker!" Jerry called down from the crane having turned off the engine so the arm paused for a moment. "I'm a bit rusty, you knew that; been a while ain' it," he added grinning. "I did *say* when you asked me to come and help you out."

Seb Rains stood looking up at his old schoolmate. "Yeah well, I thought a few years out the job wouldn't make *that* much difference!! Do you even *know* your left from your right, Jezza?" Jerry grinned, and after finishing the second half of a re-lit roll-up, started the engine again. Seb wiped the sweat off his forehead, removed his glasses and leant up against the fencing that ran alongside his site office. Once he'd cleaned the lenses with a hanky, he put them back on, fiddling with the wonky arm to get it comfy. Looking up to begin re-directing Jerry, Seb saw something black protruding from the boot of the car. As the crane arm swung forward again, a faulty boot lock sprung open with the weight of its contents, and the object wobbled, got hooked on something and then lurched wildly, swinging at an awkward angle on its way to the crusher.

"*Hey Jez! Jez – turn it off again, mate!!*" However, Jerry had the engine on full throttle and two other machines had just started up so he couldn't hear him. As the long arm's huge claw clutched the Jag through broken windows and swung its load across the yard, it tipped dangerously end on. "*Turn the bloody thing off!*" Seb yelled, running to the front of the machine waving his arms wildly, but it was too late. The long black package broke free from its 'hook' on the car's boot and plunged downwards to smack the ground with a sickening thud. Sebastian Rains had occasionally encountered the odd forgotten spare wheel or sports bag left in cars brought to be crushed, but he always made sure every vehicle was thoroughly inspected and therefore empty. He had made sure *this* vehicle was thoroughly inspected....

Up above in the crane, Jerry hadn't realised what had just happened. He'd blithely carried on swinging the car towards the crushing machine to drop it in before bringing the arm back to rest. Feeling pretty pleased with himself for hitting target, it was only then he turned off the engine.

On the ground, Seb stood rooted to the spot staring at the elongated black package secured over and over with duct tape. He was beginning to wish he hadn't watched *The Scrap Yard Slicer* the night before on Netflix.... It had landed not so far from where he was standing, and now he must walk over to it. Meanwhile, Jerry had climbed down from the crane's cabin and was sauntering over to him.

"Wass up – why the stony face? I hit target, didn't I?" he asked before following his friend's extended arm pointing to the taped bundle lying in the dirt. The end had burst open when it hit the ground and the plastic was now flapping in the breeze. A flicker show of something pale was revealed each time the loose corner shot back and forth.

"I was yelling up to you but you couldn't hear me above Tommy's and Dave's machines. It fell from the boot of the Jag. We need to check out what. . . *that* is." Jerry stood up a little straighter, no longer grinning, and took a deep breath before they walked together slowly towards the solid-looking bundle.

"Probably just some old clothes," said Jerry hopefully, standing back slightly as they got nearer.

"You *think?*" asked Seb wrinkling his nose as he lifted one corner of the loose plastic with his foot. Turning round to his friend, who was now looking a tad ashen, he thumbed backward to the bundle. "*No way in hell is that clothes....*"

TWENTY-FOUR

Annie sat in the ridiculously white, excessively clean reception area. The deeply studded green leather sofa was very chic, and the matching obligatory cheese plant in the corner to her left reminiscent of eighties' decor, yet somehow didn't look out of place. At least they weren't white. Annie was beginning to feel her tight black skinny jeans, high heels and red leather jacket were out of place. The fact six months ago they wouldn't even have made it to her wardrobe remained deeply buried in her subconscious.

She checked her watch for the tenth time – five past twelve. Sighing impatiently at the late start of her appointment, she looked aimlessly up at the ceiling. Thankfully there were at least no retro leaf prints running along the base of the coving. The plant, though. She rather liked that. Maybe she'd get one, as long as its survival wouldn't be reliant on her. Over the years Annie's flood and Sahara techniques had rarely resulted in any successful green projects, so Harry would need to see to it.

Tapping the magazine on her lap she looked around to see where the continuous faint soothing sound was coming from. Not exactly music, more swishing water mixed with random haunting noises. Annie thought for a moment. . . surely not a *whale* CD? Were they still a thing? It became louder as the door to her left opened and a very tall, very timid-looking woman emerged all in grey, mumbling thanks and clutching a sheaf of paperwork. The door closed again and the whale sounds stopped shortly afterwards. Lady Grey left the reception and exited to the lifts that would take her back down to the street.

Five minutes later out stepped a tanned, fair-haired man dressed in a pale blue open-necked shirt, sleeves casually rolled to the elbow, upmarket cream denims and a broad, appreciative smile.

"Andrea McMahon?"

Annie smiled back and stood up. Using her maiden name would prove useful just in case he put two and two together. It would only be necessary for a short while anyway given what she had in store for her new therapist. She smoothed down her crease-free tight-jeaned backside, and followed Miles into his equally white, squeaky clean consulting room. *One he would not be requiring in the near future.*

* * *

217

Jacey Pearl had just put the phone down from Retford CID and made a note of the full name she'd been given for her boss, DI Fran Taylor. Sitting back for a moment, a mental jigsaw puzzle began to take shape. She picked up the phone again, found and dialled the number for Rampton High Security Hospital, and asked to speak to the person in charge of the women's section....

Fran was just about to leave the station for an appointment when Jacey knocked on her open door.

"Come in, Jacey, will this be quick? I have to be somewhere."

"It's just that I've confirmed the full name of James Johnson's partner from Retford CID, ma'am – it's Zoe Katrina Zandini."

"Ah, so you were right then – well done." Fran smiled as she tidied a few things on her desk and picked up her bag.

"Thank you, ma'am – I actually made another call after that. To Rampton Hospital, spoke to the head of the women's section."

"Oh really – why call Rampton if you got her name from Retford?"

"Because after DS Moorcroft mentioned at the briefing this morning about Zoe throwing boiling water over Charlotte Peterson, well. . . I wondered why she would do that."

"They've all got their problems, Pearl, that's why they're in there. Not all of them are criminals but they all have mental health challenges one way or another, that's the purpose of the hospital."

"Yes, of course, ma'am, but Zoe Zandini was apparently very much in awe of Peterson, to the point where they thought she was in love with her. The staff couldn't understand why she should want to harm her, it was totally out of character. I did some digging and discovered Zoe was sent to Rampton for the multiple stabbing of a social worker. Her nickname is 'Stabby Zandini' – boiling water just isn't her style."

"Hmm... well, it's unlikely she'd be able to get hold of a sharp knife or any other blade easily, so maybe if she was on some kind of kitchen duty or something...?"

"But why do it *at all*, ma'am? If she rated her so much, I mean?"

She had a point, thought Fran. There was definitely something going on there that wasn't adding up. "Okay, thank you – keep up the good work, Jacey, see if you can find out any outside Zandini connection with Zoe, current visitors and such like."

"Yes, ma'am, I'll get on to it right now."

She turned on her heel and left the room in a hurry as Fran called out, "*Don't forget to eat something, Constable!*" The phone rang almost immediately the advice left her lips. She sighed. This would make her late... "DI Taylor."

"Hi, this is DI Janis Lane, Carlisle CID. I believe you have a big case on at the moment covering your patch and Penrith with regard to body parts?"

"Yes, that's right, do you have something for us?" replied Fran, bag now over her shoulder as she began walking out of her office.

"You could say that. We've had a call in from a Sebastian Rains of Storm Car Salvage, a car scrap yard based in our area. He's just had a man's torso drop out of a Jag from thirty feet up...."

Fran stopped walking, turned round and went back into her office shutting the door. "Go on...."

"Cumberland Infirmary has the torso of a black male minus head, arms and legs. No identifying marks. It was wrapped in a heavily taped large black bin liner."

"The mortuary at Penrith has a male IC3 leg – have you had any contact with them?" replied Fran.

"Not yet, but the coroner will be liaising, a PM's been ordered on the torso at Cumberland so checking for comparisons. A possible blood match, aging, body and limb measurement ratios, sizes, etc. I have to say I've never had anything like this in my career."

"Me neither. Has this – what's his name? *Rain?*"

"Rains – Sebastian Rains," said Janis. "He's the proprietor. His colleague Jerry, full name Jeremy Kitson, was apparently operating the crane."

"Did this Sebastian Rains have the correctly recorded ID of the person who requested the car to be crushed, their ID and bank details?" asked Fran.

"Well, he thought so – turned out to be fake."

"Doesn't it always," sighed Fran. "Honestly, Janis, we could really do with a break on this one."

"I'll get straight back to you when we have anything more worth passing on – good luck."

"I've a feeling we're going to need it. Thanks for the

heads up, anyway." Fran ended the call, went straight through to the incident room and added the information to the whiteboard. *Male body parts appearing all over the county, all in the space of a few weeks,* she thought staring at the board. . . *and Rampton seems to be the connection. What the hell is going on....?*

* * *

APPLEBY ROAD, KENDAL - 2.00 P.M.

Gina parked her car outside the craggy grey stone building and checked her mobile before getting out. Andrew had rung and left a message just to ensure she was okay. He'd already wished her luck earlier but wanted Gina to know he was thinking of her. Today was a big deal. Even if it was only lunch, it would be the first time they'd have spent any real time together since the whole thing had come out – a revelation for both of them.

She warmed at his message, put the phone back into her bag and was just about to open the car door when she saw a woman coming out of the building. It was a new business address, he'd told her that, so it was only to be expected to see people coming and going. She did *not* expect, however, to see someone she knew. Especially *her*.... The door to her Corsa remained closed as Gina watched Harry's wife walk away from her father's consulting rooms towards her own car, briefly look around, then get in and drive back down Appleby Road. Mixed in with the shock was a smidgeon of envy she was sitting in a seven-year-old teal Corsa, whilst Annie was driving a slick black Range Rover Sport. She made a mental note to add a newer more interesting car to her recently started goal list.

Opening the door again and inching herself and her bump slowly and awkwardly, she swung her legs round to the outside and eased herself up out of the seat and onto the pavement. It wasn't easy now she was seven months pregnant, and made even more difficult given the camber in the road caused a backwards slope into the kerb. She stood up and turned round to reach inside for her bag before locking up. Stretching her back, Gina rubbed the base of her spine as she walked towards the building, and despite it not being the intention of the visit, the idea of a lie down on a counselling couch sounded heavenly. . . *as long as there wasn't any actual counselling.*

An image of Annie leaving persisted in her mind as she rode the lift to the first floor. *Why would she be seeing Miles? Why? It can only be one of two things, she needs counselling or. . . or she's having an affair with him.* Gina knew she wouldn't feel comfortable even mentioning she saw her, let alone asking her father why Annie was there. She'd barely got a relationship with him herself; to ask such a personal question was simply not on. He probably wouldn't divulge patient information anyway.

The lift pinged the floor's arrival and Gina took a deep breath. The memory of seeing Miles at the pub three days before, and him subsequently asking if they might meet for lunch to get to know each other a little better, now replaced the one of Annie. She felt like running but knew she wanted to find out if there was more to Miles than the shallow, sexist womaniser she'd witnessed when working at the Petersons' surgery. He had sworn to her he'd changed and wanted to try to be the father he could have been had he known about her all those years ago. Well, now she was about to find out.

* * *

Annie had not noticed Gina waiting outside when she'd left the building. This was mainly because she was going over the last hour she'd just spent with Miles in minute detail, *who* she discovered, was very different from Christopher Mogg but slightly less irritating and had to admit quite attractive. Of course that would make her second strike a little guilt-ridden. Still. . . there was a definite tingle of excitement starting up, an anticipatory shiver that waterfall tumbled right through her as she drove down the road. *Annie was developing a liking for the planning stages.* She giggled at the thought of her 'consultation' with Miles who had noticed absolutely nothing unusual about her at all. *Clearly in the wrong profession,* she thought as the car slowed with the holiday traffic. She drummed her fingers on the steering wheel. Her mentor was going to be very happy about Miles shortly being out of the picture. Annie knew how let down Charlotte had felt when he'd divorced her and made clear he never wanted anything to do with her again. Miles had literally cut off from his wife and disappeared into the ether. . . until now.

It was nearly four thirty when Annie turned into her road and straight into the drive opposite where their house sat on the corner. It had a slightly wider plot which meant a slightly wider drive. *This always came in handy if wine ever accompanied her journey.*

It appeared Harry still wasn't home despite going in for an eight to four. She pulled on the handbrake, killed the engine and sat there mulling for a moment. Kendal to Kirkdale was just over an hour's drive normally, but tourists added to that and then there'd been the obligatory pie to pick up from the supermarket to burn later as well. Annie had resisted sticking a bottle of red alongside it in the trolley, and rewarded her hair shirt stoicism with two family-sized trifles. Now she was regretting that decision. The carrier bag slumped across the passenger seat reflected her mood, but as she reached to pick it up a light bulb moment hit followed by a slowly increasing smile. *That second one may just come in handy, though.... No good for hemlock, but probably just fine for one of the med-filled sachets under the spare room floorboards.*

TWENTY-FIVE

They sat opposite each other in a pub at the bottom of Appleby Road. Miles was experiencing a rare, almost alien feeling for him – *nerves*. He'd even surprised himself at how important it was everything went really well today, and absolutely determined it would. Not only did he feel guilty about missing the first twenty years of her life but he was torn to bits over what Charlotte had put her through – both times. As Gina's father, it was up to him to protect her and *so far he'd failed miserably.*

"I don't blame you, you know, for any of it. I mean. . . some of the comments you made when you walked past me in recep—"

"Oh God, don't," Miles interrupted her, briefly putting his face in his hands. "I can't tell you how sorry I am, love. . . I mean, Gina...." He took a swift gulp of his pint and looked sideways in embarrassment at the memory, and suspecting he hadn't earned the right to call her love yet. "If I'd known, I would never ha—"

Gina half smiled and waved the past away with her hand. "It's gone, done and dusted." She looked down and patted her stomach. "She's all that matters now, Ellena Rose Gale."

Miles smiled wistfully. He could hardly believe how lucky he was in getting a second chance at parenthood, however late, and soon to be a grandfather as well. It was like being handed a brand new life. "It really is wonderful news, and I believe you and Andy are planning a Christmas wedding as well?"

"Yes, at the little church in Kirkdale. Molly's in on all the arrangements too of course and. . . um..." she rolled her bottom lip anxiously as Miles waited for her to continue. He'd guessed what was coming....

Gina's 'don't shoot the messenger' expression looked back at him. "Emily's flying in from New York." *A pause....*

"No Gareth then?" he asked trying to appear nonchalant.

"Em's not sure, it depends on work." Gina noticed her reply had enticed the tiniest crinkling around his eyes and a very soft intake of breath, right before he cleared his throat and excused himself. She watched as he crossed the floor to the washroom. A few years ago she would never in a million years have thought even one parent would be attending her wedding. Now, despite everything, there would be two. She smiled happily. *It was a good feeling.*

* * *

RAMPTON PSYCHIATRIC
HOSPITAL - NOTTINGHAMSHIRE

Charlotte's burns from the boiling water incident had healed remarkably well. Thankfully her legs had been tucked under a table, and Zoe hadn't aimed the jug at her face, nevertheless the pain over the previous three weeks had been excruciating. Still, all things considered she knew she'd been lucky, and soon Zoe Zandini would learn to regret her actions. . . *Charlotte would make sure of that.*

Both of them had been heavily questioned as to why it had occurred at all. Charlotte could hazard a guess it was linked to Zoe's criminal background, the Zandini family who'd temporarily funded her US trip, but she'd been genuinely shocked Stabby would actually carry out any injury orders (or worse), because of the unpaid loan. As far as she was aware, Zoe had refused to give any reason at all other than she was feeling stressed and fragile – and that could only mean one thing. Her guess was correct. Raiffe Zandini's patience was running out and it was entirely possible more of the same could be coming her way.

There had been several strictly monitored meetings between the two women to hopefully initiate remorse from Zoe and forgiveness by Charlotte. Zoe had shown *considerable* remorse, but was still refusing to offer any real reasons why she did what she did. It was exceedingly clear she was more than sorry for what she'd done, to the point where she'd begged for Charlotte to forgive her in the last session, at one point even bursting into tears – Charlotte on the other hand had simply looked straight through her with that cold, lead-eyed, dead-eyed shark stare, the one that would never alter. They were currently near the end of such a meeting. . .

Zoe was holding the imitation microphone – it was therefore her turn to speak . . . "Charlotte, please forgive me, *pleeeease*. . . I wasn't in my right mind, you *know* how fond of you I am, it wasn't *me* doing it. I don't know who it was in my head but it wasn't *me!*" Her dangly spirals bounced wildly as she moved her head about frantically, tears brimming. "I don't. . . I don't know what more to *say,* I. . . it was. . . unforgivable...." She fell forward dramatically and covered her face with both hands having dropped the 'microphone.'

The meeting co-ordinator, acting as mediator, picked it up and looked expectantly at Charlotte who sat with her arms crossed looking bored and unmoved by the younger woman's emotional plea. Since Jenny Flood's brother, Jason, had murdered her horses two years ago, she'd completely lost all ability for loving, caring or empathy. Such emotions had long since been replaced with hatred, coldness and revenge, *but at least the Flood siblings had been disposed of....* However, this time Charlotte *did* eventually respond to Zoe's plea. It was a surprise to both of the women sitting opposite her. She didn't bother with the microphone....

"Have you *any* idea of the *pain* you've caused me?!" she spat, shooting out of her chair, face contorted Cruella Deville style.

Zoe looked up, and then at the mediator – scared, heart pounding. She may have been a hard nut on her estate, but Charlotte was the equivalent of Doctor Death.

"Not only *the agony* of the last few weeks, there's also the little matter *I could be scarred for life!*" She was standing now, hands on hips, eyes flashing and wanting to question her about Raiffe, but that would have to wait until she could get her alone, *which*, she promised herself, would not be too far in the future. The mediator put her hand out to indicate Charlotte should sit down. She did so – *reluctantly.*

Zoe initially opened her mouth to reply but instead bit her lip and hung her head low again, shoulders slumping. It was clear no progress was going to be made, and the mediator ended the meeting before leading a distressed Zoe from the room.

Luckily for Charlotte, those meetings, although not run by, were monitored by the sour-faced orderly Rita Lemon. There was a reason why Zoe disliked her so much, one because Rita enjoyed delivering bad news (for example when she'd told Zoe about Jimmy's death), and two because she was known to facilitate certain 'negative events' between patients for the right price. Zoe hadn't gone to Rita for 'help' in that regard and as such was not in her good books. Charlotte on the other hand. . . well, she was now in her top five. She'd not caused any trouble since her re-arrest, and at the end of the day Charlotte was the victim here. Zoe *Stabby* Zandini, though. . . well. . . there had been no special privileges, lock-ins had lasted longer than they should, and there had been several occasions where Zoe was a recipient of the '*Knockout Shout*'. Put simply, if she'd got upset about anything, even just yelled a couple of times in frustration, Zoe had ended up locked in her room jabbed and unconscious. Rita Lemon and her male assistant ruled that wing their way, and like many who are given power. . . *it was not strictly by the book*.

After Zoe had been taken out of the room and back to her own by the mediator, Rita Lemon sat down in front of Charlotte and looked her straight in the eyes.

"I imagine there's a fair bit of resentment brewing inside that head of yours, Peterson. Am I right?"

Charlotte sat back in the chair and studied the stick-thin orderly. Her pockmarked skin, her lank, mouse-grey hair scraped into a greasy bun, the small gap between her chipped top front teeth.... There was also a faint odour Charlotte couldn't quite put a finger on, but it could've been onion. Yes, Rita Lemon was unpleasant to look at and unpleasant to be around. She was also knocking sixty and physically no match for Charlotte, but hopefully there would be no need for a match despatch anyway. She had a feeling Rita was about to become very useful.

"A fair bit, but I can control it," Charlotte finally replied calmly.

"Well, the moment you decide you can't keep a lid on it you come to me, do you understand? Nothing goes down on my wing without my say so."

Charlotte raised an eyebrow and lifted her head a little higher. "Is that right? So you knew about Stabby Zandini boiling my tits then, did you?"

"No. I didn't. . . which is precisely why you will be coming to me if there's to be any kind of reciprocation. That's *any* kind, Peterson. *Do I make myself clear?*"

Charlotte kept her waiting for a few seconds, wondering just exactly what Rita would want for turning a blind eye, or even better, maybe supplying some intravenous drugs or providing her with a mobile. . . or both. She knew she was single and had heard she was bisexual. Charlotte hesitated, blinked slowly, thoughtfully, and with her head slightly to one side rolled her eyes around the woman's sallow, angular features. There was no way in hell she could even *pretend* to get it on with her if that was to be the demand for supplying certain illicit items. Still, if Lemon *did* get her the right kind of injectables, it might just be *she* who was finished, before even getting a chance at Charlotte's bits and pieces....

Finally, with the delivery of an icy breeze, she leant forward slowly annunciating every word, "As. . . *crystal,* Miss. . . *Lemon.*"

TWENTY-SIX

The local church struck five. It felt strange to be back there again. Michael Morton stood behind a hedge opposite the house, a strong breeze cutting across the back of his neck. He flipped up his jacket collar and hunched down into it as the sunny day disappeared behind clouds, and rain threatened.

He'd parked in a side turning further down and walked back. . . just in case, he wasn't quite sure of what exactly, but felt the need to be cautious if only because of *him*. There was only one car in the drive and he recognised that, so the husband had to be out, although he couldn't know when he'd return of course. One way or another though he intended to get answers. *Time was clearly of the essence.*

Annie had literally blanked him and returned to her table when they'd come face to face in the Carpenters the night before. He was so shocked he hadn't even finished his drink. Part of him had wanted to march right up to her, to *them*, and demand to know why she'd cut him off for no reason. He'd wanted to tell her husband exactly who he was, because Michael was hurt. *Really* hurt. He was her son, estranged admittedly, and they'd met in awful circumstances, but he was under the impression things were good between them and she'd wanted to continue their relationship. It was *she* who'd made that clear, that's why he'd made the journey up to the Lakes, so they could spend some time together and get to know each other properly. However, there had only been one very short, interrupted lunch. *Maybe his loser father, Kenny Drew, had been telling the truth all along....*

As Michael stepped out from behind the hedge, a silver BMW swept round the corner in front of him, crossed the road and slid into Annie's drive next to her car. The chance had passed. Harry Longbridge was home.

Michael snorted in annoyance and decided to cut his losses. He was packed and going home anyway, but had just wanted to see Annie first to find out what was going on and give her one last chance. That clearly wasn't going to happen, so he began walking back down the road to where he'd left his car. It was when he was pulling out of the side turning he saw him. Harry was walking his black Lab towards the park at the other end of the road. *Bingo! That will be at least half an hour* he thought. Michael made a quick decision not to walk back. With her husband definitely out of the picture for half an hour or so, at least there'd be no risk of him seeing his car. He drove to the house and parked beside the hedge opposite. It was now or never.

Waiting for her to answer the door felt like an eternity, but in reality it was no more than a couple of minutes before he saw a shadow through the central window. He took a deep breath as he heard the click of the lock....

Annie's face froze for a second when she saw him. "What are you . . . Michael you can't *be* here. Harry – he's upstairs, he's just got in."

"*Nooo*. . . Annie, he isn't. You know that very *well*." Michael held her eyes as she winced slightly.

"Of course he is, you can see the two cars on the drive. That one's Harry's," she said pointing at the BMW.

Michael sighed impatiently and thumbed sideways down the road. "I just saw him – *mother!* He's heading towards the park with Baxter."

Annie flinched at his derisive use of the word mother. It cut deep. Her heart was pounding, she needed to think and think quickly....

"Annie, why are you *lying* to me? Why have you been *avoiding* me? I don't understand." He threw his arms in the air in frustration.

"Michael. . . look, it's not what it seems. Harry. . . we. . . it's to do with his work, a past case, I'm not allowed to talk about it."

Michael raised his eyebrows and leant up against the door frame. "*Really...?* You actually expect me to bel—"

"It's true. It's like what happened with Kenny – I have to be careful where I go, who I see. We. . . we've had threats."

Michael held her gaze and processed her explanation. It sounded plausible given her abduction and Kenny's attempt at blackmailing Harry over it only four months ago. An abduction he'd initially been a part of. It wouldn't be impossible for another villain to be making threats. "Okay. I believe you. It would've been nice if you'd let me know; a phone call, a text, *something*."

"It was all of a sudden, right out of the blue. After what happened in March Harry's been really edgy. I'm sorry, Michael, but you need to *go* now," said Annie, looking anxiously up the road. "I can't have. . ." she shook her hands agitatedly between them, "*this. . .* on top of everything else."

Michael nodded slowly and stood up straight, his disappointment palpable. "I'm going back to London tonight then. There really doesn't seem any point in staying." He looked at her searchingly...."Will I see you again? Has it all been for nothing?"

"*Nooo* – I mean. . . yes, of *course* . . . yes, as soon as this, this case thing has been cleared up. I'll ring you. I *promise*, but you *must* go now." Annie was torn in multiple ways here. She was partly relieved Michael appeared to accept her story, partly screaming inside her head Harry may well cut Baxter's walk short because rain had started, and hammering away at both a reminder she was a cold-blooded killer, one with several more jobs to complete. Then there was the fact he was her son, and all this other stuff had got in the way of what she'd intended when they'd said goodbye at her parents' house following their escape from Kenny. She wasn't the woman Michael thought she was. *What on earth must the expression on her face look like with all that lying behind it.....?*

Michael nodded. "Okay. . . okay then, I'll go back to London and we can keep in touch by phone, but be careful, Annie, if there's someone threaten—"

"I'll be fine, don't worry, but *please* go now, I'll ring soon." She glanced down the road again, but thankfully there was still no sign of Harry. A surprised Michael then received a sudden hug. He held her close before saying goodbye and walking across the road to his car.

Fifteen minutes later Michael Morton was back at the bed and breakfast he'd been staying at. He didn't have a clue what Annie was involved in but wouldn't find out if he went home. Being in between jobs and with nobody to answer to he could please himself – *London could wait.*

* * *

7.00 P.M., CARPENTERS ARMS - KIRKDALE

Andrew, Gina and Molly sat around large bowls of spag bol and garlic bread at a table in the snug. Gina was missing her whisky and coke *(even with pasta),* and a little added reason why she was very much looking forward to the birth of Ellie Ro, was being able to enjoy her favourite tipple again. However, nothing would persuade her to let alcohol pass her lips before she was born.

She'd shortened the baby's name from Ellena Rose within days of the gender-revealing scan. They'd chosen to know the sex, and to give her the middle name of Rose after Andy's real mother who'd sadly died not long after Gina's grandmother's funeral two years before. It was there they'd been introduced for the first time in a shock meeting (as had Gina with her own mother, Emily), and Rose's many years of vagrancy had weakened her immune system which had led to cancer. Their little girl's name would always keep Rose Elizabeth Emmerson in their hearts.

Molly, on the other hand, was not so perfect, and lovingly caressed a small glass of red despite Gina's nagging....

"Have you told Molls yet, Gee, about what you saw at lunchtime?" asked Andy, pulling apart a piece of garlic bread and waving it across the table towards them both.

"What's this? No, she *hasn't*. What did you see?" said Molly nudging her impatiently.

"I went to see Miles today, just for a quick lunch."

"Oh really, how did it go? I know you've been thinking about meeting up."

"It was okay, still a bit awkward but. . . well, you know we took it gently, talked about the baby and stuff. He did keep apologising for not being there for me, not being a dad. I think he's really trying."

"Good, I'm glad for you, for both of you, especially after. . . well, everything." Molly squeezed Gina's arm.

"That's not it though, Molls," said Gina, looking over at Andrew. "When I was just about to get out of the car, I saw Annie Longbridge coming out of his office."

"Do what? *Annie*. . . why? Why would she be going to see Miles?"

"That's *exactly* what I thought," said Andrew twirling some spaghetti round his fork.

"Miles left the NHS," continued Gina. "He's started some sort of counselling-cum-natural-health business. Opened a therapy room in a house conversion over at Kendal."

"*Has* he now?. . . Did you ask him, about Annie?" Molly drained her glass in anticipation of the answer and alerted the waitress who'd just entered the snug.

"No, I wanted to, but. . . well, the moment just didn't present itself, and anyway, he wouldn't be allowed to talk about a patient *would* he, so. . ."

"Hmm. . . no, you're right, he probably wouldn't. Or he *shouldn't* anyway," replied Molly tapping her empty glass. "So why then? Why would Annie need to see a shrink? Unless. . ." Molly paused to eat, punctuating her thoughts with her fork, then swallowing said, "Unless of course she's having some mental challenges after the abduction?"

"*That's* a possibility," said Andrew. "Maybe there are some delayed issues she's having to deal with?"

"I'd say that was very likely given my recent experience with her."

All three looked at each other and then around the snug.

"*Who said that?*" mouthed Gina, eyeing the tables through the archway behind Andrew, who was already turning round to check.

Molly felt the hairs stand up on the back of her neck. In light of recent occurrences not much would surprise her anymore. The voice, however, was not in any way spectral. The man appeared from the other side of the snug near the archway slightly behind and to the side of Molly and Gina.

"I'm so sorry to interrupt your meal, but I couldn't help overhear your conversation about Annie Longbridge. I too am concerned about her, *very* concerned, and very confused at the way she's been behaving lately."

Andrew stiffened, and narrowing his eyes asked the obvious question. "And you would be. . . *who* exactly?"

The stranger hesitated for a few seconds before answering. "Michael. . . Michael Morton. I'm her son."

If that wasn't enough of a shock, what came next was like lighting a touch paper....

"Well, that's news to *me*, Mr Morton, because we never *had* any kids. *You'd better start talking – now!*"

TWENTY-SEVEN

Harry had just popped in after taking Baxter for his walk, to dodge the showers and have a quick pint. The pub wasn't exactly en route, but to all intents and purposes had become an extension of his lounge and offered an altogether friendlier environment. He also needed to prepare himself for what was due to come out of the oven later.

The Lab sat obediently at his feet sniffing the delicious aromas floating above his head, whilst hopefully eyeing the various remains of bolognaise. He also felt tension coming from the other end of the lead....

"*So* Mr Morton, maybe we should take a table away from these good people to allow them to continue their evening, and you can tell me exactly why you think *my* wife is *your* mother."

"Oh, that's okay, we don't mind at all. It's fi—" began Molly quickly, until she received a light kick from Gina.

Andrew continued eyeing the man who was giving a good impression of a rat in a trap. This was not how Michael had imagined imparting such important information to Harry Longbridge. He should be the one in control here and it definitely wasn't feeling like that.

"Shall we?" continued Harry holding his arm in the direction of the only spare table out of earshot.

Michael clenched his fists. He hated being put on the spot (much like his mother). *How much of the story should he tell? Longbridge would have every reason to arrest him if he revealed everything.* The two men left the three friends to their meal and walked over to a table near the entrance. For a split second Michael wondered if he should make a dash for it, but the moment passed when a large group of people poured through the door.

Within five minutes Molly had put herself 'on shift' and appeared in front of them with a tray carrying a pint of Harry's favourite, Ruddles, and a glass of Coke, and a bowl of water for Baxter which she put on the floor. He lapped enthusiastically sending splashes up Harry's jeans which he completely ignored.

"On the house," she said setting their drinks on the table, and to Michael, "The Coke's yours. I know Harry's on foot but I'm assuming there's a car outside with your name on it."

Michael smiled weakly and Harry thanked her. She was itching to hear what would be said but knew that was out of the question, so returned to her own table and hoped between the three of them, they'd find out in the next few days. As she walked out of earshot Harry picked up his pint, took a swig and wiping the froth from his top lip leant forward with both elbows on the table and a grim expression....

"*Begin.*"

* * *

INCIDENT ROOM -
KIRKDALE POLICE STATION
1.00 A.M., 27TH JULY

Jacey Pearl sat at her desk scrolling the endless CCTV footage DI Janis Lane had sent through from Carlisle CID. Both areas had an interest in the car boot torso discovered at Storm Car Salvage, and now it was the trainee DC's chance at Kirkdale to work her way through it. Jacey yawned as she reached for her black coffee. On tipping the lightweight plastic cup towards her and seeing it was empty again, she pushed her chair back to rectify the situation.

Pulling the hairband on her ponytail tighter, she walked through the office to where the coffee machine stood and pushed the relevant button. The whirring, clunking and eventual jamming of the internal mechanism just served to frustrate her further. She wondered if she'd ever get used to doing nights, and as usual was concerned about her mother at home alone. Although only fifty and really quite young, her mum suffered severe pain from fibromyalgia and osteoarthritis and Jacey hated leaving her at night. She had Teddy there for company but there was only so much a seven-year-old West Highland white terrier could do to help.

Having ventured into the corridor and obtaining a coffee from the machine in the office next door, she returned to her desk and the camera footage. Jacey wasn't even sure exactly what she was looking for, and after nearly three hours nothing unusual had jumped out. Ten minutes later though she nearly choked on her drink – and it wasn't due to it being rank machine bog brew. She was used to that. She put the cup down slowly and froze the screen. Leaning forward she enlarged the photo of the two figures in the bottom left-hand corner. The exchange of a package was clear. The date and time on the film was 11.00 p.m. 25.07.20. Enlarging it further she concentrated on the right hand belonging to the taller figure and her heart nearly stopped. There was absolutely no doubt. She looked about the office carefully, mouth now dry as sand. There were only a few other colleagues in doing a late turn that night. . . *and one of them was on that screen.*

Keeping her eyes on the two other officers in the room, Jacey opened her drawer and fished around for a memory stick. Her fingers closed around one and trying not to fumble, she inserted it into the laptop, screenshot the image, downloaded it and slid the stick into her pocket. Every second of those few minutes left her body awash with adrenalin, her heart pounding. The only people she felt she could trust one hundred and ten per cent now, were DCI Longbridge and DI Taylor – neither of which was on duty. She wrapped her hands around her coffee. *It was going to be a long shift.*

Having safely secured what certainly appeared to be damning and incriminating evidence of *something,* she continued running through the CCTV footage slowly, all the while noting where people were in the room. It was almost four hours later, near the end of her shift, when the actual frames of the body falling out of the car appeared. CCTV time and date read 12.47 p.m. 26.07.20. Jacey again froze the screen and zoomed in on the two men on the ground. One had his head slightly turned towards the camera. The image was grainy when enlarged but yet again she recognised something about that man too, and he most certainly *wasn't* in the constabulary. She was just about to retrieve the memory stick from her pocket when one of her colleagues left their desk and began walking up the office towards her. Panicking, she clicked out of the CCTV link and began fiddling around in her drawer pretending she was looking for something.

"Jace, you got a minute? I could do with a hand double-checking some phone data on the Mogg case."

"Sure, be with you in a sec," Jacey replied, looking up smiling, praying her breathing and expression looked smooth and normal to the man in front of her. He held her eyes. Did she imagine a questioning of her intentions there? *He knew what she was doing; had he guessed at what she'd discovered?* Jacey dreaded the thought of working with him but had no choice, and until she could get that memory stick to Harry or Fran, knew her life was possibly in grave danger.

* * *

EIGHT HOURS EARLIER
THE LONGBRIDGE HOUSEHOLD

Harry found himself in an impossible situation and not for the first time where Annie was concerned. He had absolutely no idea how he was going to deal with it. When Michael had revealed the story of how he'd discovered Annie was his mother, Harry knew Morton hadn't given him everything. The only person who could corroborate that was his wife. He'd been in half an hour and still hadn't mentioned anything, and wasn't even sure he was going to. He hadn't mentioned the burnt pie when it was served up either....

Part of him felt emphatically sorry for what that bastard Drew had put her through as a teenager, *that* on top of the abduction whilst he was in New York. But the other part, the part that made Harry who he was . . . well, he just couldn't deal with that lack of trust and honesty. Then there was the legality of it. Drew was dead. Who'd *really* killed him? Annie? Michael? *The 'other' guy Michael had lied to him about....?* It sure as hell wasn't

Baxter. Harry hadn't believed a word of what Morton had said regarding him purely turning up to the house and introducing himself to his wife as her long lost son. He let him *think* he believed it for Annie's sake, but Harry knew he had to have been involved with Drew, at least initially.

At the end of the day Michael got them both safely away, and let's face it, he wasn't about to lose any sleep over Drew's death, but the fact remained Morton must have agreed to assist him in, and be directly involved in her kidnap. It was a clear case of premeditated abduction – *that* was a crime. Yet Michael was her son, she'd clearly forgiven him, they'd kept in touch and Annie had never been able to have any more kids – *how could he take him away from her now?*

He glanced over at his wife sitting on the sofa scrolling aimlessly through her phone. At least she wasn't drinking.... *Had she killed Kenny, though?* Is *that* why she'd been behaving so oddly the last few months? As well of course as hiding an estranged son from him in plain sight? Harry barely recognised her anymore, and not just because of the crazy bleached hair. He took a deep breath in and breathed it out slowly, tried to calm his head down and rationalise things. At least she'd agreed to talk to someone about everything now and had been for her first appointment, thank God. Maybe that would help, although he hadn't dare ask about that either. *He sincerely hoped it would.*

Baxter laid his head on his dad's knee and looked up at him adoringly. Harry smiled down at him and scrunched his ear gently. At least his Lab was uncomplicated, loyal and trustworthy. . . *Dogs, he understood.*

"Coffee?" asked Annie, unusually brightly.

How does she do that? he thought. *Switch moods so fast; it had been all doom and gloom earlier.* "Yes. . . thanks," he replied absentmindedly – "Arsenal mug."

"I *knowww*...." she replied, actually smiling....

Annie left the lounge to make the coffee and Harry sat thoughtfully, still stroking Baxter whose head hadn't left his knee. He'd always wanted children. Fran losing the baby may have just made his life a whole lot easier, but it had still crushed them both. For all his railing against Annie about keeping secrets and not being honest or able to show trust, he knew full well he was no better; worse in fact because as far as he knew, she'd never cheated on him.

He sighed heavily, feeling the weight of the mess he found himself in. Lifting his head and placing a paw on Harry's leg, Baxter looked concerned. "I'm okay, lad, don't you worry," said Harry tousling his ears again. He was beginning to feel tired though. The Bonaparte case was still up in the air, there was Christopher Mogg's murder, nothing was adding up anywhere. He'd probably lost his only chance of having a child, and his feelings for Fran were stronger than ever. Now with Michael Morton on the scene *(although he'd said he was going back to London),* the plates Harry had been rigorously spinning thus far, looked dangerously close to crashing down....

Suddenly a noise made him jump. He'd slid down in the chair and dropped off for a few minutes when his phone bleeped a text. He picked it up off the side table, tapped the screen, and after reading the message was now sitting up straight and very much awake. It was from Molly.....

> Harry, it's happened again. I know you're a bit anti mumbo jumbo as you put it, but I think 2 women are going to be murdered — and soon. I saw no faces, both were like that Scream painting? It was the scariest one yet. Thought you should know — Molly.

He immediately began pulling on and rubbing his chin. What the *hell* was going on in this county? If he didn't start getting some decent leads in the next week or so he could kiss goodbye to the agreed consultancy role Fran had persuaded Hitchings to give him.

"Coffee . . ." Annie held out his mug, smile gone again. Harry took it, *and for the first time in a long time he felt like adding some whisky.*

TWENTY-EIGHT

JULY 27TH

It was 6.00 a.m. and Jacey yawned nervously as she waited for the lift to take her to the ground floor. She looked over her shoulder again – it was a relief to finally hear the lift ping its arrival so her constant pacing could stop. It was only one level but she was tired and just wanted to get home, check on her mum and get her head down. *She also wanted to offload the contents of her pocket.*

The doors opened, she marched straight in and turned to the control panel to press 'G'. . . but they hadn't closed behind her. They were about to, but a foot had prevented the action as each steel side juddered, opened again. . . and in he walked. He then held their floor level when they closed.

Jacey paled visibly. She knew it must be visibly even though she couldn't see her own face. Surely the rush of adrenalin that tore through her body from top to bottom must've dragged all her blood with it, because that's exactly how it felt. The USB stick *had* to be 'burning' a hole in her pocket too, there was sure to be noticeable smoke at any second....

"You okay, Jace, only you look like you've just seen a ghost?" He towered above her, leaning closer, his eyes scrutinising every pore on her now glistening forehead.

She side-stepped him, avoiding his gaze and quickly hit the ground floor button. "Fine thanks, just tired, not used to nights yet." Her reply was clipped. She knew she sounded defensive.

"Oh you *will* – have to, we all do." He leant back easily against the lift wall and folded his arms still staring at her.

The floor arrived, the doors opened and Jacey walked smartly out heading straight for the exit, every step heart banging like Big Ben over a microphone. She dared not look back, and once through the double glass doors ran down the steps to the car park. Unfortunately, her boss, DCI Longbridge, was not just driving in like last time, but at least today she had her car and was soon inside it. Jacey popped the locks, rammed the key in the ignition and reversed out of her space as the officer she'd just shared the lift with stood watching from the top of the steps. The shock at who was on that CCTV footage, *both images*, remained with her all the way home.

RAMPTON PSYCHIATRIC HOSPITAL - NOTTINGHAMSHIRE
11.00 P.M. - SEVEN HOURS EARLIER

Rita Lemon knocked on the door, announced her arrival and waited a minute or two before unlocking it. Her rough eczema-ridden fingers stroked the mobile in her jacket pocket and hoped Peterson would be suitably appreciative. She would need to be if she wanted the *real* prize, the one nestled in the other pocket that would seal her vindication, and rid her of Zoe Zandini for good. She knew Charlotte had no money now so there was only one thing she could do for her that would be of any value, *to Rita anyway*. She imagined her delivering that particular thing, tongue slithering over her lips as excitedly she pulled the right key for the lock.

On the other side Charlotte sat on the bed trying to work out how she was going to dissuade, or at the very least delay, Lemon from her target. She knew what she was likely to want and had absolutely no intention of serving herself up on the bedspread in return for those favours – whatever they were. The door opened.....

Rita entered and closed the door behind her. She should have been working with a colleague, but because of low staffing levels was on her own that week, lucky for her – not so lucky for Charlotte. . . depending, of course, on how much she wanted the phone. Mobiles were on the banned list; to have one would be of massive benefit to her.

"So, Peterson, how are we this evening? Think you could make use of. . . *this?*" She held up the phone and twitched it from side to side. "Of course it comes with a price." Her eyes slid from Charlotte to the bed and back again, a sick smile forming as they roamed her body.

Charlotte hesitated. She was horrified at the implication but at the same time desperately tried to think of a reasonable reply that would neither piss her off, nor appear to invite her between the sheets. At the end of the day she would dearly love that phone, and had already chosen to move to the other side of the room when she'd heard the key in the lock. "Not entirely sure what's going on here," she said, "but it's gone eleven and I was about to get some sleep. I'm sure you must have loads of work to do, especially as I notice you're on your own this eve—"

Suddenly a siren rang exceptionally loudly and began wailing hard making them both jump. Rita immediately shoved the mobile back into her tunic pocket, turned to face the door and spoke privately into her radio that had just sprung into life. It was now or never. Charlotte silently darted round the bed and was quickly behind her where she immediately began freaking out, yelling how she couldn't cope with high screeching alarms and bells, holding onto Rita hysterically, pulling her arm, yanking at her clothes and behaving totally irrationally as the woman fought to disentangle herself, finally grabbing Charlotte by the shoulders and forcefully moving her backwards to the bed.

"Sit *down!!* It's just a freakin' *bell, for Chrissake!!*" Then back into her radio. . . "Yes, yes, it's fine, I can manage, I'll be there in five minutes." To Charlotte again. . . "It'll be something and nothing, just *get* undressed and *get* into bed – *now!!* I'll see *you* tomorrow night." With that she was out of the door, had it locked in seconds and was off down the corridor to help out her colleague in a neighbouring wing. A few minutes later Charlotte was in her PJs in bed, the lights went out and shortly after that the siren stopped. The room was black. She snuggled down into the darkness, pulling the quilt up high around her head, and a satisfied smirk began forming on her face as she watched the mobile phone light up beneath the covers and spring gloriously into life.

* * *

The following evening Charlotte knew Rita would either be demanding the phone back or something worse entirely. She also knew in reality the woman couldn't do a thing about it because of risking her job. The icing on the cake for Charlotte was finding the capped syringe when looking for her trainers before breakfast. It had rolled under the plain reception-style chair next to her one small wardrobe. The room was sparse, 'suicide safe' they called it, depressing really, but that little gem of a find had made her *very* happy indeed. *Thank God for the seriously insane creating a need for sirens at the ultimate moment.*

Charlotte had not been taking her meds for quite some time now. The warders had been noticeably lax since their reduction in numbers from the recent flu outbreak in the county, and this had made her job *so* much easier. Routine medical observations were done more quickly and weren't so invasive; mouth checks were not always carried out, and of course she didn't need any meds anyway, she felt fine. Completely fine, *more* than fine.... It was her delegate, Annie who needed the tablets to carry out her practice kills, get her used to it so when the opportunity arose, *and it would*, she'd feel completely ready to despatch Charlotte's top core targets.

What was in the syringe was a complete unknown. She just hoped it would be enough to permanently finish Zoe Zandini. The thought of never having to see that pasty freckled face coming towards her ever again, framed by those ridiculous bouncing orange spirals, was utterly sublime. Her Uncle Raiffe though, he could still prove a problem regarding the money she owed his family. . . especially when he heard his niece was no more.

She'd been most careful to pick up the syringe with a tissue so her fingerprints wouldn't be on it. Of course there was no way of knowing if Rita Lemon had been as equally exacting in her handling of it, but if she hadn't, Charlotte could be in for a very healthy double despatch. Well. . . not healthy for either of *them* obviously.... Another half-smile, one that did not reach her eyes; they were more frequent again now. *No meds equals no emotion, equals no real smile.*

The syringe was now in *Charlotte's* pocket, and as luck would have it, it was time for breakfast. She fancied some of her favoured muesli with fresh fruit on top. Zoe however was going to be receiving a lot more than her usual boiled egg and soldiers....

* * *

2.00 P.M. POLICE STATION - KIRKDALE

As a follow-up from her text the previous evening, Harry had just come off the phone with Molly Fields. Whilst she was correct in her assumption of his views towards the supernatural, there was no doubt she'd been right in the past and again only just recently. This meant that no matter how much Harry may dislike it, the fact remained he felt he had to listen to and act on her visions. Chief Superintendent Hitchings on the other hand. . . *well, he most certainly didn't need to know anything about them at all.* What Harry needed to know, of course, was exactly *who* was about to meet their maker. According to his '*metaphysical expert*', on this occasion Molly hadn't got a clue, just sensed they were both women, both their 'faces' looked completely crazy and both resembled Munch's '*Scream*' painting. As far as Harry was concerned that could be absolutely anyone, female or otherwise, who was feeling particularly upset over something. She also mentioned something about seeing a 'golden glow' above

Fran in the pub the other night. That he *did* put down to mumbo jumbo, or more to the point, wine and hormones, although he didn't dismiss it entirely....

"Boss. . . ?" Terry Hackett knocked on Harry's open door and waited for the nod to enter. It wasn't an immediate pass given Harry had little time for him, but the man *was* a member of his team so had to acknowledge him from time to time.

"What is it, Hackett? Please tell me you have something *relevant*, evidence based and so water tight the CPS will bite our hands off for it."

"Well, not quite, but I do have *something*."

"So. . . what *is* it? I haven't got all day and I'm certainly not going to play guessing games." Harry already felt irritated and Hackett's presence wasn't helping any.

"Oh, you'd never guess this one, Guv, in fact it even shocked me. Jacey Pearl was on late shift last night."

"Really, how interesting, and what's so shocking about that?" Harry was already reaching for his phone, checking his jacket and generally getting himself ready to go out.

"She worked an entire night shift, yet I just saw her in the car park." He walked over to the window in Harry's office and looked down. "That girl may be a good student but she's not as perfect as everyone thinks. She keeps that up, she's gonna burn out, and *that* could mean affecting a member of the team at a critical moment."

"I agree, and it *is* a bit odd, DC Hackett. If it becomes a habit I'll have a word, but it's hardly a *shocking* incident. Maybe she forgot to take something home last night that was really important. Her mother's quite poorly, isn't she? Perhaps she'd picked up an important prescription for her and left it here."

"Maybe," replied Terry turning back from the window. "Personally I think there's more to it than that – don't ask me why but I thin—"

"DCI Longbridge – *Sir?* May I come in? It's seriously urgent and can't wait." Jacey Pearl had suddenly appeared hovering at the threshold, looking anxiously between the two men. "I *really* need to speak with you – *alone*."

Harry raised an eyebrow at Hackett then waved him out of his office. The look of fear on Jacey's face was not one he'd seen on a young officer for a very long time. "Come in and sit down, Jacey. Whatever it is – we'll sort it."

TWENTY-NINE

RAMPTON PSYCHIATRIC HOSPITAL – NOTTINGHAMSHIRE

9.00 A.M., THE RESTAURANT

Charlotte watched Zoe Zandini enter the restaurant from across the hallway before following her in. Eager fingers caressed the syringe in the pocket of her thin summer top as she felt for the protector cap on the needle end, *the end that would finish Zoe for good.* Not only that, if she could despatch Stabby without blame being laid at her door, her Uncle Raiffe, would (hopefully) no longer have anyone inside Rampton to squeeze her for the US debt.

Her heart was pounding but she wouldn't let herself become agitated; this had to be done right. Sleight of hand with zero self-attention was imperative.

She let a little dark-haired woman slip naturally in front of her as she and Zoe approached the breakfast queue, in order for them not to be next to each other. *So far, so good.* Unfortunately she realised quite quickly the lady had serious hygiene issues, but Charlotte said nothing and just tried not to breathe in too deeply. They each picked up their plastic trays, and placing them on the silver ledge began pushing them slowly along the front of the hot and cold cabinets.

As Charlotte had anticipated, Zoe slid her tray straight past all the fried bacon and eggs, fried bread, sausages, scrambled eggs and mushrooms, along to the simpler boiled eggs and toast section at the far end. This was a feat in itself given the aromas were absolutely wonderful. Even Charlotte nearly gave in. Not that Zoe's choice of breakfast would make the slightest difference *that* morning. A half-smile tugged at the corner of her mouth. Bit of a waste of time queuing really, but there you go, such is life – or in this case *death*.

Charlotte watched both Zoe and the whiffy woman in between them very carefully. Just before Zoe reached the cashier and Whiffy leant forward for bacon, she placed her hand in the syringe pocket, eased the cap off with her thumb and forefinger, and taking one step forward behind the woman's back plunged the needle through the flimsy material of her jacket-styled blouse and Zoe's equally thin cheesecloth trousers into her ample backside. She then swiftly regained her place in line as the woman scooping bacon leant back again and continued on behind Zoe, pushing her tray closer towards the cashier. Two seconds – *it was seamless perfection.* Charlotte immediately turned to the opposite side where the fruit, cereals, juices and hot drinks unit stood. She quickly poured a large bowl of muesli with plenty of milk, and with one eye on Zoe who'd initially jumped as if stung by a bee, and was now rubbing an overly large butt cheek, selected and paid for her cereal and black coffee to the cold-unit cashier. Picking up the relevant cutlery, Charlotte casually carried her tray to a table at the perimeter wall of the restaurant where she prepared to enjoy the fallout....

Setting down her tray, she sat facing the buffet bar quietly eating her muesli and watched as Zoe pulled out a purse to pay for her breakfast. Charlotte's spoon hovered over the bowl as Zoe picked up her tray and turned to walk from the queue. Suddenly. . . she stopped. The tray crashed to the floor, her knees sagged, eyes glazed and Stabby Zandini went down like a bomb-blasted chimney stack.

Charlotte swallowed hard but carried on munching her muesli whilst mayhem blew up all around her. Everyone started shouting, wardens and nurses came flying through from the hall, a doctor appeared fairly swiftly and after a quick check immediately started chest compressions and mouth-to-mouth, all to no avail it seemed, as she reflected on the exact reason *why* Zoe Zandini had collapsed so spectacularly, so theatrically, so. . . for want of a better word. . . *effectively*. God knows what Lemon had put in that syringe, but judging by the sheet that now covered the body it had certainly appeared to be very reliable. Stabby Zandini would no longer be whining and begging her forgiveness for the boiling water incident, there'd be no more cloying hero worship, sick adoration gazing and attempted stroking coming her way – *ever* again. Job done. *Lovely....*

Satisfied, Charlotte blotted her mouth with a paper serviette and watched the show unfolding in front of her. As a cold smile played on her lips, she picked up her coffee and fantasised over who'd be receiving the next shot from the handy little device nestling in her pocket.

* * *

HARRY LONGBRIDGE'S OFFICE - POLICE STATION, KIRKDALE

Harry waited patiently for Jacey to gather her emotions. She sat opposite him looking exhausted. . . *and terrified.* Slowly she put her hand into her pocket and brought it out again, placing a small memory stick onto Harry's desk. He looked down at it and then back up at her, but she was looking over her shoulder to check the door and windows to the main office. Finally she turned back round.

"What is it?" asked Harry, eyes narrowing. "I mean, I *know* it's a memory stick, but what's on it, why've you got it, and more to the point why do you keep looking round to…?" Noticing she was visibly shaking he got up and closed the door. Back at his desk he picked up the stick, and glancing at her with concern, inserted it into his laptop.

"It's the CCTV footage, sir – from the car salvage yard in Carlisle." Jacey bit her lip. "I was going through it last night when I saw it. . . saw *him*."

Harry looked over at her again wondering what on earth she'd seen on that footage that could've created such an extreme reaction. He two-finger tapped over the keyboard till he brought up the tape frozen at the place she wanted him to check out, looked questioningly palms upwards and then back at the screen. "This? *These two men in a site office?* Why are *they* so special? Who are they?"

"Magnify the image," said Jacey, elbows now on the desk and making a steeple with her hands against her nose, eyes barely peering over the top as if the sight of that screen would instantly blind her.

Harry turned back to the CCTV video and slowly enlarged the grey image. When he saw it he gasped, his fingers sprang off the keyboard as if it was on fire then shot back in his chair.

"Exactly, Boss," Jacey whispered into her hands. "*That's* why I had to come back in this morning. *That's* why I'm a nervous wreck. No doubt Terry Hackett made something of me being in after a night shift."

Harry nodded in acquiescence. "Not a word to anyone, Pearl. You did right to bring this to me. Now go home and get your head down and don't come in for tonight's shift. I'll sort it with HR. In fact, take the rest of the week off and I'll see you on Monday morning."

Once Jacey had left, Harry pulled the memory stick from his laptop, pocketed it and picked up the phone to dial an internal line. "*Sir?* There's something I need to discuss with you – and I'm pretty sure you're going to want it to be sooner rather than later."

Driving home, Jacey battled with her conscience over what she'd omitted to tell her boss. She liked DCI Longbridge. He'd always been kind to her and seemed to have her back, especially where Hackett was concerned. But she *loved* her mother, and there was no way she'd be able to cope if it came out the crane operator of the salvage yard was her mother's younger brother. They may not have shared the same father, but that had never made any difference to her mum. Jacey knew she certainly couldn't be the one to impart that information to her superiors. Equally she knew her career could be on the line if it ever came out she'd known all along her *uncle* was also on that footage – *and passing a suspicious-looking package to a serving Cumbrian officer.*

* * *

It had been just over three weeks since Annie Longbridge had murdered Christopher Mogg. Apart from the odd news bulletin asking for people to come forward with even the smallest piece of information, even if they thought it was irrelevant, there had still not been any real progress in finding his killer. This had given Annie an inner confidence. She had deliberately waited before. . . *moving forward*, despite Charlotte leaning on her at her last visit.

The appointment with Miles had been surprisingly pleasant, quite relaxing. She was actually looking forward to the next one and wasn't at all sure she could cut short his time on earth, despite originally making him her next project. She wasn't even sure she *wanted* to. However, Charlotte did *not* need to know that. *Not yet.*

Annie sat pensively in front of her secret laptop up in the spare room. She didn't want to risk Harry coming in and finding her, so hadn't used it anywhere else in the house for quite a while. He was out again that evening, no doubt with *her*, and despite their recent 'heart to heart' meal in the pub, she was feeling increasingly bitter.

On the screen, the dating site on which she'd ironically found Christopher Mogg that fateful *(for him)* day several weeks before, automatically flashed up. It seemed like a lifetime ago since that first encounter, but now she found herself in front of the bright blue and orange page once again, sitting on the floor, wine in hand, just *click, click, clicking. . .*

THIRTY

It was now gone midnight. The dating site she'd been scrolling through earlier had left her torn between two men, so she'd decided to sleep on it and make her choice in the morning. Now Annie was in bed flicking through social media on her mobile. Not that she was exactly sociable these days, more of a lurker really, but it was a habit she'd got into before going to sleep. She was just about to turn her phone off when it suddenly lit up and the thunder and lightning ringtone rang out *very loudly* considering it was the middle of the night.... Glancing anxiously at her bedroom door, she quickly answered and held it to her ear under the duvet.

"*An*-drea. . ." The voice was stony, level and quiet. There was a pause before the person spoke again — *Annie knew it wasn't her mother.*

"Guess who? Or should I say guess *how?*" A snigger....

Annie felt the hair on the back of her neck twitch. She lifted herself up slowly on one elbow and looked down at the unknown number displayed on the phone. Beads of sweat sprung out across her forehead. She swallowed hard, thinking, knowing. . . *How the hell....?*

"Ch. . . *Charlotte?* Is. . . is that *you?*"

"It *is*, Andrea, it most certainly is. And you're wondering exactly *how*, aren't you? Go on, *admit it!*"

"Well. . . yes. I thought phones were banned, and how did you ge—"

"How did I get your mobile number?" interrupted Charlotte, the smug tone seeping thickly down the line. "Your last visit, my dear. You left your phone on the coffee table when you went to freshen up. I simply. . . *freshened up my knowledge in the interim.*" Another snigger.

Annie lay back down, the phone resting against her ear. She really didn't know how to respond to that. A squeak of the landing floorboards and sudden strip of light appearing under the door warned her Harry was on the first of his two nightly bathroom visits. She wondered how sexy *that* little nugget of knowledge would sound to *Fran sodding Taylor.*

"*Andrea. . ? Are you still there?*"

"Yeah. . . yes, I'm still here. Why are you *ringing* me, Charlotte, especially at *fucking midnight?*" Annie kept staring at her bedroom door....

"Now, now, Andrea, let's not get *feisty*, shall we?"

Annie winced. She hated being called by her full name. Her mother was the only person who insisted on it not being shortened and it didn't feel right coming from an insane doctor, especially one that used it *every bloody time* she opened her mouth.

"I managed to lift a phone off one of the dumbass orderlies who thought she'd get the better of me, but I'm not into LGBT so it was one nil to me. It's a long story... *anyway, look*, having got the damn thing, I'm ringing to save you a journey and find out *exactly* how far you've got. Nothing new coming out of the mainstream media tells me that would be – *not very.*"

"I've. . . had a lot on, but I've earmarked another practice run on the dating site and should hear pret—"

"Forget him. Whoever it is – *scrap* it. Have you got a pen and paper handy?"

"Wh-what?" Annie replied as another squeak sounded on the landing floorboards and the light now disappeared from under her door. "It's ten past effing midnight, Charlotte," she hissed. "I'm in *bed!!*"

"Don't worry, I'll text you the address. It's the cousin who stole my inheritance. *I want her gone.* Do you understand, Andrea? She has to take priority now. Once you have it written down, delete my message — and Andrea. . ."

"*Yesss . . ?!*" said Annie through gritted teeth.

"Don't *ever. . . ever* disrespect me like that again."

Annie took a deep breath but did not reply. The silence between them was unnerving yet powerful. Two female killers, one who believed she would always be top dog, the other who had started circling. *The air was palpable.* Charlotte broke the silence....

"You get this done and we both benefit," she said firmly. "Rid me of this thorn in my side, and *you* will feel confident enough to move on to the thorn in *your* side."

With that, the line went dead. Annie lay in the dark, head and heart pounding. She had never given serious thought to eliminating Fran, she assumed she meant her, but now. . . *now it had been put out there, even if only in a suggestive format....* There would be no sleep for her that night. A bleep penetrated her racing thoughts. She looked down at the phone to see a text from Charlotte. It was the name and address of the cousin, her supposed next despatch. . . well, maybe. . . *then again, maybe not.* She turned off her phone.

* * *

1.30 P.M., KIRKDALE POLICE
STATION - TUESDAY, JULY 28TH

The next day there was a very different atmosphere at Kirkdale nick. It was a mixture of disbelief, disappointment, suspicion and a very heavy dose of sobriety. Everyone was quietly getting on with their work, but the normal busy air of the crime squad office, especially, fell under an extensive cloak of numb suppression.

It wasn't as though it had never happened before because it had, although it was rare in a small country town. It was more that the officer concerned was highly thought of and liked by everyone, *especially Harry....* If it had been Terry Hackett who'd been seen behaving suspiciously on that CCTV footage, given his cocky, misogynistic attitude, the shock wouldn't have been anywhere near as explosive. To be fair, *any* bent copper would be a shock, but when the news hit that Rob McPhail had been suspended prior to investigation for receiving hush money attached to the body parts case, the implosion was cataclysmic.

Harry sat in his office, one hand drumming fingers on his desk, the other supporting his chin as he stared in continued disbelief at the frozen screenshot of PC Rob McPhail, and as yet an unnamed man from Storm Car Salvage. Rob had insisted they were doing nothing illegal, but the word from Carlisle CID was Sebastian Rains had form for small irregularities, mainly paperwork related, the odd bit of weed, but nothing high level – *until now.* The phone rang interrupting his troubled thoughts, the ones telling him he was seriously losing his touch if he hadn't seen this coming....

"Longbridge – It's me." Chief Super Chris Hitchings' flat tone conveyed his feelings perfectly.

"Sir?"

"Carlisle CID is insisting on sending *their* people down to question PC McPhail over this camera footage."

"Right, yes, of *course* they are..."

"I understand you requested McPhail to be part of your team on the Bonaparte case, despite him not being a DC or even a trainee DC. Is that right?"

Harry paused and licked his rapidly drying lips.... "Er, yes, sir, on account of him having such excellent and very broad area knowledge over the years, and being a thoroughly solid. . . cop...." He stopped short when his boss sighed heavily. "Hands up, clearly my mistake," Harry continued. "I *was* also encouraging him to think about applying, coming off the beat. He had potential even if he'd started late."

"Yes, well that's as maybe. Now we know, or *likely* know the reason why he was happy staying exactly where he *was*."

"Indeed. Sorry, sir. It's bugging me big time, though. I just never saw anything untoward, *absolutely nothing*. I still can't believe it's true."

"What's your gut instinct then, Harry? Do you think it's an innocent mistake? He wasn't accepting a bung for looking the other way? There was a headless *body* in that car, for God's sake!"

"I really don't know, Boss. Until he's been questioned none of us will for sure, but I admit I can't figure out why he was up as far as Carlisle."

"Well, don't beat yourself up over it. I know you like to see and bring out the best in people. No repeating the transfer idea again, though."

"Absolutely not, sir, no," he replied holding his forehead with one hand as it slowly slid down his face to his chin, face down, eyes closing momentarily.

"How are. . . er. . . things at home, Longbridge? Okay, are we?"

Suddenly Harry's head snapped up. Eyes now wide open and alert, a vision of Michael Morton sitting opposite him in the Carpenters immediately flashed front and centre, and despite some of the team hinting at knowing about

Fran, he'd sincerely hoped nothing at *all* in his personal life had reached Hitchings. "Yes. . . all good, sir – thank you.... Actually, you've just reminded me, I need to get a nice card for Annie's birthday. It's coming up shortly." *A bit of an exaggeration date wise but it would do.*

"Right, yes. . . good, good.... well, I'll leave that one with you then. Anyway, I understand Carlisle are sending a couple of SIO's down tomorrow, so we need to accommodate them as best we can. No blocking tactics, Longbridge, even if you *aren't* sure this footage is conclusive against PC McPhail."

"Yes, sir, understood." *That doesn't stop me giving Rob a visit at home, though,* thought Harry as Hitchings ended the call.

Five minutes later he was descending the steps to the ground floor two at a time when Joe Walker called out from the door at the top.

"Sir – we've just had the name of the crane driver in the CCTV footage at Storm Salvage confirmed by the owner as a Jerry Kitson, thirty-eight, divorced, apparently not been there that long. His record checks out as nothing major, a TDA, some petty theft and cannabis use as a teenager."

"Okay, thanks, Joe – noted. Update DI Taylor when she comes in, will you?"

"Will do," replied Joe to Harry's back as his boss continued down the stairs, tapped his number into the code locked door to the front office and exited the building to the car park.

Once in his car and driving to McPhail's house, Harry started praying the officer he'd had so much faith in had a very good reason for receiving that package from crane driver Jerry Kitson, particularly as Kitson had recently dropped a headless corpse from the boot of one of Storm's scrap cars. Rob had been suspended but not arrested. . . *yet*. Before Carlisle CID arrived the following day, Harry wanted an hour alone with his officer first.

He pulled up to the three-bedroom flint cottage in Riversdale Lane just outside Kirkby, and turned off the engine. The small wrought-iron gate was peeling heavily. A rash of rusty orange patches emerged beneath curls of black paint on the trellis work as flaking pieces dropped to the ground like the devil's dandruff.

Getting out of the car Harry leant against it for a moment and looked up the path to the front door. He noticed that *that* wasn't in much better fettle than the gate, and the garden could have done with clearing of some rubbish bags, plus the grass desperately needed cutting as well. *If Rob McPhail was really bent and coining it in from seriously heavy bungs, surely his property would be in better condition?* He was pretty sure the man was a mad keen gardener too.

Harry pushed himself off the BMW and opening the gate, felt it scrape the stone slabs due to hanging unevenly against the post. *Something isn't right here,* he thought. *It isn't right at all.* But whatever was going on, he was determined to get to the bottom of it. Standing in the porch he yanked the long old-fashioned bell pull and heard the muted jingle from the other side of the door. At least that was working. A minute or two later there was a noise inside the house, and eventually the door opened a couple of inches until it snagged on the security chain. *Rob 'Big Mac' McPhail then peered suspiciously through the gap....*

THIRTY-ONE

With both her parents dead, Raiffe Zandini was recorded as Zoe's next of kin, and right now, rather than being solely the grieving uncle, he was also mad as hell. Of course this was not entirely down to tested fatherly emotions expressed due to her death. With Zoe now gone there was no longer anyone to exert pressure on Charlotte for the money she owed the organisation, money he was being heavily leant on to collect by the power at the top. Raiffe was not only angry, he was worried. He'd made the decision to put forward Charlotte's case as a good return on the US loan based on Zoe's recommendation. Naturally the head of the Zandini family never got their own hands dirty, which meant he would need to explain himself, be prepared to take the rap for the financial loss. *Maybe worse...*

Now Raiffe was nervously waiting for that 'power' to arrive and deliver their decision. Suddenly the tall, broad-shouldered and quite handsome fifty-five-year-old with the square jaw and olive skin, was no longer exuding a commanding demeanour. The controlling air and threatening smile was gone. He was pacing up and down inside a derelict industrial unit in Carlisle, heart pumping faster than it should with sweat popping across his forehead and looking altogether smaller and weaker than usual. He checked his watch for the tenth time. She was clearly enjoying his discomfort. At the end of that thought, Raiffe heard cars scrunching over the long gravel approach that ran up to the building. Walking briskly over to the heavy sliding door at the entrance, he saw two vehicles turn the corner of the unit and come into view. *Two.... that was bad news.* His stomach lurched and bile filled his mouth – he forced it back down grimacing. The turquoise Bentley slowed to a halt and the accompanying black Toyota Hilux mirrored it.

Dominique DuGuarde stepped out of the Bentley and fixed Raiffe with a diamond-hard stare. He swallowed several more times when he saw the gun in her gloved hand. The ape that had jumped down from the Hilux was dressed entirely in black and stood with his arms folded across his mammoth chest. . . *waiting.* Eventually DuGuarde spoke....

"So Raiffe, have you anything new to tell me? Or has the fact Peterson has now removed Zoe from the equation ended any chance of recovering our losses on the US investment?" She fingered the Glock17 impatiently as she waited for his reply.

"Pleece, Madame DuGuarde. . . Dom, vee don't know zat zee Peeterson voman killed our Zo-ee and eet is not my folt about zee lon. Eet voz Zo Zo's reesponsi *beel-ity*." He hunched his shoulders opening his arms wide to express his inculpability. "She assured—"

"You snivelling little *shit*, Raiffe! She was the *introduction* agent! It was *you*, *you* who made the decision! That's what you're *paid* for, to make the *right* decisions, the *successful* investment choices for this organisation. You *know* how wrong choices end up, Raiffe...."

"But. . . but Dom, vee are *fam*-eely you and I, by marriage *yes*, but steel vee are fam—"

The shot rang out. Raiffe's knees buckled as he sank to the concrete and fell forward, his face landing cheek-side down, a single bullet hole decorating his forehead, much more decorating the floor behind him....

Dominique handed the gun to the man in black. "Clear up this mess and make sure it disappears completely." He nodded not speaking a word, and Cumbria's Chief Constable turned on her heel, got back into the Bentley and drove back to her other life.

* * *

Sitting in Rob McPhail's living room, Harry was listening to a story he couldn't quite believe. He imagined trying to tell Chris Hitchings what he was hearing and the thought of his reaction wasn't good.

"So you're telling me this Slavic character's been blackmailing you for the last three months, due to a loan you got involved with and couldn't repay?"

Rob sat with his head in his hands. He looked haggard. "Yeah, basically, I got in over my head and couldn't pay him. He had me acting as a collector for other people's loans to pay off my debt."

"But what about the salvage yard in Carlisle, the body in the boot? Where does that fit in with loans?" asked Harry. "And why are you using money lenders?"

"I took a car there once. The guy who handed me that package recognised me from a meeting in a local bar with this Raiffe bloke. Turned out he was working for him too, getting rid of . . . whatever he wanted getting rid of. I'm not sure the owner knows anything about it, though. As for me using loan sharks. . . my eldest got in to debt at uni, started deal. . . doing things he shouldn't, to try and sort it and. . . well...." Rob looked thoroughly beaten, eyes brimming, head hanging low. "The guy with the package, he's got kids too and we got talking. He gave me a cut to help me out."

Harry let the drug inference go. He had far too much on his hands to worry about a wayward teenager at university, and McPhail was already buried in the darkest place he'd seen a colleague for a very long time. "Carlisle are coming down tomorrow to interview you about the CCTV footage, you know that don't you? I'll do what I can but...."

"I know. Thanks, Boss. I don't expect anything." Rob sighed heavily and now leant back in the chair staring at nothing before carrying on…. "He threatened my family. If it was just me I could've. . ." He paused and looked straight at Longbridge, "But not Carrie. . . *not the kids.*"

Harry nodded thoughtfully. "This Raiffe, have you got a surname for him? It's looking like he could be connected to the body parts case. Either way he obviously needs finding."

"I got the feeling he was part of something big, massive even," said Rob, "not the usual small-time loan shark. He never gave me his surname. I only know it was Raiffe because Jerry the crane driver mentioned it once."

"Hmmm…. that would be Jerry Kitson. Joe Walker got the name confirmed by the owner of Storm Car Salvage just before I left."

"That's him. Raiffe, the foreign guy, he made me take the payment to Kitson for some special deal. That's presumably what this CCTV business is about. I'd already paid him out as ordered, but as I said, Kitson insisted on giving me a share. He also knew I was a cop, probably wanted to make sure I stayed on side as well. I didn't know about any body in the boot though, Guv, I swear."

Harry nodded slowly, looking McPhail directly in the eyes. "Yes, it is about that, exactly that. Tell me – what does this Raiffe look like?"

"IC2, mid-fifties, six two –six three, broad shoulders, olive skin, dark hair slightly greying, a good-looking, fit man, I'd say." *Harry took out a notebook….* "Can I ask one thing though, Boss?"

"Go on," said Harry, jotting down the description. He just hoped Rob wasn't going to finally ask him the obvious. *But of course he did.*

"Who spotted me on the CCTV?"

"You know I can't tell you that, Mac," Harry replied getting up from his chair. "Look, I must go, I need to be elsewhere. I just wanted to call in and speak to you before Carlisle CID turned up tomorrow."

"I appreciate it, sir, I've been worried sick. I still am. This Raiffe guy contacts me any time of the day or night with orders for my next job."

"Don't worry about that, I'll have your house watched by one of our lot for the foreseeable, and someone will pick you up and ferry you to and from your interview tomorrow."

Back in the car, Harry was left in two minds. On the one hand he was glad he was right in that McPhail *was* at least at heart a good copper, he'd just tried to prop up his family and made a mistake. A gigantic one as it turned out. Plenty of people had fallen foul of that in similar situations. On the other, he couldn't see him not getting kicked out of the job, and *that* would be a great shame. He was just about to start the engine when Joe called....

"Sir, I tried to contact DI Taylor regarding the named crane driver and his past record as you asked."

"Yes, okay, has she got something more on him then?"

"No sir, I couldn't get hold of her. Not anywhere. She was due on at two but hasn't turned up, she's not at home and nobody's seen her. Mobile keeps going to voicemail."

Harry looked at the clock on his dashboard. It was now 3.45 p.m. Fran was very rarely late for anything. His head suddenly felt fuzzy, and it wasn't just because of his sugar numbers as Molly's recent 'golden glow' comment about her passed through his mind. "Right, thanks for calling me, Joe, I'll head over to Fran's place now, check it out. I'm sure she's fine, maybe just not feeling well." He ended the call and automatically stuck his hand into his pocket for a barley sugar before realising he'd run out. Making a mental note to get some at the first opportunity, he fired up the engine and left McPhail's cottage in a not altogether small cloud of dust Fran's racing-driver brother would be proud of.

* * *

Annie Longbridge was not a natural killer, but she was learning to be. She was also learning that part of her healing process was not to kowtow to *anyone* – especially her 'mentor'. Yes, Annie had come a long way in a relatively short time, but not in the manner Charlotte had planned. She had absolutely no intention of tracking down and disposing of Charlotte's now rather *rich* cousin following the diverted inheritance she'd received, or any other people on Charlotte's unfinished '*list*'. No, Annie had her own list now, and the next one on it, her first really *personal* one, was much closer to home. The two 'practice run' dating-site guys had had a lucky escape. . . *for now.*

She hadn't intended to, not initially, but when she'd overheard those girls in the pub talking about it, confirming what she'd suspected, or at least some of it, all the madness in her head had just got a little too much. The news of the pregnancy had clinched it though, which was why the object of her obsession was now confined to a far more restricted environment than she was used to, than anyone was used to.... Getting her there had actually proved less challenging than she'd first thought, especially as it was so close by – on site, you could say....

* * *

1.45 P.M. - TWO HOURS EARLIER

Fran was running late for work which was rare. She was chasing around the house grabbing paperwork, a slice of toast she kept picking up, biting into and putting down, similarly with a mug of tea (not biting obviously), and finally her keys, bag and jacket. Dashing down the stairs and out the front door, she would never have seen the woman dressed head to toe in black at the rear of the house. She wasn't aware of anything other than being late.

The garage was at the front. It had started raining. She flipped the door up then frustratingly realised she'd forgotten her umbrella. It only took a second. As she turned, she felt an arm around her neck, then she was dragged back into the garage and thrown hard over the bonnet of the car. Everything went black. And when she came to. . . *it was still black....*

The smell hit first. Even before the feeling of damp underneath and the crashing pain in her head. *Sewage....* Then the fact she couldn't move her hands or legs. . . *or sit up.* Her head was *killing*, but the fear of her predicament, the fast dawning realisation of where she could be, where she *had* to be, almost wiped out the pain.

She could taste it. The iron in the dried blood that must have run down her neck and round to her lips before being lain on her back. She tried her hardest but couldn't prevent a tear escaping each eye, fall sideways down each temple and soak into freshly washed hair. Hair that was now bloodstained and lay on the dirty bowed sides of the industrial waste pipe. Dread set in. The involuntary shaking began. Soon the screaming would start....

"Where the *hell* are you now, Harry? *Dear God – where are you now....?*"

THIRTY-TWO

The news of Zoe Zandini's death had made national TV within twenty-four hours. There had been several dramatic events at the psychiatric hospital over the last few years, not excluding Charlotte's escape, and now any serious occurrence generally hit the media quickly. The newsreader said it was suspected the patient had died in suspicious circumstances which meant there was no way Rampton was going to be able to hush it up. It was now under scrutiny, and an internal report by the Care Quality Commission, imminent.

Andrew was in his lunch hour with the girls in the Fields' private lounge at the Carpenters Arms. There were two main points included in the hospital interview that had kept Andrew glued to the screen. One was that Zoe Zandini had collapsed in a restaurant breakfast queue and subsequently been found to have a needle puncture to her backside, and the second was a specific patient was being

283

questioned because she'd been standing behind her. No name had been given as to whom that was. Andrew was sure he *did* know.

"It's got to be her, hasn't it?" It was a statement rather than a question. "It's got Charlotte's MO all over it."

Gina shuddered. "Will that woman *never* leave our lives? It doesn't matter whether she's on the loose or banged up, she's still causing trouble and she's *still* making headlines."

"Well, at least it's not any of us this time," said Molly, "although I obviously feel sorry for the victim and their family…" she added quickly. "They didn't actually *say* it was her though."

"Too early to put out that kind of info," said Andrew moving Gina's legs gently off his lap and getting up from the sofa. "It's only just happened. You can bet your next pay check it *is* Charlotte. I'd lay a year's wages on it. Right, I have to get back to work." He leant over to kiss his fiancée on the top of her head. "I'll see you at home later, Gee. Bye, Molls."

After Andrew had gone, Gina remained lying on the sofa stroking her now enormous seven-month belly and stuck out her bottom lip. . . "Don't you worry, little one, mummy won't let the wicked witch of the Lakes get *you*."

Molly laughed and standing sideways stuck her four-month baby curve forwards. "And *this* mummy won't let her get *you* either, my little Yankee cherub!"

Gina smiled. "We're going to have so much fun with these two."

"That we are," said Molly. "Let's start by treating them to a big squashy cream doughnut each from Bella's!"

Gina struggled to get herself from lying to sitting, to off the sofa and standing up, but she managed it. She could always manage it for cake....

* * *

Harry turned into the top of Stanger Street just as the rain started getting heavier and was forced to slow down. His dashboard clock told him it was 4.15 p.m. It was a partly sloping hill, levelling out further down and full of 1920s terraced and semi-detached grey stone properties, bay windows echoing the past and gabled windows suggesting loft conversions of the present. Parking both sides, B&Bs, a thirty mile an hour zone and holiday traffic didn't help. His heart was racing and he'd begun to get a full-on headache. Flicking on his windscreen wipers he finally reached the turning to the three new-builds and indicated.

Like Joe, he hadn't been able to raise Fran on her mobile or work phone, and was actually now thinking about Molly Fields' latest two death predictions. She hadn't been able to determine for sure whether they were male or female, only her *sense* they were female, and had a suggestion of mania about them because of seeing Munch's *Scream* painting as the vision image. *Mania, manic, craziness. . . that doesn't suggest a police officer though, does it?* The 'golden glow' thing though – *that* swam briefly around his mind.... Harry consoled himself with the fact he'd heard nothing further in the news about any more deaths. . . *or body parts.*

He turned into the lane off Stanger Street, drove round to the back and pulled up in front of Fran's new-build. Nothing looked out of place. He yanked on the handbrake and got out of the car. It was raining hard now and he hunched up the collar of his jacket and took shelter under the dual grey tiled porch that covered both Fran's and the attached semi's front doors. The bell brought nobody to answer it no matter how many times and how impatiently he rang it. No irate Fran came running down the stairs moaning at him for treating it like the blues and twos. *He wished to God she was moaning at him now....* He even tried the attached neighbours, but Fran had once mentioned they were a young couple out at work all day and he got no answer there either.

The third new-build in the mews was an elderly couple but they were unavailable too. He walked round the back of the property where he saw that further behind on the other side of some high wire fencing, a few more houses were obviously due to go up, but production had appeared to have stopped. This had left the smallish building site now looking not exactly derelict, but certainly shut down.

Fran had no garden at the rear of her place either. Looking down he saw some brownish black tram lines coming from the plain single back door of the garage. They disappeared into the remainder of a grassy area which had presumably been part of the land now cleared for additional new homes.

Harry looked through the door's window and could see Fran's car was still in there. He tried the handle. Surprisingly it opened. Something had made those lines, but having never been in Fran's garage before he didn't know what, and looking round there was nothing in there now that could have done so. All his instincts told him it was time to call this in as a missing person. If Fran was fine and well somewhere Harry knew she'd go ballistic and accuse him of overstepping the mark, but he also knew if he didn't he may regret it for the rest of his life. *(He'd be reminding her to lock the bloody back door as well as the front when he saw her, too!)*

As he tried to make the decision of whether or not to report her missing, he saw the corner of something poking out from inside the front wheel of Fran's car. He bent down to hook it out only to discover his fingers curling round her phone – the screen was cracked and the back scuffed. Harry then noticed several registered missed calls. Joe's calls and *his* calls. . .

He pulled out his mobile.

7.00 P.M., STANGER LANE BUILDING SITE

Fran was absolutely terrified. She had no idea what the time was but felt like she'd been in that pipe forever, and thought she could now hear rain. She was convinced it was a waste pipe yet to be covered over on the old building site, and suspected the chances of being found quickly were slim. Nobody knew where she was and the site behind her home had closed down. There would be no workmen turning up. Not now and not in the near future. At the end of the day she was an adult and wouldn't have been missing for very long; most people would probably just ignore her absence for a couple of days at least. Fran prayed hard Harry would go into over-protective mode and start searching for her, *and fast.* She promised herself if she ever got out of this alive there'd be no more moaning about his impatience or borderline mollycoddling.

Muted noises floated beyond the darkness. She strained to hear voices outside her circular pipe prison. . . voices, footsteps, kids, dogs barking – *anything.* What she *could* hear, or *thought* she could hear, was just muffled. Trying to scream for help with a gag in her mouth had proved impossible, and the smell of sewage was making her feel sicker by the minute. She was desperately trying to think of something else because if she vomited with the gag she knew she'd very likely choke. The black had begun to seem less dense though, and she could see a little murky light. It was as though material of some sort had been draped across the exit.

She had tried to loosen the tape on her wrists by twisting them back and forth, but could barely move as her hands were bound firmly behind her back, and feet tied tightly in a crossed position so everything was hopelessly restricted. Attempts at wriggling down the pipe towards the half-light and thus the exit by pulling back with her feet, and bringing her knees up to the top of the pipe and down again, had proved virtually futile. . . *but only virtually.* She managed a tiny movement forward which gave her some hope and persevered with this every few minutes despite the pain on her back, particularly at the base of her spine when the pipe's ridges appeared every metre or so. There was no knowing how far from the exit she was, but Fran sensed it couldn't be that far. She just had to try and clear her head, stay determined and work her way slowly down, but it was tight, and adrenalin was pumping fear through every fibre in her body making her legs feel wobbly and weak.

She fought to remember what had happened, to keep her brain active and not think about the vile smell, but could only recall a vague sense of rocking, her back hurting and a squeaking sound, *then waking to that god-awful stench.* There was nothing else apart from the initial shove. An overwhelming need to relieve herself had beaten her long ago and the initial warmth of damp trousers had quickly turned to cold, soggy material.

Despite everything she was hungry. Gnawingly, achingly hungry. Her stomach was cramping with it and bile kept shooting up into her mouth, but the need for water was worse, *far* worse, and the numbness in her arms and legs increasing. Fran could feel the tears coming again, and it was when she heard the rushing sound in the distance her fear really escalated. Common sense told her the pipe couldn't be in use as the building had stopped. . . *but what if she was wrong?. . . What if it was a different pipe?*

THIRTY-THREE

Michael Morton was determined to find out what was going on with his mother. It was why he hadn't gone home to London, and why he'd been following her as often as feasibly possible since his conversation with Harry. That conversation had not been easy, and obviously hadn't been completely honest on his part.

With Molly eyeing him from the bar wondering what had been said between him and Harry two nights ago, Michael was now back in the Carpenters nursing a cider and reflecting on that conversation. He was genuinely worried about Annie as much as himself. The detailed account of her kidnap had been heavily edited where he was concerned, as he naturally realised Harry could never know the full truth. The truth that as an adoptee, Michael had been searching for his father, Kenny Drew, and had been convinced by him to be part of a plot to kidnap Annie for a hefty ransom. Neither of them had known

Harry was in the US until later which had complicated things. *His face flamed every time he went over it in his head. Would the guilt never leave him?* Michael took a large mouthful of his cider and scanned the room. The other two he'd seen that night with the barmaid weren't in. At least that was two pairs of eyes not on him.

Michael knew he couldn't have repeated to Harry what he and Annie had told the police in South London after making it to Annie's parents following their escape. The chances of her long-lost son happening to be driving past a lock-up with his estranged father having her tied up inside, was utterly ludicrous. That he'd heard screams, managed to get her, Baxter and himself safely away, receiving a bullet to his shoulder in the process. . . *No.....* As far as Harry was concerned, all of that had happened to another guy. The police in London had not been told anything about Michael being Annie's son so there'd been no connection there, and as far as he was aware neither had her parents.

All Harry had been told was the first part plus some bent truths. That he'd been searching for his mother through the legal routes because he was adopted, turned up on their doorstep a few months ago, met up a couple of times and had gone back to London with phone calls ongoing. Nice and simple.... When contact had suddenly been cut dead, he'd become concerned until eventually she'd called and explained about the kidnap. That was when he'd come back up to Cumbria to see for himself Annie was okay and realised how different she'd seemed.

It wasn't perfect by any means, and Harry could've challenged him on what was still a hell of a coincidence considering the Drew connection, but Michael had been put on the spot. It was the best he'd been able to come up with and surprisingly Harry hadn't pushed it.

He reached for his cider again, aware of Molly still watching as she served other customers, and was reminded of how he'd held his breath behind his glass after he'd finished telling Harry the story that night. Harry had listened intently, staring at him whilst supping his pint, remaining silent. *Even Baxter hadn't moved.* Michael felt Harry had given the *impression* he'd believed him, but wasn't entirely sure. At the time Michael had switched quickly to saying how concerned he was at Annie's changed character and behaviour since their first meeting, and sensed Harry was on the same page with him on that but hadn't wanted to comment.

Now things were getting really odd, especially after the way she'd blanked him in the pub a few nights before and her reaction when he'd called at the house the other day. He hadn't told Harry about the threats Annie claimed they were receiving from a previous case, similar to Drew's blackmail attempts back in March.

So for the last few days he'd been driving around Kirkdale and the surrounding area, out to Keswick that afternoon, following Annie to various places to see if she was involved with anything she shouldn't be. He'd discovered nothing strange though, zero. . . *zilch*. Even the trip out to Kendal had appeared totally innocent. He'd gone into the building after she'd left to find it was some kind of natural health consulting company. Even though the door stencil mentioned counselling, that would have been a good thing. . . *wouldn't it?* Either way it was *hardly the mafia*. Apart from a few shopping trips, hair and beauty appointments, and the pub, there had been very little else. Michael felt he'd literally come to a dead end.

* * *

9.00 P.M., STANGER LANE - KESWICK

Andrew was on the way back from an evening game of squash, a portion of chips warming the passenger seat, when traffic in front slowed on Main Street for a pedestrian crossing. He dipped his hand into the bag and as he lifted up a chip, a trail of blue lights in the distance turned off into Stanger Street. *Interesting,* he thought popping it in his mouth. Instead of driving straight on towards home when the cars started moving, he took a right at Stanger and followed the police vehicles up the hill.

Harry's BMW was two in front. Andrew raised an eyebrow and reached for another chip. He followed them up to the Stanger Lane turning where all three had already disappeared into and round the back to the new-builds. When he pulled up there, uniform were already standing around, torches ready and preparing to door knock. Harry was giving orders and pointing in various directions, but when he saw Andrew walked straight over to him.

"What the hell are you doing here, Gale? Nobody knows about this yet."

"Saw the flashing lights on my way home, couldn't help myself. I know technically I shouldn't—"

"No, you shouldn't, son. . . but I'm glad you are." He turned and pointed to one of the three semis behind him. "That's Fran's place. . . she's *missing*." His face was grim.

"Missing? *Fran*? Missing *how*? I mean, when. . . *why*?" asked Andrew genuinely shocked.

"If I knew *that* I wouldn't have two squad cars and a van here, would I?" Harry stated, slightly disappointed at his protégé's inane comment.

"Sorry, yes, of course. . . it's just that it's a bit of a shock," replied Andrew.

"Tell me about it. She never turned up for a two o'clock shift. . . and she's never late, well, virtually never. I was down here about five hours ago and couldn't get any answer, nothing by phone either, but then I found her mobile smashed, *and* her car still in the garage. I think she's been abducted but I've got no proof, haven't a clue by whom, or more to the point, *why*."

"Shit. Jesus, Harry, you know I *literally* know how you feel after what happened to Gina – *twice!* What can I do to help?"

"Honestly? Just don't put this in the *Courier*, lad – not yet. Unfortunately I can't let you get involved officially, but if you hear anything, anything at all, however insignificant, get straight on to me, okay?"

"Always, Harry, you know that."

Harry put a collaborative arm over the younger man's shoulder. "I don't mind admitting to you, son, I'm worried sick, scared shitless if I'm honest. When you've put away as many people as we did in London, Fran and I, you never know who's out there waiting to get their revenge. That waste of oxygen Kenny Drew took Annie whilst we were in the States; maybe another past villain has Fran." He sighed heavily and left Andrew for a moment to respond to an officer's request for attention.

"Changing the subject slightly, or actually maybe not," said Andrew when he came back, "there's been a suspicious death at Rampton. It was on the news at lunchtime. Did you see it?"

"No, no, I didn't. Any names?" asked Harry over his shoulder as he walked over to another officer to point him in the direction of the building site.

"Surname was foreign-sounding," said Andrew. "Zandy, Zindiny, something like that?"

Harry swung round. "*Zandini?!*"

"That's it. Zoe, I think they said. Apparently she suddenly collapsed in a cafe queue and was later found to have a needle puncture in her backside. I said to Molls and Gina, that's got Charlotte Peterson written all *over* it."

"Maybe, maybe not. . . The Zandinis are a powerful family, they control the largest financial and identity laundering business in London and the South East, and I believe that's now spreading all over the UK. On top of that they run a massively intricate and widespread loan-shark operation, drugs too. I've reason to believe the whole shebang has crept up to the North East including here in Cumbria. Peterson would have to have a really large set of theoretical balls to take out a Zandini."

"That would be the same for anyone in Rampton then, surely?" asked Andrew. "But the needle mark shows a favourite kill method for Charlotte."

"True. Look – I have to organise this search. You get yourself home to your fiancée now and I'll be in touch. Call me if you or the girls hear of anything."

"Will do – and Harry?" said Andrew as he got into his car.

"Yep?"

"If anyone can find her, *you* can – it'll be okay. . . *she'll* be okay."

Harry didn't exactly smile, but acknowledged his comment, nodding briefly before turning back to the search team as Andrew drove off. At that moment he wasn't feeling as confident about finding Fran as Gale appeared to be, *but he knew he would die trying.*

By midnight, despite door knocking every house in Stanger Street with a light on, as well as the new-builds in the lane, nobody had seen or heard anything unusual. The rest would be knocked and questioned in the morning. There was no CCTV in the area and all local hospitals had already been contacted.

Harry was tired and needed to eat. He was heady and his blood sugar had to be low because he felt he could eat a horse. He hadn't done any checks that afternoon, and lunch had been missed. . . *again*. It was why he'd reached for the non-existent barley sugars in his pocket outside Rob McPhail's, and he'd still not bought any of those either. He needed to go home, eat, and get some sleep but felt guilty even thinking about it. The search would continue without him, though. The helicopter and dogs had been organised and he'd put one of the longer-serving sergeants in charge. He'd have to take comfort from the fact they'd continue looking for Fran through the night. It was unusual to go to those lengths for an adult female who hadn't been missing that long, but there *were* peculiarities about the scene and Harry had a *really* bad feeling about it.

After a word with the sergeant, now acting DI, he got into his car and headed for home. It was now 10.00 p.m. and Harry knew he'd be no good to Fran if he wound up in hospital through a diabetic episode or worse. He also had to be at work first thing to put in a good word for McPhail, speak to the chief super – keep him informed of the body parts case, and convey his belief the Zandinis were at the very least connected if not central to it.

Driving home his heart was heavy. Wipers wouldn't help stop the windscreen from being blurry because the rain had stopped hours ago. He dragged the back of his right hand across his eyes and swallowed hard as he caught his expression in the rear-view mirror. If Fran didn't make it he wasn't sure he would either. Whatever was or wasn't going on between them, she didn't deserve this, and the not knowing if she was dead or alive. . . well, it was killing him. It was her car and smashed mobile in the garage that was really screwing with his head. . . he couldn't get them out of it.

It screamed 'taken'.

THIRTY-FOUR

The following morning Harry was driving to work having stopped off at a local sweet shop where they made particularly nice barley sugars. He wasn't that fussed at their speciality, but Bonbon Booty was the first shop he passed on the way to the station so had popped in on the way.

He *had* checked his blood sugar levels that morning though (having been dire when he'd got in the night before), and also eaten a bowl of cornflakes before leaving home plus two slices of toast and marmalade. Well, not quite two, one of them was currently on the dashboard, but he was working his way through it as he drove along the high street to Kirkdale nick.

When news came on the radio about the fire, Harry was only half listening. His Bluetooth had just kicked back in having gone through a poor reception area, and now his boss, Chris Hitchings, was on the phone so he was trying to be attentive. The meetings that day were going to be heavy, the first one with Hitchings, which was why Harry was surprised he'd called as he wasn't late and it was booked in. Mind you, he hadn't informed him about Fran yet despite knowing he should have. He knew his boss would never have authorised a full-on search so soon. This was exactly one of those times Chris would use as an example of him not *'playing it by the book,'* particularly with exorbitant costs involved....

"Harry, it's me. Carlisle CID are coming in later than planned to interview PC McPhail. They're waiting on more evidence from the car salvage place so will be down about twelve thirty-one o'clock as opposed to ten."

'. . . fire at the cottage in Riversdale Lane. Firefighters are battling to get. . .'

". . . Harry, are you *listening* to me? I said—"

"Yes, hold on, sir – please, there's a news report coming in, a fire in Riversdale Lane. . ."

'. . . are believed to be two members of the same family still inside. We will update later as more news comes in.'

"Sir, in view of McPhail's postponed interview I'm going straight over to Riversdale."

"*Because . . .?*"

"Could you hear the fire report on my radio, sir?"

"Yes, bits, but why does that con—"

"Rob McPhail lives in Riversdale Lane. I've got a funny feeling about this, sir, given his recent connections."

"I thought you set up surveillance on his place?"

"I did. I'll see you later than we'd planned if that's okay, sir?"

"Yes, yes, of course. I sincerely hope our man is not lost, Longbridge."

"So do I, sir. . . so do I."

Harry turned the car round and pointed it towards Rob's who lived on the other side of town out towards Kirkby. Riversdale was a tiny village of a dozen or so flint cottages close to the River Kirk. . . *although now it appeared there was one less.* He'd never been there before yesterday, now it would be twice in twenty-four hours. As he drove, *Harry sincerely hoped whoever in 'B' relief had been put on the previous day shift of a round the clock surveillance, had stayed to hand over to the night-shift babysitter.*

Harry was able to see and could already smell the acrid smoke pouring across the sky well before reaching the lane. The flashing blue lights of all three services surrounded Rob's address as he drove as close as he could to the house. The heat was intense and firefighters working hard, arms around heavy water hoses aimed at McPhail's cottage, crew shouting and running from inside and outside the property, flames pouring from the windows and doors. The roof had already gone.... An ambulance stood by waiting, and as Harry got out of the car and walked the fifty-odd yards up to the scene, sounds of crackling and the strong smell hit more densely as he covered his nose and mouth with a Baxter towel grabbed from the car. A fireman came stumbling out of the house in full gear, panting hard and carrying what looked like a body over his shoulder, his beige uniform charred by soot and smoke.

Harry watched as the two ambulance crew shot forward with a stretcher and helped to lower the body onto it. A short conversation between fire operatives and medics, followed by a sheet covering the whole of the stretcher told Harry all he needed to know. His stomach tightened. Of course he still had to confirm whether the body was that of Rob or Carrie McPhail, or any other family member come to that. With a lump in his throat and eyes glazed, he approached the paramedics – warrant held up ready.

"Is that. . . is the person recognisable?" asked Harry hesitantly, snapping shut and re-pocketing his ID, "or will forensics need to clarify?"

"Well, I don't advise a close look but I can tell you we've got a man in the ambulance already, and a woman here if that helps," answered one of the paramedics.

"I think the man is likely to be a police officer from Kirkdale," said Harry. "It's really important I know for sure, not just because if it *is* him he was a colleague, but also for other reasons."

"You'd better speak to one of your lot then. They're parked in the field over there next to the end cottage – arrived about fifteen minutes ago. As you can see there isn't any room here in the lane, and an officer came over when the man was brought out and placed in the ambulance."

Harry walked over to the field. Coming towards him was Suzanne Moorcroft and Joe Walker both looking very subdued, particularly Joe. He got his answer.

"This is just gut-wrenching," said Joe, eyes glistening. "Rob was a really good bloke, never spoke ill of anyone, I. . . I just can't believe this. Who would *do* any—"

"You didn't know about the twenty-four-hour surveillance on Mac's place then?" asked Harry despondently, any hope he'd had now firmly dropped to his boots.

Suzanne jumped in immediately. . . "*Surveillance?* Why was there surveillance on *Mac?*" She looked at Joe. "You mentioned on the way over something about an officer under suspicion for bribery, you didn't say it was *Mac!*"

"He'd got himself in a spot of bother, in debt to the Zandinis," said Harry. "He was seen on a CCTV footage taking a bung. We believed he could be targeted because of the footage. Weren't you both in the office when it broke yesterday? The gossip zipped through the station like wild—" Harry stopped, realising where he was going.

Joe shook his head in disbelief. . . "So it's actually *true* then?" He turned to Suzanne. "I'd heard the rumours, Suze, but I knew you were mates and wasn't a hundred per cent certain." To Harry he said, "Suzanne was at a training thing." He looked over at her rolling his eyes, "One of those HR jobbies about health and *diversity*, wasn't it?"

Suzanne acknowledged her out-of-office day, but frowned slightly at Joe's disparaging take on it. As a gay man she thought he'd have been more pro the diversity training, but Joe disliked anything that harped on about differences however well meaning, he just wanted to get on with the job. Hence he'd given it a miss. She let his comment pass, though. *She was still trying to get her head around Rob....*

Harry knew exactly what course they were referring to and was exceedingly glad he'd managed to avoid that particular event – *again*. He brought the conversation back to the scene at hand.... "Have you any definitive proof it's Rob and his wife, Carrie, under those sheets, Joe?"

"First out was definitely Mac. He's in the ambulance. Right size and height and I could just make out part of the dragon tattoo on his right arm. What was left. . ." He looked away for a moment, measured his breathing trying to prevent the inevitable. He swallowed the lump rising in his throat.... "I had to come back to the car, suggest Suze didn't go over to ID the body. I wouldn't know about his wife, sir, I never met her. The second body's only just been brought out." Joe looked down at the ground before meeting Harry's eyes again. He found his senior officer in much the same state when he did.

Harry lifted his arm, hesitated then patted Joe on the shoulder. "I know, son, I know. Look. . . the bad news doesn't start and end here either." A flash of anticipation exchanged between Suzanne and Joe. "Fran. . . DI Taylor, she's missing."

"*Missing?* Since when?" asked Suze. "I saw her yest. . . no wait, a couple of days ago."

"Me too," added Joe. "I don't understand though, *two days?* I know I phoned you yesterday to say I couldn't get her re your message about Kitson, the crane driver."

"I know it sounds a bit. . . well, overkill," replied Harry, "but as you mentioned on the phone, she was due in yesterday lunchtime, I've not been able to contact her, she's not at home and I found her car and mobile in her garage late yesterday afternoon. All hospitals have been checked, friends and relatives rung first, etc., although I don't think she's got that big a family. An emergency search was set up and carried on through the night by 'C' relief."

Joe and Suzanne admitted it sounded very odd, especially the mobile. Still, it was only two days.... "Any news yet?" they both spoke in unison, well aware of Harry's feelings for their DI.

"Nothing." This time it was Harry's turn to look at the ground. "Look, I have to get back to the station to brief the chief super about DI Taylor, and now Mac. He doesn't know anything about the search for Fran yet and I'm going to have to fill him in." He turned to the cottage, now a steaming black mess. "I still don't understand how this happened with an officer on nightwatch, unless it was a genuine accident of course, but when I saw Rob yesterday he was a scared man." Harry paused for a moment. "Unless that officer cleared off for some grub, of course.... "

"Who was on night surveillance, sir?" said Joe, eyes narrowing in thought.

"PC Crawford from 'B' relief came over after I left yesterday afternoon, then DC Hackett was due to take over from eleven last night till seven this morning," replied Harry.

"Hackett. . ." said Joe flatly, both hands locked behind his head, taking in a deep breath and breathing it out heavily through his nose.

"I know, I know, but he's employed in our constabulary. I can't just not *use* him, Walker."

"Yes, but he's *'C' relief*, sir. If you set up a search for DI Taylor last night, maybe he got pulled off surveillance to join it."

Harry's stomach suddenly lurched. He started to feel distinctly uncomfortable and immediately heard Chris Hitchings' voice in his head.... *'By the book, Harry – the book!'* Someone must have been watching their watcher, and it was looking suspiciously like they saw them leave their post unattended. . .

THIRTY-FIVE

2.00 P.M., STANGER LANE
BUILDING SITE

Fran had woken up to the sound of barking, *lots of barking*.

She felt like she'd been lying in that waste pipe for weeks given there was no clue to passage of time, but realised logically it couldn't be that long or she'd be dead – *unless of course she was, and now actually residing in hell....*

She'd been drifting in and out of sleep, not only through sheer physical weakness, but also the frantic mental exhaustion of thoughts and emotions continuously flooding through her on a repeating loop. Fear, hopelessness, renewed determination, belief in Harry, confusion, loss, death, and back to fear again. They played on an ever running conveyor belt in her fragile mind as she lay cramped and pained in virtually complete darkness. Fran had almost given up hope, but for one thing, one *precious* thing that was keeping her going. She held on to that thought and never let it go....

The rushing sound she'd heard earlier had not materialised in water or sewage at all. This had confused her considerably but resulted in much thanking of the big man in the sky ever since. Promised weekly church attendances for the rest of her life if she ever got out had been proffered over and over again. The stench seemed to have eased off too, which was equally surprising. Either there was a loss in her sense of smell, or what she'd been gagging on for what seemed like an eternity, was farmers spreading an inordinate amount of manure on nearby fields.

But now she could hear barking, really excited barking and multiple voices, loud shouts of, "*Over here!!*" Her heart leapt as she tried to call out but still gagged and weak, could only produce a muffled grunting sound. A few minutes later when Deefa and Darcy took turns to thrust their beautiful, clever and excited Labby heads inside the pipe, barking like there was no tomorrow, she knew they'd found her. Beneath the gag Fran erupted in muted but uncontrolled hyped laughter, and entwined grateful tears, as the dogs were pulled back, and she felt the warmth of human hands on her legs dragging her out of that hell hole.

"We've got you now, ma'am – you're safe. Everything's going to be fine, you're all good."

After Harry had made her and Joe aware of Fran's situation, Suzanne Moorcroft had insisted on going from the fire at Riversdale straight back to the station and taking her own seek and search dogs out to look for her DI. The team on 'C' relief hadn't come up with anything, the helicopter had developed a fault and not gone up, and she was determined to get her little stars Deefa and Darcy on the job. They knew Fran personally which made it especially heart rendering. It was like those boys realised how extra important their work was that day.

Right then, DS Moorcroft's voice was the best thing Fran had ever heard. *But where was Harry?* Her heart sank a little, even through the enormous relief and gratitude at being found. The brightness of daylight was fierce after being in the dark and it was hurting to open her eyes, so she waited. Somebody placed something soft over them as a shield, removed the gag and untied her hands and feet. The cloth smelt strange, sort of smoky. She felt a splash of water on her cheek, then another. . . and another.... With her hands now free, she pulled the material gently down from her eyes, squinting at first, then peaking her hand against her forehead saw him crouching beside her, eyes full, unable to speak....

After Harry had spoken with Chief Superintendent Hitchings to let him know about Rob McPhail's death and that Fran was missing, he'd gone down with Suzanne to the building site behind Stanger Lane to join the day shift, and the search for her. With Deefa and Darcy given an item of Fran's clothing to use as a scent, they'd quickly got to work scouring the site, and had found the waste pipe exiting from the recently demolished agricultural warehouse brought down to make way for more new-builds. When Harry saw Fran pulled out of that pipe, he thought his heart would burst, both with love and anger. *He swore he'd kill the person who'd put her in there.*

Wiping his eyes quickly, Harry took Fran's hand in his own and turning round yelled loudly, "Get an ambulance here – *NOW!!*"

"Already on its way, Boss," called out Suzanne from the dog van where she was rewarding both Labs and giving them some water, having ensured she'd first given Fran a small bottle. She'd just returned with the boys from the other side of the site where they'd uncovered a flatbed trolley beneath a heavy and dense thicket. It had Fran's scent on.

"You'll be in hospital soon. It'll all be fine, I promise," said Harry holding the bottle up to her lips. "Not too much, take it slowly...."

It tasted sublime.... "You know you can't promise that," whispered Fran hoarsely, "but I can tell you I did a lot of praying back there."

"Church for the next ten years then," he quipped, smiling as the sirens sounded in the distance. "I'll come with you to the hosp—"

"No. No. . . I'll be okay now," replied Fran. She put a hand on his arm, "Just find her, Harry. *Find the bitch that knocked me out and put me in that fucking pipe!*"

"*Her?*" Harry frowned, searching Fran's face for answers. "How do you know it was a woman? There's blood on the back of your head, you must've been hit from *behind*."

"The strength of the shove, the hand-sized grip on my arms, I remember *that* much before I blacked out. It was *definitely* a woman, Harry."

"Boss, something you should know," said Suzanne having put the dogs back in the van and returned to Harry and Fran. "The boys found a flatbed trolley out on the perimeter of the site where there's still some thicket and woodland. They went mental when they scented it so it's definitely connected, not just a dumped random."

"I've got a trolley like that, I keep it in my garage!" said Fran urgently twisting her head back and forth between them.

"There was definitely no trolley of any sort when I checked your place yesterday, just a few packing boxes, decorating stuff, your car and phone behind a front wheel so. . ."

"It *must* be the one then. I don't remember being put on it although have a vague memory of a rocking sensation."

Harry got up when he heard the ambulance approaching, standing back as the medics jumped out and opening the back, lifted Fran onto the stretcher. His brain was teeming with some very troubled and confusing thoughts. "I'll be in to the hospital to see you later then. Look. . . I'm not saying it *wasn't* a woman, Fran, especially in view of the trolley, but we shouldn't rule out a short, lightweight bloke either."

She lifted herself up onto one arm then and looked him straight in the eyes. "Make no mistake, Harry, trolley or not. . . *it was a woman.*"

* * *

All hell was breaking loose. Jacey Pearl had been told to return to duty. News of Rob McPhail's death had gone viral on an office WhatsApp group, and obviously there were no longer any concerns over her bumping into him following her CCTV discovery. Thus she'd been ordered back in and officially interviewed over the footage herself, but still hadn't disclosed her mother's younger brother was *crane driver Jerry, 'Jez' Kitson* – the second man in the video handing Rob the package.

However, when Terry Hackett had revealed Jacey's mother was a Kitson before marriage, she'd tried desperately to deny it. . . but of course Hackett had proof. Unlucky for Jacey, he'd literally only found it that morning in the locker room. A prescription for some painkillers in her mother's maiden name must've fallen out of her pocket. She'd been collecting double the amount because of how bad her mother's fibromyalgia and osteoarthritis conditions had become. Sandra Pearl had begged her daughter to find a way to get more because the doctor wouldn't prescribe a higher dose. Jacey's Uncle Jez had managed to 'acquire' a forged prescription pad and she'd written one in her mother's maiden name. It was a week before the footage had come in from DI Janis Lane at Carlisle CID. Jacey had been worried sick she'd agreed to it at all because at the end of the day it was fraud, but she loved her mother so much, couldn't bear to see her in pain and would have done anything to help her.

She'd been searching for the 'prescription' everywhere at home, but it had obviously got stuck in the lining of her jacket then dislodged that morning as she'd pulled out her purse to buy a chocolate bar in the vending machine. Hackett had been right behind her. Now her job was on the line. Well, more than that, she would be charged with fraud – *her career, her whole life was in the gutter.*

Harry sat in his office. A large black coffee on his desk had gone cold. He was shocked to the core with what had unravelled in the last forty-eight hours – this was Kirkdale, for God's sake, not London. One colleague blackmailed into going bent, then dying in a house fire, probably murdered, another who meant the world to him abducted and could've died, in hospital recuperating, and now the trainee DC he thought was nigh on perfect, charged with fraud and due to be thrown out of the force. He just wanted to go back to bed and wake up to a run-of-the-mill day.

"Sir. . . ?" Harry hadn't heard Joe knock on his open door. "Sir, DI Lane, Carlisle CID. She's been trying to get through to you."

Harry looked down at his phone. He'd had it on silent just for a few minutes to try and process what was going on in his head. "What did she say?"

"Jerry Kitson. He's singing like a canary, apparently."

Harry smiled. That phrase sounded odd on a youngster. He reminded himself Joe liked some of the old TV police series, *The Bill*, *Prime Suspect*, *Minder*.... "Okay, I'll ring her. Thanks."

Joe smiled and left the room only to come back a few minutes later and quietly place a fresh coffee on his desk.

". . . *Really?* Interesting...." Harry signalled a thank you to Joe for the coffee and continued listening to Janis Lane.

"So the owner is denying any involvement then," he replied, "although he *did* report the body as soon as it turned up so...."

"Yes, we believe Sebastian Rains is totally innocent," said Janis. "Kitson was abusing his old school friendship with him by using his salvage yard as a cover for receiving laundered money and getting rid of anything the Zandinis wanted – including bodies. Rains trusted him completely."

"How come he's coughed so easily to his involvement?" asked Harry.

"*That's* the million dollar question, Harry. We still don't know. It was all too easy, frankly. Raiffe Zandini's disappeared, though. Kitson says his calls have just dried up. There's more to this – *a lot more*."

"Hmm... well, I suppose we shouldn't look a gift horse in the mouth, even if that horse *has* got something lurking in the back of the stable. The Raiffe Zandini disappearance though, that's *very* puzzling, especially as his niece has just been topped in Rampton. That's not even logical, certainly not the same person responsible."

"Yes, I saw that on the news," replied Janis. "I just feel there's something more substantial here, I just can't put my finger on it."

"Indeed. Well, anything you find out let me know and vice versa of course. Another thing, the Bonaparte case we're working on here, the body parts case? Now we have the link with Storm Salvage, I think we can safely assume they're all connected and the Zandinis are responsible for all of it. One of the arms and the head belonged to Zoe Zandini's partner, James Johnson, aka Jimmy 'the Lash' Johnson. The DNA from the torso at the scrapyard obviously won't test positive to those though as you mentioned three days ago Cumberland Infirmary confirmed it's black, so it's another unknown body part on our whiteboard. My theory is these are people who've either not paid their dues to the Zandinis for debts or services rendered, or not done their job properly within the family or organisation."

"There's a black leg over at Penrith as well, isn't there?" asked Janis.

"There is, in Marcus Ventnor's hospital mortuary. That's been there a good seven months or so at least. No other black body parts have come to light though, at least not yet. To be honest, Janis, I don't see us putting the whole puzzle together unless we can infiltrate the Zandinis and make them talk. On top of all this we have a solicitor in the mortuary at Kirkdale, cause of death *hemlock poisoning* of all things!!"

"Yes, I heard about the hemlock victim, very unusual. Doesn't sound like a Zandini MO to me, though. What do you make of it?"

315

"No, well, we were wondering if it was just a case of us finding the body before the job was finished in the dissecting department, if you get my drift."

"Still don't think they'd bother with hemlock, Harry. Gunshot, knife or strangulation followed by mutilation and random burial plots, that's Zandini MO." Janis Lane was nothing if not direct.

Hearing it like that something clicked in Harry's head. "I think you're right. Christopher Mogg was murdered by someone unrelated to the Zandinis, but we literally have zero leads on who might have held a grudge against him, other than Charlotte Peterson who was obviously more than a little miffed he got her inheritance diverted, but she's safely ensconced in Rampton. There hasn't been any other suspect on our radar at all."

"Well, good luck with that, Harry, I really must go now. I've got to get back to Kitson, see if I can get anything else out of him."

Harry said his goodbyes and ended the call. Finally reaching for his coffee and taking a sip, he grimaced – *bloody cold again. . .*

Later that evening, Harry sat at the kitchen table with Annie at the opposite end, sharing a not-so-disgusting-looking shepherd's pie.

"This looks nice, love," he opened safely, smiling. "Not had a shepherd's pie in a long while, nice change."

Annie returned a cool, fast smile before forking some up and eating it. She didn't feel it necessary to add any extra pie facts. The fact she hadn't actually made it herself, the fact she couldn't care less whether he liked it or not, the fact one end of it was very different from the other, and the fact she'd got one fewer bottles of hemlock under the floorboards in the spare room....

THIRTY-SIX

As Harry was about to tuck into his dinner, Baxter began whining and jumping up, pulling on his arm. Every time he lifted the fork to his mouth the Lab started barking and knocking Harry's wrist with his muzzle. At first Harry just told him to lie down. Then just as he decided it was because Bax hadn't had his walk, a text came in. He put his fork down and picked up his phone, which of course was on the table....

> Kitson's been found dead in his cell. We think it was in his food, a shepherd's pie apparently, the rest's gone for testing. It suggests an inside job so obviously an investigation is imminent. I'll be in touch
> – Janis.

Harry looked down at his plate, appetite suddenly evaporated.

"Come on, lad, let's go to the park." He pushed his chair back and walked out to the hall to fetch Baxter's lead. The Lab was at his heels faster than if he'd smelt liver cake. *Something he'd not had in a very long time.*

"What about your *bloody dinner?!*" Annie called from the kitchen.

"I'll have it when I get back, warm it up later. I'll do it, don't worry."

The front door clicked shut and the house fell quiet. Staring at the space Harry had left when he'd walked out, Annie looked down at her own plate, picked it up and with as much force as she could muster – *threw it at the wall.*

At the park Harry let Baxter off his lead and gave his red Kong toy a good lob across the green. Watching the Lab chase after it, he mentally went over everything as he walked. Fran's abduction, McPhail's death (possible murder), and the Zandini connection (particularly Zoe's suspected murder and Raiffe's disappearance). Then there was Christopher Mogg's murder, the various body parts. . . *thus far,* and now Kitson was dead too. Right then Harry seriously felt in need of something he hadn't had in twenty odd years – *a concentration smoke.* He shook his head and sighed. *What the hell was going on. . . ? What was he missing?*

Baxter ran up and dropped the Kong at his feet,

panting and wagging his tail enthusiastically. Harry picked it up and threw the toy again, this time in the other direction. The dog shot off after it towards the trees, and a lady spaniel owner Harry occasionally spoke to waved to him from the same spot. He raised an arm in acknowledgement, then stopped for a moment as something triggered in his head. Fran was insisting the person who'd abducted her was female. Who other than Charlotte Peterson could have anything serious to hold against her? It was possible a past villain down south wanted revenge but. . . no, she'd not been intricately involved in anything seriously big time, and certainly never mentioned anyone she knew personally. Well apart from Annie having a bit of a beef but that was just too ridiculous. He started walking slowly again.... Charlotte was confirmed to still be in Rampton, but could definitely be holding a grudge against Fran. She was after all one of the two officers who'd brought her back from the US, and subsequently returned her to the hospital. Could Peterson have got someone to act for her on the outside? If so. . . *might she have arranged the same for Mogg given his interference in her mother's will?* He stopped walking again, deep in thought. That would work in *theory*, but where did the Zandinis come in to it? The answer to that came at exactly the same time as Baxter's incessant barking rose from the trees. . . *Raiffe Zandini. He must've lent Charlotte the money, arranged her escape and new identity for the New York killing trip.... She couldn't pay him back because of*

Mogg…. and he got his niece Zoe to lean on her. That's it. That must be it! He started walking slowly again…. *The fact she couldn't legally inherit a penny for years, if ever in her position, had clearly passed them both by.* Now things were slotting into place, though. *Now* he just had to unearth Peterson's contact. He started walking more quickly then, just about broke into a slow run as Baxter's barking had increased to an embarrassingly high pitch for a nice village park.

As he approached the trees he prayed it wasn't another poor bastard's hacked off bits. What he found when he got there was not what he was expecting. Baxter was standing over two Kongs. . . the red one and another black one. His barking was down to not being able to fit both in his mouth at the same time, *despite now undertaking a really impressive attempt.*

When he got back to the house, Bax ran into the kitchen with the black Kong in his mouth (finders keepers), whilst Harry had the red one in his pocket. As he followed him in he saw the newly acquired 'find' now in the Lab's water bowl. A licking sound was evident somewhere in the vicinity of the dresser. Then he saw it. The pieces of smashed china on the floor and the wall wearing a shepherd's pie, or what was left of it given Baxter's efforts. *Harry's* dinner was still untouched on the table.

After a quick search it was evident Annie was gone.

* * *

RAMPTON PSYCHIATRIC HOSPITAL - NOTTINGHAMSHIRE
AUGUST 12TH - TWO WEEKS LATER

Marie Violet Osborne had been interviewed by Retford police at length, and was still insisting she'd had nothing to do with Zoe Zandini's death. The fact a hot-food server remembered Marie standing directly behind her in the breakfast queue when Zoe collapsed that morning, and a needle puncture later found in Zoe's rear, had done nothing to persuade Marie she was clearly lying.

An autopsy had concluded death was from a combined intramuscular overdose of Midazolam and Diazepam, unfortunately the syringe that delivered it was still missing, and Marie wasn't being cooperative in that direction either. The only thing not adding up was the fact Marie Osborne and Zoe Zandini had never had any behavioural issues with each other. Not a single one. Whereas the person who *did. . . was Charlotte Peterson.* However, nobody was coming forward to say Peterson was even in the same *queue.* The server had remembered Marie because she was unkindly but factually known as 'Whiffy' due to strong body-odour problems. People always remembered where Marie was, and right now that was locked in her room.

Charlotte knew she was on slightly dodgy ground owing to her beef with Zoe over the boiling water incident (known about by the powers that be), and the fact Zoe had been blackmailing her through her Uncle

Raiffe, not known by anyone. . . *yet*. So far things were relatively stable and nobody was looking her way. As far as Charlotte was concerned, this was the only reason Rita Lemon was still walking around free as a bird. She hadn't wanted to stir anything up again until certain they were concentrating on Whiffy Osborne. Now it was looking like Marie was going to be charged, despite not having a motive, which gave Charlotte room to move. *Naturally she still had the syringe....*

And Rita. . .? Well, she *knew* Charlotte must have been the one to kill Zoe. She was, after all, originally setting up that opportunity in the first place, but had intended to reap a particular reward for herself in the process. Maybe more than one.... and therefore hopefully form a bond. However, that had not happened. She'd kept her distance from Peterson since the night the alarm had sounded when realising she'd got the mobile from her. . . *and the syringe*. Which was why her bosses couldn't know what she knew, but even so, Rita was still in an extremely vulnerable position. *She knew the most dangerous woman on the wing would come for her.*

Charlotte had heard nothing from Annie for over two weeks. In fact, not since ringing her at midnight to order the hit on the cousin, who as far as Charlotte was concerned, had falsely inherited her mother's money. If *she* couldn't have it, she'd be damned if her holier than thou cousin was going to benefit from a cool million. But nothing had been reported on any news anywhere, so Charlotte had to assume spinster Phillipa was still happily splashing *her* cash.

It appeared Annie Longbridge was not delivering. Clearly it was time to lay things on the line. Either she was working for her *(also getting in practice for her own planned revenge, of course...)*, or she wasn't. Charlotte recalled the night of that conversation. She hadn't felt entirely in control; it was as though little agitated Annie had suddenly grown a pair and was standing up to her. She didn't like that, she didn't like it at all. And it wasn't going to happen. It would only take one phone call to the man who'd put her in that bloody lunatic asylum to have dear *Andrea* sitting right next to her on the lounge settee. . . as an inmate.

Meanwhile, there was Rita Lemon to see to. Charlotte couldn't allow that woman to walk around knowing the truth. However, getting close and concealed access for that particular despatch was going to prove a damn sight harder than Stabby Zandini....

The following day Charlotte surprisingly had her chance. It was risky and she'd had to be *really* creative to pull it off. Rita was on duty watching patients in the herb garden. It was a long-held hobby learning about and growing herbs, and the one area where she'd usually be quite chatty and friendly with residents instead of bad-tempered and miserable. Luckily the sun had gone in necessitating a long cardigan coat, and again the capped syringe had been buried deep in Charlotte's pocket beneath several tissues. It had – *but not any longer.*

Knowing Rita would never be able to resist showing what an expert she was in all things herby, Charlotte had already 'planted' the loaded syringe needle up next to a badly placed row of mint she'd taken from pots earlier. The opportunity came when Fiona Massey, a younger patient, came back from a toilet break. Charlotte called her over and engaging her in conversation, invited her to crouch down and look at what she'd done so far, taking care not to let her near the 'needle plant'. Rita was watching from the sidelines....

"Not sure I've done this right at *all*," said Charlotte trying her best to look helpless, one eye surreptitiously on Lemon. "Never been any good at gardening, not my thing really!"

"Oh not to worry, I think they're just a bit—"

"Oh for God's *sake*, Peterson," interrupted Rita, marching over to the plot, "they're all bunched up on top of each other, you've got them like a plate of *cabbage! This* is how it should be done!" Charlotte stood to the side, and Rita made sure Fiona was between them. She had no intention of even being within *spitting* distance of the crazy ex-GP. Fiddling around in the earth, separating the small mint plants so they were evenly spaced, Rita kept an eye on Charlotte as she worked.

"Wait, what's that?" asked Fiona leaning forward and pointing out something in the earth to Rita.

"Where, what do you mean?" replied the older woman, all concentration now on the mint.

Looking briefly around Charlotte grabbed her chance. Walking behind them and turning to face outwards, she gave Rita a hard shove with the sole of her foot. She pitched forwards hands shooting out in front to save her from falling head first into the herb garden. The agonising scream that followed was instant. Rita's right hand grabbed her left instinctively as she pulled it out of the earth and saw the syringe hanging off it. . . plunger fully depressed. Fiona looked on in horror and Charlotte immediately bobbed down to imply sympathy and support in front of anyone in the vicinity.

"Miss Lemon. . . what's *happened?* Are you *okay?* Miss *Lemon.* . .? Shall I get someone?" Rita turned sharply to look at her, stark terror on her face as she pulled out the syringe and began scrabbling backwards trying to get away, whilst Fiona looked on helplessly between the two, mouth hanging open in shocked confusion.

"Go inside *now*, Fiona!" yelled Charlotte. "Find a doctor, find *anyone!*" The younger woman jumped up and ran for the building as three other women came charging up from the vegetable garden, and Charlotte shouted at them to go inside and find help as well. The minute they'd all disappeared and she and Rita were alone, Charlotte crouched down beside her.

"Bye bye, Rita, sorry about the new '*Needle* Mint' I planted this morning; not a herb you're familiar with, I take it? *Probably should've checked closer when I was taking my meds, eh?* Never mind. At least you won't have to learn about that one now...."

But Rita wasn't listening. *She was no longer able to.*

THIRTY-SEVEN

KIRKDALE POLICE STATION
1.00 P.M.

Although Harry had seemingly worked out a great deal in the last couple of weeks regarding the body parts case, the Zandini connection including high-profile patients at Rampton, the blackmail of PC Rob McPhail and possible murder, he knew there was still a fair way to go in solving the casserole of illegal shit sitting on his desk. With this in mind (and the usual cold coffee), he was about to be shell-shocked some more due to his ever-ringing mobile....

"Longbridge..."

"Harry – Janis Lane. We have a problem. Well, *you* have a problem but it affects the constabulary."

"Go on. . . *sorry*. . . Good morning, Janis."

"Morning. . . probably won't be thinking it's very *good*, though."

"I'm beginning to gather."

"Your DC – Terence Hackett?"

"What about him?" asked Harry, now beginning to feel distinctly wary.

"I hope you're sitting down."

Harry was beginning to wish he'd never given up smoking twenty a day a couple of decades ago.... "I'm sitting – just tell me."

"We have reason to believe Hackett's responsible for Kitson's death."

"Do *what*? You *can't* be serious? Come on, Janis, I know he can be an irritating little bastard, definitely homophobic and embarrassingly misogynistic, but for God's sake – he's no *killer!*"

"He used to be attached to Carlisle about fifteen years ago. I believe you were down in London back then. His car was seen parked locally to us when he visited an old colleague the day Kitson's food was laced, *plus* he had access to the canteen. He's not popped in to 'visit' for a very long time...."

For once Harry was stuck for words. He didn't even have Fran for backup as she was still off.

"Harry? Are you still there?"

"Sure. . . yeah, I'm still here. Have you actually figured out why my officer would have any *reason* to commit murder? And what did Kitson actually have to *give* you that was so massive he had to be removed?" Harry was now feeling it necessary to throw a protective ring around Hackett, something he could never have imagined in a thousand years.

"There's a lot more, Harry, and it's not great. Have you spoken with your chief super this morning?"

"Hitchings? No, why?"

"There's been a development over the McPhail house fire. It involves Hackett. I spoke to your boss whilst trying to get through to you earlier."

Harry winced. He'd been visiting Fran that morning. She was on a long convalescent leave and he'd left his mobile in the car. Another hazy head moment had resulted in him forgetting to check it. "I had Hackett on surveillance that night but. . . well, he may have got pulled off early because of DI Taylor's abduction the same day. It's been a bloody nightmare down here, to be honest."

"Harry, it's not just Kitson. A witness has come forward. A householder in Riversdale Lane says they saw Terry Hackett feed a lit rag through McPhail's letterbox in the early hours of July 29th, the day of the fire, and then left immediately afterwards. He lives opposite. Apparently they had to let their new puppy out for a pee and. . . well, they weren't sure at first but..."

"So why the bloody hell are they only coming forward *now?!*" At that moment Hitchings was trying to get through.... "Hold on, Janis, I've got—"

"Don't worry, you go, I've got stuff to clear up here, we can catch up later."

Harry said goodbye and Chris Hitchings came on the line....

"Longbridge, why is it so damn difficult to get hold of you these days? Carlisle wanted you this morning and came through to me, and every time I'm expecting an update on the Bonaparte case, whole *weeks* go by. *Care to explain?*"

He was exaggerating but not by much.... "Yes, sir, you see—"

"You're not going to bullshit me, Harry, *are* you?"

If he'd had any hot coffee to drink, at that point Harry would have just choked on it. Hitchings rarely used the BS word – it threw him slightly....

"Erm. . . well, things took a turn for the worse when DI Tay—"

"I heard. . . and not from my DCI; that's *you* by the way, Longbridge, in case you've forgotten. I sincerely hope Fran is recovering. Mrs Hitchings sent flowers from us both, and I recommended a good rest at the police treatment centre in Harrogate. She declined."

"Yes, thank you, sir, I. . . well, I think she just wants to rest at home to be honest."

"Quite. Well, the option's still there if she changes her mind. Now tell me, what's the update, apart from losing one officer in a fire and nearly losing another from some *madman?*"

Harry decided to just tell him. "DC Hackett, sir, it seems he's well and truly bent and quite likely working for the Zandinis."

"*That's* what I wanted to speak to you about. DI Lane filled me in when she couldn't get you this morning. I want him picked up today. I've even had the chief constable breathing down my neck about all this. She's going to be making a statement on the news later due to a group of officers discussing highly confidential cases on What Is or What's That . . . or What something or other."

"Think you'll find it's WhatsApp, sir," said Harry, feeling unusually IT informed.

"Right. . . well, whatever. Dominique Du Guarde, *our chief constable*, is flame throwing in *my* direction. I want you to organise the pick-up, Harry, low key if you can. By the way, where *were* you this morning?"

"My mistake, sir, I'd left my phone in the car and hadn't checked it when I got back from. . ." Harry hesitated....

"Back *from*. . . ?" questioned Hitchings.

"From visiting DI Taylor. . . *sir*...."

"Hmm... didn't find a good enough birthday card for your wife the other day then....?"

"Not a good enough anything, frankly, sir, but I'd rather not—"

"Be careful, Harry. These things have a habit of escalating, rarely turn out well and *always* affect work. Get it sorted – *one way or another*."

What Harry hadn't told anyone was that Annie had disappeared. . . completely. He literally had no idea where she was, but her car had gone and her mobile sat at home. Presumably she had a second one, or maybe even a third, nothing would surprise him anymore.

When he'd got back from taking Baxter out that night, after Janis's text about Kitson being poisoned, Annie wasn't there. She hadn't come back that evening, or the next day, or the next. Although it sounded crazy, he'd initially assumed she was sulking about the meal he'd left. As the days went on he really didn't know what to think. But Annie was an adult, things between them had been going from bad to worse that year, and Harry had a job to do. He simply didn't have the time or the energy to juggle her anger issues, their marriage, or any of it anymore.

Fran's abduction had shaken him badly. It had taken him full circle back to March, Kenny Drew keeping Annie in the Stratford lock-up. . . and not being able to do a *damn* thing about it.

He couldn't think straight. He needed hot coffee. . . and he needed it now.

Two mugs later he was thinking more clearly and the op for Terry Hackett's arrest had been arranged for early evening with himself, Joe Walker and four on loan from 'A' & 'B' relief, given they were literally four down including the now sacked Jacey Pearl and with Fran on extended sick leave.

At 5.00 p.m. Chief Constable Dominique DuGuarde gave a media statement which was broadcast on Cumbria Live, BBC Cumbria and various local TV and radio stations including Kirkdale, Keswick and Carlisle....

> *"We are aware of serious issues within the constabulary that have been leaked through various online..."* (She began coughing.) *"Excuse me. . . through various online groups. There have been..."* (More increased coughing.) *"I do apologise, I can't seem to lose this hacking cough.... there have only been a small number of officers involved."* (Lighter

coughing.) *"But I can assure everyone this is being dealt with..."* (a final small cough.) *"Thank you."*

In Braithwaite, Terry Hackett rewound his kitchen TV and listened carefully once more, this time watching DuGuarde's lips and eyes closely. *Lose this hacking cough....* that was the signal. *They were coming for him.*

He raced upstairs and grabbed the pre-packed sports bag from under his bed. At the same time he heard banging. Terry froze. Looking out of the window he saw nothing. No police cars, no vans, no police. In fact, given he lived fairly close to town, strangely, no people at all. The banging came again. He tentatively came out on to the landing with the bag, looked over the banister and then took the stairs warily down to the hall. When the banging repeated and became more urgent he followed it to the kitchen and saw Du Guarde's 'heavy' at the back door wearing his agitated face. By the time he'd answered it the banging started again, this time from the front of the house, *and this time there were plenty of vehicles and plenty of people he would recognise.*

* * *

ONE WEEK EARLIER - B&B KIRKDALE
AUGUST 5TH

Michael was worried. He'd been following Annie around as best he could since her changed behaviour, but her car had not been at the house for at least six or seven days and he'd not seen her leave by any other means. He was torn over who he should tell, or whether he should say anything at all, and couldn't imagine Harry being very happy about him tailing his wife, even if he *had* accepted he was Annie's son.

He was starting to wonder if what she'd said about another villain making threats to her and Harry as Kenny had, were so serious she'd been advised to go to her parents' place in London. Michael had told her at the time he'd believed the threats, and he *had* thought they were viable. Something didn't feel right, though. He couldn't put his finger on it but something was definitely off. Why would her mobile repeatedly go to voicemail after they'd cleared the air? Nothing was making any sense, unless she'd been told not to answer it? *Maybe* – although she could have still rung him, couldn't she? It was like she'd disappeared off the face of the earth....

THIRTY-EIGHT

BRAITHWAITE, KESWICK
TERRY HACKETT'S HOME

Dominique's henchman pushed his way into the kitchen, barely fitting through the door frame, and eyeing the windows covering the side of the house, produced a gun from inside his jacket.

"The boss is pleased you dealt with Kitson, he was going to out her. God knows how he knew but he did. I'm here to get you away and we gotta go – *now!*"

"They're at the front, it's not easy to get round the back but they'll be here any second," replied Terry panicking, his forehead now shining with sweat. "*I can't see any type of escape working here!*"

"*This* says it'll work," said Ape Man holding the gun aloft (nobody ever got his real name).

The banging had turned into splintering at the front as Ape pushed Terry out of the back door, the gun covering him as he followed close behind. The gated sideway off the patio they'd stepped out on, led left to the front of the house and immediate arrest, and straight ahead lay a small backyard with a gated fence at the bottom through to a public pathway and woodland. They both ran to the fence and were through the gate inside ten seconds flat. It would have worked had one of the on-loan officers not lived locally and had knowledge of the pathway and quickest route to it.

Harry and Joe were waiting for them as they came through, only expecting Hackett. Ape immediately fired off a shot but instantly he'd aimed, Joe threw himself across Harry yelling "*No!*" Longbridge looked on in utter horror at the young DS who was now slumped in his arms having taken a bullet for the one officer he loved and admired above all others.

All hell broke loose then – Ape was jumped on by the four on-loan PCs, one receiving a bullet-grazed arm, another a gashed head, but with arms and legs flying, they tackled him to the ground, grabbed the gun making it safe, cuffed and took him to the van out front. It was all over in seconds.

Hackett ran off towards the woods as two men shot off after him, and Harry sat cradling Joe on the footpath doing his best to stem the blood with one hand, whilst calling for an ambulance on a spattered phone with the other.

"Don't you die on me, Walker, I need you, son. The ambulance is on its way, you're gonna be... you're gonna be fine. Do you *hear* me, Joe?" Harry's lips began to tremble and he looked away, eyes filling up and swallowing down a rapidly growing need to become an emotional wreck in front of his team.

"Not. . . not feeling too fine, sir, might. . ." he began breathing more slowly, eyes dropping, "might need. . . a few days...."

Harry shook him. "Stay *awake*, Joe, stay with me now, the ambulance is close, can you *hear* it? Can you *hear* the siren?"

But Joe didn't answer, and as the paramedics came hurtling down the footpath towards them, they found their local DCI on the ground hugging a bloodstained victim to his chest.

* * *

TWO WEEKS EARLIER
JULY 29TH

After Harry had left the house with Baxter having ignored the hemlock meal and therefore thwarting her most vengeful despatch, it had left Annie stewing over where she now found herself. Fran being discovered too soon, *way* too soon... was the last straw. *When the hell would she ever be rid of that woman...?*

Overhearing those girls at the pub talking about the baby she'd been carrying, *Harry's* baby, had not only given birth to Fran's planned abduction and acute suffering at the very least, it had finished off any last feelings Annie had for her husband. It meant what Charlotte had suggested she should eventually do, she *would* do. To feel truly vindicated, truly healed after all she'd been through with Kenny raping her as a teen, not being able to conceive as an adult, Harry and Fran's closeness back in London culminating in her dragging him away up to Cumbria, Kenny and Michael kidnapping her, and Harry staying in New York after she and Michael had escaped..... all of it.... *all – of – it!* It meant Annie needed to strip it all away so she could breathe again, feel in control again. . . *start over again.*

It was why she'd left, so she could prepare, but there was something she'd forgotten at the house, something important she'd left behind, and she knew she'd have to go back....

* * *

AUGUST 12TH (CONTINUED....)

After the ambulance had taken Joe Walker, and Terry Hackett picked up following a wide-scale search of the area with his house taped off for an in-depth inspection, Harry made his way home to check on Baxter. Annie not being there the last two weeks had meant he'd been going home regularly every day to let him out, spend a bit of time with him and sort out his food if he was going to be working late.

It was now eight o'clock and Harry was feeling very guilty the Lab had been made to wait so long for his evening meal. As he let himself into the house the silence was deafening and the absence of Baxter rushing to the door to greet him, disconcerting at best. He didn't like to think of what the worst might mean....

"Baxter, where are you? *Here, boy. . .!*" Nothing. No bouncy black bombshell with wet lollypy tongue came haring out of the kitchen – *or* the lounge. . . *or* down the stairs. Even if he'd been asleep, Harry knew he'd have heard him calling. After he'd searched the entire house, twice in case he'd managed to shut himself in a room, (unlikely given he could jump the door handles...), Harry began to worry. There was no note from Annie to say she'd come home and taken him for a walk which she might well do normally, but then things were far from normal with Annie at the moment.

He went into the back garden and searched everywhere out there as well, including the shed and the greenhouse – no Baxter. He dialled Annie's mobile and marched swiftly back up the garden, re-entering the kitchen to hear ringing and remembered her phone was still there. At least the one he *knew* about was still there. Harry sat down at the table to think. Looking around the room things didn't seem any different from when he left that morning. Dishes still in the sink from the night before, unopened junk mail he hadn't got around to checking still on the side. Baxter's bed still in the same place..... *Lead. Was his lead still hanging up in the hall?* Harry immediately got up and went to the hook where the Lab's collar and lead were always kept. *Gone....* His heart had picked up speed somewhere between the shed and the greenhouse – now it was in overdrive and thumping at what was probably an unhealthy rate. He loved that boy more than life itself. *Surely Annie wouldn't have done anything to....*

At that moment the doorbell rang and he saw two shadowy shapes through the heavy mottled glass. One tall and one very much smaller, this was *not* the time for cold callers, or a mother bringing her child for an 'official telling off' for stealing sweets from their kitchen cupboard....

He opened the door to Kate Hoffman, a relatively new neighbour who'd moved in whilst he was in New York. Harry didn't get a chance to say hello straight away as (thankfully), having leapt up at him, his face was immediately covered by Baxter's tongue.

"I thought you were. . . *away*, Harry," said Kate, slightly confused. "Only Annie asked if we could look after Baxy whilst you were on holiday. Our boys would love a dog so we were happy to have him for a few days."

"Ermm... when *was* this exactly?" asked Harry from behind Baxter's face as he eased him down, taking the lead from Kate and trying to put the Lab into a heel sit.

"Well, only this morning, she brought him round about eleven I think, said you were off to France for a week. But when I saw you drive in I thought I'd better just check if you were still going."

Harry thought quickly. "There's been a mix-up with the days. I couldn't get time off. . . work commitments. I really appreciate you offering though, Kate."

"Oh, that's okay, any time; as I said, the boys love dogs, even insisted on buying him a bed for *our* house!"

"*Ha-ha!* Right, must go, thanks again, really kind of you, perhaps I could ask for help if I get stuck another time?"

"Totally," replied Kate, smiling. "Oh, and he's had dinner a couple of hours ago. Bye now."

Harry said goodbye, shut the door and took Baxter through to the kitchen where he automatically dropped to the floor to give him a bear hug. The relief of getting him back was enormous. On the plus side it was good to know he had some dog sitting backup. *But what the hell was Annie playing at?*

KIRKDALE GENERAL HOSPITAL

Harry had heard nothing since the ambulance had taken Joe, so once he'd checked his blood sugar and settled Baxter, threw a speedy sandwich into a bag and was now eating en route to the hospital.

As he drove round the myriad of different parking areas trying to get a space, his mobile rang. Switching to Bluetooth and checking every bay, he answered only half listening....

"Longbridge...."

"Boss, it's Suzanne, have you heard about Joe?"

"I'm at the hospital now, just trying to park. Is he. . .?"

"I'm there too. I'll meet you in A&E."

"Right. . . right. . . " Harry suddenly spotted a car backing out of a space, nipped in switching back to mobile, and got out of the car. He started walking in the vague direction of the entrance whilst talking into the phone. "Suze, is he. . . did he make it?" The signal cut out as the doors for A&E finally came into view. "*Damn!! Damn it!!*" Harry shifted up a gear and began a half run until he reached the large glass frontage through which he noticed Suzanne waiting by the reception desk. Once inside she saw him and they walked quickly towards each other.

"Is he going to be okay?" Harry asked anxiously. "Bloody connection went."

"Touch and go but. . . yes, they think so. He's not long been out of theatre. They're doing everything they can."

"Can we see him? Have you spoken to a doctor? What about his parents? Are they here? Has some—"

Suzanne hesitated before gently touching his arm. "It's okay, Harr… Boss, the doctors have seen his folks. Not sure if we can see him yet though, it's this way."

Breathing a sigh of relief, Harry followed Suzanne through a variety of corridors to the family room set aside for Joe's parents. She'd been assigned as the FLO (family liaison officer), and knocked before entering.

"Mr Walker, Mrs Walker, this is Detective Chief Inspector Harry Longbridge. He was with Joe when he was shot."

Alan Walker started to move off the sofa where he was comforting his wife, but Harry stopped him.... "Please, don't get up, Mr Walker. I just wanted to come in and check on Joe for myself." Harry and Suzanne sat down in single opposite chairs.

"Mr Longbridge, I. . . we, Joe's mother and I, we appreciate your coming, we really do. Joe's often mentioned you. He thinks the world of you, you know."

Harry blushed and looked down at his clasped hands for a moment before raising his head to speak. "Your son is a fine officer, Mr Walk—"

"Please, it's Alan and Nicky," Mrs Walker interjected, fiddling with a silver cross around her neck and looking at her husband nodding in agreement whilst picking up her free hand.

"Alan, Nicky," began Harry. . . "Joe is a hugely respected member of the team, a very fine officer, we're all extremely proud of him. The whole station is praying for him to get through this." Harry hesitated. . . "Particularly me...."

Joe's parents glanced at each other questioningly, then looked back at Harry and waited.

"Your son saved my life today. He's a hero, a true hero, and I'll never be able to repay him. I'm pretty certain down the line there'll be a medal awarded to him."

Suzanne quietly produced a tissue, dabbing at her nose whilst fighting rapidly brimming eyes. She and Joe had joined at the same time and gone through their training together. She was very fond of him, but she also had a soft spot for her DCI. The whole thing had shaken her to the core.

The Walkers were just about to ask the details of what had actually happened when there was a knock at the door. A surgeon entered and acknowledged the two newly arrived officers. Smiling, he said, "Mr Walker, Mrs Walker, Joe is now in the intensive care unit. He's a strong lad and we've finally managed to stabilise him. The next twenty-four to thirty-six hours are extremely important but he's not critical. It's good news."

Joe's parents hugged each other and it took a lot for Harry and Suzanne not to do the same. The Walkers thanked the doctor for everything they'd done and were continuing to do, and asked if they could see him.

"I'll get a nurse to take you down," and turning to Harry and Suzanne, "only family for now though, I'm afraid. Maybe check tomorrow for visiting?"

Harry nodded, understanding. He would like to have seen his young officer but it could wait. Joe was going to pull through and that was all that mattered. He left Suzanne there as family liaison and walked out of the hospital into a cool and dark but thankfully dry night. Looking upwards he murmured a sincere and heartfelt thank you. . . then walking in various directions and looking around several times in confusion, swore loudly on realising he'd got absolutely no idea where he'd left his car....

THIRTY-NINE

KIRKDALE POLICE STATION
11.00 A.M., AUGUST 13TH

After a catch-up with Chief Superintendent Hitchings including how Joe was doing, Harry took the lift back to his now much slower office. It had been a serious and sombre conversation, with none of the usual quips from his side thrown across Chris's desk. Both men knew it was a very dark day when two officers were lost through murder and corruption, and a youngster for prescription drugs fraud, not to mention DI Taylor's abduction and Joe's shooting. *Maybe it was time to go back to Canon Row*, Harry thought. *It would probably be a damn sight quieter.*

As the lift arrived at his floor, instead of getting out, he pushed 'G' and carried on to the ground floor. Terry Hackett was being interviewed and he wanted an update on how that was going. With him being caught ready to flee the scene, and Ape, *real name now known as George ('Gunner') Gifford,* aiding and abetting his failed escape, Hackett had little to gain by delaying the inevitable.

He'd already admitted to controlling Rob McPhail from within the department under direction of the Zandinis, which is why he'd set the fire so Rob couldn't expose him at the planned interview the following day. What Harry *still* didn't know was who the leading light was in the Zandini family these days, but hopefully the most disliked officer in Cumbria was about to spill that information.

Arriving at ground level, and having walked the corridor to the interview rooms, he noticed room one had its light on above indicating it was in use. Harry knocked next door and entered, surprised to see DI Janis Lane leaning against a table, mug in hand, watching Hackett through the two-way mirror.

"Hi, Harry. Coffee…?"

"Always, black no sugar, thanks." He stood with arms crossed in front of the mirror analysing Hackett's body language. "How come you're here this morning then? Sorry, that sounded a bit abrupt…."

"That's okay. Don't forget your DC ended a dual prisoner-cum-witness in one of our cells. I'm here to see if he has anything else to say." She passed him his coffee. "There's something else, Harry. I was going to ring you but since your man's here in custody, I came over. We had a farmer come in to us early this morning. He found a body in one of his grain silos. Clearly an IC2 male, no head, no hands."

"Jesus, not *another* one…." Harry shook his head slowly in disbelief. "Any distinguishing marks?"

"There's a lightning flash on the chest apparently. I'm hazarding a guess he's not Harry Potter's twin brother, so for now I'm going with it being a 'Z' for Zandini." Janis shot her eyebrows up whilst swinging her now empty mug skyward in mock triumph.

"According to my conversation with Rob McPhail, Raiffe Zandini's dropped off the map," said Harry. "He was the contact blackmailing him, so you could well be right, but Rob never mentioned any kind of tattoo."

"Oh, it wasn't a tattoo – that 'Z' had been carved in...."

"Nice.... These people have such artistic talents," replied Harry dryly.

Suddenly, raised voices from the room next door had them both scrutinising the two-way mirror.

"I told you, *I've no idea who that bloody ape is! He just turned up at the house when the team crashed in!*"

"Given your actions you can hardly have expected anything *else*, Terry," answered the first interviewing officer. "He says you killed Jeremy Kitson at Carlisle Police Station, and is a second witness to your setting fire to Rob McPhail's house, causing his death."

"*He was a colleague, for Christ's sake....*" added the second officer, barely able to contain his contempt.

"None of you has a bloody *clue* who's running this. . . running *them!*" spat Hackett through clenched teeth, pointing at the two way mirror and kicking the table. "It's *not* a Zandini, but I'm not about to commit suicide by telling you who it *is!*"

Harry and Janis swapped thoughtful glances, *both* now raising their eyebrows. Through the mirror, they saw the two officers look at each other and then back at Hackett. Leaving a PC at the door inside the room, they left to re-interview the ape, George Gifford, further down the corridor.

* * *

That evening felt like most others in the last fortnight. After feeding and walking Baxter, Harry headed for the Carpenters for dinner and was now parking in the pub car park. What wasn't like most other evenings was the scene that met him when he walked inside....

"Okay, love, just *breeeathe slowwwly*, *innn* and *ouuuut*, *innn* and *ouuuut....*" Andrew was stroking Gina's back and guiding her towards the door as Harry was coming in.

"Baby's on the way," he said quickly as Gina groaned, clutching her stomach.

"Oh, good *luck*, love, can't help you with the blues and twos though, only got the old BMW out there!" He grinned, almost laughing, but on seeing Gina's glare rearranged his face immediately into a serious expression.

"Nnnn. . . *not funny, Harry!*" she gasped in between contractions.

"She's a couple of weeks early but everyone says it'll be fine," said Andrew, giving a very *good* impression he thought it was going to be anything *but* fine.

"I've rung for an ambulance. They said ten minutes," Molly shouted from behind the bar as Harry stood back to let the nearly new parents pass through to the bench seat in the vestibule. Suddenly, Gina stopped as a loud whooshing and splashing noise hit the air. . . and the floor. . . and all over everyone's shoes....

"*Oh noooo.....my waters!*" exclaimed Gina, now blushing with embarrassment and covering her face. "I'm so. . . *arrggghhh. . . owww*. . . sor. . . sorry."

"Don't *worry!*" chorused everyone, as the ambulance pulled into the car park and two paramedics ran up to the door to help Gina out of the pub.

"Let us know how it goes, son," Harry called out, as Andrew climbed into the back of the ambulance and the doors closed behind him.

After Molly had mopped up the wet tiles in the vestibule, she was back behind the bar pulling Harry a pint.

"You'll be next then," said Harry, nodding at Molly's stomach.

"Four months to go for me yet, just praying I'm on time or even a bit late so I don't miss Andy and Gina's Christmas-*ish* wedding!"

"When are you due? Come to that, when's their wedding?"

"I'm due on 28th and the wedding's the 19th. They haven't sent out the invites yet so don't worry I'm sure you'll *get* one," she said winking. Molly paused then as Danny came to mind. *He was still saying he wanted to come over....* "Just not sure how many more surprises I can take at the moment." She passed him his pint and put the money in the cash register.

He took a few gulps straight down. "Thanks, I really need this. By the way, your mention of surprises reminds me," added Harry. "Your two ummm... latest vision thingies..." He instinctively checked behind him, only to see a couple of elderly women open-mouthed and a group of lads starting to snigger. Molly rolled her eyes and then shot him a '*thanks for that*' look. *He lowered his voice....* "The first one was on the news, the second you may not know about."

"No, I don't, I was hoping I must've been wrong, to be honest. How *awful*. Was it someone at the hospital, at Rampton?"

"Yes, a warden. At the moment they can't prove anything, although Charlotte Peterson was there when it happened. Plus another patient, much younger, but neither had a motive as far as anyone knows. My money's on Peterson."

"Well, I s'pose they all have their problems, insecurities, chall—"

"Guarantee you it was *her*...." interrupted Harry sharply, holding her eyes.

Molly's own experience with Charlotte swam between them for a second; the chloroform pad over her mouth on the park bench, the struggling, the lucky escape she had.... "Yeah, I reckon you're right," she said flatly.

"Anyway. . . can I get a lasagne and chips, love? Maybe a couple of rolls? I'll sit over there at the sofa table by the bay window. Don't worry about taking it through to the restaurant."

"Sure thing, Harry, be about twenty minutes." Molly wrote the order up and took it through to the kitchen. *Visions still in full swing then,* she thought despondently.

Harry picked up a paper from the end of the bar and settled down on the sofa. Now all the excitement had passed with Gina, he began to think about the two women in his life. Annie was still absent from it and Fran very much not. The fact Annie had disappeared wasn't worrying him so much as niggling at him. His gut feeling was she'd deliberately disappeared to cause concern rather than the fact anything *bad* had happened to her. . . although he couldn't rid that from his mind entirely.

Five minutes later, Michael Morton walked in. After ordering himself a drink, he turned from the bar and scanned the room knowing full well Harry was in there. As the ambulance had pulled out of the car park he'd pulled in, having followed Harry from his house, and deliberately holding back so he didn't arrive at the same time.

It was Harry who saw Michael first. He lifted up the newspaper and sat back into the sofa cushions. It was the Fields' little mongrel, Poppy, who gave him away when she followed Molly's dad out from the private lounge and bounded over to see him. Since he'd brought Baxter in a few weeks ago, Poppy had sometimes come looking for the Lab when she saw Harry, and this time jumped up and pulled the paper down into his lap. Michael then instantly saw him and walked straight over.

"Mr Longbridge, may I join you. . . *please?*"

Harry eyed the younger man and although wasn't exactly thrilled at the idea, decided he wouldn't be asking if it wasn't important. He held out his arm indicating the free chair on Michael's side of the table.

"Thank you. Look, I know what I'm going to say is likely to ruffle feathers as it were, maybe even. . . really *annoy* you, but—"

"Just spit it out, Morton, my dinner's going to be here in a minute and I want to eat it in peace."

"I've been following my mother over the last few weeks, as often as feasibly possible."

"You've been *what?!*" asked Harry, face rapidly approaching a Hitchings' shade of beetroot....

"I knew you'd be angry, it's just th—"

"Damn *right* I'm angry, what the hell were you thinking, man? I could get you arrested for *stalking!*"

Michael looked down at the cider he was nursing. "She's still my mother, Harry." He gambled at using his Christian name. It paid off – amazingly Harry didn't blow a fuse. "I've been worried about her and came up to spend time getting to know her. She seemed to want me to but has never been available, always too busy doing. . . I've no idea *what*. One day I followed her to a therapist in Kendall, then the other day I followed her to Stanger Street in Kes—"

"*Stanger Street?*" Harry's interest was now suddenly piqued. "When *was* this?"

"Couple of weeks ago. Nothing special happened at either place. I assumed the therapist could be a positive thing. At Stanger Street she went round the back to some new-builds just visible from where I was parked, but I didn't follow her round because it was tight there. I checked Google Maps cos I don't know the area and it's a cul-de-sac. She'd have seen me."

"Do you remember the date?" asked Harry, mouth drying and slowly reaching for his drink as he recalled Fran's insistence her abductor was definitely a woman.

Michael pulled out a notebook and started flipping the pages as Harry took a mouthful of beer, watching him run his finger down one when he stopped. "July 28th, around two o'clock...."

Harry swallowed – heart tightening. . .

FORTY

KIRKDALE POLICE STATION
11.30 A.M

After having a lousy night's sleep given what Michael had told him in the Carpenters the night before, Harry was enjoying a rare *hot* mug of coffee in his office whilst on the phone to Fran. He didn't mention Michael's little bombshell exposé, deciding to save that for another time. Fran had been following orders (his), and was enjoying extended leave, relaxing at home, but was also seeing a therapist once a week to help work through her horrific ordeal. It would eventually be less often but for now she was going weekly. He'd been chatting for about twenty minutes when Suzanne knocked and popped her head round the door.

"Sir...? You've got Rampton High Security Hospital on the line, a Mark Randall."

Harry nodded and said his goodbyes to Fran saying he'd be over to see her later. *This should be interesting*, he thought, picking up the landline.... "DCI Longbridge, how can I help?"

"Good morning, this is Mark Randall, governor of Rampton Hospital. I believe you're one of the officers who brought Charlotte Peterson back from the States in March, after she absconded late last year?"

"That's right, yes. DI Taylor was the other officer. I was also the original arresting DCI responsible for recommending her case be prosecuted by the CPS. She was subsequently sent to your hospital."

"Indeed. Well, I thought you'd be interested to know she's been questioned with regard to two deaths here recently. One was a patient, a Miss Zoe Zandini and the other, one of our wardens, a Ms Rita Lemon. However, she's not being charged with either."

"You are *kidding* me! I heard she was so close in proximity to *both* women it would have been pretty much a dead cert!"

"I agree, DCI Longbridge, that's why I'm calling. I don't think Retford police have got it right. I can't prove it though it's just my gut instinct. According to Peterson, Rita Lemon fell forward into our herb garden and collapsed shortly afterwards. There was a drug-laden syringe stuck in her hand and she died fairly quickly."

"Were there any other witnesses?" asked Harry, stunned that Charlotte appeared to be getting away with it.

"Yes, a younger woman, a Fiona Massey. At first she said she saw a needle sticking out of the earth, but when questioned formerly, retracted her statement and said she was mistaken."

"You think Peterson leant on her?"

"I suspect that, yes. Retford police are suggesting the syringe belonged to Rita Lemon, and her fingerprints *were* found on it of course as she tried to pull it out. Peterson's were not. They're wrapping it up saying she was preparing to kill someone that day and fell on her own weapon so to speak. They're saying it's likely she also killed Zoe Zandini two weeks earlier, by injecting her prior to her entering the restaurant where she collapsed in the breakfast queue soon after."

"I have to admit, it does *sound* feasible," said Harry, surprised he was even thinking that way.

"It does," Randall replied, "but although Ms Lemon wasn't exactly a joyful person, she never gave any indication she was depressed, angry or planning a double murder either. We initially thought another patient was responsible for Zoe's murder, as did Retford CID. Witnesses remembered Marie being directly behind Miss Zandini in the queue. However, since Rita's death, Marie's strong denials have been listened to and finally believed."

"Lucky *Marie*...." said Harry. "Still, I take it Peterson was at breakfast the same day as Zoe? Also, she did *have* a reason to get revenge after the boiling water incident."

"Yes, she was definitely anti-Zoe after that, and *would* have been there, but unfortunately Marie Osborne has a difficult hygiene problem so was remembered. Marie is *always* remembered, wherever she is...."

Not so lucky *there* then, thought Harry. "Keep an eye on Peterson, she's a slippery one. Needles and chloroform are definitely her MO."

"Oh I'm well aware of that having read her notes, of course. The one thing that doesn't sit well though is how she would have got a med-filled syringe in the first place. Or even an *empty* one, come to that. I just can't work it out. It would be nigh on impossible for a patient or visitor to get anywhere near anything medical. This is another reason why Retford believe it must have been Rita who killed Zoe, and then fell on a syringe ready for whoever she'd planned as her next victim."

"I can certainly see your quandary, Mr Randall."

"Well anyway, I just thought I'd let you know, given your part in Peterson's residing here. I must admit I wanted to thrash it out with you. Everyone at Rampton is happy to accept the official line. I'm most definitely *not*. What worries me is if we've. . . *they've,* made a massive error of judgement here. I don't want any more deaths on *my* watch."

"Quite. Well, thank you very much for calling, it's been extremely interesting talking with you. We should keep in touch."

"Yes, of course, I feel we're on the same page here. I'll let you know if there are any more developments."

The two men ended their conversation and Harry spent the next half hour re-reading past files on the Zandinis, checking in with the hospital to see how Joe was doing, and wondering how long it would be before the suspected torso of Raiffe Zandini was confirmed. He was just about to pick up the phone when it rang. A call had been put straight through to his office....

"DCI Longbridge..."

"Oh good morning, this is Rampton High Security Hospital. I have a call for you, please hold...."

It was a woman's voice, overly bright and slightly hyper. Her approach also sounded rather old-fashioned given the more direct way calls were now made between managerial positions of different companies and organisations. And he'd not long spoken to Rampton's governor.... Harry waited. The same voice spoke again. . . *a lot less bright....*

"Hello, Harry. Long time, no see."

He froze. Switching to speakerphone, he began quickly typing a message to Suzanne in the outer office to track the call before answering. She acknowledged his email by waving from her desk. "What do you want, Charlotte? This is highly irregular as I'm sure you are well aware."

"*Is* it now? Well, if you've got your mobile there I can show you what's even more than *highly irregular!*"

Harry waved at Suzanne through the window, willing her to look up. "Do you *really* think I'm going to give you my mobile number?" Suzanne saw him and was now walking over to his door. He held up a finger to his mouth indicating she should remain silent and wrote **'Get me a spare mobile quickly'** on a piece of paper.

"I strongly suggest you do, Harry, because you're going to want to see this. I expect you also want to know where your wife has been the last two weeks."

Now he felt sick, and very cold. Suddenly his office was reminiscent of a freezer. Supporting his head with one hand and leaning on the desk, he tried to think of a response when Suzanne came in quietly with a mobile and its number on a piece of paper. He silently acknowledged her then spoke into the landline phone again. "Have you got a pen?"

"I don't need a pen, Harry, just give me the *number*."

He read it out and waited. The line went dead.

"Did you have enough time, Suze?"

She gestured through the window at the team working on the tracker device. They shook their heads.

The mobile rang with a text message. . . and an attachment. *Harry opened it....* The picture on the screen caused him to shoot back in his chair and drop a seemingly red-hot phone on the desk. It *was* red hot. A semi-naked photo of his wife in bed with Miles Peterson stared back at him. . . *and Suzanne.*

The mobile rang again.

"Pretty *damn* irregular, wouldn't you agree, Harry? Not that it bothers *me* any. Except that he's still alive of course. Now *that's* irksome."

Harry was literally speechless. He had no idea Annie even *knew* Miles. They'd been registered at different surgeries when the Petersons were practising together locally, and Miles had left the village after the court case.

"*That* shocked, huh? Well, there's more."

Harry glanced at Suzanne and shifted forward uncomfortably in his chair.

"Go on."

"Chris-to-pher *Mogg*," she said, punctuating each syllable.

"What about him?"

"Annie. . . Annie killed him. She's been rather lax with the list since, which is why I'm calling you, but she definitely despatched Mogg."

Suzanne's eyes had already widened at the photo, now her mouth dropped to match Harry's.

"I think you've been popping too many pills, Peterson. That's a ludicrous suggestion."

"Oh it's not a suggestion, Harry, it's a fact, and I've been doing anything *but* eating too many pills."

When he heard her snigger he switched tack. "Did you kill Zoe Zandini and Rita Lemon?"

Now it was Charlotte's turn to be on the back foot. There was silence at the other end of the line as something caught Suzanne's eye. Through the office window one of the officers working on tracking Charlotte's mobile signal held their hand up – *they'd traced it.* Whilst it was likely she was still in Rampton, they had to be sure. Now they were. However she'd got hold of that mobile, it could now be removed from her possession.

"We're not talking about me, Longbridge. This is about your *wife!* I suggest you find her and find her quick. She may just get back to the list. . . and I wouldn't mind betting you're *on* it. *Fran Taylor definitely is!*"

Harry flinched then, and it was as if Charlotte could sense it. There was no sniggering this time. . . *it was full on evil laughter until the line went dead.*

Annie woke up and felt the warmth of his body next to hers. It was a long time since she'd felt something so good, felt anything at all frankly that wasn't hate. Until the last couple of weeks she hadn't realised how bad things had actually got on that front, but now. . . *now* it was different. *He* seemed to understand her, and she was starting to feel happy for the first time in years.

Not being in the Job helped, or more to the point, being *obsessive* about the Job. Working for himself by running his own business, not being on call or doing shifts, it all helped. She pushed away the fact most of his clients were very likely women. He liked her, she could tell, he was really into *her*, wanted *her*....

Annie moved up onto one elbow and looked down at him sleeping. . . taut, tanned, and in a damn sight better shape than Harry. She wanted a picture.... Reaching behind to the bedside cabinet she picked up her phone, and giving her best victory smile, took a selfie of them lying there together half naked.

But that wasn't enough. She found the number, attached the photo and pressed send. It was her badly stifled laughter that woke him up....

FORTY-ONE

APPLEBY ROAD, KENDAL
2.30 P.M

Miles hadn't intended to get involved, at least not whilst she was a client. A, it was completely unprofessional and B, quite possibly illegal – which is why the woman who'd made him laugh more than any other recently, was no longer on his books.

He watched as she poured them both a coffee in his mediocre flat, still missing the space and beauty of the Victorian farmhouse he'd shared with Charlotte after moving from Bradenthorpe. An image of *why* they'd moved, *Jenny Flood*, floated momentarily. Constriction in his throat and a blurred view of his kitchen made him blink it away....

Since Andrea McMahon had come to him for therapy following a difficult few years, he felt he'd helped her quite considerably. She was at least more relaxed since the first appointment, and appeared more confident. What she *wasn't*, he was about to discover, was entirely honest about her current name or their joint connections.

At first when the police sirens sounded he'd taken no notice. The louder and closer they got, however, the more his uncomfortable memories began to sneak back in. When the noise stopped abruptly, he glanced uncertainly at her and walked pensively over to the window to see blue flashing lights and uniformed officers alighting vehicles and swarming the road outside. Residents from neighbouring properties standing in their front gardens were wondering what was going on as police ran into the office building his flat was set in.

Annie continued stirring the coffees. . . for far too long. The hammering on the door made them both jump. She looked at him then with concentrated fear in her eyes.

"Tell me quickly. Have you done something seriously wrong? Don't lie to me now," said Miles grimly, holding her shoulders as the shouting began outside the door for them to open up.

"I. . . I. . ."

"Andrea, for *God's* sake, if I'm going to help—"

"My name's not. . . well, it is but—"

"Who the hell *are* you?"

At that moment the door burst open and the room filled with police, including Harry who'd insisted on attending despite the obvious conflict of interest.

"Her name's Annie Longbridge. . . *and she's my bloody wife!*"

Miles stood open-mouthed as Annie was led out of the flat in handcuffs. Finally he found the capacity to get his legs moving and followed them down to the high street. "Mr Longbridge, *Harry*, isn't it?"

"It's DCI Longbridge to you, Peterson."

"Okay, well. . . look, I had no *idea*. She. . . you. . ."

"I know. We attended different surgeries back then. She's under arrest for suspected murder and a separate abduction, so consider yourself lucky at escaping by the skin of your teeth. *Looks like you've gone full circle, mate.*"

Annie looked pleadingly between the two men. Harry's expression lay somewhere between disgust and disbelief, Miles remained stunned at the groundhog day he found himself in whilst envisaging another six months of therapy. As the searching for evidence began in his flat, he watched Annie being driven away, *and all he could see was Charlotte.*

* * *

Harry knew he had to be taken off the case, certainly anything to do with Christopher Mogg's death and Fran's abduction. He was determined though to remain at his own house when forensics turned *that* upside down.

Hitchings had wanted him off everything altogether of course, but as Harry had pointed out, with Fran and Joe not back, three other officers down and smack bang in the middle of the holiday period, his boss would have to bring over his two least favourite senior colleagues from Penrith, George Jenkins and Douggie Judd. Those two were why Fran had managed to convince Hitchings to invite him back in the first place. Hitchings had blanched at the thought, just as he had six weeks ago. So the end result was Harry was still at work, only right now he was sitting, head low, on the edge of his living room sofa waiting to see if SOCO had found anything to incriminate his wife in Christopher Mogg's murder. Baxter sat at his feet, head resting gently on his knee, sensing something wasn't right. An hour or so later, he was up on the sofa beside him, head in his lap when one of the guys knocked on the open lounge door....

"Boss....? Sorry, sir. . ." A youngish SOCO came into the room and held out an open small cardboard evidence box with some dried scrapings in for Harry to examine. "From under the floorboards in the smallest bedroom, and also from the side of your cooker. We think it's likely to be dried hemlock traces given Mr. Mogg's autopsy results. It's not in a plastic evidence bag bec—"

Harry looked up. "Because of mould growth, yes, I *know*. You're sure it's hemlock I take it, *not bloody dried Fairy liquid?!*"

The SOCO stood there awkwardly for a moment, youth on display through fidgety eyes and a rolled lip. He reminded Harry of Joe Walker a couple of years ago, a rookie unused to his gruff manner, particularly under stress.

"Sorry. . . sorry, lad...." he sighed, interlocking his fingers. "Right. . . right, well that's, that's pretty damning then, isn't it?" It was a statement not a question.

"We still need to test forensically but it's not looking good, sir."

At that moment a second officer came in with a laptop. "We found this under the floorboards in the smaller bedroom as well. The only Internet search on this device is for a dating site. I take it there are other computers, laptops or iPads in more conventional places in the house?"

He shook his head slightly in disbelief, mouth in a firm line although nothing surprised him anymore. He wasn't feeling very good now and was getting heady indicating a need to eat. "Yes, we both have laptops. Annie usually keeps hers in the bed. . . in her bedroom. Mine's in here somewhere. Look, son, I'm a diabetic, I have to eat."

"That's fine, sir, we're finished in the kitchen. Nice dog." Baxter's head popped up and giving a wide Labby 'smile', mini whined his appreciation.

After a cheese sandwich and a mug of tea, Harry phoned Fran to let her know he'd been delayed and would be over soon. He still hadn't mentioned any of the latest news; Michael following Annie to her house, Charlotte's call and Annie's arrest and affair with Miles. He wanted to speak to her in person, especially with regard to the likelihood his wife was responsible for the ghastly twenty-four hours she'd spent in that goddamn waste pipe.

Once the SOCO team had left he was on his way.

* * *

Harry had picked Fran up from home and they were now waiting at the hospital reception desk for Joe's room number. He'd filled her in with everything that had happened since her rescue and she was understandably horrified....

"I *knew* it was a woman. I *told* you it was," she reiterated for the third time since Harry had updated her. They were now walking through the hospital looking for the corridor Joe's room was in. "The fact it was Annie is just....." she shivered, exhaling loudly. "The rest of it though. . . honestly, Harry, you must be emotionally shattered."

"Not really processing it that well, to be honest. They've obviously taken me off the Mogg murder, and I'll hardly be the one interviewing her so it's a case of waiting." He stopped for a minute and looked up at the overhanging directions. "No, it's this way, he's on Marigold Ward.... They'll have to question me, of course, to eliminate me from enquiries, with us sharing a house and evidence being found. I've got to go through that tomorrow — just hope it's short and sweet."

They turned a corner and Marigold was in front of them. As a victim of crime, Joe was in a private room just outside the main ward with an officer on the door. Harry and Fran showed their warrant cards to the security, and knocked first after seeing his parents through the window. Joe's father got up to open it and welcomed them inside.

After Harry had introduced Fran, the Walkers said they'd go for a cup of tea and let them have some colleague time with their son.

Joe looked a whole lot better already compared to the last time Harry had seen him. He sat beside the bed and took a deep breath. *How the hell could a person express enough thanks to someone who'd literally saved their life?* Harry suddenly felt totally inadequate but decided to just go for it, having first asked him how he was feeling....

"Joe, son. . . I *did* come the same night it happened, you know. I hope they told you that when you woke up. Suzanne and I *were* here but only your folks were allowed to be with you. I just wanted you to know that..."

"Yes, yes, they told me, don't worry, sir, I know you were here, I *knew* you would be."

Harry dropped his head . . . "You saved. . . " He swallowed hard, eyes filling up as Fran put a hand on his shoulder and squeezed. "You saved my life, son. . . there's no question, I can never repay you, *never*. Thank you just seems so inadequate."

Joe reached for Harry's hand and his boss covered it with both of his. Fran now had tears spilling down her cheeks and began rummaging for a tissue in her bag.

"All the thanks I need is knowing you're still here," replied Joe. "When that gun was drawn I acted instinctively – *nobody, but nobody was taking out the Magpie!*"

Harry stood up then and leaning forward, gently hugged him. "Reckon this makes us family," he said, quickly wiping an eye as Joe's parents re-entered the room. "Thank you, Mr and Mrs Walker, for allowing us to share some of your visiting time with Joe, it's greatly appreciated."

After ten minutes or so, they said their goodbyes and left Joe's parents to spend the rest of their visit with him. It was now almost six o'clock as they made their way back to the reception. They were just about to exit the hospital when they heard a familiar voice behind them and turned round to see Andrew with a big smile on his face.

"We had a little girl, Ellena Rose, eight pounds two ounces," he beamed. Shortening it to Ellie, cos it's cute and we love it, and. . . well, Rose after my birth mum, bless her...."

He paused for a moment remembering how he'd first met Rose Emmerson at Gina's grandmother's funeral, and who'd since passed herself.... "Gina's knackered but very happy, sent me out for some food so she must be okay!"

"Congratulations, Andy, that's really wonderful. Give her my best and I look forward to seeing the little one when she's home."

"Yes, it's *lovely* news, I'm really pleased for you both," added Fran genuinely. She passed a hand briefly over her still wider than pre-pregnancy waist. It wasn't missed by the two men.

"Oh God, look I'm sorry. . ." said Andy. "There's me going on about our…"

Fran flicked a glance at Harry. *"Heyyy*, don't be daft, I'm thrilled for you both – *really* I am."

"Right, well, I'd better get her ladyship something to eat or I'll be in trouble. Hope to see you at the Carpenters soon. I know Gee will want to show the baby off to Molly and her parents ASAP. We're hoping they'll both be home tomorrow. Oh I nearly forgot, I'll be taking some paternity leave, so you'll be seeing Peter Gray's wife, Stella, back as crime reporter. She can't wait. Taking early retirement was her biggest regret – I think she's missed it!!"

"Ah, the infamous Stella. Before my time; I think you'd just been upgraded to crime from sports reporter when we first met."

"That's right, I had, and now I've actually applied for the constabulary so I may even be joining you next year."

"Well, *that's* the best bit of news I've heard in the last few months. Not sure if I'll still be working though, lad. Technically they only brought me back out of retirement in a consultancy role and it just kind of escalated."

"Oh I think you'll still be needed for a while yet," chipped in Fran with a conspiratorial smile.

They parted ways with Andrew realising halfway down the corridor he hadn't a clue why Harry and Fran were there, but was too ecstatic to worry about it.

FORTY-TWO

A WEEK LATER. . .

Harry and Fran were having a quiet drink in the Carpenters when Andrew and Gina came in with Ellie Rose. Molly was on a break and came out from the Fields' family quarters to usher them into the private lounge, and on seeing Harry and Fran, beckoned them over. They held their drinks up questioningly and she indicated for them to bring them on through.

"Well, this is nice," said Harry spreading out over the extra-large comfortable couch, beer in hand. "I could get used to this instead of sitting in the bar, even better than my favourite bay-window sofa."

"You're welcome anytime, might save me having to ring through my visions!" quipped Molly.

Gina grimaced...."*Pleeease*. . . tell me you've not had any *more?*"

"You just took the words right out of my mouth," added Harry, looking weary. "*I've seriously had enough for this year.*"

"*Nooo* – everything's fine," replied Molly batting her hand dismissively through the air.

"Well, can we see this gorgeous baby of yours then?" asked Fran, keenly.

Andy was nearest the pram so gently scooped Ellie Rose up into his arms, and as he passed her over she murmured, stretching an adventurous little hand from beneath her yellow rose-patterned blanket. Fran gazed down, mesmerised by everything about her. The dinky little mouth, cute button nose, tiny fingers. . . and how strong her own maternal feelings still were.

"She's absolutely beautiful. You must both be totally in love with her."

"She is a bit, isn't she, and we definitely are," said Andy beaming with pride, pulling Gina to him and kissing the top of her head.

Harry was sitting next to Fran on the couch and placed his finger on Ellie Rose's palm. She grabbed it tightly, shaking it back and forth. Looking down at her, the two of them gradually bent their heads slowly towards each other until they touched, before suddenly springing apart and sitting upright again.

Molly and Gina exchanged knowing glances, as blushing awkwardly Harry found his beer and Andy took Ellie Rose back from Fran for a cuddle himself.

"Nibbles, anyone?" said Maisie Fields making a save-the-day entrance with a plate of sausage rolls....

* * *

Over the following few weeks and months, a lot of people were coming to terms with substantial changes in their life. Some were good, some were bad, some smaller or greater than others. Harry had already begun to go through a formal investigation due to Annie's crimes and the hemlock evidence found at their house, which was both stressful and embarrassing. His huge popularity kept him going; even Chief Superintendent Hitchings was staunchly in his corner.

Annie's son, Michael Morton, was left utterly confused and devastated at his mother's behaviour, downfall and conviction. Although having made some sort of connection with Harry, he clearly couldn't stay in Kirkdale any longer and went home to London.

Hackett was charged with corruption, arson (endangering life), criminal damage by fire, three murders (Rob and Carrie McPhail and Jerry Kitson), and anything else Hitchings could find to throw at him. He steadfastly refused to give any names other than George Gifford and Raiffe Zandini though, and Raiffe was still officially missing, although the Z-emblazoned torso in the farmer's silo was looking a likely match. Forensics were still working on that because Gifford was steadfastly denying any involvement.

Annie completely fell apart under interrogation. Despite having lived with a police officer for twenty-three years, it hadn't helped any, and she was charged with the pre-meditated poisoning and murder of Christopher Mogg, and the abduction, endangering life, and attempted murder of DI Fran Taylor.

Young Jacey Pearl, the trainee DC, had already been charged with fraud and forgery after writing fake painkiller prescriptions for her mother, supplied by her uncle Jerry Kitson, and been dismissed from the constabulary. This had been a huge disappointment for Harry who'd seen her as his new fledgling protégé now Joe was flying. Joe recovered from his gunshot injuries, spent a month recuperating at the police treatment centre in Harrogate, where both Harry and Fran had visited him to see how he was getting on, and would be returning to work in due course.

The whole 'Bonaparte Body Parts Case' had been conclusively uncovered as being the work of the Zandinis and their hired hands, initiated whenever any customers or employees failed to pay up, turned informer or otherwise betrayed them. This was finally admitted by Ape (*George 'Gunner' Gifford*), after many hours of interrogation, but like Terry Hackett, he wouldn't reveal any names of those running the Zandinis other than Raiffe. The cross-checking of missing persons with forensic information gleaned from the various limbs found was still ongoing, and their entire organisation proved to be a myriad of money-lending, sales of illegal drugs, fake ID, and a whole gamut of forgery and fraud. Harry had come across some of this when working in London, but not to the degree that had been discovered in Cumbria. What had been believed to be a problem solely in London and the South East was in fact countrywide, and was suspiciously looking likely to be an international mafia-style operation.

And then there was Charlotte.... On the face of it, Charlotte Peterson had quite literally got away with two more killings. Retford CID had concluded Rita Lemon murdered Zoe Zandini, despite no known motive, and then fell on her own weapon of choice in the herb garden, a pre-filled Midazolam and Diazepam syringe, whilst planning her next victim. At the inquest, a decision of serious mental breakdown through presumed but unproven long-term stress and depression was upheld as a reason for her actions. This was grudgingly accepted by Rita's family and supported by Rampton's governor, Mark Randall, neither of whom believed she was guilty of pre-meditated murder. *Privately, Randall still felt Charlotte was the perpetrator, or at the very least closely involved, and was relentless in keeping a very close eye on her.*

Of course Charlotte wasn't happy in the slightest. Despite despatching two of the most incredibly irritating and pressurising individuals around her, and completely walking away from their two murder investigations, her list was still long. Miles was still alive, her (now filthy rich) inheritance-stealing cousin was still alive, Emily was still alive, and that bloody DCI who didn't even have the decency to at least stay retired. . . *was still alive!* His wife, *Charlotte's carefully chosen delegate* to reduce the number of names on her behalf, had surpassed herself in reneging on the job in hand. This meant that the back-stabbing Annie Longbridge had now earned her very own place – *sitting right at the top of that list....*

FORTY-THREE

CARPENTERS ARMS – SATURDAY, DECEMBER 19TH, 12 NOON
FOUR MONTHS LATER

Molly passed the freshly poured champagne to Gina. "Careful with that now, Gee, and don't go *anywhere* near your dress with it. I can't get a replacement sent over from New York before two o'clock and they wouldn't have that one now anyway!"

Gina laughed a little nervously as she took the flute glass, and sat on her old bed well away from the stunning gown now hanging on the back of the door. "I love it *so much*, right from the day I tried it on, *even if I did end up in hospital after collapsing with dyspepsia!* I'll never forget you secretly buying it and having Gabriella's send it over after we'd left. That was both thoughtful and massively generous." She put down her glass on the side table and got up to give her best friend who was more like a sister, a huge hug. "Also for helping me get a handle on my post-baby weight too," she said grabbing a small tummy roll, "basically pouncing on me every time I even *looked* at a carb, cos there's no way in hell I'd be wearing it otherwise!"

"Well, we did sneak in a *couple* of naughty cakes, but I'm going to want *that* particular favour returned in the New Year," replied Molly looking down at her now very large baby bump. "Got a feeling I'm going to need at least as much help. For now, I'm just grateful it was only you who went into labour early."

As if she knew they were talking about the future arrival of her special friend, Ellie Rose woke up and began crying for a feed, at which point there was a knock at the door and Maisie Fields came in with a prepared bottle, ready warmed and tested.

"There you go, love. I thought she'd be wanting a feed about now. Bless her little heart, she's *so adorable!*" She cooed lovingly over the Moses basket. "Soon be you, my lovely," she said proudly to her daughter, straightening up. "Oh. . . and there's a young man downstairs asking for you...."

ST PETER'S CHURCH, KIRKDALE
2.00 P.M.

The yellow roses and white ribbons fluttered in the chilly breeze around the old arched door as the sun blazed in the bluest sky. The weather couldn't have been more perfect for a winter wedding. All that was needed were a few snowflakes to make it extra magical.

Inside, Andrew could barely hold it together as Bette Midler's song 'The Rose' began to fill the church. He turned to see Gina walking down the aisle on Ron Fields' arm in an amazing winter bridal cloak and gown. She looked absolutely stunning with her beautiful red auburn hair tumbling in waves over her shoulders, its rich colour shining vibrantly against the white floor-length velvet and faux-fur ensemble. Miles had agreed with Gina that Ron should give her away; he and Molly's mum had done so much for her over the years and it wouldn't have felt right for her biological father to step into that role now. They were however still working hard on their relationship.

Sitting in the congregation Miles caught Emily's eye. She and Gareth had flown in from New York a few days before, and it was Emily who'd brought the bridal cloak with her to go with Gina's dress. They hadn't seen each other in over twenty years but Miles would have recognised her anywhere. . . *as she did him.* They gave each other a small head tilt in acknowledgement of the one good thing to have come from their relationship all those years ago.

Harry and Fran sat together at the back, *just in case of any small disturbances....*

Sitting between her mum, Maisie, and newly arrived Danny Kellerman, father of her unborn baby, Molly held Ellie Rose, now four months old and already the image of her mother, Gina, and grandmother Emily. With a shock of auburn curls framing her perfect little face, she looked all around her, wide awake, fascinated and taking everything in. If great-grandmother Margaret Rowlands was looking down now, she would surely say, "That one's going to be just like you were, Em, fiery, stubborn and doubly determined – *you mark my words....*"

And Andrew's parents sat quietly behind him, proud and happy he'd found such a lovely girl in Gina, and had never made them feel anything other than his mum and dad when Rose came back into his life at the end of hers, after all those years. They were more than happy their beautiful granddaughter carried her name as a reminder Rose had given them a fine son they would otherwise never have had.

Gina soon reached him at the altar, and as they looked into each other's eyes the music fell silent for the service to begin....

Forty-five minutes later, after promises had been exchanged, hymns sung and the register signed, everyone filed out of the old Norman church into the bright winter sunshine. Friends and family laughed, chatted and mingled, congratulating the happy couple and gushing over Gina's fabulous cloak and dress, while the photographer was trying his best to organise all the guests for the photos.

"I'm starving," said Harry, "never got any breakfast this morning." He winced at the bright sunshine and held a hand up to shield his face. They were sitting on a wooden bench conveniently positioned where the photos were being taken, waiting to be called by the photographer.

Fran turned to him and rolled her eyes. "For heaven's sake, Longbridge, you never eat properly unless I'm around." She started fussing with an overly large bag on her shoulder and produced an oblong plastic container. Removing the lid, she offered the contents to Harry.

He glanced inside the box. "Nutritionally speaking, I don't think custard doughnuts have ever counted as 'properly', even when they *are* the mini variety. *And what on earth are you doing with doughnuts at a wedding, for heaven's sake?*"

"You don't want one then?" she replied raising her eyebrows and tilting her head teasingly.

Harry moved to grab the container as she pulled it away from him leaning in for a kiss. He obliged, letting it linger, but took care not squash their baby son, Jamie, their precious surviving 'Taybridge' twin nestling against Fran's chest. Whilst taking advantage of her weak moment, he cheekily reached round her for the box of doughnuts.

"I wouldn't say *no*," he winked, popping one in his mouth as he tickled Jamie's neck making him wriggle in delight.

And as the first few flakes of snow began to fall, with the church bells ringing all around them, Fran held his eyes softly and said, *"Neither would I, Harry. . . neither would I. . ."*

* * *

EPILOGUE

RAMPTON HIGH SECURITY HOSPITAL

MAY 2021

The rain had stopped earlier, the sun was just peeping from behind a cloud and a radio could be heard playing Chopin's *Nocturne, Opus 9 No. 2*, behind them. Charlotte and Annie were amongst a handful of patients allowed a short tea break in the garden that afternoon under the close watch of a warden. Having worked hard weeding some low flowering beds, they now sat with their drinks chatting together on a long bench facing a group of majestic firs. Gardening wasn't exactly Annie's favourite hobby any more than it was Charlotte's, but it was better than being on an enforced lock-in, *and they'd had a couple of those.*

Annie was in a sunnier mood than usual given her long-term situation, for which she most definitely blamed the woman sitting next to her. Yes, unusually, to anyone looking on, Annie looked almost jubilant.

She didn't think he'd actually *do* it, but falling in love, *really* in love, probably for only the second time in his life, had clearly had an effect. It wasn't entirely easy. He'd found them behind a light fitting at the flat; *that* part was simple. The carriage to, and transfer of when visiting was substantially harder. He'd told her that day how satisfying it was to know that finally. . . *finally*. . . he would be rid of that woman forever. Everything was her fault. *It had always been her fault.*

Charlotte drained the last drops of her tea, repeatedly wiping beads of sweat from her forehead, her icy demeanor barely detectable. The cloud eventually revealed the full afternoon sun and was now blazing down, but in the last fifteen or twenty minutes she'd begun to feel distinctly unwell. Strange given she was so rarely ill.

Opening the folded note Annie had just placed in her lap, her eyes tried hard to focus on the short message so carefully handwritten inside. Then in shock more than anything else, turned to meet her companion's accusing eyes before following their gaze to a familiar but hazy man at the far table. As Chopin reached a crescendo, the cramping increased, her focus now fading fast, she dropped the note along with her cup, and clutching at her stomach slumped forwards onto the dewy grass. Staring vacantly straight ahead, Annie lifted her tea to her lips. She watched unseeing, as a huge flock of ravens scattered noisily, soaring high above the firs into the late afternoon sun. Way below them a breeze caught the note, blowing it into a surf-hopping dance across the lawn until it came to a quivering rest. Annie's gaze dropped to her tightly closed hand. Unfurling her fingers, three empty coffee sachets lay scrunched in her palm for just a second before a breeze quickly whipped them up, causing each one to roll and bounce collaboratively alongside the note.

And at the table further along, with Chopin's now more gentle notes continuing to float on the air, Miles Peterson turned around and dipped his head in complicity. The warden came running, shouting for help as Charlotte remained motionless, arm outstretched, glassy eyes staring directly in line with her failed plans. . . and Annie's more successful ones.

The note flickered – then finally blew upright.

Oh what a tangled web you weaved when first you practiced to deceive, you never planned to pay this price – it all goes back to **Fire & Ice.**

ACKNOWLEDGEMENTS
HUGE THANKS MUST GO TO....

Nick Burrows – My long-suffering IT guy

For maintaining my laptop, keeping me connected to the Internet and generally helping me not go into meltdown – I literally couldn't write any of my books without you!

Dawn Wood (Dawnie) – A dear friend, past colleague and long-time diabetic

For all the detailed information you gave me with regard to diabetes, which helped considerably in being accurate when referring to my character DCI Harry Longbridge's own condition.

Jo Moss – My dear author friend and 'booky' companion!

For literally nagging me to dig *Blood List* out of my laptop in early 2018 after letting it 'sleep' for ten years, bring it up to date and finish it. Without you, *Blood List*,

Dead Girls Don't Cry and *The Delegate* would not be in anyone's hands right now...

Everyone at Matador – For simply being the best!
Grateful thanks for running the most professional publishing set-up in the business, giving authors worldwide choice and control.

Bruce – For his belief in me
And of course not forgetting my husband, Bruce, who has to spend an awful lot of his time living with someone who creates murder and mayhem! Also for driving me to and setting up my book stand at all my events.

AUTHOR'S LICENCE

Whilst trying to be as realistic as possible, in order to write an enjoyable *fictional* story, and despite documentary research, the specific layouts and security, daily routines and methods of working at Rampton High Security Psychiatric Hospital in Nottinghamshire are unlikely to be accurate. I hope this fact won't have spoiled the story for those who have had links with Rampton at any time.

* * *